UPLINK

BY JANE S. FANCHER

WARNER BOOKS

A Time Warner Company

WARNER BOOKS EDITION

Questar® is a registered trademark of Warner Books, Inc.

Cover design by Don Puckey
Cover illustration by Barclay Shaw

Warner Books, Inc.
1271 Avenue of the Americas
New York, NY 10020

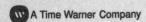 A Time Warner Company

Printed in the United States of America

First Printing: April, 1992

10 9 8 7 6 5 4 3 2 1

"Just how safe is this <u>automated</u> landing?"

The Atmospheric Entry warning flashed before she could answer. Stephen's intense gaze flicked to that announcement.

He slammed the autopilot off—and the Mini fell out from under them.

Anevai swallowed her stomach and grabbed the controls.

Lightning flashed below.

"Ridenour, what's our flightpath?"

A shrug.

"Dammit, Ridenour, are we headed into that?"

Another shrug.

"Stephen, we've got to get down—out of this. These storms get nasty. *Very* nasty."

He turned back to the window. Lightning, blindingly bright, a crash of thunder. They were right in the middle of it!

"Stephen, get us down! Now!"

He didn't move.

The next instant lightning and thunder struck in a violent series all around them. The lights dimmed, went out.

The craft tumbled wildly...

*　　　*　　　*

ALSO BY JANE S. FANCHER

GROUNDTIES

Published by
WARNER BOOKS

I

---

i

HuteEtu yawned and blinked, a flick of airy lashes that sent the morning mist down the valley in soft tendrils. In the far western sky, Winema, past her prime but still admirably rotund, dipped below the peaks, all but the edge of her silver skirts evading Etu's golden rays. Each morning, Etu reached for her and each morning melted a little more of those skirts away, never quite touching, never touched until the occasional eclipse, when Winema caught Etu and hid his glow within her darkened beauty.

Which was more than *he'd* gotten lately.

Nayati Hatawa laughed silently, and closed his eyes on the wakening world. The sun touched the treetops, rousing the birds, and warmed the air, creating the breeze, which brushed the leaves, releasing their whispering murmur. Insects and mountain rills wove complex rhythms the best of the tribes' drummers had tried (and failed) to imitate.

Underlying it all, the heartbeat of HuteNamid itself. The part of Nayati which could hear that pulse sensed its source as a man sensed the source of pain or pleasure. A different part of him (the academically constipated part) possessed terms like 'tectonic plates' and 'volcanic fissures,' 'geologic harmonics' and 'tidal forces.' But describing true global awareness in those terms was like saying a knife-edge split molecular bonds of skin and capillaries, exciting nerve endings, which notified the brain to release chemicals—when *awareness* knew a finger had been cut and the bastard who left an unsheathed blade in the pack was going to be very sorry very soon.

Recondite reality. Inner reality. Ultimate cause and effect.

A man needed a woman who understood him like that. He'd had one. Once. Unfortunately, Anevai Tyeewapi was having nothing to do with him these days, but he could deal with that. Either Anevai would come around to proper thinking or—

A new voice slipped into the euphonious stream. He smiled contentedly and stretched flat on the rock, bare chest against night-cooled stone. A wooden flute: handmade, as unique in its tone as in the hand that played it. His mind provided the musician a name and he rejected it with all other labels this morning, for all that Nigan was a friend. The flute's contribution to his recondite reality—its beauty, its power—lay within the sound itself, not the man who produced it.

—or, (his thoughts returning to Anevai) there were always other women. Others less independently inclined, others—he rubbed his still-sensitive jaw over the cool stone—with a less effective right cross.

But others were not the daughter of Sakiimagan Tyeewapi.

At the remotest edge of his extended awareness, an Alliance starship orbited his world. His Anevai was up there, whether by her own choice or Adm. Cantrell's orders, he didn't know.

And Nayati Hatawa did not *like* not knowing things. He'd grown accustomed to omniscience in all the important issues. Sakiimagan himself came to him for information: information on the tides and the weather (though Sakiimagan never questioned the source of that knowledge); on the tides of the Warrior Society (which, as they both knew, Nayati controlled); more recently, information on the condition of Sakiimagan's only son, Hononomii, lying in that starship's sick bay (information Nayati had because Hononomii had chosen to call *him* rather than Sakiimagan); and soon, very soon now, Sakiimagan would be asking him why the admiral's spy was alive when Sakiimagan had ordered otherwise.

But Stephen Ridenour was a pest, nothing more. One needn't kill pests. One shooed them away and counselled them against return.

Besides, Nayati Hatawa wasn't about to obey an old man with twisted ideas, no matter Sakiimagan Tyeewapi had been more a father to him than his own long-absent sire, no matter Sakiimagan Tyeewapi was the chosen leader of his people; Sakiimagan was also the *elected governor* of HuteNamid's *IndiGene Corps*. ComNet Alliance terms. ComNet Alliance politics. Convolute terms. Convolute thinking.

With typical white-eyed arrogance, Alliance called the People— the *Dineh*—'Ethnic Reconstructionists.' But the People didn't need to reconstruct a dead past. The People didn't need books and computer records to resurrect what they were; had been; always would be. The People were part of their universe, and the laws of the People were simple: respect of, and responsibility to that totality.

Alliance laws didn't operate that way. Playing Alliance games meant thinking those convolute Alliance thoughts. Nayati had learned from Sakiimagan himself to play those games. Games which a youthful Sakiimagan had learned from the source. Games wherein Sakiimagan's own son had no aptitude and Nayati excelled.

But mostly what Nayati had learned was not to trust those who walked that deeply in their enemy's thought patterns.

A whine of dissipation shields: discord in the morning serenade. He frowned up at the sky and a shuttle's distant foreign presence.

Cantrell was early.

Daylight. A definite sense of 'up' and 'down': they were back sunside and atmospheric. A gentle cerebral cortex nudge: patented TJ Briggs wakeup call. Cantrell forced her eyes open.

"Ground control has offered us a beam, admiral. Should I take it? It'd be faster."

She yawned and checked her watch. God, they'd *been* back

sunside for an hour. Just coming on—she pressed a button for Tunica local-time conversion—noon in the capital, and the meeting was scheduled for 1600 hours—a good three hours away.

"Admiral?"

She touched the transmit button and said, forcing sleep-slur from her voice, "Thank you, lieutenant, but no. We'll go in under our own power and in our own time. In fact, make an extra pass. Let's enjoy the view."

"That's telling 'em, Boss-lady." TJ worked his way gingerly through the cabin door, balancing two huge (covered, thank God) mugs in one hand, holding the door open with his foot, while trying to extract his ID card from the keyslot outside the door. "Wouldn't do—" He grunted. "To arrive too—" A second grunt. "Dammit!"

"Stuck again, is it?" She rescued the coffee and slipped the mugs into the armrest magtracs, leaving TJ free to wrestle with the card. "Try shoving the door past full open; sometimes that helps."

"Ha!" The door slid closed, shutting out the crew's chatter. "Gotta get maintenance on that."

She laughed as he settled into the seat facing hers. "We've been saying that for two years."

"Yeah, but . . ." He held his card up. It was—chewed.

"I didn't know it could do that."

"Neither did I." He popped the memory chip and flipped the card into the disposal, where suction took it and snapped the chute closed. "I've always wanted to do that."

"Hope you've got your backup with."

"Hey, it was useless—" She raised a brow at him and he relented. "Of course I do, Loren. I know pro-ce-dure."

He took a sip, wrinkled his nose and switched mugs. She drank hers black, sometimes, when she could get it fresh, with a little cream. The real thing, thank you, not the synthetic Wytner. She wasn't particular what biosphere produced it, so long as the sphere wasn't glass or plastic. TJ—TJ liked a little coffee to liquefy his sugar.

"Lexi coming?"

He shook his head. "Not right away. She's 'following a significance.'"

"Still wrestling with that analysis of the Tyeewapi kids' meeting?"

He nodded.

"Enough to suspect Anevai's translation?"

He shrugged. "Enough to miss breakfast."

And that was all she was likely to get out of TJ, who very carefully refused credit for insights not his. Recon evaluation was Lexi's field, and Anevai Tyeewapi and her brother, Hononomii, were Ethnic Reconstructionist to the core. For all their ease with modern technology, when they spoke in their adopted language, their minds entered a different realm. Having seen the translation program's attempts to sort out the logic and subtleties, if Alexis Fonteccio thought she'd discovered a Significant discrepancy between Anevai's translation and other possible interpretations, Adm. Cantrell was not about to tell her differently.

Another yawn; a quick calculation; a mental note to take a BioReg as soon as they landed. No sense calling a meeting if you fell asleep in the middle—and if the pill kept her wired into the wee-smalls . . . well, maybe Paul Corlaney would be available for an *un*scheduled meeting.

She chuckled to herself, winked at her Security Chief's Look. The Look deepened to frowning suspicion, and she laughed outright. "I was just thinking about Paul."

"Into brain pollution today, are you?"

"Unkind. Poor Paul—you have to feel sorry for him . . ."

"I don't *have* to feel anything for him. He used to be a drinking buddy, once upon a long time ago; now—I don't know what he is. But he made his own nest of snakes here. Let him live with it."

That much was true. She turned back to the window as sun-sparkle crossed a huge lake below, wondered absently if Paul had tried fishing it. Probably not. While he claimed to have taken up such planetary pursuits in his twenty years here, she doubted that ranked among them. Turn the Paul Corlaney who couldn't navigate a standard-config station loose on that vast expanse and you'd never find him again.

It was hard to think of Paul Corlaney as a real adversary. They'd been more than drinking buddies, much more than lovers, back on Ptolemy Station Alpha. But years of separation brought changes—undeniable fact of life—and Paul was holding out on her—another undeniable fact.

Paul would like them to think of him as just another Alliance-owned scientist dropped into a gravitywell to conduct planetary-specific research—research the results of which were the ThinkTank's payback to the taxpayers who funded their extravagant lifestyle. Only, Master GenTech Paul Corlaney was anything *but* 'just another researcher,' and somehow HuteNamid, newest and most obscure of the settled worlds, had him.

Paul claimed the lure was the local biological bonanza—and HuteNamid was indeed rich in that respect—but for a scientist whose bread and butter had been modifying GeneSets to better serve humanity's needs, a planet where everything was intensely homo-friendly seemed rather a waste of talents.

Not to mention boring to said Master scientist.

Third yawn. Paul Corlaney: one more local mystery. Along with disappearing data. Along with disappearing personnel.

On the surface, her primary purpose on HuteNamid boiled down to little more than a glorified census. Unregistered births, multiple names, individuals' entire files disappearing from 'Net records: she doubted an accurate historic census was possible now, even given the populace's cooperation—which she in no wise counted on. HuteNamid's representation in the Alliance congress might depend on accurate census records, but HuteNamid's new natives didn't seem to care.

Neither would she care, if Recon records had been the *only* records disappearing off the 'Net. Reconstructionist societies—Alliance had close to a hundred of them now, all trying to resurrect some long-forgotten ethnic past—had certain rights of self-governance; and as long as they kept their idiosyncrasies to themselves, the space-dwelling majority ignored them. The SciCorps researchers, on the other hand, were government assets, with attachments and relatives elsewhere; and somewhere in that wilderness below them, two SciCorps researchers whose records and persons had likewise disappeared, were imprisoned or hiding (or dead), and before *Cetacean* left this system, those two researchers (or their bodies) were going to be on her.

"Admiral?" Lexi Fonteccio's voice joined them from her Security Communications station at the rear of the shuttle. "Excuse me, please, but Chet's online. There's been a disturbance in sick bay. . ."

"Don't you dare negotiate, Tyeewapi! They go—or I do."

The perturbed young man on the far side of the Udirec window brought a fist down on the com button, then tapped a quick sequence on the remKey balanced on his lap. The clear wall went opaque, then flashed **Room Sealed** in large red letters.

"The little bastard!" Dr. McKenna spluttered. "It'll take SecCom to break through."

Anevai smothered a grin, wondering where Stephen figured he was going to 'go' aboard the ship. The guard next to her shifted uneasily, and she said, hoping to placate the poor fellow's embarrassment: "Look,, it's not your fault I'm not used to being stared at all the time. Stephen is, or so he claims, but now he's upset because *I'm* upset, and he's sort of into being irrational right now."

"You've got that right, girl," McKenna said. And to the guard: "Tell your boss to get his butt—"

"Gently, Doc." A slender, blond-haired man of indeterminate age joined them in the observation room. "I'm here. It's okay, Griff, you can go. Don't worry about Dr. Ridenour, I've locked him off the System." He waited until the door slid shut behind the guard, then held his hand out to Anevai. "Ms. Tyeewapi, I'm Chet Hamilton, Security Communications."

"Pleasure." She grasped his hand firmly, masking her surprise and meeting his gaze directly as she was learning they expected here. She'd heard about Hamilton from Stephen. Somehow, she'd expected the 'NetAT Master Programmer to be—taller. She gestured vaguely in the direction of the screen. "I'm sorry, sir. I honestly didn't mean to cause a fuss. Stephen's been going stir crazy, and I think maybe he's using this as an excuse to get out of here."

"I gathered.—So let's move him out. Once he's in his own quarters—"

"Forget it, Hamilton," McKenna broke in.

"I've already cleared it with Admir—"

"Has nothing to do with Cantrell. Or you! *I* don't trust him. The first thing we know, he'll be down in ZG trying to break his fool neck. The young idiot can barely walk without falling on his nose, and he's been trying to finagle a rec-release since Beta-shift. Swears a *little exercise* will do him good!"

"Exercise?" First she'd heard of it. *Down in ZG* . . . "In the gym?"

McKenna nodded.

"Well, wouldn't it? I mean, he seems a lot better today. Maybe a little exercise would be smart, and the less gravity, the—"

"Don't you *dare* encourage him! Damned if I'll have some of my best work ruined by some over-testosteroned desire to show how tough he isn't! That shoulder reconstruction is a work of *art,* and he'd damnwell better give it time to . . ."

"You haven't seen what this kid calls a light workout, Ms. Tyeewapi," Hamilton explained over McKenna's tirade.

She protested, "Surely he'd have sense enough—"

McKenna's tirade ended abruptly. *"Sense?* Sense and Stephen Ridenour parted company years ago."

Anevai hid another grin. Dr. Mo had the bit-brain pegged.

"On the other hand . . ." McKenna turned all charming and persuasive—

—Hamilton turned suspicious. "Dr. Mo, what are you concocting?"

"The main reason for Ms. Tyeewapi's escort is her brother's presence in the next ward, right?"

"Yes . . ."

"Otherwise, she's simply confined to the CivDeck, right?"

A cautious, narrow-eyed nod; Anevai decided she liked this Hamilton.

"If we moved her to DDeck, same as Ridenour's quarters, —assuming, of course, that she's willing to take on the responsibility . . ."

Anevai nodded emphatically. "I'm spending most of my time with him anyway."

"It wouldn't eliminate the observation, Ms. Tyeewapi, only

the guard's physical presence. That whole section has closer monitoring than your present quarters."

"Hey, so long as I can't see or run into them . . ." She caught Hamilton's quizzical glance and shrugged. Sure, it was a head-in-the-sand philosophy, but if it would calm Stephen down, she could put up with it. Mostly: "*And* so long as you take that special lock off my door so I don't have to ask *permission* to leave."

"Wait a minute—"

"I've got my bugaboos, Stephen has his. Cantrell told him I wasn't a prisoner, so he expects me to move with reasonable freedom. He's very—testy—about the subject."

Dr. McKenna, apparently sensing stalemate, said, "Where can she go?"

Hamilton threw his hands up in defeat. "Who am I to argue? I just work here. If Cantrell clears it, she can move this afternoon."

"This is why it's taken me so long." Lexi tapped the armrest fingerpad.

A chart appeared on the cabin monitor: a 3-D chart of language morphology both real and potential, dizzying in its complexity. "The translator practically blew a chip trying to sort this out. The percentage of words pulled from AmerInd languages other than Athabascan added to the sheer phonemic uncertainty—the boy was slurring badly during the recording— make for a very low reliability quotient."

TJ blinked and looked at Lexi instead. She was infinitely prettier; besides, it was her *job* to make sense out of the visual madness.

Several lines were highlighted. Cantrell clicked on one grouping, turning it magenta (the only unused color), and leaned forward, studying that chart. "Why the connection between *Cocheta* and *Kachina*, Lexi?"

Lexi shifted in her seat, signal of unease she rarely evinced. "Two separate words, two separate languages. *Kachina* is a deity reference. The translator's reference to *Cocheta* was a name, ostensibly meaning 'unknown.' In Hononomii Tyeewapi's original transmission to Nayati Hatawa, he quite clearly said

Dena Cocheta, 'the unknown valley,' but later, he told his sister he was 'flying with his *Cocheta*.' Dr. Corlaney indicated the term was a faction codeword, but I'm wondering if we might not be dealing with a wider concept. The *Dineh's* ancestors were highly religious—respect of elders bordering on worship, is the way I read it—and considering Ms. Tyeewapi's comments following her visit with her brother—"

Ms. Tyeewapi's comments. *Tirade* more like . . .

(*"You tell my father Nayati is responsible for Hononomii's condition . . . that his son told me to go to Nayati to get protection—for me and my Cocheta . . . Tell him Nayati has disobeyed him in the Libraries just like he did with the 'Net . . . Nayati's gone crazy and I'm not having my home, my people and my friends destroyed by some eons-dead lunatic!"*)

"You think Anevai's 'lunatic' might be some sort of religious referent?" Loren asked. "If they are—touching their gods, *could* we be dealing with local religion?"

Lexi shrugged. "It seemed a likely connection. On the other hand, perhaps it's simple phonemic drift and the correspondence to the word *Cocheta* is happenstantial. There's no direct connection with any recorded religious sect, but . . ."

Lexi seemed to hesitate, then:

"Yes?" Loren prompted.

"Many of the ancient religions used mind-altering substances, and certain sense-deprivation techniques for spiritual experiences, quests for supernatural mentors, vision quests, that sort of thing. Anevai said Nayati was going crazy. If *that's* his problem, we could be talking some local substance with a real bad interface with Deprivil. Could be that's what happened to Hononomii Tyeewapi."

It was Cantrell's turn to squirm. "Yes, well—good job, Lexi. Margo insists nothing showed up in his tests, but we'll keep that in mind." He followed her gaze out the window where green valleys and white-tipped mountains rose to meet them as the shuttle swept ever closer to the planet's surface. She said, on a deliberate change of subject, "I'd resist developer invasions, too, if I were them."

TJ scowled his disapproval, and responded drily, trying to

force her back online: "What we're up against here is no ecological-protection scheme, Loren."

"I didn't say it was." She at least had the decency to look away. "But it's part of the problem. They love their planet. They want to protect it."

"I wish you'd quit treating this like just another interCorps disagreement."

"InterCorps negotiations is my job, TJ."

"But there's nothing to negotiate *about*. HuteNamid's SciCorps is *happy* with its IndiCorps and vice versa. —Happy? Hell, they *love* each other."

"Maybe."

"But you don't think so." He pushed deliberately. Something was holding her here. Something beyond missing researchers and recalcitrant 'Netters.

"I honestly don't know what to think. We've been assuming the locals don't *care* about Alliance policies, but what if we're wrong? What if there's a damn good reason no one's ever transferred out of here—a reason not unconnected to those two who've gone missing? Maybe they're harboring all kinds of secrets. Secrets *they* dare not chance leaking."

" 'They,' who?"

"I don't know. Paul. Sakiimagan Tyeewapi. Maybe even Nayati. Who knows who's really calling the shots down here. But someday these so-called *Recon*-owned projects underway here might come to fruition and HuteNamid could become a disgustingly rich little backwater planet. The sudden power to buy people combined with the exclusive power to disrupt the 'NetDB yields a very uncomfortable—pardon me—'Net result."

Without so much as a token smile, TJ took a long pull from his coffee mug, giving her a look over the rim that made her frown and shift in her seat. "Leave us alone, will you, Lex?" He made the order sound like a request, but they all three knew differently.

Lexi had caught the growing tension, no way not, and had grown increasingly silent. She left without comment, unless an aura of relief counted. As the door slid shut behind her:

"Trying to pull one on me, Cantrell?" he asked harshly.

"I don't know what you mean."

"Yes, you do. *I* hadn't even considered the possibility of Recons making a major power play; not a fact I'm proud of, but a fact nonetheless. Forgive my prejudice, and tell me why, if you suspected anything of the kind, you haven't said something before now. I trusted you when you claimed these people are basically harmless—"

"I still believe they are," she interrupted him to say. He clenched his jaw and forced the mixture of concern and anger into the recesses of his gut.

"You 'believe,'" he said slowly. "For three days, I've had more than enough justification to pull a CentralSec override of your command, but I haven't. I've sat back, ignoring my own instincts and letting you take any number of risks with your career—and *mine*—based on that trust. We *know* the 'NetDB is compromised. We know Smith's responsible; Ridenour's even made a believer out of Chet. We know the Patent Protection Act is being used to keep important research out of communal hands, which—whatever our own opinions on the morality of the law in question—is marginally legal at best. I say we should blow the 'Link off the moon—*really* isolate these people—haul Smith, Paul Corlaney, Tyeewapi, Sr., and whoever else sneezes articulately, out to the ship and do a little mind-searching. If *that* doesn't ferret out the facts, take them back to the 'NetAT. Let *them* worry about it. The security of the 'Net is *their* business."

"I'd rather leave that as a last resort," she said, avoiding his eyes.

"Why?" he challenged, short and to the point. Damned if he'd let her sidestep this particular issue any longer. She glared at him, eyes dark and glittering in an absence of reserve only he ever witnessed.

"You know damn good and well why," she hissed. "Until I know what happened to Hononomii Tyeewapi, I'm not putting *any*one under Dep."

"You're gun-shy, Cantrell, and you can't afford to be," he said mercilessly. "Hononomii Tyeewapi cracked under Deprivil. We don't *know* the cause of that fracture. He's a self-confessed criminal and a medical anomaly: take him back to the interrogation MedEx in CentralSec. They'll straighten him out. That's *their* job.''

"You going to abdicate *all* my responsibility elsewhere, TJ? What will that gain us?"

"Maybe save your job. Maybe mine. Maybe a whole lot more. We can't afford to gamble on the 'NetDB. That goes— everything goes. Two missing researchers, who are probably dead anyway, aren't worth the risk. —*Now* I want to know why, if you thought Sakiimagan Tyeewapi was spearheading an economic coup, you didn't say something."

They swept over Tunica and into the curving bank that would take them into the final approach to the spaceport landing field, the subtle CG shift that assured landing config had successfully deployed. Cantrell's eyes closed. She swayed with those subtle shifts. "Sometimes," she murmured, "I wish I were still up in the cockpit. I was a good pilot . . ."

"You still are," he said quietly. "Just a different kind of ship."

A humorless chuckle escaped. "Yes, but now it's skin and bone rather than crylics, human convolutions instead of computer logic."

Her eyes opened and she met his gaze frankly.

"I haven't hidden anything from you, TJ. I suppose the suspicion was formulating, but nothing concrete until this instant. I don't *know* any better than you do. I'm *hoping* this meeting will reopen a dialog. Sakiimagan's current silence could be no more sinister than a conservative wait-and-see attitude. Recon/Spacer interface is supposedly my specialty. Who better to evaluate the motivations at work here? Council? Shapoorian herself, maybe? Council's a long way away, TJ. Lot could happen in the time to get us between here and there. Maybe you want me to inform them of the problem *over* the 'Net. I could do that. Open it up for transmission again and let whoever is *adjusting* it right back in. Might as well: if I pass our suspicions on to the 'NetAT that way, the entire universe is going to know anyway. Whether or not anything significant *has* been affected, users will *believe* it has, and lose all trust in the 'Net. Do you really want to be responsible for the resulting panic?''

"Dammit, admiral, there *is* no one else. Chet Hamilton can't authorize for the 'NetAT; he's assigned to *Cetacean* now, and *Cetacean* is Security."

"Stephen's the 'NetAT rep on this case."

"*Ridenour?* That unbalanced kid?" He couldn't believe she'd seriously take his advice on anything. "He's a 'NetAT Del d'Bugger, Cantrell. Nothing more. And he's already blown *that* assignment, plus everything else we might have had going here."

"That 'unbalanced kid' was the *only* ComNet expert who even noticed Smith's paper. *He* was right. He also understands what Smith's doing—"

"So he says."

"That's more than Chet can claim. *Chet* respects Stephen's judgment. If you can't trust me, trust Chet."

"I'd rather arrest Smith."

"You really think that would accomplish anything?"

"Get me a good night's sleep, it would."

"And the 'NetDB?"

"Smith'd talk under Dep."

"Not as much as we need—*Chet's* word on it, not mine. We need him awake and cooperative."

"You think this meeting can accomplish that?"

"It might help us find out where he stands. Stephen had his attention three days ago."

"Anything that moves would get Smith's attention. The local livestock probably run in terror—"

"I don't mean that way, TJ. Although—" She looked thoughtful, as though the obvious had just occurred to her. "—that weakness of Smith's might ultimately prove useful. But you saw those two together: Smith devoured every word the kid uttered; he's as feedback-starved as Ridenour. If he's still interested—"

"Don't count on it. He knows now—or will when he sees that—" TJ nodded toward the briefcase at her feet. "He'll realize precisely who and what Stephen Ridenour is. I *don't* think that's conducive to a trusting relationship."

"Which? The interview with Anevai? or Stephen's copy of Smith's paper?"

"Take your pick."

They slipped smoothly onto the runway; a far more elegant landing than she'd ever have managed. . . .

"I'm not *counting* on anything, Teej. I'm seeing what shakes out and I'm improvising. You got a better suggestion?"

When it came to mechanics, Cantrell was talented, but no artist. When it came to people—

He sighed, looked out the window, and shook his head. "Not yet."

—she was slick as silikote.

. . . Possibly, that was why Lt. Ramirez was up in the cockpit and she was back here.

He glanced at her out of the corner of his eye. "But I'll let you know when I have."

She smiled wearily. "I take it back: *that*, I'm counting on."

"Nayati, it's Sakiimagan."

Nayati lowered his bow and turned from the target glowing far across shimmering water. "You know what to tell him, Nigan."

"For the gods' sake, Hatawa—"

"Precisely. Tell him." He sensed a shift in the randomly generated wind currents within the cavern, drew as he whirled and without conscious calculation, let the shaft fly.

Dead center.

He faced Nigan Wakiza smugly. Nigan was frowning at him. He frowned back and pointed with the bow toward the phone in Nigan's hand. Nigan sighed and punched the hold button.

"Sorry, sir. I guess it wasn't Nayati after all. —No, sir, I don't. —Yes, sir, I'll tell him. —Yes, sir, I realize that. —I don't know, sir. —Yes, I told him. —Yes, sir. Goodbye, sir." He flipped the disconnect and collapsed the antenna.

"Yessir. Nossir. Let me kiss your toe, sir. —Shit, you sound like one of Cantrell's pet cops."

"Common courtesy, Hatawa. Do you recall the meaning of the word?"

"I'll remember courtesy when Sakiimagan remembers he's a Person and not an Alliance flunky."

"Log into reality, man. All Sakiimagan wants is your story

before he gets hit with Ridenour's. Only sensible, if you ask me.''

"I didn't. And that's *not* all. *You've* already told him what happened in the barn—'' Nigan's chin lifted defiantly, as if he thought that a challenge to his integrity, and defying Nayati to admonish him for that betrayal. But Nayati didn't really care. What Nigan didn't know was far more significant than anything he did. "Sakiimagan wants to coerce me into promises I refuse to make. And he wants to know what all I've changed in the 'NetDataBase. Since I don't know, I can't very well tell him, can I?''

"You've *got* to stop being so cavalier about that," Nigan protested. "We don't *know* it's safe—''

"I do.''

"And when did *you* become omniscient?''

Nayati smiled.

"Just stay off the damned 'Net,'' Nigan muttered, frowning. "At least until this blows over.''

"And let Cantrell believe she can intimidate me?''

"What is it you want, Nayati? What's so terrible about Paul's notion to get experts in—''

"Experts? Like Ridenour?''

"Yes, dammit, like Stephen. Wes says he's good. If you hadn't blown it, he and Wes might have been working on the security bypass even as we speak. Once we have safe access to the people with real clearance, *real* power, we'll have experts in all fields available for the Project.''

"Useless. Waste of time and energy.''

"You think *you* know better than the Council of Elders?''

"Of course. So could you. The Elders are as embryos in the womb compared to Them. *You* have avoided the experience, but when you take the final plunge, you know more, *feel* more, make connections you never thought possible. . . .''

"So why don't you know everything there is to know? You've been 'plunging' for two years.''

He smiled tightly. "Maybe I do.''

Concern tempered with horror replaced Nigan's scowl; satisfaction stalemated Nayati's irritation. He ignored both emotions. Someday Nigan would understand. Someday they would *all* understand and have Nayati Hatawa to thank for that knowledge.

Everyone. Even Sakiimagan Tyeewapi.

"Suffice to say, I'll do anything to protect what we have." He turned back to the target, nocked another arrow. "Fortunately, that doesn't include sucking up to 'NetAT spies." He let the arrow fly, heard metal ping as the two tips collided. He grinned. The new bow was a gem. "I think we've finally found the right glue."

ii

Lexi closed the conference room door quietly behind Sakiimagan Tyeewapi and crossed the antechamber to their temporary security station. As she slipped in behind the desk, TJ Briggs entered the final clearance code into the Security portable, ID'd with his personal, then stood back to give her a clear view of the display.

>**Father,**
>**Contrary to what you think, it was not my choice**
>**to get arrested. . . .**

She glanced up from the monitor. "Right to the point, isn't she?"

He shrugged. "Hey, she was in a hurry."

"Right . . ."

>**. . . However, I'm here now, a guest (or so Admiral**
>**Cantrell says) aboard *Cetacean*, and because I'm**
>**here, I've seen and heard things *you* need to know.**
>**So for once in my life, Dad, shut up and listen to**
>**what I have to say—not what you think I mean.**

Briggs leaned back, put his feet up on the desk of their makeshift security station, casually scanning Anevai Tyeewapi's letter over Lexi's shoulder, but concentrating on his internalized audio view of the conversation taking place beyond the closed doors of conference room B-3. Formalities mostly. Awkward exchanges between opposing factions vying for favor points and advantages. Sakiimagan Tyeewapi, Loren Cantrell, Paul Corlaney, and Wesley Smith.

King, queen, ace, and a wildcard joker. God, what a hand.

He sent a message down that nerve reserved for the security implant, and the voices in his head grew louder.

It made for an odd schizophrenia at times, the SecPlant did, but it certainly saved time, money—and lives. Valuable piece of equipment between high-ranking officials and their body-guards, especially when local politics made bugging a room impolite. Not something you could tape without duping his endocrine and nervous systems, (although someday the techno-tots would likely stuff a recorder into his skull along with everything else), but having a Central Security Voice on the other end of a Priority One Implant was the next-best thing. Anything said in there, TJ Briggs would hear, and anything he heard, he could remember, and if Loren Cantrell required any of those memories in court, they were legally admissible evidence. Better than most recordings: his brain was less easily tampered with.

He smiled grimly. Nasty trick old man Morely in CentralSec had pulled on him all those years ago. But he hadn't argued. That addition to the standard beeper had allowed him to be a *Cetacean* crew member *and* Loren Cantrell's legal backup, a position he damn sure wouldn't trust to any of his fellow Voices.

He tapped Lexi's shoulder, met her distracted blink with a quiet update on the proceedings. If Lexi had a similar personal-ized beeper, he wouldn't have to interrupt her. If Lexi had a P1-SecPlant instead of the standard-issue beeper, she could have brought that secured file up on her own.

But then, if Recon-born Lexi could be granted the Security clearance she'd earned years ago, the circumstances which prompted that letter likely wouldn't exist and the conference taking place next door would likely not be necessary.

Sakiimagan Tyeewapi's world was collapsing. He could see it happening, and at this Moment in this Cycle of Time, he could see no way to prevent it; thus his presence here in Science Complex Conference Room B-3, without a word of protest, without a single indication of his dissatisfaction.

Sakiimagan Tyeewapi was worried. His system had lost its

lifeline to the rest of Alliance. Communication cut off at this woman's orders. The loss was not, to his people, any great loss, though the SciCorps admittedly had other priorities. The fact of the shutdown—that was terrifying.

Cantrell had ordered HuteNamid's 'NetLink shut down: a supremely arrogant and radical decision made only once before in Nexus ComNet history. . . .

Outside, beyond a wall of transparent space-grown silkrylic, the rift valley and the city of Tunica provided a backdrop for the Recon governmental office towers: deliberate reminder to the researchers they were not alone. Inside, a round table topped with intricate native-wood marquetry: imagery and artform not strictly part of his Native American heritage, but certainly in spiritual keeping with those traditions.

Long before the first researcher arrived on HuteNamid, he and the building's architect had searched for such universal messages, recognizing the need to bridge the gap between the amorphous spacer heritage of the SciCorps researchers and their own Indigene Corps' increasingly homogeneous mind-set. Elsewhere in the ComNet alliance, that gap had led to internal strife, strife which had destroyed more than one fine Recon group.

He'd always believed their efforts had been successful. Relations with incoming researchers invariably grew stronger. But their subtle psychologies had never been tested as they would be today. There was no time to convince Cantrell. Nor had he the options with her that he did with the researchers. She was not one of them. Her place was solidly in Alliance.

. . . and that StarSystem had never come *back* onLine. Official reports claimed catastrophic systems failure; biological reversion; personnel relocated.

Sakiimagan's research indicated otherwise, though he couldn't prove it. —Yet.

Polite beginnings: banalities he ignored, waiting for Cantrell to reveal her true purpose in calling this meeting.

Cantrell posed a very real threat, held the power to frighten him, but since Wesley Smith had the power effectively to hold the 'NetDB hostage, Cantrell became—irrelevant.

Smith himself was—feckless, but there was no denying his

very real ability where it touched 'Net programming and 'Net data propagation. Anevai had a close friendship with the man; a friendship which had grown (he shuddered discreetly) into something like a teacher-student relationship; but a relationship which frequently proved useful. Besides, ultimately Paul Corlaney controlled Smith—

—and since Paul Corlaney *wanted* what HuteNamid (and Sakiimagan) alone could give him, Sakiimagan Tyeewapi, ultimately, controlled Corlaney. Paul also knew that separation of interest simply did not occur on HuteNamid. When it did, it was resolved—

—or eliminated. So much for irrelevancies.

"Gentlemen," Cantrell said, "I've brought you here to view a tape. Before you ask, it *has* been edited, but that edit was for the sake of efficiency, not deception. If you wish—"

"For heaven's sake, Loren," Corlaney interrupted, "cut the theatrics. What's this all about? I thought—"

"Bear with me, Paul. The tape is of a conversation, a very long interview that took place two days ago aboard *Cetacean*, after which Ms. Tyeewapi asked me to arrange this meeting."

Obvious bait.

Paul snapped. "What does Anevai have to do with it?"

This woman made Paul foolish.

"The tape is, in its way, a message from her—and Stephen Ridenour."

"How is he, admiral?" Smith asked. "Is he really going to be all right?"

"I won't lie to you, Dr. Smith, it was close. Very close. But Stephen's quite well, considering, as you'll see for yourself in a moment."

Palpable relief. Careless revelation of the anxiety which (Paul had complained) had made Smith useless for days. —Unwise. Unwise to give away so much when you had so little to gain, so much to lose.

Cantrell slipped the VD into the slot, and suddenly they were six, and his daughter's image was saying:

> *"You mean to tell me you were nothing but a Del d'Bug man?"*

So now Ridenour was an admitted spy, though not quite the

spy Nayati had perceived. Not Alliance Council. Not Alliance Security. 'NetAT: the ComNet Authority, the policing agency of the Nexus ComNet, which was itself the heart and soul of the Alliance. And Ridenour had come here to see Smith about Smith's paper on the 'NetTap. Being the 'NetAT representative, this Ridenour held the power to blacklist Smith within the scientific community—not only for Smith's lifetime, but for *all* time. But Smith didn't even blink at discovering who Ridenour worked for. No shock to him as it had been to his daughter. Not even a concern.

Perhaps he'd misjudged Smith.

"Please, Stephen, you're making me feel like a scuz. Granted, I may be, but won't you let me—"

"C–consider yourself—absolved. —Please, just go."

Ridenour, pale-faced with exhaustion, bruised and swathed in tight bandages, appeared younger than he recalled. That apparent youthfulness, combined with the spy's denial of an almost palpable, unidentified need, roused feelings Sakiimagan sternly silenced, reminding himself how easily one with training could create such an impression, and what Cantrell had to gain should such tactics prove effective against the governor's daughter's better sense.

Which, apparently, they had. Anevai did not leave, and moments later:

"Know what I think, Ridenour? I think you aren't spacer at all. I think you're Recon, just like me."

A slow nod from Paul. So Paul had suspected the truth: a suspicion he hadn't shared. From Smith—

—Wesley Smith leaned forward, staring at the screen, his face no longer an echo of his reactions. Smith had gone to Vandereaux Academy, as this boy had. Cantrell, too, was watching Smith, and exuded satisfaction in an unguarded instant.

Sakiimagan's world canted yet one degree more.

In the antechamber outside SCCR B-3, only Lexi's own light tap on the keyboard and TJ's occasional grunting acknowledgment of the next-door activities broke the stillness.

TJ's grunts she'd long since learned to ignore—he'd relay to her if something Significant transpired. In the meanwhile, Anevai's letter continued:

> **... We're all in Nigan Wakiza's debt. He was the only sane individual in the barn during the altercation—**

"Altercation, hell."

Startled, Lexi swung around to confront TJ's belt buckle. "Good way to lose something important, Teej."

"We haul the kid upstairs just short of a body bag, and the governor's daughter calls it an *altercation*." His scowl puzzled her. TJ Briggs was not usually so ill-humored.

"Stephen already explained it was an accident."

"*Accident*, hell. You going to trust what comes out of that kid's head? He was missing a few relays to begin with; after the trauma and hours under anesthetic, I sure as hell don't believe it. I can't believe McKenna let him out this afternoon. I was counting on her keeping him tied down for at least a week. I trust Chet is monitoring him."

Lexi was having a difficult time understanding her superiors' actions these days. In all her time with *Cetacean*, TJ and the admiral had *never* fought, yet ever since Stephen Ridenour had joined them, there'd seemed little but friction between them.

She probed cautiously: "Why should he? The admiral cleared his release. Besides, the whole system is locked out of the 'Net. Not much Stephen could do even if he were inclined to. And he's not, Teej, we all know that."

"Speak for yourself," TJ muttered, and tapping into planetside Security, ordered a direct link to Chet Hamilton's *Cetacean* office.

"TJ, why are you doing this? Stephen's all right. Leave him alone, will you?"

He sat tapping his foot on the floor, refusing to meet her eyes.

"Would you be doing this if Stephen weren't Recon?"

"Not fair, Lex. His genotype has nothing to do with it."

"Doesn't it?"

"He is what he is. The fact that he claims to understand Smith's system makes him potentially damned dangerous. I'd feel a hell of a lot more confident if he was a hundred years old, bald, and potbellied. Cantrell's not thinking straight about him. *You're* not. *Somebody* has to retain a sense of perspec—''

''Hi, Teej. What's up?''

He tapped the transmit button. ''Chet? How's the golden boy? Staying out of trouble? Playing any computer games?''

''Only game he's playing right now is with Anevai Tyeewapi.''

TJ barked, ''What 'game'?''

Laughter over the com. *''Relax, old man. Truthercon. The Tyeewapi girl's—oops.''*

''What oops, Hamilton?''

Silence from the speaker. TJ jumped to his feet, leaned his hands on the table. ''What—*oops*, —dammit?''

Stupid waste of energy, Lexi thought, exchanging a wry glance with the on-tap security, thankful there was no one else around to witness their superior's idiocy. *What're you going to do, Teej*, she thought, *throttle Stephen long distance?*

A pop of renewed connection. A fading chuckle from the other side of the atmosphere. *''Relax, SecMan. Didn't want to blast your eardrums. 'Less I'm mistaken, the golden boy from Vandereaux just got his first kiss.''*

TJ slumped back down. ''Stinking voyeur.''

''Want me to stop watching?''

''Want to lose your job?''

Another chuckle. *''Thought so. 'Sides, Ms. Tyeewapi's gone beddie-bye like a good girl. I'll give the kid's adrenaline time to settle, then shut him down for the night, too.''*

''You've got him off the 'Net?''

''Far as I know. Can't really be sure anymore, can we? Not after what Hononomii Tyeewapi pulled on us. But I'm not really worried about the kid. He's okay. Knows the rules.''

''Why does everyone keep saying that?''

''Cool down, Teej, your bios are hiccupping all over the boards. He'll behave. He's a good kid, and an exceedingly sick one, right now.''

''Yeah, right,'' TJ said, and flipped the transmit off. ''Not too sick to punch buttons.''

''. . . but, Stephen, if your job was to infiltrate, why were you such a . . . tode at first?''

"I—" Embarrassed eyes dropped. *"I was scared, Anevai . . . I believed any contact with Recons, or even planetary atmosphere, would trigger some genetic-level response in me, contaminate me for—God, that sounds so stupid, now."*

"So, why'd you think it? You're a lot of things, Stephen, but you're not stupid."

Impatient jerk of the bandaged head. Long fingers absently stroking the battered notebook cradled in his arms.

"C'mon, Ridenour, you're avoiding—"

A muscle twitched in a bruised cheek.

"Fuck off, 'buster-bitch."

A startled gasp. A hand raised in angry retaliation . . .

"Go ahead, 'buster-bitch, hit me. The brig's lovely this time of year. You'll love it there."

. . . and a slow revelation of anguished eyes begging for understanding.

Anevai's hand closed to an angry, shaking fist and slowly lowered. *"Don't you ever call me that again."*

"Got a problem with it, bitch?"

Same rough voice so thoroughly at odds with that Look. The girl scowled and turned away.

"Just make your point."

"I'm trying, Anevai. Do you know where the term planet-buster came from? Ever look it up?"

"Why would I want to?"

Barometric eyes dropped. The lean jaw clenched. Relaxed. And clenched again. *"I suppose my curiosity was somewhat—unnatural. It's an old term: dates from the earliest IndiCorps records. The first Terra-Engineers coined it—preferred it over their Corps designation. They were proud of their accomplishments and preferred to think of themselves as tamers of a planet, not the new locals. It wasn't until the Ethnic Reconstructionist movement that it became an—epithet."*

"Didn't mean you had to believe what they were saying."

"Don't you see? Whether or not I believed, others around me did. Others with the power to destroy the only thing I've got. I was afraid I would no longer be able to do the work I was trained for—work I love—"

"Do you, Stephen? Do you really love it? Or do you love what you could be doing, if you'd been allowed into DeProg?"

"How did you—" A startled, unfinished thought that ended with a shrug, an elsewhere look. *"I wasn't good enough, Anevai. It's that simple."*

"Like bloody hell. You keep telling me how these actions are being taken against Recons, and yet you refuse to see that they've warped your entire thinking about yourself."

"In other words, I'm crazy?"

"I didn't say—"

"Of course I am." Chillingly matter-of-fact. *"But if Bijan Shapoorian and his kind can do that to an indigene-born, think how much more effective their arguments can be on those with something to gain politically, economically—even psychologically—by believing them. What you have here—like that eclectic interCorps 'gang' of yours—it's special. But that very uniqueness could destroy it. It must be protected."*

"And what you're saying is that we can't do it on our own."

A nod: *"You need Cantrell. But what Wesley's system can do—I can't ignore that. There* must *be a way for everyone—you, Cantrell, your father, Wesley, even Nayati and the Council—to have what they really need."*

"Need, Stephen?"

Another nod. *"Need. Not what is—politically correct for them to want."*

Cantrell had left that barb in, even though Stephen had known he was being watched—probably known he was being recorded—and could well have meant it expressly for her ears. From the moment she'd known of his existence, she'd harbored—

'politically correct' plans for Stephen Ridenour. Plans she'd never actually expressed, but plans he no doubt suspected. Brilliant, Academy-trained, attractive as hell—

—and Recon: the antithesis of all the hate-mongering anti-Reconstructionist fables Shapoorian's GenMem freaks propounded. He'd have been the perfect Recon press rep except . . .

. . . except he wasn't interested. Chances were, Stephen Ridenour would never willingly breach that security hold on his personal files and reveal to the universe who and what he really was. Besides, once the 'NetAT got him back, between their own low-profile policy and what he now knew, he might well never get into public again.

She supposed she couldn't blame him—he'd been a target for most of his life—but she had had hopes on the way here. Now—

—now she'd be satisfied if the mere fact of his heritage—coupled with his undeniable personal appeal—helped to manipulate the single problem sector of HuteNamid. Afterward, she'd deliver him wherever he wanted to go. He'd have ceased to be of value.

> "And what about you, Stephen? What do you want?"
>
> "I told you: to clear Wesley's paper."
>
> "That's for Wesley. Adm. Cantrell said you're not pressing charges against Nayati—or me. Is that a political move? Wouldn't you like . . . revenge?"
>
> The boy shook his head slowly.
>
> "Certainly not against you. You couldn't have stopped him—we both know that. Against Nayati—" Dark lashes dropped, concealing the boy's expressive eyes. "Nayati couldn't help himself."
>
> Anevai looked distressed.
>
> "Gods, Ridenour. I wanted to stop him. I knew—everyone watching must have—that you were telling the truth. That you didn't know—"
>
> "Don't you see, it didn't matter. . . . It wasn't Truth he was after. Not even a confession. I doubt Nayati

knew why he...'' A visible shudder. *"I remember thinking that any moment the knife would begin to cut more deeply and that soon I..."* The imaged eyes hazed, the recorded voice dropped to a whisper. *"...soon I would be looking up from the ground at my own headless body: God's—retribution—for..."*

A roll to face the wall; shaking hands pulling the covers up over bandage-shrouded shoulders. A faint request for Anevai to leave.

At the door, a hesitation. An abrupt return to the bed to pull Stephen up into her arms, saying nothing, ignoring his protests, rocking him gently, holding him until he quit objecting—

—and for a long time after.

God, he was just a boy. Paul caught that thought, cut it down before it gained too firm a foothold, and concentrated on other, more disturbing impressions. *Headless body? God's retribution?* What kind of deranged viper had Loren loosed among them? Recon, without a doubt; no spacer would think in those terms. Remarkable he'd retained any vestige of the beliefs after all these years—

—If he had. If they weren't *all* planted thoughts in a superbly trained actor. Best to have Wesley check his records thoroughly—*hang* the security flags.

"Well, governor," Loren said as the images faded and the lights came up, "do you begin to see how far we've all gone wrong in our dealings with one another? Stephen was attacked and nearly killed—"

"According to his own statement, admiral, he was caught spying. And those who caught him tried to ascertain why their rights to privacy were being violated. You speak eloquently of injustices to Recons, yet you yourself—"

"—Did not instruct Dr. Ridenour to follow your daughter to that barn. Stephen's no spy. He's a student. A young man eager to do the best job he possibly could, who misinterpreted instructions and put himself into a situation he was in no wise trained to handle. This Nayati Hatawa nearly killed—"

"Ridenour nearly killed himself—again, by his own admission. You have the weapon: whose presence did you detect on it?"

Without a flicker, Loren answered, "Stephen's. Before that, your daughter's."

"Have you *any* solid evidence to substantiate Stephen Ridenour's claim that my nephew was even present in the barn that night? And what of the others Ridenour claims were there?"

"Your daughter's statements—"

"Hard evidence, admiral. The sort admissible in *your* courts of law. Was her statement made under Deprivil?"

A flicker of eyelid. "No."

"And such a statement made now, so long after the fact, would be subject to her personal bias, would it not? Lacking absolute veracity, and therefore legality, would it not?"

Loren didn't flinch. Neither did she answer.

"You've disrupted the research facilities, had your investigation teams crawling around the barn and surrounding area for days. What have they found?"

"You know it's impossible to link any of the findings to anyone specific until we've got the person. Yes, we have certain readings. So far, we've been able to identify Dr. Ridenour's presence, your daughter's, and Nigan Wakiza's. At the same time, we know others were there—others without proper 'Net records. That's why we *must* have this Nayati. Perhaps we are accusing him unfairly. If that's the case, let's clear him and be done."

"Clear him? I've heard no formal charges," Sakiima said. "Not even the 'NetAT can do anything without filed complaints."

Her jaw tightened. "Dr. Ridenour has chosen not to press charges."

"Doesn't that suggest to you that perhaps Nayati is *not* the guilty party?"

"What it suggests to me is a young man who's been taught so long his rights don't matter that *he's* come to believe it. A young man who has chosen to forfeit those—*virtual* rights, as he calls them, in favor of some esoteric Greater Good. Personally, I think he should sue the pants off your Nayati—*make* him explain himself in a court of law. Do them both good."

"You've no grounds to judge what is best for Nayati. You've never even met him."

"Haven't I?" Uncharacteristically, Loren was allowing her growing impatience to show. Possibly because she'd met her stony-faced match in Sakiimagan. "I've met him a hundred times on a dozen different worlds—and *stations*. Your people are not so unique as you'd like to think, Sakiimagan Tyeewapi, and the type is not confined to planets."

"If that's true, then you should understand why I ask—respectfully—that you grant his own people the right to judge him."

"His crime was not against one of his own people! Hasn't Stephen rights also?"

Sakiima sat silently for a long moment. "All right, admiral. Suppose I arrest Nayati. Have him brought face-to-face with Ridenour—in the presence of a Peace-maker Justice. Would you be willing to abide by the Peace-maker's decision?"

Paul met Loren's glance with a helpless shrug. He had no idea what Sakiima was up to.

She asked cautiously: "What's a Peace-maker Justice?"

"Someone who knows both parties, can listen to both sides, interpret from both points of view. Make a ruling according to true justice, not some faraway court's interpretation of irrelevant laws. We have our own Justices—the wisest of our people, chosen by the locals. None of them, of course, would know Dr. Ridenour."

"A single person's judgment? One of your people who knows both parties? Anevai, perhaps?"

"Or one of yours." Sakiima glanced toward the oblivious Wesley, and beyond Wesley to him. "I'm sure we could find someone."

Loren silently looked from one to the other of them—connections being made, tested, and broken. Finally, "I don't think so, governor. At least, not yet. I'm not talking about arresting Hatawa—yet. I'm talking answers. Resolutions. —Mutual satisfaction. Nayati Hatawa attacked Stephen for a reason. I want to know that reason."

"You say Dr. Ridenour is here to investigate Dr. Smith's paper. What Wesley Smith decides is his business, not mine.

Nayati's judgment and his honor are in question. Those are my business, not the Alliance Council's, not their representative's."

"Yours, Sakiima?" Paul asked, uncomfortable with this allocation of power and responsibility. "Isn't the assessment of his judgment—the ramifications of his actions—the Tribal Council's business?"

Sakiimagan stared at him, then dipped his chin noncommittally, and with a chill that had nothing to do with room temperature, Paul felt his old friend retreat—felt himself thrust into the role of Unfriend, if not outright Enemy.

"This means you're not going to let us have him?" Loren asked Sakiimagan.

"He's not mine to give you, admiral. If Nayati chooses to give himself up to you, that's his business." Sakiima's response was cool and hard. "Touching though Ridenour's personal story has been, it has nothing to do with our situation here."

"All right," Loren said slowly, "let's talk about *your* business. Tell me, governor, have you ever been off this planet of yours?"

"I was born in space, admiral."

"You know what I mean."

"What difference does it make?"

"A great deal. Politics. *Real* politics, not the stuff you read in Sociology class. For the moment, this paradisiac, but isolated, corner of the universe is of little interest to the rest of Alliance. You and your people have eloquently expressed your desire for it to remain so. But I can't help wondering how you intend to enforce that isolation. I could have helped—had fully intended on doing so—but Stephen Ridenour is an authorized representative of the ComNet Authority, and your Nayati Hatawa attacked him. Under those circumstances, I can't see how to keep you—and this beautiful planet—from offWorld attention."

"Should that concern me?"

"You tell me. You would have me believe your people are different—that here Recon and researcher coexist in harmony and mutual respect. But there's a reason for that, isn't there, Sakiimagan Tyeewapi? A reason you have, perhaps, *forgotten* to mention."

"None that I can think of, admiral."

"You accept only the researchers you personally invite in, don't you? Everyone else remains spacer—and the Enemy. Isn't that right?"

How had she found that out? Another chill as Sakiimagan's gaze flicked toward him and back to Loren. Sakiimagan suspected *him* of telling her . . .

"Clever scheme," Loren said. "You've used your Recon connections to lure particularly creative researchers down here where your Recon immunity keeps your Recon/Researcher co-op projects hidden for over twenty years. Clever, but you've bucked the system—and now you're going to draw the 'NetAT's fire in a major way; a fire I can't help you duck. I represent the Alliance *Council*, and we all know the *'NetAT* is the true power where it regards the 'Net's access to information. Stephen Ridenour was—*is*, dammit—the 'NetAT representative in this situation. —And your people tried to kill him."

"No one tried to kill him, Loren," Paul interjected quietly, hoping to show Sakiimagan he was no traitor. "And his welcome might've been different if he'd been here openly. Trying to sneak in as a fake transfer with faked credentials was—"

"Bullshit, Corlaney," Wesley broke in.

"Decided to wake up, did you? —What's bullshit?"

"You should learn to keep your trap shut when you don't know shit, Dr. C. Stephen Ridenour's credentials are more legitimate than yours."

"Let's not get nasty—"

"Your Nayati's motivations," Loren interrupted them, "won't make a bit of difference to the 'NetAT evaluation of the situation here, not unless we can manage an attitudinal turnabout right now. —Four days ago, Stephen wouldn't even acknowledge his Recon birth. Now, rather than press charges against Nayati Hatawa, he said *Don't cloud the important issues*. He's changing. Maybe others can change, too. —And let's talk power. *He* has the power to influence the 'NetAT on your behalf; I don't. You can't afford not to court Ridenour now."

"What exactly do you want?" Sakiimagan asked cautiously,

and Paul pleaded silently to Loren not to ask again for Nayati, drew a relieved breath at her response:

"Stop withholding vital information, for one thing."

"Such as?"

"Where Drs. Bennett and Liu are. What's happened to them."

"And?"

"That'll get us started."

"I haven't yet agreed to tell you anything. I want my son back. You've made no formal charges—I want him released into my custody."

"That's not possible. He's under his physician's constant supervision."

"His *physician* is his grandfather."

"I'm sorry, governor."

"Then he *is* a hostage."

"No, governor, he's insurance; at the moment, my only resource for information. Your daughter has spoken with him once and learned enough that now *she's* cooperating. She's trying to get *your* endorsement and support before she commits fully. I respect that allegiance. I'm *not* pressuring her. I don't *want* to pressure your son. But I might have to. Do you understand me?"

"You're very—persuasive, admiral. However, you overlook one very real possibility."

"And that is?"

"Perhaps Councillor Shapoorian *is* correct. Perhaps the *Dineh* do not belong in Alliance Council discussions. —And perhaps that Council should likewise stay out of ours."

For a long moment Loren sat silent, studying Sakiimagan like a puzzle with no ready answer. Then: "And perhaps you, sir, are not seeing things quite so clearly as you believe—or as all your people would see them, given the chance."

She extracted an envelope from her briefcase and slipped it across the table. A glimpse of familiar handwriting: Anevai, Paul thought. And Anevai had requested this meeting.

"I understood your people were highly democratic," she said. "I suggest you take the decision to them."

Ignoring the envelope, Sakiima rose to his feet, effectively ending the meeting. "I want my son back, admiral, then—perhaps—we can talk."

"And your daughter?"

A glance at the table. "I'm no longer certain I have one. Much as Dr. Ridenour feared, yes, he *has* changed in his short time here. And as much as I would like to deny it, if what you tell me is true, if Anevai is, indeed, 'cooperating' with you, my daughter has been equally contaminated by her contact with him."

Without a backward glance, he left the conference room.

A message was waiting when Anevai arrived in her quarters. From Stephen. Considering the condition she'd left him in, she was surprised he could *find* the keyboard, much less use it.

>**Thanks for the game, confrere, but you left without explaining your last throw. Was that payment Truth? or Consequence? Either way, I think I finally won a round.**

>**Till tomorrow, sleep well.**

>**Soberly yours: SR**

Anevai read it through several times before wiping it, feeling more than a little guilty, wondering exactly how he meant her to take it, remembering a lighthearted good-night which had turned into Something More.

She shouldn't have let him have the Scotch, no matter the high water ratio, but Truthercon didn't make much sense otherwise, and Stephen had insisted on learning the silly game once she'd been stupid enough to mention it. And you had to pay *something* if you guessed wrong. Trouble was, Stephen had never guessed right.

Maybe he hadn't wanted to. Maybe he'd gotten in exactly the condition he'd wanted to be in tonight. Maybe he'd been far too serious for far too long.

Muscle and bone settled on the bed. Somewhere, far across the room, was a bathroom with a medicine cabinet and lots of little vials clamped securely against vector shifts. She could find something there for the aches and pains, could even find something to tell her body it was the perfect time to go to sleep and that when she woke up, it would be 'morning.'

But she'd have to make it across the room first, and some-how, she thought her body might manage sleep all on its own.

She unzipped her borrowed *Cetacean* shipsuit, stood just long enough to let it drop into a puddle around her feet, hooked it with a toe and flipped it over the swivel chair.

A spark of light fell from its pocket, *pinged* off the chair-base and landed in the carpet. She stretched out her foot, captured the spark between her toes, and rolled back into the pillows, transferring the spark to her hand.

The bed-lamp, dialed to a single narrow beam and angled at the cut-crystal button, sent tiny rainbows scattering throughout the otherwise darkened room. A roll of the button between her fingers and the rainbows chased each other on a spiralling dance reminiscent of the jacket this button—and two more exactly like it—had once graced. An all-over rainbows jacket. Pale-blue iridescence that had made its wearer seem like something made of moondust. But he *had* been real. All too real. And as fragile as the jacket itself: quality tailoring which when stressed had come apart everywhere but at the seams.

She sighed. Kisses, even when they came from one of the universe's better-looking bit-brains, were not supposed to affect sensible adults this way. She recalled thinking once (it seemed long ago and far away now) that they (*all* the gang) could cure the academy-clone 'NetHead of his cool aloofness. She just hadn't anticipated quite so much—personal—involvement in the process.

Sleep well? —*Ha! Wesley, we've created a monster!*

iii

"Did Stephen ever tell you, Adm. Cantrell, what the title and tag were on that paper of mine?" Wesley Smith leaned forward and rested his elbows on his knees, letting his hands hang between free-swinging feet. He was too tired—and too de-pressed—to bother sitting up—to bother finding a real chair rather than the tabletop.

He had good reason to be depressed. Stephen Ridenour was

gone. Irrevocably torn from his side by the idiosyncrasies of Alliance law.

And by the stupidity of one Nayati Hatawa.

Loren Cantrell didn't answer. He glanced toward the window where the setting sun highlighted sculptured cheekbones, traced the slick teal fabric stretched over arms crossed beneath a measurement the tailored uniform did nothing to disguise. Loren Cantrell was Alliance Security and military spit-'n'-polish to the core—

—failings Wesley Smith could overlook when they came packaged in such a body. Wesley Smith could be thinking very lascivious thoughts—

—if only he weren't so depressed.

At the moment, a frown line marred the elegance of her dark-skinned features. How nice. He'd found a Question without some quick and easy response. Faith restored in his own superior mind, he graciously granted her time to formulate an answer.

Somewhere behind him, Paul Corlaney grumbled. Paul was pissed because Sakiima had taken offense and bolted. But Paul had been pissed about one thing or another all week. Besides, Wesley was pissed at Paul, so who cared?

Paul was at the core of all Wesley's problems, Paul and his smarter-than-thou decisions. As the responsible party, Paul Corlaney *might* prove useful in rectifying the mess Paul had created, but until Wesley Smith saw what form that usefulness might take, Paul could go suck a rock. In the meantime, the Wesser and Admiral Loro were going to talk about the Wesser's concerns, not Paul's.

And if that perturbed Paul Corlaney, so much the better.

Still wearing that becoming look of confusion, Admiral Loro moved into the chair nearest his perch, and looked up into his sad eyes. (He knew they were sad, knew that he looked wretched—miserable—utterly pathetic. It was one of his most believable Looks.) She was ignoring Paul's grumbling. (Served Corlaney right. *He* took Loro for granted, just because he happened to have the advantage of prior *acquaintance*.) Unfortunately, she didn't appear in the least sympathetic to *his* woes, either. One might even say she appeared—amused. That she didn't believe his Look in the least—

—insightful brilliance which merely sharpened the game. It made her such an *excellent* foil. Wesley *liked* Adm. Cantrell. Wesley *liked* Adm. Cantrell a great deal. He'd be quite happy at the moment—

—if only he weren't so depressed.

Loro was saying: "I don't recall Stephen's mentioning it, Dr. Smith, and I never thought to ask, but..."

What was she talking about? Oh, yes. His Question.

"...I'd assumed it was just another reference piece under the 'Net-applications tag. Was I wrong?"

His mouth wanted to twitch upward. Good touch. He let it twitch. "You could say that. You see, I hadn't planned to publish my ideas—somehow, I didn't think it was the sort of thing the 'Net Authorities would want to hear, being the conservative lot—" *Of asses.* "—they are. But Paul—"

"Dammit, man, watch what you're saying!"

"—Paul thought," he continued smoothly, noting the answering twitch in Adm. Loro's mouth, the crinkle at the corners of her eyes: appreciation of his stylish handling of Paul's lack of couth, no doubt, "—and correctly so, I think now, though I—mildly—disagreed at the time, that I could use a partner here. —Someone off whom I could bounce my ideas. Someone reliable enough, and clever enough, to remove some of the day-to-day *I-need-it-now* pressure. Being one of the smaller egos here—"

Over in his corner, Paul snorted. Appalling sound.

Wesley cast his eyes heavenward, compelled to excuse his associate's crudity. "As I was saying, being one of the smaller egos, I would certainly not begrudge another's input. However, I wanted someone who saw beyond the physicalities, and into the...poetic, you might say."

"Good lord, Wes, say it and be done!"

"Shut up, Paul," Loren said affably, obviously entranced with his narrative.

But: "Perhaps he has a point, admiral," Wesley said, thereby proving his superior breeding. "Perhaps I should." He allowed his voice to drift off Significantly. "The title was

Harmonies of the 'Net, and I flagged it to *Philosophies of the 'Net*."

Nothing.

Several long moments of nothing.

He looked down at her through his lashes. Waiting.

Her full lips twitched. Twitched again. And stretched into a definite smile this time, a rich chuckle vibrating deep in her lovely long throat.

He leaned back, balancing on his tailbone, lacing his fingers behind his head. Somehow, he'd known she would appreciate the sheer elegance of his humor. One of the most—hell, what use modesty?—*the* most significant paper ever to hit the Nexus Communications Network, and he'd squirreled it away among the inner-system shaved heads and sniffers of questionable substances. A move which had infuriated Paul, but a move he'd never regretted.

Because he *hadn't* wanted anyone in on his research. Since he'd never met a 'NetInterLink designer—or a 'Netter of any *other* discipline—he would let shine his shoes, he certainly wasn't about to let one put his or her grimy little codes into his *programs*. And giving one of the big academy's A-K clones the power to adjust the 'Net DataBase was unthinkable.

Unthinkable, that was, until Stephen Ridenour came along. Until an academy clone with the soul of an Ethnic Reconstructionist Indigene came into his life. And the thought of working with that—*God!*—it sent chills along his spine. He *wanted* the kid back down here. He *wanted* to lock him in a back room until Adm. Cantrell's *Cetacean* left the system. He *wanted* to study a great deal more than 'NetInterLinks with Stephen Ridenour.

Loren's rich laughter faded, but not the appreciative grin. "I begin to see why Stephen's so crazy about you, Smith," she said: jolting dislocation of his carefully choreographed itinerary. "Not one 'NetTech in a million would dare look under that tag for fear Someone might catch them at it and revoke their license. No wonder— What is it, Dr. Smith?"

"Is that—" His voice broke. Disgusted, he collected his scattered composure and tried again: "Is that true, admiral, or are you just saying it?"

"Which?" Awareness dawned in her dark eyes. "That Stephen's crazy about you?"

He nodded, soft-headed bit-brain that he was.

"You saw the tape. Meeting you and (incredible as it might seem to us) Paul—" Corlaney twitched, and she paused. "Yes, Paul? Did you want to add something?"

Paul snorted. "Not bloody likely, Cantrell." The man was smart, definitely smart, but an ass with the manners of an Albion wargel. Manners which put *him* back in balance, back in control of the situation—

—and of himself. "Good lord, Paul, when did you become such a . . ."

"Prig?" Loren supplied.

Wesley grinned at her. "The term I was considering, while similar, was somewhat less—genteel. But that'll do."

"Don't mind Paul." Loren laid her hand on his knee. Like the rest of this woman, it was strong and decidedly shapely— well-defined tendons and muscles an intrinsic part of its beauty. He'd wager she knew how to use those hands. Paul could probably testify to that. But she was ignoring Paul utterly now. Now, her attention was far more intelligently directed at Wesley Smith. Foolishly, Wesley Smith was more concerned with what she was saying about young Ridenour than with the latent talent of those shapely hands.

"You've studied under Victor Danislav, Dr. Smith. You should know better than most how stifling Vandereaux Academy can be, and I suspect Stephen experienced the worst it had to offer. A mind like yours, ready to consider what his had to offer—" Her hand moved to his wrist. "I think you should know—Stephen was in the midst of sending you a message that night—he was intending to come to your room . . ." His pulse increased; she smiled and released him. "However, you must also realize that he must go back to Capital-Station with me. He has no choice —*I* have none. Not now. He did ask me to tell you . . ."

A pregnant pause; he held his breath.

". . . that he wished it could have turned out differently."

He released the breath in a rueful huff. "Do you know, Adm. Cantrell, there are four or five thousand papers under that tag:

all—save one, of course—pure drek. There's something special about a person willing to chip through the coal to find the diamond. Stephen was doing that when he found me."

"Found you?"

He shrugged. "Found my paper. Same difference." Stephen had tried to come to him—would have but for Nayati. He looked down at his hands hanging limp between his knees. Matching fingertips, he flexed the fingers up and down. "Know what this is, admiral?"

Another snort from the corner, but he didn't care. Loren asked gently, "Why don't you tell me?"

"A spider doing push-ups on a mirror."

"Why would a spider do that, do you suppose?" she asked, admirably straight-faced.

Somehow, he didn't feel like laughing either.

"Perhaps because he fears only his reflection will ever follow where he leads." He let his hands drop. "I asked Stephen, that afternoon in the bar, why he bothered—not to read my paper, naturally, but to sift through that muck to find it. He said an Indigene lecturer had asked him a question that made him view the 'Net in a new way; he thought that perceiving it as a non-designer might help him better understand the 'Net. I didn't fully appreciate that reason until now." He nodded toward the screen. "Considering his personal phobias, that indicates a special mind—a very special mind indeed."

"Good God!" Paul exploded, shifting Cantrell's attention to his corner.

But Wesley didn't care. Stephen had tried to send him a message . . .

Paul headed for the door. "I can't take any more of this."

If only they'd had more time together . . .

"Hold it right there, Corlaney," Cantrell said sharply.

. . . even now they could be talking via the 'Tap. . . . Privately.

Of a sudden, a shiver ran down his spine. Familiar sense: the Key to a Design presenting itself. Paul had stopped, but Paul didn't matter. Loren didn't. Loren was concentrating on Paul. Excellent.

He assumed his *Look* again and said, "If you will excuse me a moment..." And had brushed past Paul and out the door before she could object.

Wesley Smith slipped out of the conference room and shuffled past their station. A decidedly wretched Smith—
—whose head came up and whose pace increased with each stride.

Lexi blanked the screen with a touch, glanced at TJ; he was Listening to Cantrell.

She stood to follow.

"Sit," TJ said, "Barney can—"

"So can I. —My butt's going to sleep."

TJ tapped an answer, and said, "Boss says he's to come back, but give him a chance to do it on his own."

"You got it."

Paul closed the door behind Wes and slapped the palm of his hand against the frame, anger and resentment a cold fist squeezing his throat. When that fist relaxed enough to let him speak:

"How long have you known?"

"About what, Corlaney? There's still too damn much I know *nothing* about."

"Ridenour's connection with Councillor Shapoorian's brat, for a start."

"That bothers you, does it?" She moved around the far side of the conference table and leaned casually against it—a hairsbreadth out of his reach. Just as she'd been two days ago. Just as she'd been twenty years ago, right when he'd needed her most.

"You *know* it does—you aimed the shot carefully enough. The woman's a plague. How she keeps getting reelected . . . but other than her constant string of Special Interest Bills, and that eternal genetic memory crap, she's seemed relatively harmless of late. Now this. Is Ridenour her latest atrocity? What's she up to? And why haven't you told me before now?"

"Why should I?" Her indifference set his teeth on edge. "You haven't exactly expressed an interest in anything outside this planet since I got here. You've been so absorbed in your little cover-ups, I thought perhaps you'd forgotten there's a lot more to Alliance than HuteNamid's little corner.''

''If you'd open your eyes, woman, you'd realize this little corner of the Alliance deserves a maximum of attention.''

''What the *hell* do you think I'm trying to give it, *man?*''

He glared at her, slammed his fist against the wall and aimlessly paced the conference room. On rethinking, it should have come as no surprise that she'd uncovered Sakiimagan's recruitment program. She had resources they couldn't guess at, and they hadn't been all that careful. After all, they'd done nothing illegal—just unusual. But Paul held out little hope of convincing Sakiimagan of his own innocence. As for Ridenour . . .

So the kid was Recon. That explained Loren's interest; she'd never been one to waste much time with children, and Ridenour was little more. He'd been jealous once; now he knew better.

But there was also . . .

He recalled a moonlit cliffside, Loren in his arms . . .

. . . and the kid's whisper on the night breeze . . . *I remember Rostov's moons—three of them. I remember asking papa who painted them and . . .*

She'd shushed him, but not before he'd revealed more than enough to make an ex-Rostov researcher wonder.

He stared at the now-blank screen. Rostov. Was *that* the kid's homeworld? If so, why in hell was he on the loose and here on HuteNamid?

''Classified, Paul—''

He blinked over his shoulder at her.

''—Even you can't break that particular Pandora's box open.''

''I didn't realize I'd asked a question.''

The corner of her mouth tightened. ''You didn't have to, Corlaney.''

Caught off-balance, he turned away from that knowing stare. ''You always were a spook, woman.''

She took a step forward, throwing him further off-balance. ''Does the name Stefan Ryevanishov mean anything to you?''

A chill hit his gut. ''Can you give me a hint? From where would I know him? I've met a number of people over the years.''

''A planet called Rostov. Ever hear of it?'' A hint of sarcasm.

"I stayed there for several months back during my 'Tank-hopping days," Paul said slowly. "I—think I might remember him. Why?"

Disappointment. *Extreme* disappointment that radiated through visible indifference.

Of a sudden, he realized what a fool he was, but it was too late.

"Why now, Paul?" That disappointment permeated her tone. "Why did you choose now to start lying to me?"

Wesley keyed in the disconnect code and leaned back against the mirror, waiting for the 'Tap to weasel back through the interweaving security codes, seeing, for the moment, not the patterned tiles of the bathroom walls, but dark curls framing liquid crystal: opal eyes: a gem the like of which he'd never seen before and never expected to find again—not in this Universe.

A gem and more. A bud moments away from blossoming.

A bud. Seeds. He liked that. A glance at his reflection; it was smiling. The smile widened. He'd planted seeds just now.

Leads plucked off his pocketcom and stuffed into his pocket, folded the PC and tucked it in next to his heart. Cover grid snapped back over the intercom. Order restored, he strolled from the restroom, humming to himself.

A woman was sitting in a corridor window seat, apparently enjoying the view. *Cetacean* teal-blue. One of Cantrell's shadows.

Wesley stopped in front of her, and when their eyes met, "Aw, shucks, ossifer, I thought you were going to join me."

The woman's mouth twitched. Wesley leaned close to her face, staring at the twitchy mouth. Pretty mouth. Pretty lady. He stilled his hormones and encouraged the twitch: "C'mon, you can do it."

The twitch broke into a full-blown grin.

"Much better." He patted the officer's cheek lightly, winked as she controlled a justifiable urge to break his arm. He'd always wondered what a broken arm might feel like. Maybe today his luck would run dry and he'd find out—

"You realize I'll have to search you before I can let you go back in." Po-lite, apologetic ree-quest.

—Then again, maybe he wouldn't. "Hey." He held up his arms. "I'm all yours."

"Wouldn't you prefer to do it in private, Dr. Smith?"

"Oh, good. A strip search?"

She pulled out a scanner. "Sorry to disappoint you, sir."

Wesley sighed and held his arms out straight. The guard ran the scanner quickly, but thoroughly, around his body. Cleared him with a respectful nod and a Sorry, sir.

"It was wonderful. TTFN." He kissed his fingers toward the bemused guard and sauntered back toward the conference rooms.

It was all so amusing; all part of the game they played. Everyone knew the rules, and knew what to expect. Everyone except Stephen Ridenour, and Stephen had suffered because they'd all been exceedingly stupid and narrow-minded in their play.

A pat of a pocket, a slight smile. Sometimes, rules could be changed.

"I'm having you moved into the rooms next to mine. I want you where my people can keep a close eye on you." Loren's voice was like a laser scalpel, cutting him in half, cauterizing feeling on its way through. "Do me a favor and don't try to shake them."

"Loro—" His voice cracked. He coughed. "Dammit, *why?* Because of Stef? What has he to do with this?"

She said nothing, seemed to be listening, then tapped behind her ear. TJ. That damned beeper. He took the distance between them in three strides and, grabbing her wrist, forced her hand down, knowing he was courting disaster, frustrated enough not to care. *"Why, dammit?"*

She gazed significantly at his grip; he released her.

"I know you were there before you came here," she said. "I know Sakiimagan contacted you *through* Stefan Ryevanishov. I know you opted to HuteNamid because of that letter. Anevai said she'd take us to the libraries—her brother claims he's 'flying with his Cocheta.' *You* claimed *Dena Cocheta* was nothing but a kid's password. What the *hell* is going on here?

What kind of *games* are these *kids* playing? Chemical ones? Something *you* brought from Rostov?"

"Lord, *no!* How could you even think—" He fought hard for control. "Stef was just a friend, Loro. A good kind man who passed on a letter from Sakiimagan. *Sure,* it was a propaganda letter: Sakiimagan wanted the prestige of my reputation. Hoped it could help recruit other researchers. He wanted—"

"Prestige, Paul? When you came here under an assumed name? A secret transfer?"

"Private letters, Loro. Quiet. Like everything about HuteNamid is quiet. I *told* you: it's why I came here. Don't make more of this than exists. Whatever Stef's gotten into, I haven't seen or heard from him in twenty years."

There was a pause as she took a turn about the room, then, with seeming irrelevancy, she asked: "Why has no one ever left here?"

He didn't believe in irrelevancy where Loren Cantrell was concerned.

"What's that have to do with Stef's—"

"In thirty years, no researcher has ever transferred in and then decided they wanted out. Why?"

"You've seen this place, met the people—would *you* leave?"

"Frankly, yes."

He ran a hand through his hair, the depth of her animosity confusing him. "I—Sakiima's careful who he chooses. Screens them. Questions Recons who've dealt with them. Oh, there have been a few who thought about leaving; they talked about it a day or two, then decided against it."

"And that didn't seem strange to you, Paul? You know how these assignments fluctuate."

"Not strange at all. I tell you, no researcher could find a more pleasant situation—there aren't any better facilities, certainly no richer biosphere, and the IndiCorps—"

"Spare me. I've had all the sugar I can stomach."

He bit back a retort and scowled.

"You asked me why I'm having you monitored, then presumed the answer. You're wrong, Paul. You're being watched because of what I'm about to tell you. If you've been playing it straight with me, you've nothing to worry about—it's classified, but not that high. You're even free to discuss it with Sakiimagan—just no one else. The relocation is for your protection as well as for my peace of mind. Once we know we can trust you *and* these people you call friends, you'll be back on your own. I'm running out of time and patience. Tell Sakiimagan how Rostov's people 'just disappeared' during their final few years; ask him if that doesn't sound familiar. Then tell him a whole planet's out of the 'Net because of a massive civil war—''

"*Not* a techno/bio breakdown?''

"That was part of it—a *result* of that war. Everyone was killed, Paul, —after years of unusual cooperation between SciCorps and Recon. Ask him if he wants that to happen here, and if not, tell him he knows where to find me. I'm through chasing after him. *Through* courting his goodwill. Either he contacts me within the next two days—I'll even make it convenient: *planetary* days—or I'm declaring martial law. I *will* have those two missing researchers. I *will* have Nayati Hatawa. And I *will* have the truth about this Cocheta. I *won't* have another Rostov.''

iv

Lexi had left the station as a cautious tail. She came back on her quarry's arm.

TJ raised an eyebrow as she released Smith's arm, gave him a pat on his butt.

"So,'' TJ said, as she slipped in behind the desk. "He do anything exciting?''

"Sort of depends on your point of view.'' She paused, seemingly absorbed in the disappearance of Smith's patched jeans behind the ornate double doors. Then grinned at him. "Went to the John.''

Point, Lex. "Anyone else in there?''

"Scanned clean and not a peep. —Still.'' She frowned. "He took a while.''

"Yeah, well, what can I say?''

"Looked remarkably happier coming out.''

"Hey—when you gotta go . . ."

She glared at him. He laughed.

"Relax, kid. How much could he do in a bathroom? Let it rest, okay?"

"Sure —when you ease off on Stephen."

Set. "Covering my blindspot?"

"That's what makes a team, Teej."

And match.

The lowering sun cast long shadows on the rift valley outside the window. The Rostov he'd known had had rolling, grass-covered hills—no mountains, not like these. But there'd been deep river-cut chasms lined with twisted trees . . . Rostov dead? Stef, Ylaine—little Nevya? Paul hadn't thought of them in years. Had assumed them safely lifted out and making a new life for themselves elsewhere. There'd been no mention of 'civil war' in the news release. But of course there wouldn't be. Loren had said that was classified. But what about the relocation reports?

"Anyone rescued?" he asked at last, searching for the clever questions, not the one his gut demanded.

"No."

"Damn." He'd learned years ago not to look back, not even to find Loren, once he'd severed that connection. It was kinder to oneself and old friends to let memories survive rather than pollute them with unwanted reminders of one's own increasing mortality. Why'd she have to bring up Stef? What could Stef possibly have to do with—

"Loren, *is* young Ridenour from Rostov? Is that why—"

"*I* could tell you, Paul, but I won't."

He swung around. Wesley: standing beside the closed door, holding up the wall with his shoulders. "Where the hell did you come from? And the hell you can! Tell me what? How? And why not?"

"There are more things on heaven and earth than are dreamed of in your bit-brain, Paul." Wesley swayed away from the wall and sauntered over to the table, basking in the attention. He perched on the table and leaned toward Paul, elbow on his knee, chin resting in upturned palm. "I can get most anything I want out of the 'Net—if I don't mind leaving tracks.''

"And the other?" Paul asked.

"Because *I* don't trust you anymore, Paul. Not where Stephen's concerned." The smug facade didn't slip, it vaporized. "Dammit, I *told* you to be careful with him, and you sat back and let this happen. *You knew* Anevai planned to lure him to the barn that night, didn't you? You knew and you didn't make a move to stop her. You set Stephen up as much as Nayati did."

"Back off. Your brainchild's no innocent. Perhaps it got a little out of hand—"

"A little—*God*, Paul, what ozone are you living in?"

Wesley shot Loren a grim smile. "My sentiments exactly, admiral. —I told you, Paul, we need him—*I* need him— badly. And now—"

He slumped, deflated, staring sightlessly at the polished hardwood floor. "—Now, damn you, Paul Corlaney, he'll never come back."

Paul felt a rush of anger, a rush he didn't pause to analyze. "So *what?*" Wesley's head flew up, his eyes wide. Paul felt a cold satisfaction and pressed his advantage. "You're not the only one smarting, Smith. So your pretty-boy's gone—there'll be others—there always are. Isn't that what you've been telling *me* for years? Well, it's *your* turn in the cold showers for a while."

Wesley's shock changed to a wide grin. "So *that's* your problem, Corlaney! After twenty years you couldn't get it u—"

TJ's feet thudded to the floor. He pitched forward in his chair, elbows on knees, staring intently into nothingness, remained in that odd position for several moments, then leaned back again, returned his feet to the desk and raised a brow in Lexi's direction.

"Well, m' dear," he said, "the shit, as they say, has just hit the fan."

Wesley Smith was thoroughly disgusted. Wesley Smith was thoroughly disgusted and lying in an undignified, painful tangle of arms and legs on the floor under the table. Undignified didn't matter.

Pain did.

He didn't like pain. Not in his jaw, which had absorbed the brunt of Paul's fist's momentum, not in his butt, which had absorbed the brunt of his body's potential energy gone kinetic.

He untangled that tangle and sat up, hitting his head on the underside of the table, cursed roundly and looked up—

—into Paul's white-with-shock face.

"Shit, man," Wesley complained, "what's *your* problem? Who hit—"

Paul turned on his heel and left the room.

He crawled out, met a hand, and let Cantrell pull him to his feet. He rubbed his jaw and slumped into a chair as she muttered to the ozone.

"Having Paul followed, admiral?" he asked, when she shut up.

"What do you think?"

He shrugged. "He's just going to go sulk. Made an ass of himself in front of a class act and he knows it."

She chuckled. "Class act? Thanks, Smith. I assume that's a compliment."

He grinned. "The best."

"So we'll let Security get some exercise. Can't let them sit around and grow fat, can I?"

"I can think of worse fates."

"Serious, Smith? Not exactly your style."

"Hey. Man's gotta do."

"Did you mean what you said?"

"Usually. Which?"

"That you can get anything out of the 'Net you want, if you don't mind leaving tracks?"

He controlled another grin—more a smirk, this time, he thought—and let that *control* show. "More or less."

"I don't appreciate the humor, Smith. Have you been into *Cetacean's* Security Files? *Can* you?"

"Now, admiral. That's not how the game's played. Valuable information's traded, you know that. Paul was trying to give it away, like a fool."

"And you, I take it, are no fool."

"I'm many things, Adm. Cantrell, but a fool's not one of them."

"So, if we're trading information, tell me, what would *you* like to know?"

"Well, therein lies the—bug. You see, there's not much you can tell me, if I'm telling you the truth. So, if I ask for information, I give away what I can and can't do, don't I?"

"I see you intend to make this a long exercise."

"Not at all. I might be willing to trade, say, information for favors?"

"Of what sort, Smith?"

He leaned forward and said straightly, "I want Stephen back."

"And if that could be arranged?"

"No ifs. Either I get that or you get nothing."

"What if he doesn't want to come back?"

"I want a chance to convince him. *Down here.* In *my* directory, not yours."

"I'll have to think about that. What do I get in return?"

"I'll have to think about that. I'll let you know."

"Careful sonuvabitch, aren't you?"

He grinned. "I didn't know you'd met my mother, admiral."

A cough of surprised laughter. "Tread carefully, Smith. I'm not nearly so restrained as Paul. I've decked several people in my life—without the slightest qualm."

"I'll remember that."

"Will you tell me one thing? No advantage. Just to satisfy my curiosity?"

"Try me."

"How the *hell* did you come to be here? You're more out of place than Paul."

"You wound me. You think I don't belong in Eden?"

She collapsed onto his tabletop. "You *dare* hand me an opening like that?"

"If I had any hangups about the answer, woman, I promise you, you wouldn't get the opening. —Sure, why not? Like everyone else, I was asked."

"You're slipping, Smith. You might be handing me a piece of the puzzle I didn't already have."

"Oh, I am, either way. Either you didn't know: in which case, I've told you; *or* I knew you knew, in which case, you know something I had already discovered. Of course, you *don't* know if I got that information from Paul . . . or from the 'Net."

"So educate me."

"Oo-oo, the opening the woman hands *me*. —Again, why not? I hate the system. I also hate the role of dutiful eldest son." He laughed. "Lord, if *mein papa* ever heard me use that phrase, he'd die laughing." And on a second thought: "I've got to get the folks here. They'd love it. Damned if mum wouldn't disappear into the mountains and never be heard from again. Hadn't thought of that before, admiral. Thanks. Maybe I'll suggest that as a fifty-seventh second honeymoon."

"You're welcome. And my education?"

He leaned back in the chair and pursed his lips. "Any time, Admiral Loro. Any time at all."

She slid off the table and toward him. "Can I pick the topic?"

Her voice was low, seductive. Her fingers touched his hair. He was right: definitely talented hands. He leaned his head toward her, blinked up at her as her fingers traced a pattern down his nose to his mouth. He kissed her fingertips and said against them, "Sure. Why not?"

She leaned over and kissed his lips, then whispered, "How 'bout Smith's 'NetTap 101?"

He closed his eyes on the doubled image and began to chuckle, felt her echo it, lips to lips. "Touché, Admiral Loro. For that, you deserve one: the Cocheta Libraries."

She pulled away. "What about them?"

"I can tell you where they are—"

She twitched.

"—but not how to get there."

"There's a difference?"

"Absolutely. I can tell you, they're somewhere near Tunica and underground, but where and how to get to them—no. And

I, like Paul, have been there. But we were taken. Only a few know how to get to them. Part of the deal we made with Sakiima when we came here. The other part was to keep our mouths shut about them.''

"A deal you've just broken.''

He grinned. "Hell, somebody else has already. I'm counting on you to help us renegotiate.''

V

Ridenour was alone now. A rather bemused Ridenour who'd begun playing computer games for real, his every keystroke echoing to a window superimposed over his vidim on Chet Hamilton's monitor.

From the anonymity of his office, Chet watched the kid casually create a sim of Truthercon: a sim that accounted for bias in the dice, air currents and tilting lap table with elegant simplicity. In a stupid game of chance this twenty-year-old kid considered levels of complexity some economists wouldn't bother with in futures-market predictions. And he did it without backtrack, without hesitation.

He wondered if Sect. Beaubien over in 'NetAT central had any idea what he'd come so close to losing to HuteNamid. Somehow, he doubted it, for all he was responsible for that last-minute transmission from the 'NetAT containing the kid's final exams. Written responses and completed programs, no matter how good those answers, meant little when compared to the casual ease with which Ridenour operated.

He'd had his doubts once, when he'd read that paper of Smith's and scanned Ridenour's Vandereaux records; because Ridenour's early evaluations were—dismal. Had the academy been in a position to dump him, they undoubtedly would have. But Stephen Ridenour, aka Zivon Stefanovich Ryevanishov, was a 'disadvantaged Recon orphan,' and his legal guardian, Victor Danislav, Dean of 'NetScience at Vandereaux Academy, wasn't about to let his nevvy flunk out. So instead, they'd poured money into special-education programs, given him unprecedented time on the exceedingly expensive, state-of-the-art Editorial VRT's just to bring him up to standard baseline work.

Later . . . He grinned at the unsuspecting young man and asked aloud, "Did they ever guess, kid?"

Because some*where* some*time* some*thing* had clicked in that young Recon brain. Just what those 'somes' were would require some*one* with a lot more time and interest in the subject than he had to figure from Ridenour's personal files. The Academy's much-touted Mentor interface system controlled so much of each student's program, he doubted Danislav and the other Vandereaux profs had even suspected how *much* the kid was grasping until those finals crossed the Board members' desks. Since they'd had the audacity to demand additional testing before they'd grant his degree (which automatically sent the results on to the highest legal authority in the field—in this case, the 'NetAT) they had *then* been forced by the 'NetAT's evaluation of those tests to grant the kid an unprecedented Fourth Echelon rating.

In the way of academic institutions, they were now probably dislocating their arms patting themselves on the back.

And according to this talented youngster, Smith's paper, which to *him* had appeared so much gibberish, contained a theory that was going to make the existing NexusSpace Network obsolete. Not the most welcome revelation to a SecOne Communications man who was also a 'NetAT Master Programmer. Made a man feel older than he really was.

He certainly couldn't deny that someone from this system had used the 'Net in an uncomfortably unusual fashion. Physicists claimed the 'NetDataBase *couldn't* change, that you could read it, even write to it, but once written, you'd never catch it again, and even if you did, to change a part could destroy the whole. Not a theory one would care to test casually, with all the recent history of mankind on the thing. Yet records from this remote system had disappeared—not garbled, not random, and without destroying the 'NetDB.

If Ridenour was right, if Smith's hypothesis *did* hold cosmic water, the replacement of the 'NetOS with something more flexible, more exotic—and less absolute—could prove the most all-consuming project ever undertaken by one civilization. He'd often thought the transition to the 'Net must have been a mess—had thanked his lucky stars he'd not been a part of it.

Perhaps that temptation of the stars had been too much.

The window no longer displayed probability games. Instead, lists of test ratings and psych evaluations scrolled almost too rapidly to read. A quick query: Ridenour's own school records.

That was strange. In lieu of his deceased parents, those files should belong to the state until he reached full legal age, and Stephen Ridenour was a long way from twenty-five.

He cut in a second window and tracked the access trail. The files were in Ridenour's personals, all right. Transferred (a third window for a file history) along with all his other personal files the day he boarded *Cetacean*. Authorization: (further check, same file) Vandereaux 'NetSciences—old Danislav himself. He supposed it must be all right. Possibly a part of Stephen's unusual status—

—but he made a note into his personal MEM to check into it when they returned to Vandereaux.

An angry whisper issued from the long-silent speakers:

"Why didn't they tell me? Bastards! Danislav, you could have, damn you. Give you a thrill, did it? watching the 'buster-boy bust his butt in terror? Hope it was worth it."

Not a happy boy. Getting himself riled. Some people—like Doc McKenna—weren't going to be pleased.

He sent an interrupt to Ridenour's comp access:

>*Hey, kid, bedtime. Turn the vid off and go to sleep now.*

A sharp, startled glance in the general direction of the camera pickup, a swallowed *"Shit,"* a blushing return to the keyboard.

>**Hello, sir. Didn't know you were there. Sorry for the language.**

>*Ha! Remind me to teach you some really good ExD's sometime. Stuff you don't learn in the dainty a-ca-de-my life.*

Ridenour's expression threatened argument.

>*BED!*

"All right!" The kid's voice came over the speakers, and his image shoved the keyboard onto the desk. *"All—"*

Chet blanked Ridenour's access, and the kid stopped in the middle as if sound, as well as keyboard, communication had been interrupted. Maybe (bittersweet thought) for Stephen, they were the same.

Ridenour cut the lights, the view option defaulted to infra, and within moments, the ghostly image was breathing the long slow evenness of sleep.

Chet grinned. Ah, for the clear conscience of youth again. "Enjoy it while you can, kid," he said. "You won't be able to pull that off a year from now."

He yawned widely; Ridenour wasn't the only one who'd had a long day. "Guess you're safe for the night, kid," he mumbled. "See you in the morning." And put the room on auto scan—his crew had better things to do with their time than watch a kid snore.

Sleep, Chet Hamilton had said, as though it was the simplest thing in the world, as if he were a child to be reminded.

Stephen kept his breathing easy, relaxed, feigning that sleep with tricks gleaned from a lifetime of monitoring: a Recon 'NetTech—even a trainee—couldn't *possibly* be trusted to keep off the 'Net on his word alone.

As if he would *do* anything. While Wesley Smith's concepts posed certain *theoretical* capabilities, he certainly wasn't stupid enough to experiment with it himself. He valued his mind—had grown quite attached to it over the years, for all its odd ideas—and he didn't care to empty it onto some tape and spend the rest of his life scrubbing floors for the 'NetAT kitchens because what neurons remained might be too dangerous—or embarrassing—to let loose in public.

Besides, the only files he was really interested in were all Secured files, requiring specific passwords and biological clearances, which not even Wesley's *theoretical* system could break into, and he wanted into *those* only because he was curious whether or not he'd just qualified for bit-brain of the century.

He'd really rather not get out of hospital only to discover he'd landed there playing the straight man for a twisted hoax.

What are you planning to do? Put that transfer through for real? Confused, traumatized memories: Cantrell and himself beside a fire in a pit of sparkling star-stone, Cantrell's reference to the bogus transfer that had gained him temporary entrance to the 'Tank below. She'd invited him to use it, and in the next breath, had told him about 'NetDB tampering and undetectable transmissions.

If he were a suspicious sort, he might think that exceedingly convenient timing.

Because Cantrell had a fetish where it came to Recons, and the possibility that Vandereaux's token Recon graduate might elect to stay on a frontier planet rather than make a splashy return to Vandereaux might just prompt her to take action, maybe even to say things that weren't quite true.

He scowled into the dark before he remembered viewers and relaxed his face again.

Try downright lies. Certainly wouldn't be the first he'd been handed on this cursed-from-the-beginning mission. If he thought God would listen to him at all anymore, he'd pray to have just one truth made known to him. He'd like to know just one thing he'd actually accomplished here.

Five minutes alone with Wesley Smith: that was all he needed. Five lousy minutes.

But he'd done more than enough in the name of survival to alienate that inflexible God of his parents long ago, and the academy certainly hadn't provided any substitute—unless you counted the Mentor whose psychological and educational evaluations dictated a student's future.

His stomach churned, which made him think of the pills on the bedside table, which made him think of Chet watching and the questions Chet would ask should he reach for those pills.

Theoretically, the Mentor files were government property. Theoretically, no student ever saw theirs. But somehow, his had transferred with his personals, therefore he had the right to review them. But Chet had been watching. Chet had told him to go to bed, as if he couldn't make that decision for himself, and *dammit!* he hadn't finished!

Stephen clenched the fist hidden safely under his pillow, keeping his visible hand relaxed.

Early on, those scores were as bad as he'd feared—worse, if that were possible—but later on, especially the last few years . . .

Once—just *once*—someone could have told him. *All right* would have been enough. The sadists probably assumed that he would lose his edge, lacking parental pressure, but that only proved they'd never understood him—never even tried to understand him.

Danislav, at least, should have known better.

He'd often wondered, in some ungrateful corner of his soul, who had paid Danislav, and in what coin, for his sponsorship. It couldn't have been the distant relationship to his mother. While Ylaine Ryevanishov had certainly used that connection to lodge his initial application, Danislav had made his refusal to acknowledge their relationship abundantly clear from the moment Zivon Ryevanishov arrived at Vandereaux.

Not that he cared, not really. Even willing, Victor Danislav would have been a poor substitute for the father he almost remembered. He appreciated, now, the wisdom of young Zivon's self-induced amnesia. Far easier to forget Stefan Ryevanishov than to live without him. At least young Stephen had had Dev . . .

(*"Why the* hell *are you here alone? Trying to kill yourself?"*

(*Himself, barely thirteen, a test he was sure he'd failed, and a stolen afternoon in an empty gym.*

(*A man he knew only from the newsvids catching him as he missed a dismount, surprising Truth out of him. . . .*

(*"I—I like being alone, sir."*)

He'd expected well-deserved chastisement, but after a moment's frowning deliberation:

(*"Your name's Ridenour?"*)

(*"Y—yes, sir."*)

(*"You know who I am?"*)

(*"Coach D—Devon, s—sir."*)

(*"Do you know what that last move you made was?"*)

(*"Y—yes, sir."*)

(*"Well?"*)

(*"A th-three and a half T—Thomas—"*)

("And the pull out?")

He recalled blushing furiously, then saying, still with that damnable stutter he'd never quite mastered:

("I—it wasn't very good, sir. You see, m—my sh—shoulder caught and to pull out I had to half-twist to the ripple and—"

("Can you do it again? —Right this time—with the half-twist?"

(Not allowing himself to wonder what was behind this new type of examination:

("I—I think so."

("Well?")

He'd done it—quite creditably, as he recalled—good enough anyway that Devon had ordered him to report for the team workout the following day—then terrified him by qualifying that order: *If you want to.*

He'd never been given a choice before.

And he did want to. *God*, how he'd wanted to.

He should have known better.

Both fists clenched this time as he fought impotent anger. Vandereaux Academy Athletics Department had the finest medical facilities in Vandereaux System available to them, and a StarShip emergency surgery team had managed what Vandereaux claimed was impossible?

Not in this universe.

He wondered who had made the decision not to operate—or more accurately, to tell *him* that reconstruction would make gymnastics impossible. Because reconstruction was the *only* option he'd had. Replacement, while a someday consideration, had been economically unfeasible at the time: he couldn't possibly have paid for it out of his student stipend, and since any 'non-original body parts' would have made him ineligible for competition, it was 'unnecessary surgery' as far as Vandereaux's Budgetary Committee was concerned. His other option, rest and physical therapy, had at least gotten him back in the gym. It had taken nearly two years, and he'd never again be remotely competitive, but he *had* started flying again, had even regained some skill—

—just in time to come to HuteNamid and blow the shoulder out all over again. Then, without *asking* his permission, McKenna had done the restruct and he'd awakened with her well-intentioned gloat ringing in his ears. *Be careful with it and it should be good as new when it heals....*

Not a single dire warning about partial paralysis or unpredictable joint seizures.

One more Vandereaux lie: that's all the Meds' *choice* had been. But someone must have advised them. Someone who knew that gymnastics meant far more to him than the competitive aspects. Someone with the power to convince Dev as well....

He thought of those files sitting in *Cetacean's* 'banks. *His* files. Personal information which had followed him from the academy. Files he hadn't known existed before tonight.

Sleep, Hamilton had said—

He reached a hand from under the blankets, snagged the keyboard by touch in the darkness and pulled it back under the blankets.

—because, *dammitall*, he wasn't sleepy!

Wesley Smith waved to his Security tail and closed his apartment door. The guard wouldn't do much good if he really wanted to get out, but they needn't worry about him. Not tonight, anyway. He wasn't about to go anywhere—tonight.

Tonight, he had work to do.

He pulled his sweater off over his head and drop-kicked it across the room. Whistling tunelessly, he waltzed into the bathroom and flipped the shower on, parked his elbows on the countertop and said to his reflection, "You, my dear, are a genius. *Some* people might think you heartless scum, but we know better, don't we?"

He kissed his finger and touched the tip to his mirror-imaged lips, kicked his slacks out the door and stepped into the shower.

Cantrell was off making up to Paul. Better than Paul deserved, but he wished them both luck as he leaned into the hot, wet massage.

It really wasn't fair, you know. Paul had his Admiral Loro— if he didn't screw up; Anevai was up there with Stephen all to herself—

—Who'd J. Wesley Smith have?

Nobody, that was who. No body at all.

He should have guessed Anevai would get through to the kid first. She had all the luck. Probably a good thing—he'd never have convinced the kid to talk the way she had. Never would have gotten around to it. Too much else to discuss. Some that even had to do with *Harmonies*.

For the Del d'Bugger he'd expected, he had a special file squirrelled away, ready to implement the instant the Bug had gone after it.

And a bigger pile of shit would never have hit the 'Net.

Green glow lit the underside of the sheet and his fingers on the keyboard. Slow going, and you needed a good memory to use the one-line remKey-display, but any academy student learned that trick his first year. It was the only way to 'beat' curfew: the covers 'hid' you from the vid-scans and no comp-monitor would ever dare blow the whistle.

Hamilton was Academy—maybe even Vandereaux—and Stephen was gambling now Chet would know those rules and play by them so long as he kept to his own files.

Medical files: 17.03.70 CNS, the day of his accident.

Reports flashed across the screen a line at a time, some keyed, others illegible stylus hand-scans. He didn't waste time on analysis. Nothing. Nothing. More nothing. Until a handwritten memo at the end of a routine status report to Victor Danislav:

>Surgery auth: denied.

So they'd never really *needed* to convince him. Danislav had already made the decision. But under that note:

>Ref: Cristof Devon: Attitude problem. High danger potential; low yield.

His hands started to shake. He lifted them off the keyboard.

Someone who knew what flying meant to him—Devon? Something inside him considered that possibility and choked. Had Dev decided *he* didn't want a Recon planet-buster representing Vandereaux? Low yield?

Olympic contention wasn't good enough for you, Dev? Or did you figure I couldn't make it back in time?

Mama. Danislav. Now Dev. A cold, deep fury dispelled the pain in Stephen's gut. Well, damn them. Damn them all. He didn't need any of them. He and Wesley Smith had found their own truth, their own purpose. A truth that fancy *Fourth Echelon* rating was going to help him broadcast to the universe. He'd play Cantrell's game to the max. Make the Vandereaux Board regret they ever heard—

The sheet billowed from his escaping sigh. Who did he think he was kidding? He'd be lucky to get the *'NetAT* to listen, 4E-rating or no. The media would have a field day with the Recon brat taking on Vandereaux Academy, then laugh all the way to the bank, leaving him with a libel suit on his hands.

Frustrated, he slammed the keyboard with his fist. The machine beeped a complaint:

>**I beg your pardon?**

He drew a breath, *Cetacean's* too-cold air stinging his lungs, and felt an insane urge to laugh. Chet was *not* watching him. Chet would never let him treat *Cetacean* equipment that way.

He ran apologetic fingers over the keys. Fourth-echelon. That was a joke everyone at the academy would appreciate. But those ratings were evaluated by unbiased computer, though the Board and the Council had to approve them, and one point was undeniable from those final test scores: he'd been good. Damned good.

But good enough for a fourth? or had that rating been granted to impress the HuteNamid leaders; could the Council revoke it as quickly and easily as they had awarded it? He'd never heard of such a case, but there was so much he'd never heard of.

His heart sped. He schooled himself to calm indifference, even while he knew he had to know.

He keyed in the string that would bring up his official Doctoral certificate, closed his tired, burning eyes on the cycling menus, found his head drifting toward the pillow and jerked awake as the system beeped an alert.

He opened his eyes, not on his Board certification, but on a flashing, neon-lit message—

>**Hey there, kiddo. You want me, you got me.**

"My God," he whispered. "Wesley!"

* * *

Damn, he was good.

Shampoo ran down his face. Wesley leaned forward, letting the water stream the bubbles away.

It was an elegant little piece of programming, that d'Bugger decoy, designed to insert dates and abortive thought experiments throughout the records for the last five years—and would do it so no one could tell the difference. Had nothing to do with the true story behind *Harmonies*, but it was a damned sight more than enough to haze the eyes of someone primed for the job while lacking true understanding.

Too bad it was going to go to waste.

That was why he wanted Ridenour back. He didn't give shit about the 'Net. Didn't give shit about retaining rights over *Harmonies*, or even the process it represented. Didn't give shit about the money, didn't *want* the notoriety or a spot in the history files. But Stevie was too damned good to be wasted on the data-diddlers back in Vandereaux, both inside and outside the 'NetAT.

He finished rinsing his hair, tapped the shower off and combed his hair with his fingers as the man-made tornado of warm, drying air whipped it about; grinned at his reflection, blew it another kiss and kicked the door shut behind him; flopped on the bed, propped his keyboard on bare knees and pulled up his own private 'Net access: the one the 'NetAT would fry him for using.

They'd *have* to fry him—they couldn't fry the access. Couldn't keep him off the 'Net when any common phone was a potential link for someone who knew.

And Jonathan Wesley Smith knew.

He had homework to do. Seeds had, after all, been planted. Given light, they might even grow. *That* depended on the fertility of the ground upon which they'd been cast.

And that . . .

(If Jonathan Wesley Smith was any judge at all—
—and he was.)

. . . was fertile ground indeed.

vi

>Are we alone?

Stephen removed his hands from the keyboard before the sensitive instrument took his sudden chill for an answer, and tucked his hands under his arms to restore feeling.

Alone? What do you mean alone? My God, Wesley, what are you trying to do to me?

This was invasion—evidently undetected—of at least lower security levels on a system that supposedly required direct physical link to access, and Wesley had done it to slip this message into *his* personal archive—a message that could get them both arrested if detected. And for what? What could such a move gain Smith now?

Unfortunately, his horrified mind could supply all too many reasons. Reactions running too high for quiet reconciliation; negotiations going badly: Smith could be setting him up—tell him one thing now using the system Smith *knew* would be an irresistible lure—tell Cantrell something else—make him the sole recipient of information which—true or false—would make him a traitor to Wesley if he gave that information to Cantrell, to the Alliance if he failed to.

Or it could be simple revenge. He'd betrayed Wesley and Wesley's friends, and Wesley could be setting him up for arrest right along with them. At least that made some sense.

Except . . . *You want me?* . . . Smith must realize by now what he was. Could it be the notes he'd come here to find? The actual step-by-step evolution of the theory hinted at in *Harmonies?* Possibly Wesley didn't hate him. Possibly Wesley understood his motivations as they seemed to understand each other in other ways. Possibly he *wanted* to give Stephen the information required for his 'NetAT report. *Wanted* to justify his paper.

Whatever Smith's motivation, he couldn't let this opportunity slip. Wesley's 'Net tapping system was too dangerous in the hands of a vengeful enemy.

Always assuming it's for real, he thought. Danislav had always told him he was too ready to trust his own opinion.

Alone? God. He gulped, closed his eyes briefly, then typed:
>*Yes*.

>**Before I tell you where to find me, be certain
there's nobody watching. I've got to trust you on
this, Stevie-lad. If there is anyone in the room with
you or any bug capable of monitoring you, do
not—I repeat, DO NOT execute. For God's sake,
son, THINK. YOU know what Cantrell's Security
is capable of. Don't worry about internal monitoring
(I've taken care of that) only direct observational.
This is between the two of us. It's a one-time
access, kid, with no Capture, so don't waste it.
>One more chance, Stevie-lad. Are we alone?**

Unless there was much Cantrell wasn't telling him, there
were still things the admiral didn't know—things she *couldn't*
know because *he* couldn't figure them. If getting at the truth
behind *Harmonies* was why the 'NetAT had sent him here, then
either she was deliberately truncating his mission, or she didn't
realize how ignorant he still was.

Did he have the right *not* to call Chet in to monitor?

Smith could be lying. This might be nothing more than one of
the infamous practical jokes of the sort that had gotten Wesley
Smith thrown out of Vandereaux. What if it was nothing more
than an elaborate Get Well card? He'd look a proper fool then,
getting Chet out of bed. Maybe *that* was Wesley's goal: embarrass
him in front of *Cetacean's* 'NetAT representative. Wesley knew
how little credence the 'NetAT gave his paper—knew it because
they sent a just-barely graduate to check it out.

And if it wasn't a trap, if Wesley honestly meant to let him
in on—everything, it was just possible there was *reason* to
keep the information out of Cantrell's hands. Possibly even
Chet Hamilton's. Adm. Cantrell had said his job here was
done, that she would take care of everything from here on out.
Adm. Cantrell had said the important job was to get the *secret*
of Wesley's Tap back to the Council and the 'NetAT.

But which secret? Its mere existence? How it worked? Or its
extent and capabilities? Cantrell worked for the Council. She
might even want to use his ignorance to let the Council have
first crack at Wesley.

His duty was to the 'NetAT, not the Council, and Smith knew that—he must know it.

Wesley, what are you up to? A one-time access? Damn!

If Wesley knew why he was here—if Wesley *wanted* to legitimize his research in the eyes of the 'NetAT—didn't he owe Wesley that? And if this file was Wesley's working notes, and Wesley wanted the admiral ignorant of the contents for reasons of 'NetAT security in a game at a much higher level—then, by God, Stephen Ridenour would keep her ignorant until Stephen Ridenour determined whom he *could* trust and in what degree.

If, on the other hand, Wesley Smith wanted to use him against Cantrell, Smith had better think again. Stephen Ridenour had been a reluctantly consenting patsy in games all his life, had learned when to argue and when not; but he'd never been a weapon and was damned if he'd sit back tamely and let anyone use him *that* way: if he was to be a weapon now, he'd be the use-er as well as the use-ee.

Cantrell's Recon obsession made her easy to handle—

—And damned if he couldn't handle Wesley Smith as well.

Dry, scratchy eyes: he blinked. Teeth aching: he relaxed his jaw.

All right, Smith. You're on.

Monitors. God, he hoped vid was all he needed to worry about. The covers draped over his head and the keyboard would keep anyone from seeing what he was doing—

—and get him fried if that screen message had, in fact, echoed elsewhere in the ship.

In the meanwhile, so what if he felt like a damn fool, answering a distant query while lying in bed with a blanket draped over his head, waiting for Security to arrive at his door?

>**Are we alone?**

>*Yes*.

>**4.5793 minutes. Took you long enough, brat. Tell Annie-girl to keep her hands off you until you're both safely home.**

Insidious warmth at that: he hadn't had a 'home' in a long time. HuteNamid certainly was not, and never could be; but that Wesley should word it in that way—

—Warmth dissipated. Too friendly, he thought. *Dammit, stop believing when it makes no sense, bit-brain!*

>I've set this to automatically read off certain re-
cords which, if you've half the brain I think you
do, you'll understand soon enough.

>As far as the in-comp monitors are concerned,
you're still perusing your old records, you egotistical
little thing. Seriously, Stephen, I knew you'd check
them out sometime. I know how uneasy your rating makes you: you turned bright red every time
Anevai mentioned it. Trust me, kiddo: you deserve
it, and more. The Evaluation Board hasn't the
brains to assess MY ability, and I'M not yet certain
of yours. Believe me, I intend to find out.

>But that's for later. For now, let's go on to the next
page and see what you deserve.

>C.

Stephen scowled at the screen. He did *not* like these games
Wesley was playing. This was serious. *Damned* serious. But he
hadn't any choice now.

He tapped PgDn.

>The following message will self-destruct in ten sec-
onds, shweethawt, so memorize it. Word for word,
kid.

>Don't disappoint me:

And after a moment:

>Remember what lies between us, Sparkle-plenty,
and hit that ol' Enter button.

The screen went blank then:

>Password:

*Password! Smith, what are you doing to me? Is there a
failsafe? How many attempts before the access is terminated?
Remember word for word?* —God!

'What lies between us?' Everything *lies between us. Space,
years, the 'Net itself! In what context? Vandereaux? The Academy?*

Nothing ventured—

>*Vandereaux*

>Vandereaux?!? Glug, brat.

>Access denied.

—nothing gained.

>**Strike one. Two more, and you're out!**

What the hell did that mean? What kind of strike was Wesley talking about? But the second part was clear enough.

Two more, and you're out. Whatever a strike was, he had three of them.

Remember what lies between us,   —Sparkle-plenty,   —and hit the ol' Enter button.

Three strikes. Three parts . . .

Is each part a clue then, Wesley?

Why *Sparkle-plenty?* Wesley had called him many names during their brief association—most of them embarrassing—but he didn't recall that one.

Suddenly, he found himself grinning like an idiot. Wesley, you two bits for brains bastard! He typed—

>**Button**

—and hit Enter with a flourish.

Paul Corlaney threw his shirt and underwear into the laundry bin, kicked it closed, kicked his shoes out of the way, and kicked the bathroom door open; all of which was psychologically satisfying, but left his bare foot throbbing as badly as his head.

He leaned against cool tiles and groped blindly for the shower handles, opening them to full with a vicious twist that jammed his thumb against the faucet. Damned undersize generic apartments . . .

Cantrell's goons had better have stocked the liquor cabinet. He planned to feel no pain RSN.

Swearing at the world in general did nothing for his head, or his foot, or his thumb, but it did put him in a perfect frame of mind for responding to unwanted visitors.

"Get the hell out of my life!" he yelled. "You've got the whole damned place wired, what *more* do you want?"

The light knock at his door stopped. He was congratulating himself on accomplishing one thing tonight, when a click (which sounded suspiciously like a lock disengaging) had him into the bedroom with his foot blocking the inward swing of his door.

"Dammit, Cantrell, get out of here!" Only she would have the gall to bypass a privacy lock. Change that: *his* privacy lock.

"Sorry, Paul. I'm playing courier tonight."

Once, not so very many hours ago, he'd have done most anything to get her through this door. Now, his friend had gone missing, he'd discovered she'd withheld significant information from him, and (so far as he could tell) had *never* trusted him, had *never* been honest with him, had never *meant* to work with him. Perhaps not even all those years ago.

"Paul . . ." Gentle reminder from the hall.

"So shove it under the door," he snarled.

"Paul, for heaven's sake, stop acting like a child. I need to talk with you."

"You should like me this way. You seem to have developed a taste for children."

"There are a couple of teenaged *children* up in my ship whose father's deserted them, and who damn well deserve better. *Try* being better to them than Sakiimagan."

"Low blow, Cantrell. Besides, it won't work: Hono's no teenager, and Anevai's no child. You get Sakiima back, then *maybe* we'll talk."

"Paul, I'm not going to stand out here in a hall and discuss secured information with you, so stand back, or I'll break your foot."

"Forget it, woman. I'm bare-ass naked."

"Sounds good to me. Step aside, Doc. —It's okay, Teej, you can—"

"*T*—Dammit, woman, you could've—" He reached blindly around the door, and grasped what he trusted was her arm, pulled her into the room and stuck his nose around—

—to an empty hallway.

He leaned his shoulder against the door, pushing it shut slowly. Turned with equal deliberation to find Loren standing behind him holding out two envelopes.

Ignoring the letters, he said, "Hand me that robe." And gestured with his head toward the chair.

"I'm not your servant, Corlaney. —Get it yourself."

"*Please*, Adm. Cantrell." Through gritted teeth. *Damned* if he'd let his bare skin anywhere near her under the circumstances.

"Certainly, Dr. Corlaney." With a damned pretty smile. A smile the woman painted on with her morning makeup.

He shoved his hands down the sleeves, gave the sash a vicious tug as he brushed past her to the corner bar. Stocked—Thank God. He slammed a glass down. The shower's hiss stopped. He poured a whiskey. Raised the glass—

"Don't mind if I do." Dark-skinned fingers reached over his shoulder, plucked the glass from his hand.

Seething, he poured another, drained it without turning, and poured a third.

"Whiskey won't make me disappear, Paul. Please, sit down and be civilized."

"Damned if I will." He tightened his grip on the glass and said bitterly, "Sakiimagan's a good man, Cantrell, and you've all but destroyed our friendship—certainly any trust he might have had in me. I might as well leave all that I've found here, and go back to your damned Council, if that's what the bastards want."

"Do you know where he is?"

"No!" He twisted around to face her. "You mean you don't?"

"Maybe at these Cocheta libraries?"

He glared at her. "Curse you, woman, I already told you I don't know."

"Paul, just for tonight, will you stop fighting me?"

The weariness in her tone pulled at him, made him look squarely at her for the first time since she'd entered the room. She was leaning back in the chair with her eyes closed, cradling the untouched drink in lax hands. Something inside him gave, and he dropped to his knees beside her.

"Are you all right?"

Half-closed eyes met his, and she set the drink aside to stroke his wet hair. "Just tired, Paul. BioRegs help adapt to local time, but they don't replace real sleep. Can't remember the last time I had a non-chemically induced rest."

He sighed and rested his head on her lap, feeling his blood pressure drop ten points. They'd been so close, the night Nayati was pummeling Ridenour into something resembling raw steak: twenty years of waiting, and adolescent stupidity had to ruin everything. Tonight, they were both too old, and too cautious, and too damned tired to transcend the barriers Ridenour and Nayati had placed between them. He rose to his feet, closed her fingers around her glass, picked his own off the floor and sank onto the edge of the bed.

"Where's the letter, Loro?"

She nodded toward the desk.

"Anevai?"

Another exhausted nod. "Paul, she's trying to save your collective ass. Asses. Whatever. And she's right—you *know* she's right. And now her father pulls this disappearing act . . . I'm not trying to screw you people—I'm not trying to drag you personally back to the Council. I don't know what the hell they pulled with you this time—if you're not willing to explain to me, I suppose I'll just have to go through channels, but—"

"Not unwilling, Loren. Can't. They'd have my hide—not to mention everything else I hold dear."

She chuckled wearily. "I don't think they care that much about your—"

"You don't know the Council." He thought a moment, then: "To hell with them. It's the virus, Loro."

Her brow twitched into a slight frown. "The restoration virus?"

He nodded. "They *made* me issue those reports."

"They?"

"Council. The 'NetAT. SciCorps. —Hell, who really knows any more? Power is power and they all want more."

"The 'Unexpected Complications' reports?"

He nodded again, old bitterness sitting sour in his mouth. "There's not a thing wrong with the process. Funny how those 'physical and sociological ramifications' didn't keep *Council* members from utilizing my—services."

"Wonderful. Meaning we're stuck with Shapoorian forever?"

"Hell, we'd have been stuck with her regardless. She's too pickled to croak. But, yes, she's had the evaluation, and as far as I know, been on the stuff for the last fifteen years."

He sighed, took a sip from the glass. And another, not a sip.

"Why, Paul? Why'd you agree?"

"Simple. If I cooperated, I got my choice of 'Tanks. And so

long as I never worked on the virus again, I was free to work or not, as I pleased, at government expense for the rest of my life. Such a deal. How could I refuse?''

"And if you had?"

"I'd be doing laundry on Capital Station, I imagine."

"Why didn't you tell me?"

"Why didn't *you* find out? Anyone got higher clearance than you?"

"Lot of files out there. I've got to *suspect* something to locate it on my own."

"Don't waste your time. The question was rhetorical. Nothing on the 'Net. Nothing in the SecFiles. All private, face-to-face negotiations. And part of the deal was that I stop seeing you. —or at least not go out of my way to contact you."

"Why?"

"Because the Council knew where you and your career were headed. Knew we were—friends. And I—" He raised his hands helplessly, dropped them back in his lap. "I knew you. Knew you'd fight them. You had too much to accomplish. I didn't want to ruin your career."

"What about your own?"

"It wasn't ruined, just—redirected. Sure, I was bitter. At first. —Not now. I wouldn't be saying anything—"

"Bastards!"

His heart thudded to the pit of his stomach. "Loro, —for God's sake, don't—"

"Hypocritical, lying bastards. Chalk that one up to the list of things Kurt Eckersley has kept from me. Right along with Stephen."

Ridenour again. So much for old time's sake. "You mean you didn't know the boy was Recon?"

She frowned. "No. And I want to know what else Kurt's been keeping from me over the years. How the *hell* am I supposed to do my job—forcing me to work with half the available facts—Serve the bastards right if we *do* have another Rostov in the making."

Rostov. Again.

"Loren, what's this all about? What really happened there?"

"You mean you honestly don't know?"

"How would I?"

"Good Lord, Paul, not tonight. I know you people are accessing files you have no business getting into, so let's not waste time on that. But somehow, I doubt Rostov's are among your successes, otherwise you wouldn't be asking. Am I right?"

He nodded. "We tried. Wanted leads on the researchers and Recons that were supposedly lifted out."

"Who tried?"

"Sakiima. Myself."

"Smith?"

"Not in this. Sakiima likes to keep the recruitment personal. When we reached the Rostov SecFiles, we knew there was more to the story, but—Loren, you can't tell me my friends are dead and leave it at that. *Is* Stephen Ridenour from Rostov? You implied as much, then Wesley—"

"I should think you'd be fairly certain by now, but—yes, he is."

"*Is* he Stefan Ryevanishov's child?"

A queer look, then: "No."

He felt disappointment at that. Stefan and Ylaine had wanted children badly. Somehow, he'd hoped, for their sake, Ridenour was theirs. Then he realized: "Of course. He couldn't be. He's a graduate, so he must be—what—twenty-three? -four, at least?"

"Twenty-one. Just turned." Still with that queer look.

"Early graduation, *and* a 4E. Bet you couldn't wait to shove that down Shapoorian's throat."

She shrugged, relaxing again. "Actually, his ratings only came through the day we arrived insystem. But I *do* wish I could have seen her face when she had to authorize that standing."

"I'd be willing to wager he should have been higher, if she agreed to that one."

"Possibly. It's also possible she just wanted him out. I suspect he'd become a potential embarrassment to her platform—that she intended him to put that faux transfer through for real, and Kurt sent me along to see that he didn't."

He drained his glass, mouthed an ice chunk. It was too big.

It clinked back into the glass, its icy novocaine deadening his mouth.

"I'd almost forgotten the dance. I wonder if politicians ever remember it's people they're manipulating."

"I don't think that goes well with the territory." She sipped her drink. "What made you think Stephen was the Ryevani-shovs'?"

"I don't know— A sense of justice, I suppose. They wanted children of their own—"

"Their own?"

"They had a little girl staying with them—Stef's niece, I think—Stef never explained. They were good people, would have made good parents. Something about Ridenour—felt familiar. But he couldn't be theirs. I left there..." A quick calculation. "...eighteen—maybe twenty NS years ago. Not long enough, anyway."

Her brow knit. "And she wasn't pregnant?"

"No. In fact, Stef had us run some tests—he didn't want to go to a Recon medic: secrets were nonexistent among his folk. But everything checked out okay. No reason they couldn't have kids. I figured it was only a matter of— Why? You told me Stephen wasn't theirs, are you telling me now that—"

"I said he wasn't Stefan Ryevanishov's."

"I told you. They had no children. And they'd been married for years."

"Come now, Paul," she said dryly.

He frowned. "Even if she'd had someone else's, Stef would have raised it as his own."

"Not according to Lexi's study. She says the Rostov Recons were quite touchy on the subject."

"I don't care what Lexi's 'Net records claim. Stef adored children—and his wife."

"And how'd she feel about him?"

"Dammit, Loro, what are you—what difference does it make?"

She stared at him for a long moment, then handed him the glass and pushed herself to her feet. He made no effort to stop her. They were both too tired to argue.

At the door, she glanced back, then turned and leaned a shoulder against the wall.

"How well did you know Ylaine Ryevanishov, Paul?"

"Not as well as Stef. She wasn't quite as—"

"You're standing by that?"

"It's the truth, dammit!"

"If you say so, Paul." He could feel her upset past the blank face she gave him. But it couldn't be jealousy, they hadn't been together for years—since well before his time on Rostov.

"Loro?"

"Stephen was *registered* as ten when he entered Vandereaux."

"So?"

"He's Recon, Paul. His mother filled out the application."

"So *what?*"

"Rostov's years are short, Paul. I leave *you* to figure the math. —Good night."

A sudden draft of cool air brushed the back of Stephen's neck. He straightened abruptly, glanced down the rimway, one direction and the other, straining, in the sleep-cycle minimum lighting, to spot the origin of that breeze.

Nothing. No one. He wished his nerves agreed. He shivered and returned to the security board outside Anevai's quarters, fingers shaking so badly he could hardly find the keys. He finished the feedback loop to the monitors, cancelled the LokCode and detached the leads from his PC.

Likely he was a fool to risk everything this way, but if he was right, if Smith's paper *was* a setup, he was ruined anyway. He'd already played into Shapoorian's hands—and if Wesley, if Anevai were simply players in one more convolute political powerplay, what did *anything* matter?

Three more heartbeats of silence. He released his breath, touched the door open and slipped through, whispering, *"Anevai?"*

The panel slid shut behind him, cancelling the hall's ambient light. He restored the lock with a fingertip touch, turned—

—and froze. He'd expected absolute darkness within the room. He was wrong. He traced that glow to bathroom lights set for minimal cool, used that dim light to guide him to Anevai's bed. He'd expected her to be awake—had counted on it. But there'd been no sound from her, no hint of movement.

The shadow on the bed stirred sleepily, shifted onto its side. He dropped to his knees and held his breath. When the shadow made no further sound, he rocked up onto his toes and inched closer to settle on his heels beside the bed.

The hand he extended to touch her arm shook. He paused, touched his own cheek instead. Cold—even to him. He tucked it under his sweater to warm it first—

—and found himself flat on his back on the floor, a decidedly female body holding him there, a sharp point at his throat, and a low voice in his ear, "Take the hand out and open it, Spacer-man—" Pressure surrounded his wrist as he jerked the hand free. "—*slowly.*"

He eased the hand open and the pressure relaxed, the weight on his chest shifted.

"Don't you *ever* sneak up on me again, Spacer-man. You want to share my bed, you ask po-lite-ly, hear?"

For several hard-won breaths, a confusion of startlement, embarrassment and anger held him speechless. Finally, he gasped, *"Dammit, Tyeewapi, I'm not a spacer, and—and I'm not here t–to sh–share your damn bed! So get your f–fucking knife out of my neck, and get off me!"*

Her weight lifted, and from somewhere above his head: "My, my, Spacer-lad, such language."

Light flooded the room. He shoved himself upright, drew in his knees to sit cross-legged on the floor, resting his back against the bed, squinting and blinking his eyes against the sting of adjustment. "Will you be serious," he muttered, and rubbed the spot on his neck where the sharp point had pricked the skin. "Dammit, what is it about you people and kni—"

His eyes cleared; the shadow beside the door gained edges and detail. Feeling the heat rise in his face, he looked elsewhere. "Anevai, I . . . Would you mind getting back into the bed, please?"

A chuckle. A pad of bare feet. The rustle of sheets. He noted with clinical indifference it was a stylus, not a knife, she tossed onto the bedside table beside a presspad, and wondered if all Anevai's people shunned nightclothes or if this was a personal preference. Noted, with a thoroughly unprofessional relief, that Anevai had tucked the sheet up under her chin.

With an innocent blink, she asked: "Is this more to your liking, Spacer-man?"

Warm oil dribbled onto Cantrell's shoulders, oozed down her spine and puddled in the small of her back. Sure strong hands squished and popped in the puddle, then pushed the slime back to her shoulders.

She groaned, felt her head sink farther into the pillow as TJ's hands convinced her neck muscles to relax, felt clenched hands loosen and drift across the smooth sheets as that practiced touch moved to her shoulders.

"So what do you think, Teej? Was Paul involved with Ylaine Ryevanishov?"

"Dammit, woman, don't tense up!" A sharp, squishy slap to her rump. A grumbled: Make my work difficult, will you . . . "Of course he was. We're talking Paul here, Loren. You've seen the pictures of the kid's mother." Another trickle of oil, a second pooling, and the massage resumed. "So what?"

"So what? Look at the ti— *Ow!*" She glared at him over her shoulder.

"Relax, Boss-lady. What about the timing?"

"You know what Danislav said. They ran the tests at Vandereaux. Stefan Ryevanishov was *not* Stephen's father. Paul's presence on Rostov, his involvement with the Ryevanishovs, his libido—dammit, everything points to it."

"So run the specs. Find out."

"I'd rather not."

"Why? What difference does it make? You're not in the market for a kid—Paul's or anyone else's. Who the hell cares?"

"*I* care, dammit! *Ow!* —All *right.*" She lay back on her stomach, took several deep breaths and forced muscle to relax. "Don't you see, Teej? If Stephen *is* Paul's son, he's useless— worse, fuel for Shapoorian's crowd: they'll claim the only reason he made it through the Academy is his spacer genes. Better the 'NetAT *should* swallow him . . ."

His hands stilled. The mattress shifted. She twisted around

as he settled back on his heels at the foot of the bed, concern, and a faint distaste on his face.

"What's wrong, Teej?"

"Useless, Loren? Is that all you've cared about? His use to *you* as a Recon academy clone?"

"Of course not, but—"

"A kid practically kills himself trying to prove he's got the balls as well as the brains to do his job—*for you,* Loren Cantrell, —and all you can say now is he's useless because his father might—*might*—be spacer?"

"I never said . . ." She caught his look, replayed her statement, and: "God."

"And while we're on the subject, what about that implication you made to Smith?"

"Implication? *What* implication?"

"About Stephen's intentions that night."

"I had to know. And you should have felt his pulse. He's *ours*, Teej. No question. The man's—"

"So what? The *boy's* not interested."

"You know that?"

"I think it's none of my business." He stood up, still with that Look, and rested a hand on the bedpost. "Loren, I respect you highly, you know that. I know you're exhausted. I also know you'd never have made that statement cold sober. But *in* exhaustion *veritas?* I think you'd better examine your own motives a bit more carefully before you take on the GenMems for real. I think you'd better start thinking more like the Loren Cantrell I met years ago and less about what's—how did young Ridenour put it?—*politically correct* for you to think. Stop manipulating ideas and start remembering those ideas revolve around people."

Her support arm started to shake. She leaned back and pulled the covers up over her shoulders, chilled. Oil cooling on her back? Or cold truth striking deep?

Either way—

"TJ, I—"

He raised a hand. "No need, Boss-lady. I've had my say, except: there are other possibilities. Paul's association with the Ryevanishovs could be incidental. It's no surprise they knew each other. Nor was Paul the only Rostov researcher Sakiimagan contacted through Stefan: that decade between Paul's transfer and the massacre on Rostov saw more than seventy-five percent of Rostov's SciCorps replaced. Several of them are here.''

A touch of anger eased the chill. "When did you discover that?''

"Same time we discovered Paul's link to the Ryevanishovs. —It's hardly surprising. They're all T-Class EcoSpecs: not that many options in other 'Tanks.''

"Why didn't you say something before now?''

"To paraphrase a very smart, very single-minded woman, you haven't exactly expressed an interest in anyone else since we got here.''

"Been pretty focussed on Paul, have I?''

"You might say that.''

"Damn. —I assume you've spoken with the researchers in question?''

He nodded briefly, meaning nothing of significance *had* come out of those interviews: no esoteric point of ethics would have kept TJ from telling her immediately if it had. He knew when to make a point—

—and when not.

"How many are we talking about? Enough to focus attention on HuteNamid?''

"I doubt it. There are four other than Paul who did time on Rostov, all multiple transfers: typical ex–Rostov researcher pattern: they don't seem able to settle—''

"Except here.''

"Except here," he amended. "They left Rostov because of 'growing unrest'—nothing more specific—and they all transferred here within the last few years, since the Rostov investigation was closed, and at a renewed invitation—from Corlaney this time. Their first invitation, like Paul's, came through the Ryevanishovs. *All* claimed the Ryevanishovs as 'friends' and all were on Rostov at the time Stephen would have been conceived.''

She chuckled and lay back into her pillows. "Not going to cut me any slack, are you, Teej?''

"Have I ever?"

She shook her head. "And you'd better not start now. Good-night, Teej."

" 'Night, Boss-lady."

vii

Dear Dr. Paul,

Adm. Cantrell seems to think this letter is an unnecessary precaution. I wish I could agree with her. Unfortunately, I know Dad better than she does and I'm quite sure that without coercion he will refuse to read my letter to him.

I'm counting on you, Dr. Paul.

If *you* don't understand what I'm trying to say to my father, *talk* to the admiral. Get her to make you understand. Then, if you can't get Dad to read my letter, or if you think you can put it better, please try to explain to him yourself. The Dineh are not alone in the universe, no matter what we would like—and I no longer think we want to be. I don't think it's healthy. I don't think it's smart.

Please, Doc. Not just for me. For you. For Hononomii. Even for (the tode) Nayati.

Love,

Me.

The carefully handwritten pages struck the edge of the desk and spilled to a jumbled pile on the floor. Paul ignored them, finding the shadow patterns on the ceiling of far greater significance.

Twenty minutes later, he was studying the inside of his eyelids with the same interest, while rubbing the pounding in his temples to dormancy.

The girl made sense; in her naive way, more sense than all the so-called adults had been making. Life was rarely as simple as youth would have it, but rarely as complex as age tried to make it.

One final hesitation, then he picked up the phone. A moment's anxiety when the screen remained dark, a longer one when Loren, blank-faced and chill, appeared on the monitor.

"Yeah, Corlaney? What do you want?"

Harsh. Abrupt. And he felt like laughing out loud.

He was tired. He was frustrated. He was confused. He *thought* he wanted sympathy.

She knew better.

"I want to talk to you, Loro. As soon as it's convenient."

"You have anything to say that I want to hear?"

He looked at the letters on the floor. Took a breath, and looked back at the monitor.

"Yes, admiral, I believe I do."

Her face softened. Not so far as a smile, but a ghostly dimple appeared in one cheek.

"Not tonight, Paul. You look like death warmed over. Get a good night's sleep, and I'll see you first thing in the morning. No rush." At last the smile broke through and she finished softly. *"Not now. G'night, love."*

"Yeah, right." Why did he feel as though he'd been had? "First thing tomorrow. 'Night."

Her image disappeared, and he almost called her back. Almost begged her to see him right now. For what purpose, he wasn't sure, only that he either wanted to follow through on his betrayal of Sakiimagan before he had time to think, or he wanted to bury his guilt in her intoxicating presence.

Instead, she left him to his own conscience for the night, forcing him to consider what he was about to do, forcing him to do it in full control of his faculties.

No excuses later.

Thanks, Cantrell.

"...Then it accessed Wesley's personal notes from his private files," Stephen floundered, trying not to reveal how little he really understood. "Not all of them, of course, just excerpts, but enough to show there *is* no meaningful link between *Harmonies* and Rasmussen's 'Net theory. He–he referenced, among other things, a note he received from one Anevai Tyeewapi that was—his words—the key to the whole concept.''

Down the length of the bed, Anevai sat cross-legged, a blanket drawn around her bare shoulders, a lumpy mound of pillows propping her elbows, her chin cupped in her hands. She hadn't moved or said a word since he'd begun his convolute question. If those brown eyes of hers weren't open, he'd swear she was asleep.

"Anevai!" Dark eyes flickered in his direction— "Is *Harmonies* as much yours as Wesley's?"

—and narrowed. "That so hard to swallow, *Spacer-man?*"

He flinched, but didn't protest. That epithet either endorsed his fears or proved how thoroughly he'd undermined any growing understanding between them. "I didn't mean it *that* way. But how could you . . . Where did you . . . I mean—God *dammit!*" All the frustration festering in him burst. "Four *years* ago?"

His breath deserted him. He brushed his face with a shaking hand, remembering his own four-years-ago, feeling himself VOSsing out and unable to stop it as the room faded to the blackness of a deprivation tank—the computerized images, electronically induced senses. Hour after hour of *being* what he was not—from a charm to a black hole— experiencing Reality as only the VRT's could present it. Content with the games, until the Voice insisted those games were real, ordering him to release his 'wrong-headed notions' and accept.

"Stephen?"

Accept.

He'd done the work, played the game, but he'd never really believed. *Never.*

And all that while, Anevai had been pouring radical ideas into Wesley's receptive mind. Ideas which had, ultimately, generated *Harmonies*.

"Stephen?"

He'd been truly jealous of very little in his life. *This,* he was jealous of.

"Stephen!" Anevai's hand clamped on his wrist, snapping him into RealTime. "Are you all right?"

He stared at her and asked, trying desperately to hold his thoughts together, to take advantage of her softening expression, "Please, Anevai, you've *got* to tell me what a girl like you had in common with an introverted Recon misfit who—"

"You?" Softness vanished. "What makes you think we have anything in common?"

"Had." He slumped, suddenly aware of every bruise. Every healing stitch. He felt . . . deflated. "When I was a kid."

"Because you're Recon? Hardly, Ridenour."

He scowled, her disinterest absorbing the last of his own urgency. "Has nothing to do with Recon, Tyeewapi. Has to do with *thinking*."

"About what?"

"For God's sake, the *'Net*. What else?" He caught himself—while he'd fooled the monitors with that fractal-loop, he hadn't soundproofed the whole ship. But he was tired of her act. She'd sat next to Wesley and himself in the bar while they talked 'NetTop for hours, acting lost, asking truly *basic* questions. Either she was pretending an ignorance she didn't have, or Wesley was lying. And either way, it reeked of one more damned setup.

You'd think he could smell one coming.

And damned if he would leave here without *some* admission of Truth. He tried to ignore the hand clamped on his wrist, concentrated instead on breaking through that indifference. "Don't you see, Anevai? From the day I arrived at Vandereaux, Danislav tried to get me to settle for BasicTech."

She looked skeptical. "A TT10? Fourth Echelon material? Try again, Ridenour."

"You never saw my 'Net Topology tests. Profs used my answers for *bad* examples for years—still do, for all I know. I manipulated the system well enough—I had that frightening nonchalance children have when they've no concept of the havoc they can create if they mess up—but my perception of it was all wrong. Or so they said."

"So they said?"

He clenched his fists, his pulse pounding against her forgotten grip. "That's the *real* reason—I'm here. To *hell* with the Del d'Bug business. *Harmonies* drove Danislav crazy: he'd worked damned hard to eradicate my *fool notions.*"

"What's one got to do with the other?"

"When I read *Harmonies*, I— Don't you see? Those 'fool notions' about NSpace were more like Wesley's—*your* perceptions, than Rassmussen's." And if *that* wasn't an understatement..."Don't you see? It *feels* like a setup— Shapoorian's genetic-memory crap with a vengeance—and she's been after my hide for years. And if it's planned, if you and Wes..."

But she wasn't listening, was staring right through him.

His hand twitched under her grip. Hands. Always so damned many hands. Pushing here, prodding there; do this, do that, don't ask why, just *do*. He'd *never* understand why people couldn't keep their hands to themselves.

"Shee-it," she whispered. "Maybe Shapoorian's got it right."

A coldness in his gut: verification he hadn't really wanted.

He jerked his hand; she released and leaned back. The blanket slipped, baring one brown-skinned shoulder. She ignored it. Still OTL.

He asked harshly, "Why are you here?"

A blink, and she was RT and tracking. "What does that—" "*Why?*"

She scowled. "I told you, I was worried about you. I—"

"Bullshit. Cantrell had you arrested in connection with my assault. *I* didn't press charges—not against you, not against your precious Nayati. I'm not asking why you came aboard *Cetacean*, I want to know why you're here now. Cantrell goes back, but you stay here. You have the run of the ship. And of me. *Why, goddammit?* Who are you working for?"

Her fists clenched in the blanket. "I don't have to answer that, and I don't have to sit here and listen to this. Get the hell out of my room, Spacer."

"Gladly!" Anger-blind, he jolted toward the door, but: "Dammit, no!" He slammed the wall with his fist and whirled back to the bed, desperation making his voice shake uncontrollably. "Can't you just tell me, does Cantrell know your connection with Wesley? With *Harmonies*? *Are* you hers?"

An openmouthed What the hell makes you think that? eased some of the hurt he only recognized in its abatement. He *wanted* to believe her protestations of friendship—*wanted* to trust her . . .

. . . And in the next breath, he stifled that want.

"It just doesn't add up." He dropped back down beside her, never taking his eyes from her face, searching for any sign of imposture. "Nayati tries to kill me for no apparent reason—*you* save my ass."

"I didn't. Nigan—"

He brushed that qualification aside—they both knew better. "Same difference. But then Cantrell tells me about missing data and a tap of the 'Net. I *think* I understand—tell her I do. Then you show up—get me to spill my guts—personal shit I've kept strictly private for damned good reasons; you act like you know nothing about the 'Net, and then *he* calls you the key to his new system. Cantrell leaves you here, within my easy reach . . . Cantrell is the Council's; Shapoorian is on the Council, and she'd give a great deal for my liver on a platter. Please, you've got to tell me, is all this—Wesley's paper, your presence here, God, the whole damned planet—just some elaborate scheme to finally drive me insane? To prove some political point?"

He reached for her hands, wanting to make her listen, pulled back at her scowl and wrapped his arms against the churning in his stomach, wishing for his bedside pharmacy while knowing no pill would solve this problem. He muttered, Never mind, and shoved himself to his feet. No matter others' motives, Anevai Tyeewapi, if that was even her name, was just doing her job. Same as Cantrell. Same as he.

But as he reached for the door-release:

"In answer to the question, Ridenour—" Soft-voiced from the bed, tempting him to turn back. "—No."

An insistent beep greeted Nayati as he sauntered into the Library's Main Control room. In contrast to the tunnel's glow, the only light here came form the monitors. His eyes adjusted to an image as irritating as that beep: Nigan Wakiza, lounging in a chair, bare feet tapping the counter in time to the drumbeat escaping the earphones he wore.

"Nigan, answer the phone."

Nigan's eyes remained closed. His toes continued to tap a complex pattern, his fingers to dance along the holes of an invisible flute.

The beep went on.

"Dammit, Wakiza!" Nayati jerked the transmitter from the deck, and raucous noise filled the room. "Shit!" He brought a fist down on the power button.

Blessed silence.

Beep!

Nigan sipped his beer.

Beep!

"So get the damn phone."

Nigan swallowed and licked his lips, plucked the transmit from Nayati's lax fingers and punched it back into the deck.

Beep!

"Busy. *You* get it."

"You *know* who it is."

Beep!

Nigan grinned. "Sure do." He toed the power on again, leaned back and closed his eyes.

Nayati swore and sat down before the console. He flipped the acknowledgment and the screen came to life on Sakiimagan's impassive face.

"Ya'at'eeh, Nayati Hatawa." As though nothing had happened. As though he'd not been avoiding the governor for three days.

"Ya'at'eeh, Sakiimagan Tyeewapi." He matched Sakiimagan's calm, speaking the Old Ones' tongue. Fluent as only they two could be.

"It's good to hear your voice, nephew, but there's no need to mince words. My daughter has made allegations."

"Such as?"

"Nothing you can't account for. I need specifics. I need to understand your reasons. Meet me at Spirit Lake in three hours."

Three hours. "There are guards with sensors in the woods," he cautioned.

"I've seen them," Sakiimagan said contemptuously. "I

wonder what these much-vaunted Security Agents would do without all their little machines to replace their own senses. I was tempted to walk past them openly—"

"Uncle, no—"

"Of course not. I used the shielded tunnels. I'll leave the same way."

"Ha'goo'nee, Sakiimagan Tyeewapi."

"Ha'goo'nee, Nayati Hatawa."

"What made you go into 'Net studies, Stephen?"

"Why?" he asked, suspicion flaring anew.

Anevai shrugged, nervous fingers pleating the blanket, smoothing it flat and pleating again. "Trying to answer your question."

Fair enough.

"I don't really . . ." But he stopped that almost lie. He did remember, though he hadn't thought of the reasons in years. Beyond Anevai's nervous fingers, a silent bedside presence: the monitor and keyboard no alliance residence could survive without, link to the central nervous system of an entire civilization . . .

(*"Papa, how does it know?"*)

Back to the wall, knees pulled up to his chest, he rested his chin on crossed forearms and closed his eyes on the monitor, letting the memories surface . . .

(*His much younger self craning to see the screen over the table's edge. Papa lifting him to his lap, letting him stretch his fingers over the keyboard. Himself touching fingers to the screen, laboriously reading words in the Other Language—the only one Mama let him speak nowadays.*

(*Papa's hug making him gasp for breath. Papa's cheek, pressing against his, smooth and cool and smelling—a closed-eyes sniff—like the flowers in Mama's garden. That was Papa early in the morning. Later his cheek would get rough and he'd smell of the fields, and later still of soap and vodka. That was Papa, too, but Zivon liked the morning smell best of all.*

(*"I wish I knew, my little Zivon. All I know is how to get it to tell me some of what it knows and how to record what we've done. Only the 'NetTech specialists over in SciComp really know how it knows."*

(*"Can't you ask them?"*)

Naïveté upon naïveté. But his papa hadn't answered, and later, he'd gone alone to the Rostov Science Complex—a long walk for an adult, it had seemed endless to a seven-year-old—and asked to talk to the people who knew about the 'Net.

They'd laughed in his face.

"Why?" He remembered the wistful note in his father's voice, remembered mama's punishment when he'd returned from SciComp long after dark, too humiliated to explain where he'd been. "I think . . . I think maybe it was so I could tell papa how the 'Net worked. It seemed so unfair that someone should know and refuse to tell him."

Her expression said the reason made no sense. He supposed it sounded crazy, but it was the only answer he had to give. Staring off into the blankness beyond the wall, remembering that wistful note, he sensed an emptiness that could never be filled. Papa was dead. He finally understood how the 'Net worked, but he'd never be able to explain now.

"How did you learn?"

"What do you mean 'How'?"

"Wesley taught me—took me on in desperation, I suppose. Was there a Wesley for you?"

"A Wesley?"

(*"No, Papa! I don't want to go!"*

(*"Zivon, Richard has invited you to SciComp. Says you've got potential. They've never volunteered to work with one of us before. Twice a week, son! You must go. Show them how bright our children are."*

(*"I–I'm s–scared, Papa. Th–they . . ."*

(*"Because they laughed? They're sorry, now. They want to make it up . . ."*)

"Mostly," he answered slowly, refusing to give Richard or any of the other Rostov researchers Wesley-esque status. "I think I taught myself."

"How?"

"From the *'Net*." He took a deep breath. Curbing irritation. She couldn't know the old wound she prodded. "There are plenty of references if you're persistent enough."

"Why?"

The blanket had slipped. He took his eyes from exposed

cleavage, met hers, and looked elsewhere, uncomfortably aware of her silent laughter and deliberate rearrangement of the blanket.

"Why–Why do you ask?"

Her brow puckered. "I've been thinking about your original question. Councillor Shapoorian maintains—"

"I don't give a damn what any Shapoorian thinks."

"Shut up and listen. She maintains Recons become Recons because they haven't got the brains to understand spacer technology."

"That's bullshit, Tyeewapi. I'm proof of that. *You* are."

"Are we? Or are we her best argument . . . not that she'd appreciate the extrapolation. And I'm not implying she's right in everything. I mean, the specific memories and all get pretty crazy, but if the actual process by which the brain works can be inherited, couldn't humanity have bred itself into a—conceptual dead end? Couldn't they have—"

He was *not* interested in extrapolating *any* of Shapoorian's ideas. "I'm not *into* biology, Tyeewapi."

She paused and stared at him, the pucker turning quizzical. "I know. Too bad."

It took an embarrassingly long consideration, but when he finally took her meaning, his face grew hot, and he muttered, "Just make your point, Tyeewapi."

She chuckled. "All right. Point: Why you? Why were *you* the one to spot Wesley's paper?"

"Coincidence."

"I don't believe in coincidence. Not when Wes went to such pains to bury that paper."

"Bury it? That's odd. I thought it quite logically flagged—"

She giggled. "Can I tell Wesley that?"

"Why? To give him one more reason to despise me?"

The giggle faded, her head cocked. "What makes you think he despises you?"

"More than enough cause, Tyeewapi. I'm a Del d'Bugger. If he didn't realize that before, he does now—or will soon: I won't lie to him anymore—*can't*. That means I came here to discredit his claims. I've lied, spied on his friends, gotten you arrested, and probably, before this is all over, will get him arrested, too—"

"I think it safe to say, Ridenour, that all of the above doesn't mean squat to Jonathan Wesley Smith. If I know my Wesser—and believe me, I do—he's counting the minutes until he can get you cornered to discuss *Harmonies* in private. If you *knew* what he's put me through for the last four years trying to *create* you—"

"Huh?"

"Remind me to work with you on self-expression. —Wesley *wants* someone like you—badly—though I don't think he himself realizes it. Someone with the mathematical and scientific training to . . ."

Stephen tried not to listen—either to Anevai or to the persistent tug inside him. It was all irrelevant. Except . . .

How could he face the 'NetAT now, knowing how little he understood? He'd come here as their rep. What was he going back as?

If Wesley Smith really *had* been looking for him, if Wesley *would* still talk with him . . .

The blanket was slipping again. Stephen, always cold on the ship, waited for her to shut up and notice. When she did neither, he edged closer and quietly pulled the blanket up over her shoulders, overlapping the corners under her chin. Her hands appeared from under the blanket and closed over his before he could release his hold.

She'd stopped talking.

Startled, he met her crinkle-eyed gaze.

"Very good, Ridenour," she said softly. "One of these days you'll even manage that without blushing."

"I'm *not*—" he protested: at which, naturally, he did.

With nothing to hold it in place, the blanket settled into a puddle around her hips. He tried not to look; tried (equally difficult) not to look pointedly elsewhere.

She giggled and released his hands to pull the blanket up, then paused, and threw her arms around his neck instead.

"Why bother?" she said, her voice tripping on that same light laughter. "Why don't we work at completing the cure instead?"

It was a lip-lock that would have done the Wesser proud. Anevai had hoped to change the mood—she'd been given the job of keeping Stephen relaxed, a job she was failing miserably. Anevai had hoped to distract Stephen's thoughts, and her own, from profitless speculation—if Cantrell's plan succeeded, Stephen would soon be happily occupied with someone far better qualified to answer his questions. Anevai had hoped to recall a flicker she'd thought kindled in Stephen's room not so very long ago.

Well, two out of three wasn't bad.

She paused for breath; Stephen jerked away and rolled off the bed. She grabbed for the desk's edge to keep from falling, then threw up an arm to catch the fabric flung in her face: her jumpsuit, the one Cantrell had given her to replace the torn and blood-stained garments she'd worn aboard.

"What's this?" She smiled up at his white, tight-jawed face, seeking a better humor: "Prefer to do the unwrapping yourself, maybe?"

"G–get your mind out of the—" She lifted her eyebrows, and he stopped in mid-sentence. Then: "We're leaving. Tonight."

"Leaving? The *ship?* You're crazy! Why? How? To go *where?*"

"Because—" He seemed to be searching her room for something. "Because—"

"Shit, Ridenour. You don't want to have a little fun, just say so. —Take off. Leave. Don't make up elaborate nowhere excuses."

His search ended—straight on her. "I must talk with Wesley."

"Why?"

"Because . . . Just because."

"Why the hurry?"

"Who knows what's happening down there right now?" His hand swept a vague gesture through the air. "The admiral went down this morning, and whatever her plans, she means to move fast. She must. She's got a hold on local 'Net usage. Soon—I don't know exactly what the law is this week—only the Council can lift the ban. And she doesn't understand—how *can* she? *I* don't, and she depended on me to—"

She should tell him Cantrell's plan—but he'd been so set all along on keeping Wesley free of the ship. He'd insisted Wesley did *not* want back in space—

"Slow up, Ridenour. Why can't you just call her? Let *her* arrange a meeting with Wesley so you can figure out—whatever it is you want to figure out."

"Because I'm no longer convinced I should trust her." The vague gestures, the searching, ended, and silver spook eyes made her feel more than skin was exposed. "I'm no longer convinced I should trust *anyone,* or of what's right. I need—I need *time*, dammit. Time to think. To understand. *Before* I face the 'NetAT. I *don't* want her monitoring and controlling everything that's said between Wesley and me."

"But we can't just leave without Cantrell's security knowing. They probably know already. They've heard everything we've said and done here, haven't they?"

He looked vaguely sick at his stomach. "You could believe that and still *do* what you just did? Still suggest what you—"

"What did I . . . ?" Puzzled, she thought back, felt a moment's queasy embarrassment herself, but realized: "If they make a habit of invading people's privacy, wouldn't be the first time they've seen a bit of friendly cuddling. Besides." She winked, hoping to loosen him up a bit, get his mind clear off this dangerous track. "Let's give the natives a thrill."

His lip wrinkled. "Let's not. —I took care of the monitors before I came here. As far as Sec's concerned, you're snoring away same as you were an hour ago. The systems in this section are pretty basic."

"Okay," she said slowly, not certain who was crazier at the moment: Stephen, for suggesting the scheme, or herself, for inclining to go along with him. "Say I'm convinced of the why." She stood up and began pulling on her jumpsuit. "And the how?" Again, that desperate glance about the room. She sank back onto the bed. "Shit, Ridenour. You haven't the foggiest. —Next time you offer to spring a gal from the pokey, have a plan, will you?"

He blinked, shook his head confusedly. "P–pokey?"

"Add it to your list of Things-to-ask-the-Wesser." She kicked her boots across the room. One bounced off the wall, the other off Ridenour's shin. He swore softly, shifted his weight to his other foot and bent to pick the boots up. He straightened, face to the wall, and froze.

"Ridenour?"

He didn't answer. She leaned over, tried to look around him to see what he found so mesmerizing.

"—Ridenour!"

A silver eye glared over his shoulder. "Move over."

He threw himself down beside her and slammed the keyboard on his lap. She shrugged the jumpsuit up over her shoulders, and said, "That's a limited access..."

He looked back at her, a quizzical glance, then without a word, fingers flying across the keyboard, accessed not only *Cetacean's* Computer-main, but Requisitions as well.

Requisitions?

A check of the wall beside the door. A small sign: emergency craft assignment and directions. She swallowed hard, forcing her heart back out of her throat.

"Ridenour, you wouldn't dare..."

If he heard her, he didn't acknowledge, his concentration glued to the screen.

"You're *not* going to get me into one of those."

A blinking stare followed her accusatory finger to the sign on the wall. "Of course not, Tyeewapi. Don't be ridiculous. But there are several other automated vehicles—in a variety of sizes. Some as easy as your bubblecar shuttles. That's what I was just checking. Now, *shut up.*"

She moved back to his side, felt a prick in her foot: the stylus, half-hidden in the rug; beside it, a spark of crystal, both apparently flung to the floor with Stephen's angry possession of the keyboard. She swept them up and tucked them absently into her pocket as she sat down beside him, felt a chill as he used *Cantrell's* personal Security Key to requisition a small cargo craft.

"I thought those Security Keys required about a dozen physiological matches..."

"So did I—an hour ago." Absently, as menus and forms flashed and filled faster than she could read the titles: "Is there any place other than the main spaceport we can safely land and meet Wesley? Some place less obvious?"

"Not really," she said faintly, the ramifications of his absentminded confession registering. "Though at this hour of the night..."

"Never mind. Doesn't really matter. They won't trace this for a while. Long enough, anyway. We'll go there.... Safest anyway to..."

"Safest? Ridenour, what are you—"

The screen went blank. Popped back with:

>**Craft: DBO/MINIBUS7/40.**
>**Designation: ASCET397MB.**
>**Course Destination: Tunica Air and Space.**
>**Coordinates: Chart 35/Detail C/D2.**
>**Course Status: Laid in.**
>**Type Launch: Semi Auto.**
>**Type Landing: Full Auto.**
>**Launch 3000CNS.**
>**Window: 00:20CNS.**
>**ETA: 0330CNS.**

3000h. It was, by the readout on the screen, 2845h now.

"In a hurry, are you?" she asked, trying desperately to cover her jumping nerves.

"Naturally." A look that indicated she was crazy for thinking otherwise. "Now, just one more thing—"

The screen went blank, and with his eyes closed, Stephen typed rapidly for several seconds. Flying fingers stilled, rested lightly on the keys; a hint of satisfaction crossed his face.

His spook-eyes opened. "Let's go."

"But—"

He was already at the door. He swung back and held out his hand. *"Come on!"*

"Just a damn minute, Ridenour!" Anevai grabbed her boots. Hopping on one foot, glaring up into his face while she pulled one on and yanked the lacing tight at the knee. "What did you just do?" she demanded, pulling the other boot on and pointing at the computer with her chin.

The frown deepened: "Don't go crazy on me now, Tyeewapi. I called Wesley, that's all. I warned him we were on our way. To meet us at the—"

"You used the 'Tap!"

"Of course. Now come on."

"But Wes didn't—couldn't—*wouldn't* have—"

Stephen grinned: an impish grin she'd never have credited him with. "He didn't have to."

"—Damn—"

That imp-grin widened. "C'mon, friend."

viii

The haunting strains of Mandisa's *Fantasia on a Theme* filled the room. On the screen, a slow-motion collage wedded music with the lyricism of the human body. From floor to five-bar to Mobius Band, from ZG compulsories to fifth-level specialty, one motion flowed to the next in a single routine only clever video editing made possible.

But that clever editor had had the advantage of an unusual subject. The gymnast moved from one apparatus to the next with, as one color commentator put it, "... a singularity of style—a uniformity of grace that was unusual, if not unique, in the gymnastics field. ..."

Translation: God, he was beautiful.

Wesley hit the replay and settled back against the pillows to view the video essay for the sixth time. Toes tapped off rebound pads with an uncanny sense of precisely the degree of lift those randomized pads would lend, and exactly what could be accomplished with that boost; taking arcs that created a regularity of motion and line independent of the viewing speed.

It was that regularity the video artist had sensed and used to such advantage. For once, the 'color' sportscaster correctly analyzed performance. Stephen Ridenour had been good—possibly even great, given time and intersystem experience—but no training could teach that extra sense of poetic timing and movement that had set him apart.

He'd needed an edge. He'd been a head shorter than most of his competitors: LowG experts tended to tall—1 mete 8 and above emphasized the long arcing trajectories—and Stephen was slightly under Wesley's own perfect 1.75m. He'd looked almost like a child—until he'd started to move.

Amazing how the kid could glide like that in a gymnas**ium** and trip down a simple flight of stairs. Luckily for Stephen, Anevai had been there to rescue his exceedingly attractive ass.

Attractive, yes, but not what it had been. Damn shame. In a way, Anevai was right: compared to Stephen Ridenour, Vandereaux gymnast, Stephen Ridenour, Vandereaux graduate, certainly was 'too skinny.' And the relaxed face, the occasional shout of laughter as he soared from one bar to the next, bore little resemblance to the stiff-backed, pinch-mouthed Academy-clone he'd first seen at the *Watering Hole* door.

He scanned through other broadcasts pulled up from the 'Net and *Cetacean*'s Vandereaux files. Contrary to what he'd implied to Cantrell, he'd not been into Stephen's files before. Now, he didn't care if he left tracks. Let her wonder.

The 'casters had started paying attention to Stephen when he was still a JV. His so-called comeback from a 'childhood injury' to his shoulder had made him a natural human interest story. A year or so later, even the 'casters had begun to realize the skill and difficulty that lyrical style camouflaged.

Longer hair, too. Better keep this one away from Anevai once they got him back. With hair, *she'd* demand equal time—

If they got him back. Damned frustrating state of affairs. If Ridenour had just been another bit-brained CodeHead like most Del d'Buggers, keeping him would have been simple: a transfer request had been filed as part of his 'NetAT cover story. All they'd have had to do was accept it.

Unfortunately, the 'NetAT wanted him back to expose Wesley Smith for a fraud, among other things. Danislav probably wanted him back, too, possibly for the 'glory and honor of Vandereaux.' (Read: Danislav.)

All of which made things slightly more complicated, but hardly impossibly so. Besides, if Stephen Ridenour had been one of the CodeHeads with vaporware for brains, Wesley Smith wouldn't *want* him.

For scenery, he could look out the window.

He sighed, and scanned the files at random. Sometimes, life was very difficult.

A closeup of Stephen winked past. Not in action. Talking. Complete with network commentator. He cycled back, surprised the Vandereaux powers-that-be had let the Recon kid loose to talk. But as the interview ran—standard Hi, Mom! fare: something about a message to his folks—he realized a shy, embarrassed Stephen Ridenour, complete with stutter and long-lashed opal eyes, could have been one of the best PR numbers Vandereaux ever had.

Bet that *brought him a shit-load of fan mail,* he thought.

An auto-search for related material found no further interviews, only a brief memo issued the week following that first one:

>**Vandereaux PubRel/Victor Danislav.**
>**Subject soliciting excessive public interest. Possible exposure potentially detrimental to Vandereaux image and Subject's studies. Recommend limiting coverage of sporting events in which Subject is involved. And under no circumstances shall the Subject be granted further public interviews.**

Figures: Public Opinion on the kid's side would undermine if not eliminate the Academy's stranglehold control of his life and career. Private-sector interest: product endorsements, personal interest stories—lord, the kid was natural vid-fodder.

Ridenour's final appearance was three days following the 'accident.' Stock footage with Danislav (the old media-leech) personally announcing the kid's retirement from competition. Cristof Devon should have made the announcement. But there was Danislav, big as life and twice as asinine, acting as if he knew what he was talking about, Sincerely Sorry to have to make the announcement. Bull-shitting about how proud the Academy was of Stephen, and how *sorry* they all were to lose him from the team, just when he was coming into his own.

Damned hypocrite. He pulled up the vid poem again before he puked, and anger dissipated as his heart rate increased for altogether different reasons.

''God, he's—''

Suddenly, the image disappeared. In its place:

>**Tunica Air and Space.**
>**0330.**

>**Be there.**
>**Button.**

A quick stop-off at Stephen's room for 'the necessaries.' Bed made, keyboard tucked neatly under the desk, not so much as a paper clip left out . . . She didn't dare sit down anywhere— something might wrinkle or fingerprint. Anevai settled on the edge of a chair while Stephen pulled on a thick sweater and disappeared into the bathroom.

"Haven't you got anything warmer than that? It can get cold this time of year."

An indeterminate mutter drifted from the cubicle, then more clearly: "Thank God. They brought my stuff back up. —It'll be enough. We won't be outside much."

She glanced around the room. "Assuming all goes as *you've* planned."

Stephen's head appeared. "What can go wrong?"

"Shee-it, Ridenour!" she said. "Talk about famous last words!"

He emerged with a double handful of pill bottles and tossed them onto the bed. They bounced—three times.

He cast a puzzled look her way. "Whose last words?"

"Gods. —Never mind." She pulled her own fur-lined jacket snug and buttoned it all the way up.

"Best I've got, Tyeewapi." He pulled a hip-pouch from a drawer and began stuffing pill bottles in it. Not so much as a two-drawer search. She didn't know *anybody* was that organized. He hesitated over one slim vial, then, a rather sick look on his face, added it to the pouch as well.

"What're all those for?"

"Mostly stuff McKenna ordered me to take—" A sardonic lift of his brows. "—on pain of death. The others—well, they'll keep us going."

He popped a vial open, swallowed one of the pills dry and offered the vial to her. She stepped back, hands behind her back.

"You ever hear of food, Ridenour? Thanks anyway. I'll do without."

He shrugged and clipped the belt around his waist, a single

tug draping the sweater gracefully over the bulge. On his way to Grand Theft MiniBus and *he* looked like a model for some Family's designer. "C'mon. Let's get going."

"You planning a fast turnaround?" At his puzzled glance: "A toothbrush? Change of socks, maybe?"

"I'd rather avoid encumbrance."

"Encumbrance?" She stifled half-hysterical laughter. "Sure, why not? Borrow from Wesley." The image of this fashion plate wearing anything of the Wesser's choosing truly boggled the mind—but then, this whole scheme was a guaranteed mind boggler. She just hoped they survived long enough to get caught. "Lord, let's go."

A pause by the desk, a glance at her; a blush and a step toward the door.

"Stephen?"

Another glance, then he spun back and pulled a battered notebook from the drawer.

"I thought you wanted to avoid *encumbrance*."

His mouth tightened defiantly. "It's mine, and I'm not leaving it in anyone else's hands! There's stuff in here I can't remember how to read—yet. I want it with *me*, not up here, if—*when* I do."

She held up both hands. "Hey, Ridenour, you want to mess with it, it's your problem. Just don't blame me if it gets dirty."

His eyes narrowed, and he hugged the book to him. "It won't."

Out the door and back down the darkened rimway, this time to a lift. Their goal lay at the stationary core of the monstrous ship: the rimside emergency vehicles would draw too much attention—or so Stephen claimed. Anevai followed somewhat blindly, dazed by the speed at which events were flowing around her. If Stephen was right not to trust Cantrell, she supposed they should get out of here while they could. *If* they could. If he was wrong . . .

. . . If he was wrong, she still didn't want to stick around without him. If anything happened to him, Cantrell would rightfully blame her. And if he actually did manage to get them down to the planet's surface in one piece, she could keep him that way.

But she still half-expected—or half-hoped—someone would pop out and arrest them at any moment.

The floor of the lift pressed hard against her feet for a long acceleration. Surprisingly long compared to her trip from the main shuttle bay. Sure, it was a different shaft, and they were core-bound rather than rim, but the ship was *round*. So why—

"Hang on to this." Stephen thrust his notebook into her arms.

"Ridenour, what—"

He grabbed her around the waist, whispered, "*Trust me*."

A control touched—"*Three*"—a ring on the side of the cabin gripped—"*Two*."—

And suddenly, she knew.

"*Ridenour!*"

Pressure on her feet stopped. She was falling headfirst—

—or rather, feet first toward what had been the ceiling. She didn't know quite what he'd done, but decel hit their feet, not their heads, though evidently harder than even Stephen anticipated. His knees buckled and he fell, his hold pulling her down on top of him.

"Sh-*Shit*!" A whispered gasp; not hers. She rolled away, leaving Stephen propped against the wall. He was holding his arm. His left arm. All they needed was to foul up McKenna's work, too.

"Stephen, are you all right?"

It took a moment before he got it out, but his answer seemed steady enough. "I'll be fine." —No. I don't need help, just jarred things a bit." He used that ring ladder built into the wall to pull himself to his feet. "Stupid stunt to pull. Forgot the ship is smaller than Vandereaux. Emergency express means business here. . . ."

"Stephen, shouldn't you be wearing your brace?"

He shook his head. "Don't have it anymore. Between Nayati and the meds there wasn't much left of it. Besides, McKenna says I won't need it—"

"Once it heals. I don't think she intended—"

"Here we are."

They coasted to a civilized halt, and drifted out into the coreway. It bore no resemblance to the main shuttle bay, though they must connect somehow, and one direction looked much like the other.

For a long moment, Stephen hung there, looking rather helplessly one way and the other, up and down—at row upon row of entryways into this central ring.

"Lost?" She honestly tried to keep the sarcasm out of her voice.

Unsuccessfully.

He glowered at her. "Just don't let go of that book." And grabbed her wrist.

A sequence tapped into a numeric pad on the wall next to a series of rings, his lean fist closing tight on one of those rings as it began moving along a fine track: one of an interlacing series of tracks forming a geometric lacework on the inner wall.

She heard him mutter: "I didn't want to use this. Whole damn ship could find us now..." But she refrained from answering: she didn't think he meant her to hear.

Another spook-eyed glower aimed her way. Then again...

It was a small ship. A *very* small ship, the interior walls all cupboards and storage racks. If ten people could fit in it any way but stacked, she'd like to know how.

Anevai bobbed in the cockpit doorway as Stephen floated into the pilot's seat and pulled the safety straps around him. "Do you know how to fly this thing?"

"Of course not. I told you, I haven't been off-station since I was—"

"Yeah, right." She swallowed hard and entered the cabin rather more gingerly, eased her way into the co-pilot's seat, eyeing the complex array of controls. "Stephen, maybe this isn't such a bright idea. How 'bout we just contact the admiral in the morning and—"

"For heaven's sake, Anevai, it's all automated. The course is set. It'd complain if I *tried* to touch controls. And no, I can't wait. By tomorrow, the admiral could have Wesley up here, asking me to explain things I can't, then she'll keep me from him—after using me to trick him aboard the ship. I've got to go now!''

For the first time it occurred to her they might actually succeed and of a sudden, she remembered what *should* have been her *first* consideration when Stephen proposed this mad scheme. ''Hono! —Stephen, I've got to go back!''

''What? —Why?''

''My brother. Hononomii. He's still up in sick bay. I've got to go get him.''

She shoved off the seat and back out into the cramped airlock, hitting her head twice before getting the trajectory right.

''Anevai, wait!'' Stephen's head popped through the hatch. His hand caught her ankle. ''You can't go back!''

She jerked free, spun and bounced off the far wall. His hands caught and steadied her and they bobbed together in the lock. What steadied him, she didn't know or care.

''Who's going to stop me?'' She panted in his face.

''We haven't time!''

''So reprogram this thing.''

''I *can't!*''

''Like hell,'' she said. And recalled, of a sudden, a bed made, an orderly room, *everything* precisely where he expected it to be . . . Not coincidence: a clear intention of leaving. ''I don't like this, Ridenour. You reschedule that launch, or you go without me.''

He *looked* desperate. ''I can't take the risk.'' Didn't *mean* anything. ''You don't realize what the admiral might do—''

''Yet you expect me to leave my brother up here?''

''I—''

She reached for the core-lock rim and pulled out of his hold. ''Well, I won't do it. Stay here if you want. I'm going back for my brother.''

''Anevai, wait! You can't do anything for him even if you get him free, and you can't *do* that. He's under high security lock. Even *I* can't get past it.''

'*Even I* . . .' She recalled his casual use of Cantrell's personal key and ignored that desperate look. ''You didn't even try.''

She jerked at the rim and sailed through the lock.

"All right!"

She caught the rim with her foot, a ring with her hand, and waited.

"All right, Anevai." A much lower voice said, "I'll try to get the locks down—"

She glanced back eagerly.

"—from here!"

Her body drifted slowly. She stopped its rotation with a hand to the other side of the lock. "Guess again, Ridenour."

"If I can get past the locks, we can go to his room and get him. If I set off alarms, at least we've a *chance* of getting out."

"You release them from here. Just give me time to get to his room first."

"It's useless my going downworld without you. *Please.*"

"No." She ignored his protests and kicked herself off in the general direction of the lift with more energy than finesse. A body shot past, twisted and hit a blue spot on the wall with a foot. He rebounded straight at her and stopped her with a hard grip on her arm, one foot to a red spot on the inner wall, the other hooked in a ring. She swung at him furiously—an awkward blow he blocked easily, definitely with the advantage in this upside-out environment—a fury which eased at the sight of his terrified face, his obvious restraint of that advantage.

"Anevai, p–please try to understand. If *you* get caught, Adm. Cantrell won't touch you—except, maybe, a question or two under Dep. If *I* try to free your brother and get caught, with what I know, with my training, and with no more justification than I can give right now, I won't stand a chance. They'll mindwipe me so fast, I won't have time to wonder what I've forgotten." His shaking voice faded to a desperate whisper: "I've got so damn little to call my own, Anevai, please don't ask me to risk that too. I *want* to help you. I—I suppose I even want to help your brother, even though maybe he deserves—"

She kicked free at that, from his startled gasp getting him somewhere important, and sent them rebounding off opposite walls. She ducked, spun wildly, disoriented, grasping for a handhold—any handhold.

A hand caught her, stabilized them both—some damned unfair instinct seemed to tell them where those rings were—

then released her gently, though not before she felt the trembling in his fingers.

He drifted apart from her, stopped his motion with a touch, floated there, wide-eyed desperate, but making no further move to stop her. And while she refused to believe they'd wipe a mind like his (even if they had that fabled ability), she supposed that in Stephen's case, such a fate might well be the ultimate threat.

Hononomii. Stephen. Why should she have to choose?

"All right. All *right*." She tossed her hands up in defeat, starting another crazy tumble. Stephen steadied her again and she caught at his hand. "See what you can do from here."

She settled into her seat, feeling a twinge of guilt as he worked his way past her, white-faced, and pressing a hand to his side. This was crazy. He shouldn't even be out of bed.

"Stephen, let's forget—"

But he wasn't listening. He accessed *Cetacean's* computer, searched menu after menu, muttering to himself and casting desperate glances at the chrono display blinking ever closer to the far end of the launch window.

"Just *cancel* the launch request!"

"It's not that easy!" He passed a hand over his eyes—a very shaky hand—and said in a strained but milder tone, "Anevai, I'm sorry. That's not a terrifically safe maneuver I pulled, using the admiral's Security key. If I don't have to..."

"Well, you do have to. It's too late to get Hono out and back before the window closes."

"Maybe not. We've still got almost fifteen minutes, if you'll shut up and let me..."

She shut up.

Two minutes later, she regretted that silence when Stephen muttered, "Here goes nothing."

The next instant, all hell broke loose, CompuLink speaking.

"*Dammit!*" Stephen's voice broke on the expletive, and acceleration slammed Anevai back into her seat as the MiniBus exploded out of its bay.

II

i

"You're telling me you had the clear opportunity to finish Ridenour and *waited* for Cantrell's medics to show?"

Sakiimagan's words froze the air even in these climate-controlled caverns, but they hadn't the power to disturb Nayati Hatawa. He simply smiled calmly in the face of that fury and said, "He intrigued me, uncle. A stubborn will that deserved a chance to live."

"And in so choosing, you have put me in a position of either protecting you and the Cocheta or my own children. I do not appreciate your timing, boy."

"Now, uncle, let's not start calling names, shall we? I sent Ridenour back with a message for the admiral—a much clearer one than his disappearance would be. I exist and she can't do anything about it. When the *Cetacean* leaves HuteNamid, it will not carry Nayati Hatawa. I am my own man and I've done no wrong; so I sent her an Alliance Academy message: payment in kind: damage one of ours, we damage one of yours. Leave us alone, we'll leave you alone. Her interrogation methods are responsible for Hononomii's condition, mine were responsible for Ridenour's. Hono remained alive—so hers did."

" 'Your own man.' " Sakiimagan sat back in the carved stone seat. From hidden sources, Cocheta phosphorescence reflected off the pool's still surface, the occasional ripple making shifting spirit shapes across his chief's strong features and opalescing the stalactites dripping behind him. "I'll grant you that. 'Done no wrong?' Are you, then, your own judge as well?"

He shrugged and let Sakiimagan take that gesture as he would. *He* took his orders from a higher source than Sakiimagan Tyeewapi; higher, even, than the Tribe's Council of Elders.

Sakiimagan said, "You were to stay away from the Libraries,

yet I find you here. You were to stay off the 'Net, and yet you freely admit otherwise.''

"There's no need for caution where it concerns the 'Net. I know what I'm doing."

"So you say." Sakiimagan frowned. "Anevai was right about you. Arrogance shall prove your downfall."

"Anevai's acting like a bitch in heat." The words erupted from righteous indignation, indignation his uncle failed to share. He turned away, but revised his tone. "I'm not trying to defy your authority, Sakiima. Not at all. There *are* times when I must trust my own judgment—am I not a grown man? —and this was one of them. Had Ridenour died there in the barn, there was nothing to link me to it. Since he survived to make accusations, I'll simply disappear until the admiral and her minions leave the system."

"Which Cantrell won't do until she has you in hand, and frankly, I don't blame her."

"You said yourself Ridenour's not pressing charges—the so-called crime was against him."

"You don't think she's interested in what he overheard?"

"He heard *nothing*. Only what Anevai said."

"Which she says *you* pushed her into saying."

Nayati smiled into the pool. "Of course. She was refusing to commit; everyone could see it. I couldn't allow that. Besides, it doesn't matter. He heard nothing."

"How can you be certain?"

"He was in no shape to remember anything."

"You didn't know that when you let him live."

"We're back to that, are we? All right. Let's be honest. I *wanted* Cantrell to know. *Let* her try to burn us the way she did Rostov!"

"*She* was not at Rostov."

"Her counterpart was."

"We don't know what happened there, Nayati."

"We know the 'Link was shut down."

"After a prolonged silence—not quite the case here."

"Enough you were nervous three days ago. —And we know the evacuation stories are lies."

"We *suspect* they are. Dammit, boy, temper your thinking! We don't want Cantrell overreacting and creating the very situation we hope to avoid."

"Let her. She'll regret it."

"You're betting our home and our lives on untried systems, boy."

"Untried, uncle?"

"Nayati!" Nigan's voice burst from the glowing tunnel and Nigan himself followed it into the cavern, running over water-smoothed stone, skidding to a halt before them.

"I'm here. You don't need to frighten the fish."

To Sakiimagan: "Pardon me, sir. —Nayati, it's the ship."

"Cetacean?"

He nodded vehemently. "Alerts all over the place. A small shuttle launched—"

He ran for the tunnel and the control room, Sakiimagan close on his heels, and Nigan panting at the rear.

"Briggs? Where's the admiral?"

Chet's voice in TJ's head overrode even the curious sensations Lexi was generating somewhere below his knees. He sat up and swung his legs over the edge of the bed, disengaging her and clearing his head for business.

"In bed where she belongs, Chet." Lexi's arms wrapped around his waist, her whisper in his ear demanded enlightenment. He pressed her hand, signalling patience. "I'll be screening all her calls until she's awake enough to tell me to go to hell."

Lexi punched him in the arm. He pressed her hand again. Whispered out of the corner of his mouth, for all that wouldn't keep Chet from hearing, "Sokay. Chet's one of the old hands." And to Chet: "Wait a second. Switch to the audio before my arm turns black and blue, will you?"

He flipped the Security Com to receive, cleared with a bioscan and got the go-ahead from the ground team. "Okay. You're cleared. What's up?"

"I think we've had an escape attempt."

"You—think? What have I got up there? A ship full of—"

"We got an alarm on an attempt to bypass the locks on Hononomii Tyeewapi's room. Can't trace the origin. Tyeewapi's still sound asleep—even through the alarms."

"You *did* remove the ComLink from his room, didn't you?"

"Naturally. But for all we know, the attempt could have come from your end. We simply can't trace it, TJ. You ready for the good news now?"

"There's more?"

"A Mini launched within seconds of the alarm."

"Before or after?"

"After."

"Requisitioned?"

"Seems to have been."

"Seems? It was or it wasn't, Chet. Who cleared it?"

"That's why I wanted to talk with the admiral. Her requisition. If it weren't for the coincidence of the timing, I wouldn't have noticed. Looks like a routine req for extra transport, and we've got a lot of folks down there."

"I'll guarantee you the admiral didn't authorize that release."

"Theoretically, no one can get past bioscan checks."

"Theoretically. Course logged?"

"Auto to the Tunica spaceport. Should pick up a beam in twenty minutes, give or take. —You've got some weather coming in."

"Track it anyway."

Lexi reached over his shoulder to tap into the com. "Chet, what about Stephen and Ms. Tyeewapi?"

"Hi, Lex. We checked them, first thing. Who else on board other than Hononomii himself might pull a stunt like that? But they're asleep."

"You're sure?"

"Looking right at them."

"Everything quiet?" TJ asked.

"For the moment."

"Figure the Mini's course and keep me posted. We'll pick it up down here—and whoever shows up to meet it. See if there's *anything* in the SCs to give us a clue. But keep it under wraps, Chet. If anyone asks, the system hiccuped, right?"

"Right, boss."

"Okay. Keep me posted. Briggs . . ." A tap on his shoulder. "Wait on, Chet." He put a hold on transmit. "—What'cha thinkin', Recon-lady?"

"Have him try a scan on Stephen's frequency. See if his *beeper* agrees he's in his room. Better yet, have him check Stephen's room directly. Seems to me, one part of the system's compromisable, the rest might be as well."

He twisted in her hold to kiss the inside of her elbow. "Knew I kept you around for something other than your body." The elbow evaded his lips and he said hurriedly, "I'll ask Chet."

Moments later:

"He's gone, boss."

"Dammit, Ridenour, wake up!"

An open-handed slap startled the black comatose fog from his head. Stephen groaned, and raised a blind hand to intercept the next strike, received instead a grip on his shoulder which hurt more than the blow. A voice cried out. His voice. He gulped and bit his tongue on a second protest.

"All right, Ridenour. You're awake. Now, *do* something!"

He rubbed a hand over his eyes. Felt every half-healed wound protesting separately and in concert. Fool. Stupid, stupid fool.

"How—" he croaked, coughed, and tried again. "H–how long have I . . ."

"Less than five stinking minutes. Get on that thing, and get us back."

He could see now, though his head throbbed and lights danced behind his eyeballs.

"Back? Where?"

"Wake *up*, you VOSsed-out CodeHead! *Cetacean!*"

They couldn't do that. The course was set. Besides, they'd set off alarms and—

"Like hell we can't."

Can't what? What was she talking about?

"Damn it, you spacer sonuvabitch, you did that on purpose. You *know* you did. *They* know you did. So turn this bucket around and take me back to my brother."

"On p–purpose? What did I—"

"You set those alarms off just so we'd leave within your *window*. Alarms pointing straight at Hono. Well, I won't walk into whatever trap Cantrell has set up down at the spaceport, I won't provide her 'incident.' So turn this tub around. Hear me?"

He felt a prick in his side, looked down to see the stylus she'd threatened him with in her room disappearing into dark-blue mohair, and wondered absently if StylWrite's marketing department had ever considered such a use for it. The slender point disappeared further, and his brain cleared quite miraculously.

"I hear you, Tyeewapi. But I'm not about to do it. Your brother will be fine. Certainly safer than we're going to be. Regardless of what you think, I did *not* set those alarms off on purpose. —Go ahead. Kill me, if you really think you can with that thing."

Increased pressure in his side. "Think not?"

He swallowed hard. "I—don't know, but at the moment, I'd rather be dead than back on the *Cetacean*. Know how to fly a MiniBus, do you? Know how to reprogram its course?"

Her mouth tightened.

"Good luck, Tyeewapi, but don't blame me if I opt not to watch."

He folded his arms and closed his eyes. After a long hesitation, the prick in his side disappeared.

"All right, Ridenour, guess we play it your way."

He resumed breathing and eased his eyes open. "Anevai, I honestly did *not* do it on purpose. I do *not* know how Wesley infiltrates those levels—or even if he *can*. I *tried* to warn you."

She squeezed her eyes shut and muttered under her breath.

"I'm sorry, Anevai, what was that?"

A narrow one-eyed look. "Damned spook-eyes." And the eye quickly closed again.

"Huh?"

"Eloquent, Ridenour. —You. You and your damned spook-eyes. It's bad enough my brain tells me one thing and my gut something else. Then you look at me with those spook-eyes of yours and I can't think straight at all."

"I—" What could he do about his *eyes*? "I'm s–sorry, Anevai. Should I not look at you?"

To his further puzzlement, she gave a bark of laughter. "I give up, Ridenour." She sobered quickly. "But I've got my eye on you. If you want to keep breathing, don't double-cross me."

"I have no intention of double-crossing anyone—although I suppose I'm double-crossing the admiral at the moment—but that's only because I'm sick and tired of half-truths and downright lies."

"You're a fine one to take offense at that."

He felt the heat rise in his face.

"You'd better blush. How do you think I feel, hearing one contradiction after another from you, each one of which means life or death for me, my brother—for *all* my people. You think I don't want a few truths myself?"

"But—"

"There is no *but*, Ridenour. What makes you special?"

Desperation made a cold lump in his chest, made breathing difficult. The stylus floated between them. He reached for it, too hard, had to catch it on the rebound.

"Well, Ridenour?"

"Nothing!" The angry explosion was out before he could stop it. Breathing deeply, he repeated, quietly this time, "Nothing. All right? Not a single God-damned thing. But a few months from now, regardless of what you, your father, and your brother, and Nayati, and all the others do to salvage or destroy your standing with the Alliance, I'm going to be in the custody of the 'NetAT because of what I've learned here—probably for the rest of my life. Because of what I've just done, I'll be damned fortunate if I'm still alive two years from now—if you can call being without ninety percent of my brain being alive."

His fist clenched on the stylus. The sheath snapped; he felt pain, dampness when he eased that grip. "The only thing of meaning I'll ever do is this report to the 'NetAT. So excuse me if I want to make sure I get it right."

He ignored her then, wrapped his hand with a wipe from a dispenser in the side of the chair, caught floating drops in a second one. Anevai expressed what might be concern, but he ignored that too; just handed her the bloodied stylus pieces and sequenced into *Cetacean* communications.

Secured Line transmission. He didn't need to hear what they were saying. He turned the com off—no sense listening to static—and said, "Well, they're onto us. By the time we planet, I guarantee there'll be a party waiting."

He rubbed his forehead, and tried to think through rapidly growing mental fuzz. He'd had no business taking *any* Sud'orsofan and that last one was running out fast.

"Is—is there somewhere—*any*where—else we could land? Someplace I could indicate to Wesley without saying outright? —In case Hamilton hears us?"

"I don't know! I already told you that." Her hands were shaking as she pulled the disposal door open. She jerked back as the suction whipped the stylus pieces away and snapped the door shut, then stared at that door as though she'd never seen one before and muttered, "I suppose we could...I don't know coordinates, but I can take you from about any point within forty kilometers of Tunica."

More evasions and half-truths. "Take me where?"

"My grandparents' village. That's the safest place I know. Wesley knows it real well. Just tell him—" She paused. "—Tell him to meet us at the waterfall. He'll understand."

"The waterfall. You're sure he'll know *which* waterfall?"

She nodded. Then muttered: "He'd *better*."

"Ridenour's on board. And Anevai. They're headed for Tunica Air Space."

Sakiimagan looked sharply at his nephew. "How do you know that?"

"I feel it." Nayati might well be serious, but his intense gaze could also be taking in details from the instruments Sakiimagan himself imperfectly understood.

"Cantrell must have called him down, then. Evidently he's not as badly injured as she would have us believe."

"No, —and no."

"You grow cryptic, Nayati."

Nayati raised an eyebrow. "Not at all, Sakiima. I simply meant he's not coming at Cantrell's request."

Sakiimagan scanned the room. Automatic processes all around

them. Processes he knew nothing about. His jaw clenched; he relaxed it before his too-observant nephew could notice.

"All their communications?"

Nayati's mouth quirked. "Enough. Getting the direct translation codes for the Secured communications—that's a bit more difficult. Smith could—if he would."

"Dammit, boy, you *will* cease and desist as of this instant. I have no time to analyze your actions here to determine the consequences or even the legality of—"

"*Legality?* —Gods, don't give me that. I follow your example, *sir*, in everything I do. *Everything!*"

"And has it never occurred to you I might be wrong?"

Nayati's stricken look gave him hope at last—time to leave him with his own conscience. Rising to his feet, he said, "I must get back. If you are correct, Cantrell will be moving and my absence will cause unnecessary complications for our people."

Nigan said from the doorway, "You'll stop in Acoma on the way, won't you, sir?"

He hesitated, unsure of his own wishes, even less certain of Cholena's.

"She deserves to know, sir. —Anevai's her daughter, too. And—" Nigan swallowed hard. The boy was treading where he had no right, knew it, yet held firm under Sakiimagan's scowl. "She wants to see you, sir. *Please*, stop?"

His resentment faded in the face of Nigan's obvious concern. Nigan's family lived in Acoma, as did Cholena's parents—

—As did Cholena herself, at the moment.

He nodded. "I'll stop, son." He set a hand on Nayati's shoulder as he passed. "Promise me one thing, beloved brother to my son."

Muscle tensed under his hand, then Nayati looked up and smiled. "I'll do anything I can, uncle, you know that."

"Tell me what you've done."

"I've done many things."

"You know what I'm speaking of. Eventually, I want to know everything you've done on the 'Net and what these instruments are capable of. But right now, I want to know what you've done to my son."

"Hononomii? I've done nothing."

"If you say so." He studied his nephew's handsome, arrogant face, unable to read Truth, this longtime companion of Hononomii's suddenly become a stranger to him. Perhaps Anevai was right—

—in many things. He paused again at the door. "One more thing. Remember the first rule about Library use? If you've broken it before today, I grant you pardon for that. If you break it from this moment forward, nephew, you are no longer of the People. Do you understand me?"

Nayati's chin raised a notch. "I hear you, Sakiimagan Tyeewapi."

Hearing was not understanding, but it would suffice.

For now.

Nayati watched Sakiimagan disappear in the tunnel's glow, love and hate warring in him.

Brother of my son: How dare he? Hono was nothing! —*Less* than nothing. Hononomii never thought of anything except reestablishing the ancient lifestyle of their long-dead ancestors here. *He* relished the gifts of *this* world the way Sakiimagan did, had dared even *more* than Sakiimagan. One day Sakiimagan would realize that link.

He headed toward the back rooms.

Nigan called after him: "Where are you going?"

"An appointment."

"Dammit, you heard Sakiimagan!"

"So?"

"Please, Nayati, be careful. Let me—"

"No! I don't need monitoring. —And don't try. I'll know, Nigan. Believe me, I'll know!"

ii

Wesley glanced at his watch. 0410h. He pressed the side button. 0107h 'NetStan. Which had the kid meant? Did he even consider a second possibility? He'd been born Recon, lived spacer, but he'd never experienced the unique schizophrenia of dealing with two independent time systems simultaneously.

Everything occurred at two different times: 'NetStan and real. You arrange meetings—you specify.

Dammit.

Had Stephen even left the ship yet? But he must have. He'd waited in his room until the launch window was long closed in either reckoning and Stephen hadn't sent word—

So where the hell was he? Was he alone? Surely he'd have the sense to bring Anevai.

"Dammit!"

One more round of the observation lounge, to the window to stare out into the storm. Leaning his forehead against the glass, he shaded internal reflection with his hands, trying to pierce the darkness for a glimpse of the tiny craft; flinched and closed his eyes as lightning chained across the sky and thunder rattled the windows.

Bit-brained brats had no business trying this on their own. Sure, he'd set bait for Stephen, but to establish contact so they could work out the details together. He'd intended to divert Cantrell's attention until the boy was well, then finagle Stephen back to HuteNamid.

But, *no*. The kid had to do it all himself. And now he was late. God-awful late.

The least he could have done was check the local weather report. Stay in out of the damned—

"Dr. Smith?"

He controlled the impulse to whirl and run, performed instead a nonchalant turn to—

—Alliance Security teal. Surprise, surprise.

"Yes?"

"Would you mind coming with us?"

"Have I a choice?"

"Not really."

"Then I'd be delighted, naturally. Mind telling me where we're off to?"

"Mind telling me what you're doing here at this time of night?"

"Would you believe sleep-walking? —No? —Then I suppose I would mind. I'll wait and talk to your boss directly, thank you."

"As you wish, doctor."

> >FLIGHT OPTIONS: fully automated planetary
> landing.
> >A) LGS landing base: *Current Operational Mode*.
> >B) Coordinates _____ × _____.
> >C) Emergency Descent.

"I'd hoped—" A tiny whisper Anevai nearly missed.

"Hoped *what*, Ridenour?"

He blinked in her direction, and anxiety shifted to studied unconcern. "Nothing, really. It's just that—" He shrugged, flashed a rather forced grin. "Shall we say, I wish we could stick with *A?*"

"Well, you just said we can't, Ridenour. So get a move on. I just hope to God Wes got the message before Cantrell's goons got him."

He cycled past coordinate options, brought up a detailed contour map of the Tunica area. She oriented herself, then pointed out Acoma. He clicked on those coordinates, then tried to reprioritize the autopilot.

The computer protested. Vehemently.

"Oops," he said sheepishly—while *she* swallowed her stomach. "Sorry."

"Oops? *Sorry?* Gods, Ridenour, you trying to give me a heart attack?"

"I said I was sorry. I just should have taken it off auto first."

"Do you mind not making mistakes when it's our *lives* at stake?"

His face hardened . . . "I never guaranteed anything. Just to get us off that ship. Only way I knew, Tyeewapi."

The Atmospheric Entry warning flashed before she could answer. Stephen's intense gaze flicked to that announcement and—

—"*Shit!*"

He slammed the autopilot off—

The brakers protested—

And the Mini dropped from under them.

Anevai swallowed her stomach and grabbed the controls.

"Dammit, let go!"

"Just shut up and reset those coordinates."

"You don't *know*—"

"Neither do you! Dammit, Ridenour, a *bit-brain* could hold this steady. —Set the damned coordinates!"

He set the coordinates; Anevai relinquished the controls to the autopilot with a sigh of relief. The low hum signalling their drop into the atmosphere disappeared as the dissipation shields kicked in. A beeping light advertised the extension of the stabilizers, and soon after, lift joined the brakers' thrust in giving direction within the small cockpit.

Anevai knew how the aerodynamics and engineering worked, had heard shuttle crews talk about it for years, awaiting her chance. If she weren't scared half out of her mind, she'd be fascinated. And if her companion hadn't entered his own wait-state, staring vacantly out the side port—and gripping the armrests harder than she was—she might not be quite so terrified.

A lifetime later, lightning disrupted the blackness below.

The Mini bucked again, steadied and continued its descent.

Anevai swallowed hard and asked, "Ridenour, what's our flightpath?"

A confused, over-the-shoulder glance.

"Dammit, Ridenour, are we headed into that?"

A shrug. Another flash.

She controlled fear, controlled anger. "What time are we supposed to land?"

"I don't know. —Soon." Back to the window.

Minutes later, storm winds battered the light craft. Lightning, blindingly bright, a crash of thunder before her eyes could clear.

"Stephen," she said. And when he didn't respond: "*Stephen!*"

He turned slowly, wide-eyed and white-faced. She felt a distinct chill, not at all certain he even saw her.

"Stephen, we've got to get down—out of this. These storms get nasty. *Very* nasty. Just how safe is this *automated* landing?"

His face hardened. Took on a chilling intensity. "I have no idea. Shall I call up the stats?"

"Dammit, Ridenour, we're right in the middle of it! Get us down! Now!"

He didn't move. She grabbed his arm, hauled him around and slapped his face. Hard. Hard enough to rock his head back, hard enough to split a lip.

"Dammit, Ridenour, wake up! We've got to do *something!*"

He lifted a hand to his mouth, looked at the blood it came away with, then said, remotely, "No."

"No, *what?*"

"I'm through doing. I've made my move. The next is His. I think, perhaps, He's finally getting his chance at me. I think maybe I've been safe from Him in space. Planets are where He lives, you know."

"What the hell are you talking about?"

He stared through her. " 'Hell.' Maybe you're right. Maybe it's not God's doing at all. I'm sorry, Anevai, you shouldn't be with me. I shouldn't have made you come. I'd forgotten old—debts. . . ."

"You're crazy, Ridenour," she whispered, of a sudden, truly believing it. Of a sudden regretting a whole lot of choices.

He shrugged and turned back to the window; she turned to the controls and brought up the flight options as she'd seen Stephen do.

"What are you doing?"

"Stay out of it, Ridenour. *You* may be ready and willing to bite Wesley's big one, but I'm not."

"No!"

He grabbed at her wrist. Lightning chained a violent series around the tiny craft. Thunder reverberated through the cabin. The lights dimmed, went out.

The craft tumbled wildly . . .

"Dammit, Ridenour, let me go!"

His grip tightened, cutting off circulation.

She struck blindly in the dark, located him in a lightning-strobed instant, and roundhoused to his jaw with every ounce of leverage his hold on her provided.

Two thuds in the darkness, and his hold slipped. *Hope he broke his damn fool head*, she thought sourly, even as she flicked the tiny red button blinking on the instrument panel.

Emergency light flickered in. No time to take account of their position or how much damage they'd taken. The remaining gyros screamed alerts. The options blinked on the monitor.

Without hesitation, she punched '*C*.'

The metal beast ripped through his world. Agonized screams: ancient trees and young alike. The ground trembled, echo upon echo, as the intruder struck. Unlike the branches dying on rain-soaked ground, the metal seams held.

Save one.

The ringing of the World ebbed to the subtlest vibrations. Life within the metal stirred. Feet tapped the World's surface like ants upon his arm. Even in this dreamstate, Nayati felt— satisfaction? Relief? Anevai was not dead. The heartbeat within the other was strong, but other weakness made his footsteps drag.

He was radiating. Did Anevai know? Had she sufficient Sense to feel that tether line to the ship? There was a haven within reach. Would she remember? Would she feel it? She'd moved so far away . . .

A sound—a touch.

His World-sense collapsed and Nayati was back in the Cocheta rooms, isolate in his own body. Nigan was there: it was he who had caused the collapse.

"I'm sorry, Nayati. It's Anevai and Ridenour. Their ship—"

"You *idiot!* You think I didn't know?" He slipped from the safety straps and jerked off the bench, the silken caress of the Cocheta suit insulating him from the World. Reluctantly easing it off, he yanked on fringed leather leggings, lacing them as he ran barefooted for the control room. It would take far too long to reform the matrix. The Cocheta machines would have to complete the saga.

iii

(Lightning chains across the sky. Demonic eyes stare at him, vanish with the light.

(Bare toes feel in the darkness for one step and the next. The *unlatched door swings open at his touch, leaving no chance to knock, no chance to ask permission to join the laughter within.*

("*P–Papa?*"

(*Laughter stops. Lightning flares. Bare skin shines.*

("*What's wrong, son?*"

("*Why aren't you in bed?*"

(*One and the other. Thunder booms, making the house shake, making him jump. His knees quiver, but pride keeps him on his feet.*

("*S–S–S–*"

("*Don't stutter!*"

("*—Scared!*"

("*It's only a storm. Go back to bed.*"

("*Ylaine, it's Nevya, not the storm.*"

("*Nevya's gone; time he accepted it. —Zivon, go back to bed!*"

("*Y–yes, Mama.*"

(*Retracing the steps to his room, carefully avoiding the storm-demon in the hallway mirror. Pulling off his nightshirt to be like Papa, to make him brave enough to laugh at the storm, too.*

(*But it only makes him cold.*

(*He burrows under the covers. Lightning can't reach him here, but Thunder does. Finally, he pulls his blanket off the bed and crawls under his clothes to the back of the closet, wraps himself in his blanket and dreams of ice shooting from the clouds and slicing blackened skin.*)

The storm was one of the worst she'd ever seen . . . or perhaps it was just that she'd never come quite so close to dying in one before.

Anevai shivered and huddled into a tighter ball under her blanket's heated folds. Stephen had settled in a pocket at the back of the Cave, well out of the light from the glowlamp, except for a blanketed foot.

Thunder crashed through the cave; the ground shook; the glowlamp flickered in the static discharge.

Stephen cried out, and the blanketed foot disappeared behind the rock. Anevai shifted the lamp as far as she could without disrupting her cocoon. Even so, it barely caught the shadowy huddle.

"Relax, Ridenour," she said, breaking the silence for the first time since she'd hauled his catatonic butt from the Mini's wreckage. "Go back to sleep. These caves are the safest place on all HuteNamid to be right now."

Spook-eyes turned to her. Dubious, frightened spook-eyes that impacted her anger and frustration squarely, destroying the one and severely damaging the other.

She said softly: "Park it, 'buster-boy. This here's good old planet-buster special effects. Put on 'special for the tourists. We Recons know better, right?"

The grin that tried to meet her halfway failed miserably, but he lay back down, and eventually his breathing regularized—rest, if not real sleep—and she drew the light away.

She hadn't had time to search for much. Their precipitous landing had left Stephen less than helpful and rain pouring in through a broken seal. She'd grabbed a couple of emergency packs from a locker that had opened automatically on impact, stuffed Stephen's damned notebook into one of them (his one coherent thought an obsession not to leave it behind) and hauled him out through the storm.

The only piece of luck they'd had was the proximity of one of the Caves. Besides being dry and out of the wind, once the Cave detected their presence, they could count on a fair degree of climate control. *Which can't happen too soon*, she thought, shivering again.

A booming roll of thunder; blinding chain lightning; she squeezed her eyes shut and pressed her hands to her ears.

"Zivon?" Nevya's voice pulled him from the fascination of gathering clouds and he jumped to his feet as she appeared over the rise, running through the obatsi herd, the wind whipping her hair free of its braids.

"Zivon! We've got to get them home right away! Didn't you see the storm coming?" Nevya ran up to him, grabbed his hand and pulled him after her until they were running together toward the herd. They spread apart, calling to the sobaki who were off chasing Smells.

Frenetic minutes later, they had all the obatsi milling in the pens and Nevya ran into the barn to get the feed in the mangers, leaving him to fasten the gates.

He struggled with the latch on the last one. Papa had said he'd fix it, but he hadn't gotten his Round-tuit yet. The metal latch was stuck, rain freezing to an icy coating. He grabbed it and leaned with all his weight. It moved a little bit and he tried again. This time, his hand slipped off, slicing a frozen finger on an ice-covered edge.

He stuck the finger in his mouth and kicked the stubborn gate, as Nevya's voice called for help. He scowled at the halfway-down latch—good enough for a couple of minutes—and ran into the barn out of the freezing rain.

Together they dumped another bag of grain in the bin, then she left him to finish graining while she let the obatsi in. He was running from the feed bin to the stalls filling the grain buckets and dodging the first line of obatsi when he heard Nevya scream. He dropped the bucket and ran to the last door. She was standing in an empty pen.

"I—I d—d—didn't—Th—the latch w—w—" He couldn't get past the stutter, but Nevya didn't scold him.

"Go inside. Get your papa—he should be home by now. Quick, Zivon! Tell him I'm taking the sobaki with me to find them."

Hours later, he was sitting beside his bedroom window, trying to see through its ice coating, when he heard Papa come home. Other men had come back long ago with the obatsi—all but Meesha. He'd seen that, before the ice covered his window. But no Papa and no Nevya.

Mama had told him to go to his room and stay there. Mama was very mad at him, he knew she was, but he didn't hear Nevya—only Papa—and he had to know Was Meesha all right? so he ran downstairs anyway. Mama always said Don't run, you'll fall, but he ran anyway, so of course he fell down the last four steps.

Papa, sitting by the fire, ice from his hair melting into dark, widening puddles on the blanket around his shoulders. Mama was kneeling beside him, rubbing his hands and crying....

* * *

"Nevya? *Nevya! Don't*—" A penetrating shriek through the ringing in her ears.

Only the trailing corner of Stephen's blanket was visible now.

"Don't be dead, Nevya. Please, don't be dead." And panic rising: "*Don't*—"

Anevai squirmed over to his corner, moving the glowlamp till it reached into Stephen's hideyhole. He pressed against the stone and tucked his head away from the light.

"P–Papa?" Zivon coughed, remembering to cover his mouth, and tried again. "Papa, where's Nevya?"

Papa looked up. Mama looked up. Papa looked cold and tired and worried. Mama looked mad through her tears.

"P–Papa?" He tried to stop the stutter. Mama didn't like him to stutter. "Nevya's all r–right, isn't sh–she?"

"I don't know, son," Papa said quietly. "I couldn't find her."

"P–Papa?" The stutter reached his hands, then his knees. He took a step into the room. "P–P–Papa?" He wanted Papa to hold him and tell him everything was going to be all right. But Papa was shivering, too. Papa needed someone to hold him, but Mama was doing that. Vodka. Papa needed vodka. He picked up the jug from its spot beside the door.

But Mama said, "Get up to your room! This is all your fault! You and your daydreaming! Meesha's gone and Nevya went looking for her—useless breeder that she is—for you. Nevya's hurt and cold and lost, and it's your fault! Go to your room and think about it while you lie warm and safe in your bed."

He looked at Papa, but Papa wouldn't look at him. He couldn't feel his fingers. The jug slipped, crashed to the floor, and broke into a zillion pieces. Papa looked up at that, and he could see Papa blamed him, too, could see it through the exhaustion in the soft brown eyes.

He turned and ran.

"Stephen? Stephen, are you awake?" Anevai touched his shoulder cautiously, the sweater cold and damp beneath her fingertips.

"Who—?" A breathy whisper from the shadowy face.

Thunder interrupted: final snit of temper from the sky. Nothing compared to the violence of the storm just past, but enough to send Stephen cowering against the cave wall, frantically searching the dark shadows surrounding them.

"Stephen," she said firmly, "this is Anevai. Do you hear me, Ridenour?"

A blink of tear-blurred eyes.

"A–Anevai?" A whisper that might well be nothing but mindless repetition.

"Do you hear me?"

A second blink. "I—I hear you, Tyeewapi."

"Good. Now listen to me. You were dreaming. The storm's over. Everything's all right. We're safe now. Got it?"

He breathed deeply, nodded, rubbed dirty hands hard over his eyes, leaving streaks of dirt behind, tiny drops of red where grit punctured newly healed skin.

"You want to talk about it?"

He shook his head. Pulling his knees to his chest, he crossed his arms over them and buried his face. The blanket tangled with his legs, leaving his damp sweater exposed to the cave air. Warmer air than when she'd dozed off, but not that warm.

She caught up her own blanket—with her fur-lined coat, she'd grown almost too warm anyway—and knelt at Stephen's side. He ignored her when she wrapped it around him, made no effort to halt its inevitable collapse to the floor.

"C'mon, Ridenour," she said, sharp and clear, her best no-nonsense voice, and picked the blanket up, this time holding it in place and giving him a shake. "Snap out of it."

His near hand clenched. One agonized eye appeared over his arm. Her gut twisted, squeezing sympathetic tears from her.

"Oh, gods, Stephen," she whispered, "won't you tell me what's wrong? *Please*."

The fist relaxed. Reached out to touch her cheek, explored the tears.

His fingers were freezing.

Another rumble from the outside, a flicker of far-off lightning. Stephen drew his hand away, pulled the blanket higher, cocooning his ears and chin, and looked into the rock shadows.

"I killed her." An ever-so-slight movement of his lips. A quiet admission which chilled in the instant before her gut refused to believe it. Stephen Ridenour was a scuzzy, lying indi-turned-spacer, but he was no murderer.

"Who, Stephen?" Then she remembered: "Nevya?"

He nodded—

"Who was Nevya, Stephen? What happened to her?"

"Lightning. There was a storm and I—" He shuddered, buried his face again. "I f–found her after..."

"Gods," she whispered.

Those dark-rimmed eyes looked at her over the blanket, dry now and unblinking. "It was my fault. I killed her."

She was out of her depth, she knew that and as she searched helplessly for some easy phrase, some simple answer, silvered, no-longer-dry eyes turned away. She prevented that with a hand to his cheek, slid it to the back of his head and pulled him to her. He didn't resist. He didn't relax either. She felt him fighting for control, knew the depth of his pride—having met it head-on before—but could only suspect the depth of the guilt.

"Go ahead and cry, Stephen. It's healthy—nothing to be ashamed of."

A sullen mutter answered. She brushed her fingers lightly over his hair, urging him to relax. "What was that?"

He shook his head irritably. "Cut it out."

She didn't stop, having met the stubbornness that was Stephen before, too.

He tried to pull away.

She tightened her hold. "C'mon, Ridenour. Relax."

"I said, *Cut it out!*"

"Okay. Okay." She let him go, and he jerked upright, his face dark with anger. "But you've *got* to learn to talk to people."

"The hell I do." Sullen turn toward the shadows.

She grabbed him by the shoulders, forced him to look at her.

"Maybe not *people*, Stephen, but me. Please? I want to help you, and it seems to me if you'd just—"

"Good *God*, Tyeewapi, *let it rest!*"

His shoulders were inflexible as stone under her hands, his clenched fists trembling in his efforts to control them.

"Go ahead and hit me, Ridenour. But I'm not about to—let it rest."

"All *right!*" He hissed, narrowed eyes glaring at her. "My *mother* used to say God gave me a supply of tears when I was born, and if I wasted them, there'd be none left for important things—like when *bugs* flew in my eyes. You happy now?"

She realized her mouth was hanging open. She closed it. "That's a *joke*, right?"

"Is it?" He wasn't laughing.

"Shit, Ridenour, your mom was kidding you."

"Was she?" He seemed perfectly serious. Without a blink, he said, "Sorry to disillusion you, Tyeewapi, but she was right—absolutely. I ran out some five years ago."

For once, Anevai had nothing to say—no unwanted sympathy, no absolution, no smart quips.

Stephen rubbed at the white scar on his finger, curled the hand into a fist. He'd never explained to his parents about that stuck latch. When infection set in, he'd lied about how it had happened. Because by then it had been too late: Nevya was dead and no excuses would bring her back. The pain when his mother lanced and treated the finger, the fever that followed were the only payment he could make for that death.

One thing he could say about Vandereaux, the academy had given him plenty to crowd that particular guilt out of active files. It had taken this planet's storms and Anevai's damned inquisitions to resurrect it.

Another flash of lightning. Anevai looked at him, a worried look. Probably figured he'd freak out on her again.

Without comment, he pulled her blanket off, shook it out and handed it back to her; when she made no move to take it, he folded it and set it on the ground between them. The pill bottles made an uncomfortable lump in his side. He unclipped the pouch and placed it near his head, approximately where a night table would stand, to remind himself to take them in the morning.

He felt Anevai settle close at his back, but said nothing. He was too tired to object, and cold enough to welcome the added warmth of the blanket she threw over them both.

iv

For the first time in his life, Wesley Smith felt utterly, frustratingly, hopelessly impotent. Locked in an empty room with no explanation, no accusation—

—and no terminal. Nothing but an overstuffed chair, an overhead light, a small table, a couple of stupid journal PO's he didn't give shit about and a magazine of no social value whatsoever.

He'd never felt so blind, deaf and dumb in his life.

He tossed the magazine in the general direction of the table. It missed.

"*Shit,*" he muttered, and pulled himself out of the too-soft chair to pick it up. As fate or a mentally disturbed gremlin would have it, the thing fell open to an ad featuring an opal-eyed gymnast in full flight:

'*Highlights of the '68 Olympics—available at last through your local 'Net Distributor!*'

The magazine hit the far wall, rebounded to a crumpled pile on the floor. "Dammit, boy," he muttered, "why didn't you contact me first?"

"Come now, Smith—"

He whirled to face the door, scowling.

"—he obviously contacted you at some time. Otherwise, what were you doing at the Tunica Spaceport at such an ungodly hour of the morning?"

"About time you showed, Cantrell," he growled. "Ever hear of unjustified detention? My lawyers will love this one."

She spoke quietly with someone outside, then eased the door shut.

"Oh, I imagine we could come up with half a dozen good excuses for holding you. Actually, I was hoping to avoid official charges—that your cooperative gesture was real. Now, however—"

"Now?" he demanded, cutting through the bullshit.

She obliged him:

"You lured the boy back down, didn't you—when you left me alone with Paul? And right afterward had the nerve to intimate you were on my side."

He threw himself back into the easy chair. "Never said that, admiral, just that Paul and Sakiima are acting like fools."

"Do you deny you enticed the boy to attempt this escapade?"

"I certainly do. What I did was inform him that he was *not* in possession of all the facts."

"And what are those facts?"

"I'm sorry, admiral, but you're no more equipped to understand and act on those facts than Stephen is to pilot a starship." He hooked a toe around a table leg and dragged it around in front of him, kicked the journals onto the floor and replaced them with his feet. "I'll talk to Stephen and no one else. Now, where is he?"

"I was counting on you to provide the answer to that."

The table tipped, spilling his feet to the floor. "He did leave the ship?"

"Yes."

"Anevai, too?"

"Yes."

"So why are you asking me where they are? Surely you can track the MiniBus. Your handymen let them slip past at the spaceport? That's where he . . ."

"Where he told you to meet him?"

He nodded.

"Of course we can. And have. He kicked in a diversionary, tried to foul the tracker, but that didn't accomplish much. We know *where* they landed. But they're no longer with the ship."

"*How* do you know?"

Narrow-eyed consideration, then: "Stephen's beeped. We know he left the landing site. We tracked him for a time, but the storm—seems to be disrupting his signal."

Storm disruption? Not likely. Not a beeper. Anevai must have taken him into one of the Caves. Wesley grinned, caught a suspicious look from Cantrell; countered with blithe innocence. Right about now, Stephen's signal likely appeared to be coming simultaneously from about nine contradictory points around the planet.

Some disruption.

"So? What do you expect me to do about it?"

"You expected to meet them. Did you have a contingency plan?"

"If I did, do you honestly think I'd tell you?"

"You'd better, Smith, if you care about the boy."

"You keep calling him that. I suggest you stop thinking of him in that light. He's a highly talented Nexus 'Net scientist that you'd do well to respect and treat very carefully."

"I throw that back at you, Smith. You want that *scientist* protected, you tell me where he's going. There's a hell of a storm out there. The Mini's stable, but no miracle worker. And *he's* no pilot. Unless Anevai is . . ." She seemed to be probing for a reassurance he couldn't give her. "Well, there's every chance their landing was not without incident. And Ridenour is still far from well. He's quite extraordinarily delicate, Smith, in many ways. Now are you going to tell me where we can find him?"

Naturally. When he was ready. When *he* called the shots. "I don't know, admiral, but I can find out."

"How?"

"Get me a terminal. He'd leave a message."

"Done."

"And no monitoring."

"You've got to be kidding."

"You want your boy back?"

"Damn you, Smith."

"Undoubtedly. Do I get my privacy?"

"All right!"

"And—"

"You expect more?"

"Certainly. But it's so very little, really. If I give you his destination, I go with you to pick him up."

"What kind of fool do you think I am?"

"If I thought you were a fool, I wouldn't be dealing with you. The kid expects me to be there. You want him to behave, I'd better be."

Her jaw tightened. "You'll work with us?"

"On one condition."

"The hell! You've already set three." She frowned, then shrugged. "What's one more? What else?"

"To meet him first. Alone."

"No."

"Then find him yourself."

"Not going to work this time, Smith. You want him safe, too."

"Damn right, I do. Which is why I want to meet him first. Safe he is, as long as Anevai's with him. Safe and available requires a bit more. Do I get my meeting?"

"Why?"

"Because I don't want a damned *audience*." He felt his face grow hot, recognized the unfamiliarity of a blush too late to stop it. "I'm fond of him, I believe he's not unfond of me. You say he's walking a thin edge, I'm assuming you're right. I don't want to embarrass him in front of God and everybody. And—And I want to explain to him *why* I showed up with—"

"—All right, Smith. All right. But controlled conditions. I'm not giving you two the opportunity to disappear together into the woodwork."

He grinned, back in control of the situation—and his blood pressure. "Or the 'NetWork, as the case may be? No problem, Admiral Loro. Now, hie me to that terminal."

("Zivon? Where are you, son?"

(An escaping whimper shames him. The closet door opens.

("Zivon? Is that you or a bannik?"

(Papa wants him to laugh, but laughter sticks halfway up. The clothes part to reveal Papa's warm, brown eyes, not the evil-eye of some vengeful spirit impersonator.

("Poor, frozen little bannik. It's morning and the storm's gone. Does it want to come in out of the cold?" Papa says, raising the tail of his sweater.

(He bites his lip against another whimper and squirms under the sweater, wrapping his arms and legs around Papa and burying his face against Papa's chest, warm—and safe—at last.)

Sunlight in her eyes, muttering in her ear, how was a body supposed to get any rest?

Anevai yawned widely and captured a corner of the blanket

escaping over her shoulder, rolling half-consciously toward nearby warmth. Hands, grasping blindly, found her and pulled her into arms that closed around her, squeezing to the point of pain, then relaxed accompanying a shuddering sigh.

Not an altogether unpleasant position to find herself in. On the other hand . . .

"Shee-it, Ridenour," she murmured into the curls in front of her nose. "Least you could've done is let me in on the party."

He pushed himself away and up on one elbow, his puzzled gaze drifting down to the tangle of blankets and legs. He blinked, brushed an unsteady hand over his face. "Lord, Anevai. E—excuse me."

He reached to unwind the blankets, but she pulled at him. "Did you hear me say Go away? It's still raining out there— hear it? We've got some time to kill. You know a better way?"

She brushed his cheek with her lips, figuring to make up for last night's tension and harsh words. She didn't figure for more than that, wasn't sure she wanted more. But they'd been friends. She wanted him to know, as far as she was concerned, they still were.

In lieu of immediate rejection, she migrated to his mouth. His lips softened and responded, but triumph was short-lived. He pulled away *again* and sat up, a deep frown line between his brows.

"Are you saying—do you *want* me to—"

She stifled laughter, and caught at his sleeve, using it to pull herself up beside him, to pick up where she'd left off.

Still no objection. No response, either. He seemed to be considering the matter. Damned researchers had to analyze everything. She set about distracting his higher brain.

Finally, he whispered, "If you're sure . . ."

She grinned, and swayed toward him, determined to show him just how sure she was. His arms wrapped around her, easily this time, as they sank into the tangled blankets.

Some undetermined time later, one surprisingly dexterous hand left her. A rattle beside her head took a moment for her distracted higher brain to recognize. When it did . . .

"Shit, Ride—"

His mouth closed on hers, stopping her objection. Seemed like the fool had to have a pill for everything—

"I'm sorry, Paul, it'll just have to wait."

Paul grabbed at Loren's arm as she passed his office door, fell into step beside her when she refused to stop. She had her security case with her—Official, then. "What's happening? Can I help?"

"Stephen's down here again."

"Loren, this is hardly the time—"

"Not *my* choice. His."

"Where is he?"

"We don't know. With the Tyeewapi girl—we hope."

"Good lord, woman, you should tie him down. The kid's a walking—" She halted in front of Wesley's office. "What're you stopping here—" The door burst open, slamming him against the wall.

Wesley's head popped out. "Admiral, I've been waiting— Why're you blocking my doorway, Corlaney?"

He rubbed his bruised shoulder—he'd make Wesley regret that—and countered: "What're you doing up so early? Your mind doesn't function before ten o'clock. Go back into your hole, Wesley. I'm busy."

"So'm I. Go 'way. —Admiral, I need to talk to you."

"You got a message?"

Wes nodded.

"What do you mean, a message?" Paul asked. "What's going on?"

"Go away, Paul. I'll talk with you later."

"Loro!"

"Paul, we've got it under control. We'll talk after I get that boy back. I'm leaving..."

"Loro, *please*, just give me a minute."

"Don't press me. I told you, as soon as Stephen's safe. We're on his trail and—"

"Ever think I might have something to add to that?"

"You know where he is?"

"No."

"How to get him back?"

"No. —But—" He was being pushed, and he didn't like being pushed—

"Smith?"

Wesley glanced at him. "I'll tell you once we're on the way."

"What's wrong with now?" Paul demanded, already suspecting (and resenting) the answer.

"Corlaney," Wesley said coolly, "you've already caused more trouble than you're worth. I don't want you running to Sakiimagan with this bit of information and creating more. So leave us alone. *Go away.*"

"Go ahead, Cantrell, see how far you get with this infant brigade and their old-enough-to-know-better ringleader." With a glare toward Wesley: "Since you've got so damn much spare time, Smith, there's a stack of info-reqs taking up space in my office. I want them *gone* tomorrow."

He whirled back toward his office.

"Paul—"

He ignored her and kept walking, felt the security guard's touch and whirled back.

"Sorry, Paul. I'm keeping you under wraps until we get back."

"Loren, listen to me." He held up a hand as she began to speak, hurried back to her and lowered his voice. "Just—listen. Sakiimagan's back. —Or will be soon."

"How do you—"

He held up his hand. "The main thing I wanted to tell you was I'll try to get him to read those letters. Try to get you Nayati. But I want to do it in private. Listen in, if you insist, but let us *be* alone. You can arrest him, put *me* away for the duration after that, for all I care. Just give me one more chance with him."

She frowned. "Paul, don't try to double-cross me in this, for God's sake. Too much is at stake."

"And you only know the tip of the iceberg, admiral, sir."

"What do you mean by that?"

He turned away. "Goodbye, admiral. Good hunting."

"Dammit, Paul! This isn't a game."

"I never said it was." But he paused nonetheless, right

fighting with pride; as she and Wesley headed the opposite direction: "Loren, wait, dammit."

She kept on walking.

"Barb and Will."

She stopped. "What about them?"

"You want them?"

"That's a stupid question, Corlaney, and you're not a stupid man."

"Acoma. Inyabi and Matowakan Tyeewapi."

She raised her chin: acknowledgment of his—defection.

"We'll do that."

"Quickly, Loro. I don't know how long before Sakiimagan knows I told you. He might move them. I don't know what his resources might be."

She nodded, said to the guard as she passed on her way to the tube, "Take care of him, Buck."

V

The coolth of evaporating alcohol replacing the clammy chill of sweat brought Anevai drifting back into RealTime. Stephen, with a KlenzWipe. He didn't linger over that as he had—other things, except to pause, while fastening her jumpsuit, just short of the base of her neck to brush the pulse point with his lips, before running the zipper the rest of the way up and turning the collar down meticulously.

All done. She sighed and let her eyes drift shut. Rain was over. They should be up and moving, but somehow a lassitude in direct proportion to her earlier response had taken over, and she lay, contentedly unproductive, while Stephen's hands cupped her face for lip exploration.

"Had me fooled, Ridenour," she murmured against his smooth cheek.

"Hmmm?"

"Thought I had to run interference for you. Looks like I was wrong."

His gentle touch slowed— "I'm no child, Anevai."

She blinked lazily up at him. "So I've discovered."

—and stopped. A final brush of his lips over hers and he sat up, pulling his own clothes to rights, insisting on dealing with it himself, making his own rearrangement equally sanitary, but far more cursory.

Puzzling. But solving puzzles required thinking, and at the moment, thinking was far from her mind. When he'd finished, she caught his elbow and pulled him back down, using his chest for a pillow, the fuzzy sweater dry now beneath her fingers. He'd never removed that sweater—never *removed* much of anything. Just—artistically rearranged things. And yet . . .

It had all been for her. No question of his own marginal involvement, now she thought about it. She'd been beyond caring at the time; she wasn't now. She moved her hand down the fuzzy sweater. "Stephen, are you sure you don't want me to—"

His hand caught hers, returned it to his chest and held it there. "I'm fine, Anevai. I got what I needed last night—and before. —What I've needed for a long time."

She thought about that a moment—several moments, the speed at which her mind wasn't working—then shoved herself upright. "Do you mean to tell me that that was *payment*? For *listening* to you?"

He made no attempt to deny or justify. He just looked—hurt.

Different customs, Tyeewapi, she thought, reminding herself firmly of mom's favorite lecture. Indignation melted and she stroked his cheek. "You pay real well, Spacer-man. Guess someone to talk to has been in pretty short supply for you for a long time, hasn't it?"

He didn't answer, but he didn't have to. She curled against him, wrapping her arms around his waist, settling her head against his chest. "Well, Ridenour, looks like I owe you now. Listening comes pretty cheap here. Consider my ears your own personal property for the next—say—fifty years."

He was silent for a while. Then the chest beneath her cheek began to vibrate. "Stephen, I didn't mean to . . ." She looked up—

—into laughing spook-eyes. "Is that 'NetStan years?" he asked softly. "Or planetary local?"

* * *

Two *Cetacean* search vehicles were waiting for them at the Spaceport. Cantrell hurried Smith aboard one, TJ and a security team boarding the other. Within minutes both vehicles were airborne, the one heading for Acoma, the mountain village where (according to Paul) the two missing researchers were being held, the other—

"Well?" She demanded of Smith, who leaned back in his seat across the aisle and waved his hand airily.

"Oh, just follow them."

Sudden suspicion: "Ridenour's heading for Acoma?"

A smug closed-mouthed grin.

"Damn you, Smith," she said conversationally. "We don't need you at all, do we?"

The grin disappeared. "Oh, yes, you do, admiral. Believe me."

Lexi moved up the narrow aisle from the tracking station set up in the equipment bay and Cantrell nodded her toward the seat next to her.

"What did you get on Inyabi and Matowakan Tyeewapi?"

"Local MedTechs. Tyeewapi's wife's parents. Not much more than that. Their home doubles as a clinic—easy access from the village landing strip for emergency cases. Various facilities in the back for Recon folk medicine—"

A snort from across the aisle.

"Yes, Smith?"

"Not 'folk medicine.' Damned fine physicians. I'll take them over Vandereaux's witch doctors anytime."

"Did I say otherwise, Dr. Smith?" Lexi asked mildly, and Smith had the decency to at least *appear* chagrined.

"MedTechs. —Smith." She leaned forward to catch his eye. "Are Bennett and Liu ill?"

He shrugged. "I don't know, admiral. I don't *know* what happened to them. I do know Inyabi and Matowakan. If you'd like, I'll introduce you."

"I'd like to give a *positive* first impression."

Smith pressed a hand to his chest. "You wound me!"

"Impossible."

He shrugged and slumped down, doubling his legs up to rest his ankles on the forward seat.

"Have we received those details of the landing site yet?" she asked quietly, keeping one eye to Smith's performance.

Lexi handed her a packet of surveillance photos.

"Admiral?" A glance toward Smith; Cantrell nodded the go-ahead. "It's a long way from Acoma."

"Meaning: do we trust the dear doctor?"

Her own glance at Smith intercepted a worried look. A look he quickly covered with a nonchalant shrug. "Up to you, admiral."

She eyed him a moment longer, then asked Lexi, "And the area where his signal disappeared?"

"Third one down."

Nothing but trees and rock and more trees.

"Analysis show *anything* unusual? Any sign of them at all?"

"Solid rock there, admiral. No idea yet what might have happened to his signal."

"How far from Acoma?" she asked Lexi.

"13.47k."

"Not that far."

"I can't believe Stephen can do it. Not through that country. It's rugged going, and the crash—"

"—Admiral?" Smith. "May I see the photos?" An unusually diffident Smith who'd heard the word 'crash' used for the first time. She passed them across the aisle. He glanced at them, turned pale under his tan. "You're sure they got out of this?"

She nodded.

"How do you . . ." A hard swallow. "How do you know he was alive and it wasn't simply the body being transported?"

"The beeper is connected with the subject's nervous system, Dr. Smith. If the subject dies, an indicator superimposes on the signal. I'm surprised you don't know. I thought communications was your specialty."

"I suppose I might have, once upon a long time ago. But I'm a 'Net man, admiral. I've no interest in RealSpace toys." A sharp, sideways glance. "Stephen's signal is still going crazy?"

She nodded. His dark eyebrows twitched, a not-quite-steady

hand passed the pictures back to Lexi, and he slumped back into his seat, staring glumly out into the sunlit clouds.

Sunlight filtered down through the trees, glinting off wet rock, making colored sparks of dripping needles. Anevai chewed on an emergency ration stick and watched from the cave as a *wi'iswanik* hopped from treelimb to treelimb, loosing prismatic droplets along the way.

A quick intake of breath at her shoulder. She turned, propping her back against stone. "What'cha think of storms now, Mr. Spacer-man?"

A ghost-smile touched his mouth. His eyes flickered in her direction, but he didn't move his head from the scented breeze which stirred the curls falling over his forehead.

"Worth every minute, Ms. Planet-buster," he murmured, and spook-eyes flicked back to the outside.

Definitely easy on the eyes, he was. She studied his profile as she chewed on the ERat stick—not a half-bad breakfast, all things considered—watched those silvery eyes reflect blue and green as they tried to take in everything at once.

"I wonder if they're dominant or recessive." He cast her a puzzled look, and she elaborated: "Spook-eyes."

The spook-eyes under discussion dropped as the skin around them reddened.

"I almost hope my timing *is* off," she said, only half-joking. "I wouldn't mind at all if my first had them."

A slow take. A start. "Do you mean you don't . . ."

She laughed outright. "No, Stephen. And you pick a fine time to ask!" She held out the rest of the ERat stick. "Here. Lunch."

His jaw clenched, his face death-white now. His shoulder brushed her as he retreated into the cave. Puzzled, she followed, found him on his knees beside the packs, rocking slowly forward and back, crossed arms pressed against his stomach.

"Stephen?"

His head came up as she squatted on her heels beside him, but he didn't look at her—just stared straight ahead into the depths of the cave, his backlit face unreadable.

"Stephen, it's all right. *Really.* I'm regular as clockwork, and it's not the right time. Not even close."

"It's not that..." His head tipped toward her. Sunlight edged his cheekbone, revealing his expression at last.

He looked ready to throw up.

"You won't get p–pregnant. Not from m–me."

It took her a moment to realize: "You mean you've *already* decided—"

"S–say it was decided for me." Again, while she heard the words, comprehension took longer. She reached for his hand, but he drew away. "Long time ago, Tyeewapi." His voice was steadier now. "Doesn't matter." He faced her at last. "But how could *you* run that risk? *You* didn't know. You might have... don't you s–see what you'd have put that child through? He'd have had *no father*, Anevai. E–even if s–someone here agreed to take him on. He'd *always* know. He'd always..."

It didn't take a mind reader to read between these lines. She stopped him with a hand to his lips, replaced her fingers with a feather-light kiss. "It's all right, Stephen. We'd know who his father was, and he—or she—would be proud. We value new GeneSets as we value new life. Whoever they owe their chemistry to, every child here has more parents than they ever know what to do with. And if you won't give it to me, I'll creep to your bed and steal a bit of blood, like a vampire in the night, 'cause *I* want a kid with spook-eyes." She ran her fingers through his fine, silky hair. "And if he—or *she*—has to have hair like this and a skinny neck too, that's okay by me."

His mouth moved, but no sound came. She laughed and plugged it with the ERat stick. His mouth clamped around the stick: vain attempt to hold it in place as his shoulders began to shake. She pulled the stick and the plug on his silent laughter.

"No, Anevai," he said, when laughter eased and she tried to give him the stick again. "I can't."

"Ate earlier, huh?" He shrugged, and she gave him a quick hug. "Wesser's waitin', Spacer-man. Let's get—"

But a glance revealed nothing left *to* pack. His head cocked in silent question as he hitched one of the packs onto his shoulders. Upside-down.

"Never mind." She showed him how to carry it properly,

adjusted the straps, giving the one around his waist an extra pat, then tossed the other over her shoulders, settled it with a shrug, and headed out along the trail into the sparkling trees, tugging the straps tight as she walked.

Booted feet, crossed at the ankles, barred her progress down the narrow aisle. Lexi resisted the temptation to kick them out of the way—after all, Smith did at least *appear* to be asleep— and stepped carefully over them.

"Admiral?" At Cantrell's tacit invitation, she slipped into the seat next to her. "Chet's onLine."

Cantrell glanced at Smith, then nodded toward the seat monitor. Lexi signalled ComStat with a raised hand, and Stoddard transferred Chet's incoming to screen.

> >Ridenour's signal just turned up again, strong and steady.
> >*Figured the problem?*

Cantrell responded via the armrest fingerpad. From Smith, a twitch, a flicker of eyelid. He'd caught that move, Lexi would swear to it.

> >Nothing in the system, I know that. Just all of a sudden, the signal quit tripping around the cosmos and settled into place.
> >*Moving?*
> >Slow, but steady—right on a line for Acoma.
> >*Got them on vid?*
> >Yessir. —When you can see them. Rough country. Seem all right.
> >*Keep monitoring. I'll have TJ check in for exact coords. —Thanks, Chet.*
> >Got a message from Dr. McKenna, sir.
> >*Go ahead.*
> >Rather cryptic. Just: Don't push Ridenour. And: Wet TNT.

Not a common referent, but Lexi knew: highly unstable and ready to blow. Stephen Ridenour was that, all right. She based her opinion on gut instinct. She wondered how McKenna knew.

Another glance toward Smith; he was watching them openly now.

Cantrell knew it, said aloud, "Tell her, message received and understood. —Cantrell, out."

"They've found him, haven't they?" Smith asked, his voice low, sober.

Cantrell nodded.

His mouth twitched: humor or something else, she couldn't tell. That was the problem with Smith: you couldn't take anything he did or said at face value.

She wished she knew why he insisted on coming along, on meeting Stephen alone. More, she wished she understood Cantrell's agreeing to his terms.

Lexi didn't trust Smith, for all she chose to play along with his games. She couldn't read him, couldn't understand his motivations for playing them. Born rich enough to stick his baby rattle up any political nose, brilliant enough to flout the toughest academic system, he opted for out-at-the-elbows sweaters, mismatched socks and this undeveloped world as far from the social epicenter as a man could get.

And he'd opted for work. Hard work. She'd seen the performance quotients on all the researchers, and no one could complain that the man sat around on his butt seven days a week. A true cynic might claim he'd stacked those quotients in his favor, but twelve hours of fielding pleading demands for his time from Recon and researcher alike did not exactly support such cynicism.

With his posturing, the jocularity he slipped on like a cloak, Smith used people's better natures and in doing so, mocked it, parodying the guileless naïveté a Stephen Ridenour exuded as naturally as breathing. The question was whether that mockery was aimed at those who fell prey to his performance, or at a personality trait he simply did not believe in.

The one indicated a cruel streak. The other...

For Stephen's sake, Lexi hoped Smith could learn to accept the real thing. There was no denying Smith made Stephen happy. She'd seen them together, had seen Stephen truly laugh for the first time. For that, she'd endure Smith's posturing, and gladly.

But if Smith compromised that happiness, he'd learn what *vendetta* truly meant.

Because Stephen Ridenour's happiness had become, for Alexis Fonteccio, a high priority. She knew Cantrell's interest in Stephen had waned, and understood the reason for that disappointment. But Cantrell failed to realize that Stephen had accomplished everything necessary to further the Recon cause— regardless how his story ended. No matter what happened now, Recons had a precedent. Stephen was destined to be a legend, like it or no. The only question now was whether he was to be a martyr or a Cinderella.

Cantrell wanted a spokesman, someone to fight a public-awareness campaign. But Recons didn't need another Julian Rebellion. Vocal, political, inciteful, Julius had done every-thing to raise awareness—and resentment. Recons, Spacer sympathizers, Separatists and GenMems. He'd alienated them all.

But he *had* made them think.

Stephen was—Stephen was hope.

Stephen's importance hereafter was not to make a stand. He'd done that. While the Julians had fought, and killed, and gotten themselves killed, he'd endured the system. He'd sur-vived and reached the top. It didn't matter if Stephen never spoke to a reporter. It didn't really matter if the system chewed him up and spat him out now. It didn't matter if he faded out of sight forever into the depths of ATStation or the forests of HuteNamid.

Martyr or Cinderella. Personally, Lexi would prefer the latter. She'd seen one too many idealistic dreamer used for political appetizers. And if she had to play the tyrannical fairy godmother, she'd damnwell do it to keep Smith or anyone else from making a martyr out of Stephen Ridenour.

And on that thought, she asked, "Shouldn't you have TJ send a team out to pick them up?"

Before Cantrell could answer, from across the aisle:

"May I make a suggestion?"

Cantrell silenced Lexi's protest with a hand on her wrist and said, "I'm listening, Smith."

"Let Stephen come to us."

"Why?"

"He jumped into this—planned it on his own, for all you

think I'm behind it. If he can pull it off—let him. Let him accomplish it on his own."

"If you're pulling one on me, Smith—"

"No reason to. I'm worried about the kid, but I also think this is not the time to help him."

"Lexi? What do you think?"

Lexi stared hard at Smith, wondering whether this appealing, caring analyst was the true man behind the foolish facade, or simply another manipulative mask.

Either way, the point he made was valid. Stephen was breaking free of the crippling hold Vandereaux had had on him. To allow him to play it out . . .

She caught Cantrell's eye, tried to express caution, and nodded. "*If* he's really okay."

"Good enough. We'll give him his chance."

"I misjudged you, Ridenour." Anevai's voice drifted around the tree supporting his back.

"When?" They'd stopped for a rest. She was sitting. He didn't dare. He'd never get back up.

"Aboard *Cetacean.* Room spotless. Bed made. Everything right where you looked for it. Figured you'd planned our escape before you ever came to my room."

He edged around the tree so he could see her, braced his legs slightly apart, put an unsteady hand on the trunk to balance against the swaying landscape. "I still don't . . ."

"I figured nobody would make their bed before going visiting in the middle of the night. I see now, I was wrong. Anybody who packs blankets and glowlamps before his eyes are open would never leave his room with the bed unmade."

He chuckled, wiping sweaty film from his face. "Academy training. I fear I'm stuck with it for life."

"Oh, if that's all it is, don't fret. You grow out of the habit rapidly, if the Wesser's any indication. I promise you, neatness is not his greatest vice. You'll be a good influence on him—if he doesn't corrupt you totally first."

He felt a knot tighten in his chest, coughed as the world went liquid around the edges. A steady arm wrapped his waist under the pack. Anevai: on her feet and solid as the tree.

"Are you okay? You want to sit down?"

He shook his head slowly, carefully, felt her arm tighten as his balance wavered.

"No, you're not okay? or No, you don't want to sit?"

He pulled free and started walking. His head was clearer when he was moving, no matter his knees wanted to sit.

"Shit, Ridenour, don't blame me if you fall on your nose."

But a moment later, she was at his elbow, a light, steady support until his balance returned.

"Thanks," he muttered, when her hand dropped away.

"I hate to be a pessimist," she said, "but what if Wes didn't get the message? What if he's already been arrested?"

"Then Cantrell will just have to release him, won't she?"

"Why? I hate to burst your self-delusions, Ridenour, but who are you that she'd—"

"I'm the one with the answers." She frowned darkly and he qualified: "Or, I should say, the ability to get the answers. I'm also the one with the 'NetAT's ear."

She kicked a stone out of the path. "Then you *are* going back. I thought, maybe, you wanted to stay here. I mean, Cantrell could deliver your report, couldn't she?"

"You don't seem to understand. Much as I might want to stay—and that *is* a might, Tyeewapi, —I've got to go back. It's my responsibility to make the 'NetAT understand Wesley's system and why you all have done—what you've done with it. Might mean the difference between Wesley's arrest or freedom. Between *your* arrest and freedom."

She shrugged and started walking again, hands shoved in her pockets, scuffing a dust cloud from the trail. "What of your own freedom?" She threw a half-glance over her shoulder. "Or was all that stuff last night just to shut me up?"

"If you mean about the 'NetAT owning me, no, that was truth." He drew a deep, straggling breath. "I'm not free to stay here. I never was. I don't know what *my* chances are back at Vandereaux, particularly after what I pulled last night, but there's a chance I can save Wesley's career, considering who and what he is, but not without—"

Swift movement across the trail. He tried to track it, which succeeded only in making his head spin again, held his balance by instinct alone, and started over:

"But not without knowing what's going on here. There's too much I don't know. I don't know *why* Wesley kept his ideas so secret. I don't know why Nayati hates me. I don't understand why Cantrell left you up in the ship, or what she intends for Wesley. I've got to understand *everything* or nothing makes . . ."

Of a sudden, his breath just disappeared altogether, the trail ahead grew dark around the edges. . . .

Or maybe it was just clouds shadowing the sun.

Clinging desperately to their conversation, he gasped, "Anevai, why *did* Nayati want me dead?"

A long silence—so long he despaired of an answer. She didn't stop, didn't turn to face him—patently *avoided* doing either. Suddenly:

"Well, it *wasn't* just so I could—'save your ass.' "

His accusation aboard *Cetacean* thrown back in his face. He couldn't blame her, but it was no time for . . .

"Why?" All his energy, all his anxiety exploded in that one word.

She did slow at that, and one worried eye appeared briefly. "I just don't know, Stephen. He didn't used to be like that. He's . . . gone crazy the last few years—the last few months, it's gotten . . ."

"Crazy, how?"

"You saw—uncontrolled, irrational. That's not the Nayati I grew up with, Stephen. Honestly."

There was no denying her sincerity, but there had to be more to it and somehow the rationale behind that seemingly irrational attack was assuming overpowering importance. Pain-hazed memories couldn't supply what he needed. Anevai couldn't—or wouldn't . . .

He swallowed hard as the shadow spread to obscure all but a narrow window on the trail, and placing his feet exactly where Anevai's vacated suddenly required vast amounts of concentration. In some vague, unoccupied corner of his mind, he realized:

"I've got to talk to Nayati."

The feet stopped—

turned—

—too suddenly for him to stop.

He caught at her for balance; she slapped his hands away, and shoved him back.

"So that's what this is all about." She spat the words out. "To get your hands on Nayati."

"No—" He shook his head, instantly regretting the action as the remaining world spun around him. He caught at a tree limb. The limb snapped. He grasped the trunk instead.

"Tell me, when does Cantrell show up?"

"Don't go crazy on me, Tyeewapi." He was tired, sore, and not, on the downside of Eudoxin, in a frame of mind to explain anything. But he tried, nonetheless, only just realizing how he must sound to her. "I'm after *reasons*. That's *all* I'm here for. You insist Nayati's attack in the barn wasn't over Wesley's system, but you won't say what it *was* about; that Nayati's crazy. Well, I don't think he *is* crazy, and if you won't tell me, maybe he will."

"If I tell you, will you forget about Nayati?"

Rough bark scraped his cheek as he leaned wearily against the tree. "I can't promise you that, but I won't turn him over to Cantrell—I'm doing this to keep away from her. I thought you understood that."

"I'll tell you what I understand and who I believe. Nothing and no one. I'm waiting and trying to figure. Just like you."

Anger radiated from her, threatened to engulf him. She turned abruptly and stalked away at a pace he couldn't hope to match, and soon she'd be beyond that small patch of reality remaining; he clung to his tree and called after her: "*Will* you tell me?"

"Tell you what, Ridenour?"

"Why Nayati wanted me dead. What he's trying to hide. What Wesley's system has to do with it."

"Dammit, I *told* you; he's—" She swung around, staggered, and sat down abruptly, holding her head with both hands.

"Anevai!" He released the tree and stumbled toward her. "Are you all right?"

An accusing stare met him as he dropped to his knees beside her. "What did you do to me in there, you spacer-scuz?"

"In where?"

"In the damn cave! You took something before you—did whatever it was you think you did, and I'm starting to think straight for the first time since I woke up this morning. Now, *what did you give me?*"

"Nothing!"

"Damn you, Ridenour!"

He saw her fist coming, tried to roll with it, overbalanced and tumbled backward into the brush. He heard her scream again and scrambled away from that anger, saw through a haze her leap for him and jumped farther into brush—

—that gave beneath him. And gave. And gave. He threw an arm across his face to protect his eyes, and caught a limb that broke, a second that didn't with his other. He hung for a moment, his feet swinging freely as splintering wood bit into his palms: painful, but a good grip. Not quite a five-bar's, but under the circumstances . . .

"Stephen!"

He looked up through a broken tangle of undergrowth.

"Don't look down!"

Of course, then he had to. . . .

vi

"How soon will you be leaving, Sakiima?"

Gravel shifted, crunched softly under his feet as Sakiimagan and Cholena strolled the garden path behind the clinic. He put his arm around his wife's waist and wished he could answer differently. "Right away. I told Paul I'd meet him this afternoon. I'll try to get word to you regarding Anevai. But I don't know how soon that will be possible. I dare not focus their attention on Acoma."

She pulled him to a stop, turned in his hold to face him. "Perhaps it would be best if we simply gave Barb and Will to them—"

"How can we?" Momentary distraction as a stray wisp of hair blew across her face. He brushed it aside, denying the urge to kiss her. It had been too long, there'd been too many harsh words exchanged, and no time in this hurried morning for reconciliation. "We must solve their—problem before giving them over to Alliance. We must prove we can handle it."

"That's the point, Sakiima, we can't." She turned her face and brushed his palm with her lips, tacit forgiveness for those past words, then urged him along the trail. "I'm out of ideas. Nothing I try does any good. They remain—well, they'll be out in a few moments and you'll see them for yourself."

At the pond, he stopped beside a bench formed of a fallen tree, brushed a loving hand across its velvety, oiled finish. He and Cholena had made it together, before politics, before her psychiatric training, before the Libraries. They'd been children then, and there had been other projects in the years since—two children of their own, among others—but this bench was special. He sat down and drew her to sit beside him.

"I wish I knew how everything has gone so wrong. Hononomii reacting to Deprivil? It makes no sense. Nayati is—Anevai was right, the boy is challenging me . . . Why didn't I listen to her?"

"I've waited for years to hear you ask that question, Sakiimagan Tyeewapi."

He looked at her in surprise; she raised a brow and continued calmly:

"You've been seeing our children ass backwards for ten years. You want Hono to be a leader—he isn't, and never will be. His head's in the clouds of ancient Earth."

Impatience surged in him. . . . "Nonsense! Anevai's the one—"

"Keep your blood pressure down or we'll start up where we left off a month ago. You're a wonderful leader, the People love you—so do the researchers."

. . . and drowned in a sea of doubt. "With a little help from the Cocheta."

"Sometimes. Not all. And if they knew your reasons, they'd understand."

"Because they can't help otherwise."

Her hand sought his and squeezed gently. "Because you've issued your invitations wisely. What you've not done well is to push Hononomii to replace you. And Anevai—"

"—Is a dreamer who fills her head with the old tales."

The squeeze became a gentle, but chastising slap. "Anevai's

a storyteller—a creator, not a believer. She listens to you—hears what you say about Alliance and Alliance politics. She sees how those old stories apply to our new world and our new situation and tries to pass your wisdom on to others through her stories. Hononomii . . . Hono's a spiritual, brave man—an inspiring example—but no leader. He doesn't *want* to be, Sakiima.''

"And Anevai is? Does?"

"You'll have to ask her. Hono has come to me with his concerns, she hasn't. I simply judge on what I've observed."

"And Nayati?"

A thoughtful look crossed her face. "*He* speaks to you, Sakiimagan."

"Perhaps it's because he wishes to be leader of the *Dineh.*"

"Perhaps. But—"

A *Cetacean* VTOL entered the valley from the north, low and fast. A second one followed, veering off to the east side of the village. Somehow, Cantrell had traced him.

"Dammit, Ridenour, wake up!"

"I *am* awake." Stephen groaned and struggled to sit up, the throb in his jaw echoing the pounding in his skull, the ache where his back had struck a rock.

Hands pulling at him. He knocked them away. "Don't *touch* me."

He braced his sore back against the tree responsible for the latest bump on his head. He'd hit quite nicely, rolled as he'd been taught . . . if the stupid tree hadn't moved . . . "Shit, Tyeewapi, why don't you just tell me when you want me to fall down and shut up? It'd be a helluva lot easier on your fist—and me."

"Well, I'm not about to apologize. You had *no right.*"

Her voice sounded right in his ear. He ducked away from that voice, caught an elbow on a rock and bit back a curse, frowning toward where she squatted on her heels.

"I'm telling you I didn't give you anything."

"Like hell. You can't lie worth spit." She slapped dirt from her knee, raising a cloud, and brushed her hair back, leaving a filthy streak across her forehead. "Dammit, Ridenour, I try hard to trust you, then you pull something like this."

Resentment flared. "If you weren't enjoying it, you certainly disguised it well."

She rose slowly, glaring at him. "That's low, Ridenour. Damned if I'll cry rape under the circumstances, but you and I both know I wasn't in full command of my faculties. I want to know what you did."

His stomach jolted. He tasted copper-edged bile, and swallowed hard.

"Anevai, I—I'm sorry. I didn't mean for you to—but then you started in about the pills—I just wanted to shut you up—but I swallowed it. You shouldn't have gotten enough to—"

"You're sick, Ridenour. I hate to disillusion you, but normal people don't need to take a damn *pill* to make love—though that sure as hell isn't the word I'd use for what you did, considering."

According to his diary, his father maintained a person should learn at least one new thing each day.

He didn't think Anevai would appreciate the humor.

"I've already apologized. What else can I do?"

"You can tell me what it was, dammit!"

He ground his teeth and stared at the ground. "Nothing you'd know. Nothing that will hurt you."

A long, glaring silence. Then: "Damn you, Ridenour. Damn you to whatever hell you believe it."

He met that glare, his own face under control at last. "I already am. Several times over. Do you suppose we can continue on now? We've wasted enough time here."

"You mean, I'm free to go?"

Sakiimagan Tyeewapi glanced down the path toward the clinic, as close to ill at ease as Cantrell had seen him. A call from Chet: they had a positive ID on the researchers in the clinic garden. They weren't moving; TJ was closing in. Left time for manners.

"Did you think otherwise, governor?" Cantrell asked, sending a silent query to TJ.

"*I'm listening, Boss-lady.*" TJ's voice whispered, "*Want us to tail him?*"

"I—assumed you were looking for me. I was on my way back to Tunica anyway. I'd rather fly than wait on the 'Tube."

Hold, she signalled back. "Certainly, if you don't mind waiting."

"Waiting?"

"We do have our own purposes here, governor."

Another glance down the wooded lane. "I'll go with you, of course. This is my wife's home town. I'll introduce you to anyone you'd care to meet."

"Thank you, of course, but I'd prefer to handle the introductions myself."

For a moment, it appeared he might protest, but when security closed in beside him, he hesitated only to ask: "Admiral, how is my daughter?"

"I thought you'd renounced her, governor."

"Please, don't play games with me. Is Anevai all right?"

"Shouldn't she be?"

He didn't bite. The man was worried about his daughter, knew *something*, but not enough, and was still reluctant to admit his resources. He left without further comment.

The wooded lane opened out on a wide drive. In one direction the hint of buildings: the village Acoma's outer edge woven into the trees; to the left, the clinic and across a gravelled lot, a stone and log house grew out of the ground and faded into the garden behind. Young voices drifted on the wind.

"Wait here," Smith said, and took the clinic steps two at a time. The door opened before he reached it.

A woman stood there: a stately woman, her grey hair framing her face with two thick braids. Inyabi Tyeewapi. Though the photo on record had to be thirty years old, save for the color of those braids, Cantrell would think Paul had been disobeying the Council's directive.

Inyabi greeted Smith with an indulgent smile, a composed Hello, Wesley, it's been too long, and looking past him: "Adm. Cantrell." *Not* a question. "Welcome to our home. I assume you're here for Barbara Liu and Will Bennett?"

Somewhat taken aback, she answered cautiously, "In part. They are here, then?"

"Of course. In the garden. —Won't you come in?"

Cantrell exchanged a glance with Lexi, then said, "I hope you won't take this amiss, Dr. Tyeewapi, but—"

"If you please, admiral, 'Inyabi.' There are three *Dr. Tyeewapis* in the general vicinity causing no small confusion, if we insist on formality."

"Inyabi, then. —Three?"

"My daughter, Cholena, brought Barbara and Will here three months ago. But, please, come in."

"If you don't mind, I'd like my people to—" A warning beep in her ear. Her people already had. "Thank you. We'd be delighted."

With Smith and Lexi in tow, she accompanied Inyabi through the outer offices and back into the wide hallway between several treatment rooms, all of which were empty. The far end opened onto a large garden, a gravel pathway between flowering bushes and under trellised archways to a bubbling pond.

Beside the pond, three individuals worked. One, a mature version of Anevai Tyeewapi, rose from a carved bench and joined them, leaving a notebook and a PC behind. The other two appeared oblivious to their presence.

"So. You finally made it here." An oddly welcoming note in the woman's mellow voice offset any implied criticism.

Inyabi said, "Lena, your manners leave much to be desired. —Admiral, this is my daughter, Cholena. I assure you, she has been taught better."

Cantrell laughed. "No offense taken, I assure *you*. However, I assume you'll both understand my impatience to meet these elusive researchers." She nodded toward the two seemingly oblivious individuals. "That them?"

Cholena nodded. "Come with me, admiral, I'll—introduce you."

She led them to the pond's edge where the two researchers sat side by side before an easel, hands clasped. They were working on a single painting: a landscape, though definitely *not* the setting before them (and from the red-hued sky and vegetation not one they'd seen on this *planet*), one with the left hand, the other with the right—

—both with their eyes tightly closed.

* * *

"Well, Ridenour, we're almost there. Only a couple of kilometers to go."

"Thank—" Stephen's relief at Anevai's announcement ended in a bitten-off gasp as he raised his focus from the trail and looked up. And up. And up.

"I told you: this way's a bit tougher."

He caught her look, clenched his jaw, and, shifting packstraps to a less raw spot on his shoulders, said, "Shall we—" He had to pause for breath. "—be going?"

But Anevai had shrugged her pack off and was settling on a rock-seat. "I don't know about you. I'm hungry and I want a breather before tackling that. It's not as bad as it looks, but it's not easy either."

She left him little choice. He slumped down, leaving his pack right where it was, his arms and back so stiff and sore he'd never get it back on. Thanks to that thoroughly senseless fall, his shoulder was beginning to feel like old times. McKenna was going to kill him.

If he lived that long.

Thinking of Dr. Mo, he worked the belt pouch to the front and dug through it for the 3XDailies, choked them down, glanced again at the trail ahead and took two Sud'orsofan as well. Exceedingly stupid, but so would falling down that cliff be.

He stifled a cough. A mountain stream had provided drinking water some unknown age ago, but his small canteen had long since run empty and his mouth was uncomfortably dry: another charming 'Doxin side effect.

"Here." A packet of liquid ERat struck him in the arm and fell unchecked to the ground.

"Can't." He leaned over and picked it up. Tried to hand it back.

But Anevai looked elsewhere, and the hand holding the packet began to tremble.

"Dammit, Ridenour. Those stupid pills . . . how do you expect to—"

"Damn me all you want, Tyeewapi." He struggled to keep

his voice steady. "It won't make me eat that stuff." And at her scowl: "*Can't*, Tyeewapi." He rolled to his feet. "Let's go."

"Not until you eat that."

"*You* eat it!" He whirled and flung the packet down the path behind them, grabbed his arm as pain shot through his shoulder.

"Ridenour, dammit—!"

He ignored her and started up the hill, grabbing for any handhold he could find. Stone crumbled beneath his fingers, a backward slide left his fingers bruised and bloody, but he kept on, focussing down to each separate hand and foothold, concentrating on getting to the top.

It was, after all, not so different from the gym—*reach and pull, reach and pull*—it wasn't even straight up—*reach and pull, reach and*—

—an impact to his ribs, hard and sudden. Concentration shattered. His extended arm contracted, instinctively protecting his newly healed side. His other handhold slipped . . .

vii

"*Stephen!*"

Anevai hooked an elbow around a tree and reached for Ridenour as he tumbled past. She caught his pack, felt a jar in her supporting arm as her hand hooked a packstrap. He collapsed against the rocky slope, breathing in sobbing, panting gasps.

And she matched the bit-brained tode gasp for gasp—

—thanks to *his* CodeHeaded stupidity.

A dirt-rimmed, furiously accusatory eye glared up at her, and a voice that was little more than a whisper croaked: "Why?"

She struggled for breath to answer.

"*Why, dammit?*"

She pointed with her chin in the direction he'd been taking, where relative ease of travel became sheered-off stone. He dropped his head back into the dirt with a smothered expletive.

"I tried, Ridenour." She gasped. "I tried to stop you—to get your attention—but you wouldn't listen. —*Now* will you follow me?"

He nodded without looking up.

"Are you okay to go on?"

Another nod.

She settled her pack properly, now she had the leisure, then backtracked a step or two before starting upward again—on a back-and-forth route which, though longer, was far easier than the one he'd attempted. For a time, he kept right beside her, tracing her hand and footholds precisely. Then, apparently getting the idea, he dropped out of her peripheral vision, leaving her free to concentrate on finding the best and easiest route. With each meter gained she asked Was he all right, but his answers grew breathless and finally, she ran out of breath too, and quit wasting it.

Her hand closed on a rock at the top of the climb, and she gasped, "Almost there, Ridenour!"

No answer. With a sinking feeling, she looked behind. And down. And cursed softly before she started back down. . . .

With a good ten meters to go, Stephen had wrapped his arms around a tree, possibly to rest, and apparently frozen there— eyes closed, cheek pressed hard against the bark—he certainly evinced no awareness of her return.

Anevai flattened against the ground, propping herself on a rock, gathering her own strength. There was no going back down—unless one did it the hard and fast way, but if Stephen would keep his shit together . . .

"Ridenour?" He started, his eyes fluttered open. She eased up behind him, and muttered firmly: "Ridenour, you freak out on me this time, and I'll kick your ass clear back to Tunica." She put her arms around him *and* his tree, pressed against his back, heard a gasp as that support eased the strain on his arms. She said, right into his ear: "You hear me?"

"I—" On a gasp. "—hear you, Tyeewapi."

"Okay, Spacer-man, now listen up. You're almost there. I want you to lean against me—don't worry, I won't let you slip—and look up. You can see the top from here."

His head tipped back against her shoulder, sweaty curls poked her ear. From the corner of her eye, she saw him blink into the sunlight shafting over the cliff-top. His breath caught in a little gasping sob, but he pulled himself back up to the tree, taking his own weight again.

"Go ahead, Anevai." A shaky breath. "I'll make it now."

"Not on your own, hotshot," she said, still right into his ear. "You see that rock up there? You're going to move to the other side of this tree, then wait for me to get set up there where I can help. Step at a time, Ridenour. Step at a time. Hear me?"

He didn't answer; she nudged him. "Hear me?"

"I—hear you, Tyeewapi."

She pulled Stephen bodily up over the edge, hugging him and laughing as they rolled back onto flat ground. His arms wrapped around her, and his face pressed into her neck, his gasps harsh and hot against her skin.

"Somehow," he whispered, when those gasps eased, "I don't think this was what Dr. Mo meant when she said Take it easy."

She laughed and hugged him again before remembering she currently hated his guts. "Someday, Ridenour, you're going to push me too far and I'll dump you over a cliff myself."

"I appreciate—your restraining your—justifiable urges—today, Tyeewapi."

His gasping whisper blew dust in her face. She sneezed and shifted her arm under his head, getting his nose out of the dirt. His stupid stunts made it increasingly difficult to remember he was just out of hospital; he had no business even being out of bed . . .

Shit, Tyeewapi, you want me to shut up . . .

Wonderful, she thought. She, who'd berated Nayati for attacking an unarmed man . . .

She pulled herself up, leaving Stephen rag-limp on the ground. She brushed the filthy curls back and murmured, "So help me, Ridenour, you get out of this and I promise I'll keep my fists to myself from now on."

But he didn't hear—dead to the world, he was. She patted him again and dug into the pack for a KlenzWipe to ease some of his sweat-smeared filth. As the 'Wipe touched his cracked lips, the tip of his tongue appeared and chased the quick-drying dampness.

"Shit, Ridenour," she muttered, for all he wouldn't hear, "that stuff'll kill you."

She'd had her concern thrown down the trail, once, but now the semicomatose idiot was going to eat something. Just because he didn't like the taste was no reason to refuse to eat what they had conveniently at hand.

"Worst time of year for you to drop in, Ridenour." She pulled out an ERat packet. "Food all around us—good food— if we could afford the time to make it edible," nipped it open with her teeth. "Meanwhile—" and held it to Ridenour's lax mouth, squeezing a bit of the fluid out.

As she'd suspected, the tonguetip reappeared to lick it off, and she squeezed again. By the time he roused enough to protest, most of the packet was gone. He shuddered and turned his face away and she didn't press the issue—a little of the stuff went a long way.

She was tucking the empty back in the pack when:

"Anevai?" Stephen's hand touched her arm. "H–help me s–sit up—please?"

But only so he could fumble for more pills. "Dammit, Ridenour, *stop it*." She grabbed the pouch away from him, resisted the impulse to throw it over the cliff—there were important prescriptions in there as well—and stuffed it into her pack.

"You don't under—"

"I understand better than you think, Ridenour. Damned pills don't solve everything."

"N–not—" He coughed, a choking kind of cough. "Sh–shit!"

He twisted away and up onto his knees. She grabbed him before the wrenching heaves rolled him right over the edge. Everything he'd just taken in and more—the last with a frighteningly red tinge. The coughing eased, and Stephen grasped desperately at her pack, and Anevai, finally understanding, pulled the pill pouch out and spilled its contents in front of him.

Shaking hands found the one he wanted, but couldn't manage the safety cap. She took it from him. "Two?"

He shook his head slightly.

"Three?"

A violent shake.

"One?"

A nod. A careful Thank you, as she shook one into his hand.

"Can you take it dry?"

Another nod. A sad attempt at a smile. A whispered Think *pickles*, which drew a reluctant chuckle out of her.

A patient delay through another coughing fit before taking the pill. Tears at the corners of his closed eyes as the pill worked its way down what had to be a raw, dry throat dissipated as he relaxed and began breathing normally.

Spook-eyes met hers, crinkled at the corners, and he whispered, "I *hate* pickles."

But she couldn't laugh with him. Instead, she asked quietly: "The emergency rations?"

He nodded.

"Why didn't you just say something, Stephen?"

"T-tried..."

Can't, Tyeewapi. "Gods, I could have killed you."

He shook his head, groaned and raised a hand to his head. "Not—not *that* bad."

"You just need pills to keep it down, right? —Shit, Ridenour, I'm *sorry*—"

"Not—not... fault."

He touched a hand to his mouth, fingered the red moisture mixing with the dirt on his fingertips. His hands were still shaking as he wiped them on his filthy, torn slacks, and the look on his face was one of quiet, contained terror.

Not that bad? I hate to think what you consider worrisome, Ridenour. Gods, what have I done to you?

She gathered the pill bottles carefully into the pouch, tucked it into his pack.

"Listen, Stephen. There's a bit of a way to go yet, but I've got an idea. —Shut up and listen." As he tried to interrupt. "If we don't head right for my grandparents, but go to the spring—we can *crawl* there in five minutes—" His shoulders shook again. "You okay?"

"I—" he breathed, "I might h–have to."

"You'll make it if I have to drag you. You can wait there and I'll go get help. Okay?"

A long consideration. "Wh—what's . . . ss—a . . . s—spring?"

She brushed sweaty hair off his forehead. "You'll see, hotshot."

One with the left hand, one with the right; mirror image palates, mirror image strokes. Occasionally two pair of eyes would open simultaneously to examine the canvas, then drift shut again. Odd behavior, to say the least.

But not the only odd behavior she'd witnessed lately. Cantrell turned away from the disturbingly fascinating tableau. Oddity was hardly proof. "Is this an act? This is no time for prevarication, Dr. Tyeewapi, your son's health might be at stake."

"Hononomii?" Cholena asked. "How does he—"

"Answer me first. Please."

"If it's an act, they've fooled me for months. I'm completely at a loss. I've wanted to call Central in on this for weeks."

"And your husband stopped you?"

"Sakiimagan has no such hold on me, admiral. It was a Tribal Council decision. Now—what bearing has this on Hono?"

"You said Bennett and Liu collapsed in the midst of an argument—went catatonic."

"That's right."

"And your Recon MedTechs handled—"

"Our hospitals are neither one or the other."

"I stand corrected. I assume their vital signs have been closely monitored?"

Cholena nodded.

"Was there anything—unusual in those readings?"

"Unusual how?" The Recon woman's face gave no indication of her thoughts.

"Highly unusual. Like a pattern over time? A repetition like a—like a tape on instant replay?"

"Is that what's happened to my son?"

She didn't answer. Cholena's eyes closed briefly.

She set a hand on Cholena's arm. "*Is* that what happened?"

"For a time."

"And now? With this mirror image behavior? Has this been monitored?"

"It's being monitored even now." Cholena gestured to the

PC on a stand beside the bench. Split-screen, side-by-side displays. Identical displays.

"Nice little piece of equipment, Dr. Tyeewapi. Remote patches?"

Cholena nodded. "Since this painting business began, their signs are identical as long as their hands are in direct contact—as if they're both painting both halves at the same time. Once they separate the—tape starts up again."

Suddenly, in her ear: *"They're a half kil or so from you, admiral. At the hot springs. Out of visual, but his signal's there."*

Cantrell tapped acknowledgment, said aloud, "Your daughter is safe."

"I'm not surprised, admiral. Once you assured me she'd landed safely, I wasn't really concerned. There's very little on HuteNamid my Anevai can't handle."

"Your husband doesn't seem to share that sentiment."

"My husband is the father of a daughter. The combination is frequently confusing—for both father and daughter."

"I can attest to that, admiral."

A man appeared behind Cholena, resting square, large-knuckled hands on her shoulders. A tall man with long black hair held back with a strip of red and black cloth. He leaned over Cholena's shoulder, holding out his hand.

"Welcome, Adm. Cantrell. I'm Matowakan." Cholena twisted in his hold, looked a question at him. "They're at the bathhouse, Lena. The boy isn't doing well."

Smith jumped to his feet. Cantrell controlled the urge to pull him back by the seat of his pants and met Matowakan's hand instead.

Cholena asked, honest concern on her face. "Not well how, Dad?"

"From the bios, mostly tired and hungry. Inyabi's fixing a room for him now."

"Unnecessary, Dr. Tyeewapi," Cantrell interjected quickly. "Ridenour won't be—Smith!" Her attention shifting to Smith's rapidly retreating backside. "Where do you think you're going?"

Forced to stop when one of her men stepped into his path, Smith swung back. "To Stephen."

"Not yet, mister. It's *my* call this time. I want to know what Stephen's next move will be, not yours."

Anevai cast one final glance at the steaming water and left before temptation won out, trudging down the well-worn trail toward the clinic: a five-minute walk that would probably take an hour the way she felt right now.

She hoped her grandparents would understand. She'd been 'too busy' to visit for months, and now she finally showed and what did she bring with her but a fistful of trouble. Wesley had better be there. Wesley better have everything arranged already—or Cantrell better have him under lock and key.

A cheerful whistle on the path ahead; she ducked into the trailside underbrush.

The whistler appeared around a bend in the trees, evidently, from the towel slung around her shoulders, destined for the hot springs. Fortunately, it was Leotii Wakiza, the clinic's night-shift EMT—and Nigan's sister.

As Leotii approached, Anevai hissed her name and stepped onto the trail.

Leotii grinned and grabbed her in welcome. "I thought you were hauled up to the big ship. When did you get back?"

"No time to explain, Leo. And—" She grimaced. "—you might want to forget you saw me. I'm not exactly supposed to be here."

Leotii's grin didn't waver. "I'm not even going to ask."

"You still got a pipeline to Nigan?"

Leotii nodded. "Sure. He doesn't dare go *that* silent. Nayati's got him pretty nervous."

"You better tell him to lie low. I didn't know where else I could come, and once Cantrell finds out . . ."

"I understand. I'll get the word to him."

"Answer a question?"

"Sure—but I expect a full confession eventually."

"If I'm around to give it. Is the Wesser up at the clinic?"

"Smith?"

She nodded.

Leotii's face fell. "Poof. No confession. —Can't tell you. Just finished my workout; haven't been there yet." Her face lightened. "But I heard somebody landing on the pad behind the clinic. Maybe that was him."

Cantrell. Sure as the rains followed the Miakoda. She didn't need another problem. She'd had a more than sufficiently eventful day, thank you. But problems had had a way of finding her ever since she'd met Stephen Ridenour.

"Thanks. That's all I need to know. Have a good..." Shit. Ridenour. "Leotii, one more favor?"

"Cost you."

"*Anything*. Just—stay away from the bathhouse, okay?"

"Ooooo—sounds good. Who're you hiding there?"

"Trust me—you don't want it."

"It? —I'm disappointed in you, girl." But Leotii smiled and nodded. "I'm headed for the lake anyway. —See you later?"

"Yeah, sure..." She hoped.

Cantrell hadn't picked them up. It was possible she was here for another reason, but somehow Anevai doubted it, and while she trudged the last few meters of forest trail, she cursed Cantrell for making them work so hard getting here.

A moment's pause just inside the clinic's back entrance, listening, waiting for a move from anywhere: outside, inside, even above. The hallway was empty, the treatment rooms open and silent. A rustling of papers, file drawers opening and closing: someone in the records room.

She silent-footed her way down the hall and glanced through the door. Her mother, at the table leafing through a stack of files. What was she doing here? She was supposed to be with Dr. Barb and Will. Did that mean they were here in Acoma, too? What had she led Stephen into?

"*Mom!*"

Her mother, imperturbable as always, looked up at her whisper, smiled and held out her arms. Anevai stumbled across the room to her, not realizing until then how much her father's rejection had hurt—

—or how frightened she'd been for the last several hours.

"I knew you'd be safe, of course," her mother said, releasing her at last. "Once I heard you'd left the crash site." She looked past her shoulder. "Is Dr. Ridenour with you?"

"Just me." She didn't want to give Stephen's location away yet. "Is Cantrell here?"

"But Dr. Ridenour *was* with you—"

"Mother, *is* that Cantrell?"

"How else would I have known you were coming?"

"How'd she know to come here?"

"Wesley told her."

"*Wesley?* The stinking—"

"Now, Anevai, I'm certain he did as he thought best. He's here, too. And a number of *Cetacean* personnel scattered about. Adm. Cantrell seems sincerely concerned for you two—youngsters, as she calls you."

"I'm not surprised. I imagine we've loused things up pretty well."

"Why'd you do it, Anevai? It sounds as if you had things quite well under control aboard the ship."

"I—don't know." She rubbed her eyes, wishing for a more reasonable answer. "Seemed like a good idea at the time."

Voices in the hall. Panicked thoughts of escape, thoughts Cholena's eyes counselled against. So she stood quietly beside her mother as Cantrell entered the room, Wesley and *Cetacean* security close on her heels.

"Hello, admiral," she said. "Lovely day for a walk in the woods, don't you think?"

Wesley searched the corners of the room, bored with the banal little rituals of would-be politicians. Anevai was here, so where was Stephen?

"Who the hell cares about the weather?" he demanded finally. "Where's Stephen? Why isn't *he* here?" Anger, indignation, and amusement turned on him. "One of the two most brilliant minds of the century and you leave him out on his own? Who knows what might—"

"He's perfectly safe, Wesley, and a whole lot more comfortable than he'd be standing here putting up with your asininity. Shut up and behave, or I'll leave him right where he is."

"But we won't, Ms. Tyeewapi," Cantrell said. "My men are at the bathhouse now."

Anevai didn't look surprised. He was.

"Damn you, Cantrell." Wesley Smith *hated* surprises. "What about our deal?"

"You'll get to talk to him, Smith. —We've been following your progress, young lady, and I was curious to see what you intended to do. What part you've had in the entire proceedings. —Why'd you do it? I thought we had an understanding."

Anevai had no business making deals with this woman. Anevai had no concept of what to demand in return for her services.

"I honestly don't know, admiral." Anevai collapsed into a chair. "Stephen was going whether I did or not. . . . The bit-brain would have killed himself on his own. I couldn't just leave him."

"What put the notion into his head? What's his problem?"

"Have to ask him, admiral. I can't presume to explain. Only. . . don't take him back, admiral. Not yet. He wants so badly to do this 'NetAT report right. He's taken it into his head it's the only worthwhile thing he'll ever do."

Wesley harrumphed. "That's ridiculous. Let *me* at him. *I'll* straighten him—"

Of a sudden, Anevai was out of her chair and around the table pushing him up against the wall and waving a fist in front of his nose. "You do, Smith, and I'll flatten your face. I've been dealing nonstop with a crazyman for two days, and I'm not putting up with any more shit. You're going to go to Stephen. You're going to be nice to Stephen. You're going to *listen* to Stephen and answer his goddamned questions. You're going to help him figure out whatever it is that's making him crazy and then you're going to talk him into going back quietly to the ship like a good 'NetHead and quit causing everybody ulcers. *Do you understand me?*"

He looked over Anevai's shoulder to where Cantrell lounged against the table, her useless security officers arrayed behind her.

"You going to stand there and let her talk to me like that?"

She crossed her arms, and raised an eyebrow. "Yep."

viii

Stephen drifted in the hot, bubbling water, letting it soak out the aches and pains, letting it wash away the filth, contemplating the nature of the universe and his place within it—

—*in other words*, he thought, *severely, totally VOSsed. Definitely a virtual operator in residence.*

Fine impression he'd make on Smith this way. *Hello, Dr. Smith. Lovely weather we're having, and by the way, don't you think that cloud of steam bears a remarkable resemblance to the Venezian multiplicity?*

On the other hand, maybe Wesley wouldn't come. Maybe this *Acoma* didn't even exist. Maybe Anevai didn't. Maybe he'd be stuck in this strange little stone hole with its wonderful hot pool for all eternity, drifting forever in the shifting, bubbling currents.

He propped his neck against the pool's stone rim. He'd never used the hot tubs at Vandereaux. They'd always been too full, regardless of the hour. Nor had he had the leisure . . .

Never enough time . . .

Water closed over his head. He reached frantically for the edge of the pool, felt rock slip from under his hand, got a second grip and pulled himself gasping to the surface. He clung there, sneezing, cursing and laughing at the same time.

He couldn't keep his head above water. How the hell was he going to keep his tail out of—what had Anevai called it . . . the *pooky*? Silly word, pooky. Another fit of laughter—

A faint scratching at the door.

—that halted abruptly.

"Anevai?" he whispered. "Is that you?"

If it was, she didn't say so. The scratching continued. He crawled out of the pool, drew the blanket around him, and moved cautiously toward the door. "Anevai?"

The door clicked open and he jumped back, stumbled into a wooden bench and thumped to the floor on the far side. A hand holding a shapeless drape of blue cloth appeared and an almost-familiar half-forgotten voice chimed, "Anybody here need a robe?"

"Wesley?"

"Have I got a—"

"Wesley Smith, is that you?"

A lecherous grin peered out from behind the robe. "—deal for you. —Hi there, good-lookin'. What'll you give me?"

"So I left him in the bathhouse. What else could I do?" Anevai slumped down on the front steps; her mother settled behind her.

"You did fine, Anevai." Cantrell's hand touched her shoulder before she and Fonteccio discreetly left her alone with her mother.

Not that it made a difference; there was probably someone listening anyway.

Gods, she was starting to think like Stephen.

She'd told Cantrell everything—everything except about this morning in the cave. She didn't know what drug he'd taken—didn't really want to get him into trouble, and since she'd had no lasting effects from it, what difference did it make?

Her mother's hand stroked her hair, pausing occasionally to pluck a leaf from her hair.

"A mess, aren't I? Sorry, Mum. Not a very good example of your parental talents."

Her mother just laughed and hugged her—leaves and all. "It sounds to me as though you handled the young man quite well, under the circumstances. However..." She laughed lightly. "I'll admit I'm looking forward to meeting this character."

"It appears, Dr. Tyeewapi, you're about to have your wish."

Anevai blinked up the lowering sun glaring in her eyes, making a haze-edged silhouette of Cantrell. "Stephen and Wesley are on their way?"

"We're here, Anevai." Stephen's soft voice preceded him out of the garden. Wesley followed close at his heels, the admiral's Security Chief bringing up the rear.

She jumped up. "I'm sorry, Stephen. I told them...I didn't know what else to—"

Stephen placed a hand on her arm. "It's all right, Anevai."

"Are you okay?" He'd gone in the pool: his hair was still damp. The robe she'd sent with Wesley was damp and filthy around the edges, but Stephen himself looked better, certainly fresher, than when she'd left him.

Until you saw the exhaustion in his eyes. But his smile, while tired, was steady. "Clean, anyway. —Admiral, may we talk in private, please?"

"We don't have anything to talk about, Stephen. You're coming back to the ship with me. McKenna's worried sick about you. After what you've just put yourself through, you'll be lucky—"

"I tried to explain to you that he—" Anevai began, but Cantrell interrupted:

"I understand you're trying to help, but if Stephen wants answers, he can find them where he's safe and under his physician's care. Smith can come up to the ship with us."

She expected Wesley to object, but it was Stephen who said:

"I'd appreciate it if you two wouldn't discuss me as if I weren't here. Admiral, I'm asking again, will you please come with me . . ." His voice lost a little of its assurance. He glanced at her. "Anevai, is there somewhere we could talk—alone?"

"Our home is at your disposal, Dr. Ridenour."

Anevai knew that voice. "Granfa!" Matowakan was standing in the doorway. She ran up the steps and hugged him, then turned back. "Stephen, this is—"

But Stephen didn't wait for the introduction. "Thank you, sir. —Admiral?"

"You're pushing, Ridenour," Cantrell said bitingly.

"Absolutely. Will you join me inside?"

My God, admiral, Lexi thought, *be careful.*

Cantrell was fuming, and justifiably. Stephen was challenging her. Calm and collected, not a hint of the stutter that so frequently plagued his speech . . . such grandstanding tactics might have served him well in the Academy, but it was *not* the way to handle Loren Cantrell.

A collection that was costing him dearly to maintain, and Cantrell couldn't see it.

Without taking her eyes from his arrogantly tilted face, Cantrell barked: "TJ, is he clean?"

Stephen's robe slipped into a pile at his feet. "I don't exactly have any place to hide a weapon."

More senseless grandstanding: the boy blushed scarlet when caught without a shirt. Lexi ached for him, wished she'd gone after him rather than Smith, who did nothing but pick up the robe and hold it, the tilt of his head as defiant as Stephen's. Made a person wonder what had passed between them before TJ's arrival. Made a person exceedingly nervous about what *other* examples Smith might provide.

Lexi quit trying for Stephen's attention, he was far too focussed on the admiral, and concentrated on Smith instead. Smith sensed her, she was certain of it, but ignored her completely.

"I'm not impressed, boy," Cantrell said. She glanced at TJ. He gave her the All Clear. "But Briggs says you're clean. —*Him*, I believe."

"S–so, w–will you t–talk with m–me p–privately? Leave B–Briggs and . . ." He looked at her at last; she shook her head ever so slightly. His expression didn't alter. ". . . L–Lexi here?"

Not his usual stutter: chill. He'd put himself in hospital at this rate.

"Put your clothes on and we'll get back to the ship. We can talk there," Cantrell said, in what was clearly an order.

Stephen didn't answer in words. He simply stood obstinately on the step, his lips turning blue.

"Damn you, Ridenour. —Briggs, check the place out." TJ disappeared into the house. "—Ridenour, put the blasted robe back on! You've made your point."

"Please, Stephen," Smith spoke sense at last, and held the robe out.

Stephen's obstinance relaxed and he turned to Smith, pushing his hands into the sleeves. Smith pulled the robe together and tied the belt. A tap kicked in her beeper's audio augmentation enough to hear Smith's murmur: "What're you up to, kid?"

And Stephen: "Just trying to get us out of this any way I can. Trust me?"

Smith glanced toward the admiral. "About have to, won't

I?'' He grasped Stephen by the shoulders. ''Don't make me regret it, fella.''

''I'll try not to.''

Cantrell tapped behind her ear, acknowledgment of some message from TJ, and jerked her head toward the house. ''All right, boy. Get in there.''

Stephen went without another word. Without a backward glance at any of them.

''What's this all about, Ridenour?''

The admiral was mad at him.

Stephen noted that fact through a haze of exhaustion, noted at the same time he felt truly at ease with her for the first time since boarding *Cetacean*. He understood anger, it was pseudo-friendship that was confusing and difficult to deal with.

''Trying to do my job, admiral.''

She sat in a straight-backed chair near the fireplace, her briefcase in her lap, her expression colder than the ashes. ''What job? You've done it. Then practically gotten yourself uselessly dead. That you're alive now is thanks to a very talented team of medical experts. Experts another ship might not have had. Council diverted *Cetacean* and her crew just so you and your mission could have the best backup available. In return, you've stolen and destroyed a craft you were in no wise fit to pilot, endangered yourself and an innocent colonist, and undermined all our credibility with the locals, and for what? Get it through your head, boy, this is no game, no test of courage. It's not only your life that's at stake. It's the security of Alliance *and* the futures of these people you call your friends. So stop this nonsense and get your tail back up on that ship.''

''No.''

''Don't push me, boy. —Get over here and sit down. You couldn't get through my men if you grew wings, so stop making me shout.''

''I've never considered my job here a game,'' he said, moving slowly across the room. ''But there's far too much I still don't understand. For all I know, you have the answers and you're refusing to tell me.''

"So ask me."

"No." He ignored her imperative gesture toward the couch; he'd had enough of being ordered about. There were rights the admiral had and those she did not. Those were the rules—the absolutes. In between lay most of reality—and reality belonged to those who played the game best. He knew most of Cantrell's personal rules now. The power she would willingly bring to bear—

"Why not?"

—and where she would draw the line at using that power.

"Because I don't trust you anymore, admiral. I certainly can't trust your answers."

He, on the other hand, had a weapon she'd not seen. One he'd quite willingly bring to bear once Stephen Ridenour succeeded in overruling Zivon Stefanovich's desire to kneel before her and plead with her to let him stay with these people who claimed they wanted him.

"Whose *do* you trust? Smith's? The man's a professional smartass, boy. After the past few hours, I'm not at all surprised he came up with a way to bypass the communication network: it's right up his larcenous alley."

Mildly amused at how little that undoubtedly correct assessment mattered to him, he said calmly: "He's the senior half of the most innovative research team in 'NetStudies today. Nothing else matters."

"High opinion you have of yourself of a sudden. That due to him, too?"

He clamped his jaw on a protest. He'd been thinking of Anevai, but he wasn't about to give the admiral additional justification to confine Anevai or anyone else.

"Go get your clothes on. I'm taking you and Smith upstairs where Chet can keep an eye on you both until this is all settled one way or the other."

"No."

"I'm getting exceedingly tired of that word, Ridenour."

"All right. Try these: I quit."

"Not in the job description."

"Admiral, everything I know about Wesley's 'NetTap will be in Chet Hamilton's personal files—including the steps I'll use to put it there—by the time you're back aboard *Cetacean*. He'll know everything I do and the decision to tell you or not will be his."

At last he had her full attention. "What have you been keeping from me, boy?"

"Up till now, I've answered all your questions as thoroughly and as honestly as I could, but you're Council, not 'NetAT, Adm. Cantrell. What I've done and can do impacts on the nature of the 'Net itself and is not something to be shared lightly. Chet has the authority to deny you access on a cross-professional judgment call. —I don't. Putting the knowledge into his hands is the best I can do."

"You can go back up where you belong and *discuss* the matter with him personally."

"Not an option, admiral."

"Why not?"

"The moment I enter that ship, my freedom to speak, my access to certain records can be curtailed. There are aspects about Wesley's theory that bother me. That have to do with my original purpose here—my *'NetAT* appointed purpose which neither you nor Chet has the right to supersede."

"You mean the sources for Smith's paper? I already told you: forget it! It makes no difference."

"It makes a great deal of difference."

"Only to you, boy. Worry about restoring the 'NetDB and protecting it against further infiltration, not about who discovered the method of infiltration and how."

Boy. Stephen stared at a painting on the opposite wall, a painting of people riding some sort of spotted creatures across a barren land far different from the tall trees and rivers outside the windows. A land much more in tune with his own child-hood memories. He made himself remember that child, focussing on the differences between Stephen Ridenour and Zivon Stefanovich.

"I'd appreciate it, admiral, if you'd stop calling me that."

"Boy? —Didn't seem to bother you when Smith used it."

"*He* doesn't try to make me feel like one."

"Really. What does he make you feel like?"

"That's hardly your business. I'm not a boy. I'm not a child, and I'm not Zivon Ryevanishov."

"Of course you're not. That's the whole point!" She leaned forward intently. "Stephen, it's not just Smith's Tap, haven't you figured that yet? It's you. We simply can't risk you."

That was almost funny, considering the *we* she represented. He moved to the far side of the fireplace and rested a hand on the carved mantel. "There is no 'we,' admiral. *You've* been inordinately interested in me from the beginning: dinner every cycle, probing my interests, my goals, pointedly sharing your onWorld experiences, giving me things—"

"What *things?*"

"The picture—that Kairol spacescape I admired, the cologne, the maroon robe—"

"I was tired of listening to your teeth chatter, you silly young fool."

"I'm not as silly—or as *young*—as you seem to think, admiral. All that special attention, yet never a move toward the obvious goal. What's in this for you? —personally?"

"I—" She drew back. "Nothing for me, personally. It's for—"

"It's because I'm Recon, isn't it? That's why you want me back. You've got a stake in this—in me, specifically, and I want to know what that stake is."

"I have no idea what you're talking about."

"Don't you? Don't you want to parade me around as a Recon success story? Some kind of spokesman for Indigene rights? You and Eckersley against Shapoorian's crowd?" He shot her a deliberate challenge. "Or are you *really* Shapoorian's?"

"You do drop that name a great deal. Gotten a lot of mileage out of her blind spot over the years, haven't you?"

"Actually, I never appreciated the potential until *you* pointed it out. Now, I'm wondering why you did that. Because I'm not, you know. I'm not Recon—not Rostov Recon, certainly not HuteNamid. Being something means belonging. Belonging means someone claims you. Rostov can't. You claim it's gone, and it threw me out anyway, at least my parents did, and my parents, also according to you, are dead. Vandereaux certainly doesn't claim me. I'm not Recon, I'm certainly not Spacer, so what use am I to you?''

Silence. A frowning, angry silence. She wasn't hearing him. She was going to insist—force him back to the ship. *Not yet*, he felt Zivon cry inside him, *Please, God, not yet*. And tried to silence that voice.

But the admiral *wanted* Zivon Ryevanishov. Perhaps...

He stopped pushing Zivon aside, let Zivon kneel beside her chair, let Zivon say, ''Admiral, I *want* to work with you, I want to find answers and solutions for you. And if you'll just give me a chance—time to sort out *what* the questions are—to find out *what* I am, I'll *be* that spokesperson you want. *Do* whatever you want. Just let me do this one thing for me. *Please*, admiral.''

Her cold gaze didn't waver. ''Oh, that's good, b—pardon me—*Dr*. Ridenour. You can tell Smith for me *your* little-boy-lost beats his all hollow.''

It took several moments for her implication to filter past Zivon's confusion. When it did, the ache in his gut told him how much he'd counted on Zivon Ryevanishov's appeal succeeding—

—and how much that—*person*—was still a part of him.

Shoving that ache aside, he jerked to his feet. When he answered, he had Zivon under control and matched her tone for tone. ''Frankly, admiral, in a purely rational sense, I sympathize with what you're trying to accomplish for the indigenes, though it's all a mental game to me. I've lost any personal stake—''

''I doubt you've ever been frank with anyone, Ridenour.''

''—But I believe in what you want to accomplish well enough to make you a deal.''

''A deal? Good God, you *have* been talking to Smith, b—''
He raised his chin.

She snorted. ''—*Dr*. Ridenour. So, what's your—deal?''

''Simple, really. You leave me here—''

''Not on your—''

''Life? That's what's at stake, ultimately, isn't it? *My* life. Which, ultimately, is mine to spend or keep. You can force me back up on that ship. Force me to tell what I know about

Wesley's system. But you can't force me to speculate further. You can't force me to go into the system and determine what's been done and how to rectify it. You can pass what I know on to others and *hope* they can manage. But do you want to gamble the integrity of the 'Net on that hope? I can tell you straight out, there is no one out there who has published on the 'Net who is going to be able to accomplish what Wesley and I together can do.''

''Cocky little devil, aren't you?''

''If you want to look at it that way.''

''And if I don't leave you here to do as you please, you'll die.''

He shrugged.

''What will you die of? Unrequited love?''

''Your sarcasm is wasted on me, admiral.'' He shoved his hands into the thick robe pockets and walked over to the painting, realized it was made of finely ground stone, not paint. He refrained from touching it, though his fingers imagined that strange texture. ''I resigned myself a long time ago to a fairly short time in this universe. If you want to force me back to *Cetacean* right now, I can't stop you. I won't even try. But I won't be there long. If I can't pursue this—thing—I've discovered here, nothing I do will have any reason—any purpose—for me ever again. Everyone has priorities. For me, Wesley's theory— and how it came to be—is one. *The* one.''

''Sometimes we can't *have* everything we want, Ridenour.''

He clenched his fist inside the pocket, wanting to strike out at something, anything. But violence would change nothing. With his luck, it would break his hand. He reached out to touch that alluring surface, denied that urge at the last minute and swung around to face Cantrell.

''I don't know about everyone else. I only know about me. I've never *wanted* anything before. Never *dared* to want. Can you *possibly* understand that? Force me away and I won't live long enough to provide anything for Eckersley's pet project— or Danislav's—or yours. Not a threat, admiral, a prediction. A person needs purpose to live. Bullshitting the 'NetAT isn't purpose. Convincing them of the truth is.''

* * *

"Are you under arrest? Are the Grans?" It was all very confusing to a tired brain. What was legal. What wasn't.

Ever since the *Cetacean* had entered the system, Anevai had been watching every word, fearful she'd slip and reveal something she shouldn't. Now, Cantrell knew more what was going on than she did, and instead of the declaration of martial law she'd feared, instead of her entire family being packed off into space, there was this quiet sorting of loyalties.

It was all very confusing.

"Not as far as I can tell," her mother answered calmly. "The admiral told us she's not going to arrest anyone—yet. She's leaving mother and father here because they, quote, are needed here. But technically, they are accessories to the cover-up."

"You're going back to Tunica with Cantrell?"

"I must."

"Why?"

"Barb and Will won't speak to anyone else, and the admiral very correctly wants to take them with her for observation. As you know, I disagreed with the Council on that issue from the beginning."

"And what about Hononomii?"

"She very carefully reminded us he's still under her control and that remaining available would be highly advisable."

"I can't believe she'll leave it at that."

"I suspect she'll leave her security all around. But I'm not concerned. This entire situation has gotten out of control. Barb and Will need more than we can give them."

"They're getting worse, aren't they?"

Cholena nodded. "And the admiral thinks it's similar to what is happening with your brother. If we can save him, I suspect we can save them all. Perhaps the *Cetacean*'s PsychTechs will have answers we don't."

"I don't know. Seems to me, if you want to solve the problem, you should get Nayati to undo what he did, for starters."

"What did Nayati do?"

She shook her head. "I don't know exactly."

"Your father says he's told Nayati to give himself up."

"He won't."

"We should give him that chance."

"I'll give him the chance. But if he doesn't show, I'll personally go haul his butt to Cantrell."

Cholena chuckled softly and stroked her hair. "I believe you could."

"What about—" She glanced up at her mother, then back to the design she was etching in the dirt at her feet. "Dad misses you—wants you back home, but he's no better, Mum. Worse, if anything."

"I know. I saw him this morning."

"What was he doing here?"

"Ah, now, that's *our* business, Miss Snoop."

"I suppose." Anevai poked a hole in the middle of Rainbow's head. "Do you suppose the Cocheta were a bunch of chauvinistic jackasses?"

"I don't know. Why?"

"Because of the way Nayati—and Dad—have been acting."

Cholena laughed. "No, child. Your father can't transfer the blame for his actions. He's always been overly fond of wielding power and getting his own way. It's getting worse as he gets older, but I won't make excuses for him. I certainly hope I'll be able to talk sense into him."

"You will see him, then? You *are* coming home?"

"Of course. He's behaving foolishly. One way or the other, the admiral's people will find the Caves. It's only sensible we introduce them politely rather than begin a war over a foregone conclusion."

"Mom, what can I do for Stephen? He's truly, severely warped. I don't think he wants to be, but—"

"Why do you feel that?"

Her face grew warm. "A lot of things. There's a tape—"

"Your father told me about it."

"Well, if you get a chance, take a look at it, will you? The whole thing, not the edited version. I'm truly scared for Stephen, and I'm in over my head. I told you about his ravings during the storm. But mostly . . ."

"Mostly?" her mother prompted gently.

"It's his pills. He's always taking something, and in the Cave, after he—kissed—me, I felt—" Her blush deepened.

She'd never had trouble discussing anything with her mother. Not from the first time she'd noticed she and Nayati weren't quite so similar as she'd thought. But this—

She took a long breath, even the memory caused a glow. "We–we—" Even now, she couldn't use 'love' to describe what had happened. "Every time he touched me, I felt it all through my body. Especially—you know."

Her mother was smiling indulgently. "He's a very attractive young man, Anevai. I'm not sure I've ever received quite so *intimate* an introduction." Her mother's hand cupped her face and she smiled reassuringly. "I'd be concerned if you *hadn't* reacted."

"Intimate, indeed," she said sourly. "He didn't expose that much skin in the Cave." Her mother looked a question. "Usually, he's more modest than the hill people. —Don't you see? He *took* something—just so he could . . . And when he kissed me, I could *taste* it. —And he won't tell me what it was."

"And you think you got some into your system, and that's what caused your reactions?"

She nodded.

"Don't *you* go searching for excuses, young lady. I've heard nothing to chastise you—or your young man—for."

"He's not *my* young man! *I* don't want him. He's totally VOSsed out and can't even touch me without taking a damned—"

"Gently, Anevai. If he did take a drug and you honestly believe you might have gotten some in your system, let's check it out. But *judge* his reasons. Was it his intent to hurt you?"

She thought of his stricken look when she'd collapsed and shook her head. "No, I'm certain of that. And I didn't notice any side effects, other than a muzzy brain at the first. After I ate and got moving, I seemed all right."

"Well?"

"I'd still appreciate it if you'd check it out."

"I'll clear it with Sgt. Fonteccio. Bother you to have her there? I'm sure it would make Cantrell's people happier."

She shook her head.

"All right, I'll suggest she go into the clinic with us. You want me to take the samples, or mother?"

"No offense intended, but I'll take Grams."

If Stephen Ridenour was not in absolute control, he faked it exceedingly well.

"Egocentric, aren't you?" she said, finally. "All that matters is *your* life and satisfaction of *your* curiosity. Haven't you any sense of social responsibility?"

"At the risk of losing any credibility I may have with you, none what-so-ever. —Now, which is it? Do I stay or do I go?"

"Before I answer that, will you answer me something?"

"Possibly. Probably."

"What happened to your signal?"

"What signal?"

"Dammit, boy, this is no time to play games. What did you do to your beeper signal?"

"I don't have a beeper."

"This has ceased to be amusing! Your signal spent all last night playing williwisp around the planet. Now what did you do?"

"Admiral, I don't . . ." His brow puckered. "When I was in surgery? Did you have Dr. McKenna put it in then? Is that how you tracked me here?"

"What do you think? After losing you twice in one day, and hauling you back in pieces the last time?"

"You had no ri—" Flashing eyes closed, fists clenched and when he had that temper of his under control, he started over. "I don't know what happened, admiral. I suppose Wesley might have—"

"Smith was with me all the time. —Stephen, listen to me. If you're telling me the truth, if *you* didn't do anything, someone else did. Someone here who knows you're carrying a beeper. Someone with the capacity to disrupt it. Now where did you spend the night?"

"It was just a—hole in the mountains—a cave—somewhere."

"Could Anevai have done anything?"

His mouth tightened stubbornly.

"My God, Stephen. This is no time for misplaced chivalry. Have you *any* concept of what you're dealing with?"

"More than you, admiral. Please, I'm tired of this. Go? Or stay?"

"You don't leave me any real choice do you?"

"Depends on how you look at it, admiral."

"Do you even know how to signal with the beeper?"

Stephen shrugged.

"There's an implant in your skull behind your left—no, you're left-dominant aren't you?—your right ear. We can signal you with it—a beep only you will hear. There's a code. One you haven't time to learn, dammit. If you hear the beep, tap the implant—echo the signal if you're all right. If you're not, or if you need help at any time, just hit SOS."

"SOS?"

"SOS. Three short taps. Three long—never mind. Just tap it—any sequence. Chet's got your channel on constant monitoring—he won't expect coherency."

"I suppose."

"You stay, you use the damn beeper."

"Whatever."

"This had better be worth it."

"It will be. Maybe not for you. Maybe not for Alliance. But it will be worth it."

"How long?"

"One day? Two? Who knows? I'm sure you and Paul Corlaney can keep each—"

She grabbed his arm, jerked him around to face her. "You want to be treated as an adult, boy, you start acting like one. You give me a time, or by God, I'll—"

Stephen pulled away and knelt on the hearthside furs. "Goodbye, admiral. Send in Wesley, will you, please?"

For an unresponsive moment, she considered forcing him, but that was senseless, and at the moment she mistrusted her own motivations. She reached into the briefcase for the copy of Smith's paper—Stephen's copy—she'd brought with her as Smith-bait. Now, perhaps a different sort of—bait.

"Del d'Bugger!" she said sharply.

His head jerked up.

She dropped the notebook on the floor.

His eyes glittered at her.

She raised an eyebrow. "You left it in your room—that night. Open. Careless of you, don't you think? Perhaps you thought SciCorps janitors wouldn't recognize it for what it was."

The glitter disappeared.

She allowed herself a tight smile. "I thought it *might* prove useful."

Without waiting for an answer, she turned on her heel and left the room.

i

Wesley paced the wooded pathway, two of Cantrell's security clinging leechlike to his shadow. Both wings of the Tyeewapi complex were ominously silent. Damned unfair, leaving a fellow all alone with no company other than disgustingly polite security guards. Bad enough Cantrell ran off with Stephen, Anevai had to disappear into the clinic without a word of explanation.

Anevai returned first, showered and changed into jeans and a loose cotton shirt, her mother and Fonteccio at her elbows. They worked their way down the clinic stairs deep in conversation. Wesley hurried toward her, breaking into a run at the last and skidding to a halt in front of her.

"You okay, kid?"

She nodded, glanced toward the house. "Stephen not out yet?"

"Not yet. Why, Anevai? Why didn't you wait? You knew I wouldn't leave you on your own."

"Can't answer that for sure, Wesley. Stephen's notion, not mine. What did you say to him?"

He registered Fonteccio's silent presence, and shook his head. "Not important."

Cantrell exited the Tyeewapi home. She wasn't happy, but she was alone. He exchanged a look with Anevai, took the three steps in one jump.

A heavy hand intercepted him. "He asked for you."

"So let me go!" he said, and pushed against Cantrell's hold.

"Before you go in, I want you to know one thing."

"I'm listening."

"I don't like the changes I'm seeing in Stephen Ridenour. That boy has a hell of a future if he doesn't blow it. You can make or break him with what you do over the next few hours. He's nothing but a child, much as he likes to think differently. You, Smith, have no such excuse. I expect you to act like an adult and counsel him wisely. *And* protect him. If anything happens to him, I will hold you, personally, responsible. If he's not up to facing the 'NetAT, *you* do. He's your only insurance against instant arrest. Do I make myself clear?"

"If anything happens to him, admiral, anything I could have stopped, I'll turn myself in."

She grunted skeptically. "One other thing. He knows nothing about those 'Cocheta Libraries' of yours, or of anything else going on here. See that it stays that way."

The Libraries had been momentary leverage to convince Cantrell his goodwill was worth cultivating; he hadn't considered mentioning them to Stephen. Still: "Pretty unreasonable, if you want his help."

"I don't," she said firmly. "Not any longer. Now I want to keep him out of everything I can. For his sake, Smith: the more he knows, the more his freedom is compromised." She released his arm and stepped out into the twilight. "—Dr. Tyeewapi, are you ready to leave?"

"Any time, admiral."

"I'll have security meet you in the garden."

"Fine." Cholena hugged Anevai briefly, and left.

Wesley met Anevai's eyes, saw his own confusion mirrored there as Cantrell told Briggs to have Paul meet them at the Spaceport.

"Admiral? What—"

She swung around. "Why are you still here? I told you, your precious Stephen is waiting for you."

"You're leaving me here?"

She spoke around him to Anevai. "I'm taking your mother and the two researchers back to Tunica, but I'm leaving a portable SecCom with you: direct link to Chet Hamilton's crew aboard *Cetacean*. I can have people here in minutes if you need help. Don't fail me in this, girl."

"I'll try not to, admiral."

Wesley looked from one to the other, not liking the sound of that exchange at all. But Anevai faced him without flinching, and Cantrell ignored him, signalled her guards and left.

Wesley's hazel-eyed gaze burned Cantrell's back until it disappeared into the trees, then darted to her. That parting shot of Cantrell's had him worried. It should, Anevai thought. Had her worried too. Cantrell had purposely placed her in the hot seat. Had given Stephen the freedom he demanded while placing responsibility for his safety and anything else that might go wrong directly on Anevai Tyeewapi's head.

Wesley harrumphed, and turned toward the door.

"Wesley?" She touched his arm. He twitched away.

"Leave me alone. You heard Cantrell. He asked for *me*."

"I don't really know if I should."

"You make some sort of deal with Cantrell and figure that gives you *rights*?"

She shook her head. "It's not about Cantrell; no *deal* anyway, just an agreement to keep her informed. —Only smart, Wes. It's for Stephen, as you'd realize if you'd listened to what Cantrell said."

His back thudded against the door, his hands thrust deep into his pockets. "I'm listening now. What about him?"

She thought about screams in the night, pills and making love, about that manic single-minded climb, and wondered how to explain to Wesley that his long-awaited partner in crime was a doper and a lunatic. Wesley reached forward, tilting her head to face him, that suspicious look tempering. "Hey, kid, we're friends, right?"

She nodded.

"And we're always up front with each other, also right?"

She nodded again.

"Well? What's the problem?"

But the words just wouldn't form.

He put his arms around her waist and pulled her up against him, swaying gently. "C'mon, kiddo, out with it."

"Stop it." She shoved him away, and backed up to lean on the railing, hands thrust into her pockets, realized her unconscious echo of his previous stance and straightened, shaking her hands out.

"Hey, Anevai, this is me. The old Wesser. What's going on?"

Finally, using the only argument that might work: "Take it easy on him, Wes. He's very—fragile right now."

"You, too, kiddo? How can *you* think I'd do anything to hurt him?"

"Not on purpose, maybe, but . . . Just give him time, Wes. Don't be surprised if he's a little . . . Shit, just let *him* come to *you*."

"Is he *mad* at me?"

"Not mad, Wes. Scared. At least I think that's what's wrong."

"Of me? *Why?*"

Ordering a fish not to swim would be simpler. "Every time you come near him, Smith, you're all over him."

"Am not!"

Could he really be so unconscious of what he projected around Stephen? That would be a first. "From his point of view, you certainly are. So cool it awhile, hotshot. Stephen . . . lost out on an awful lot somewhere along the way. Got some funny notions about . . . people."

He stared into the twilight for a long time. From beyond the trees, children's voices shouting, the occasional call to supper: life returning to normal in Acoma. He smiled sort of sadly, then turned silently toward the door.

"Wesley?"

He didn't look back. "Have to figure it out some time, don't I? Give me a few minutes alone with him before you join us, will you?"

"Sure. I'll go get something liquid and healthy for Stephen— grans said she'd leave stuff in the kitchen. Want some?"

"Yeah. —Sure." Distraction. A distracted Wesser, particularly where food was involved, was a frightening contradiction in terms.

"We've got the run of the place. The grans are staying in the hogan in the—"

"Yeah. —Sure."

Shit. "Be careful, Wes. I don't want either of my friends hurt."

With an absentminded, in-passing pat on her arm: "Neither do I, kiddo. Neither do I."

A dark lump topped with madly curling hair huddled beside the nonexistent fire, hugging something to its chest. Wesley tossed the two packs in a chair near the door, wondering what to do, now they had the privacy he'd worked so hard to achieve.

But Stephen stole the initiative from him again, said, without looking up, "Have I just ruined everything, Wesley?"

Ruined everything? Just what *had* he told Cantrell? He responded cautiously, "I don't know, son. Can't really say till we see the results, can we?"

He crossed the room and knelt on the stone hearth, waited until Stephen lifted his eyes. Saw gut-deep terror in that look and relaxed a notch. The kid had just blown the entire situation out of proportion, was seeing monsters where none existed.

"Besides," he said, "why should you have to trust my judgment? From what I've seen, yours is pretty sound."

A shaky smile rewarded his effort. "Because I believed in you?"

He relaxed another notch. "That, too, kid."

A dimple: irresistible temptation. He brushed that hint of smile with the back of a finger. Contrary to Anevai's warnings, far from avoiding his touch, Stephen melted into it. Wesley forced a grin, and pulled his hand away.

Stephen's multicolored gaze followed that withdrawal, then dropped to the ashes. One long-fingered hand left the notebook it was hugging, reached out and touched the cold hearth, sweeping through the empty air above—until the opal eyes flickered and caught Wesley watching, then the hand tucked in against his side, and he turned his face away.

"I'm sorry, Wesley," he said quietly. "I didn't mean to cause trouble. Not for you. It's just—I had to talk to you— away from the ship. I—"

"Let it ride, kid. You didn't cause problems. Not really. Bit of excitement is all. Cantrell will come about."

"I—" An unsteady breath. "—hope so. Can *you* understand? Anevai doesn't—though she pretends to. I don't want Them to make me someone else. I—I don't like me very much, but strangers—scare me. I can't imagine getting to know— someone else—from the inside."

He didn't understand. Not at all. What were they, if not strangers? "Stephen, I—"

Stephen said, staring into the ashes, "Sometimes, I want to be dead."

"Stephen, I—"

"But mostly, death terrifies me. —My immortality is gone."

"Your—" Never long on patience, he was losing what little was left. Enough was . . . "What the *hell* are you talking about?"

"My immortality. My—reason for being," Stephen explained to the ashes. "I'm not papa's; mama disowned me; I—I can't create a new line, so I'll die and be nowhere. Nothing."

He should laugh at the whole ridiculous conversation, but somehow couldn't. Because Stephen *wasn't* laughing. *Sometimes, I want to be dead.* Not that unusual a sentiment in youthful academicians, but Stephen Ridenour was out of that race now, his future a clear shot to success—until this most recent escapade. In a Wesley Smith a maneuver like the theft of the Mini was all part of the game: a challenge to the authorities to try their best against his father's lawyers. In a Stephen Ridenour, it *was* a form of suicide. He could be one of the numerous overachievers terrified of real success, or he could be downright crazy.

Crazy he understood. The other—lord, he used to have those for breakfast. And *he* had to make Stephen see sense? How in hell had he ever gotten queued for this program?

Finally, in a halfhearted attempt at humor, "I could use a reason for being. You want to be mine?"

Opal eyes lifted, filled with something he didn't *want* to understand.

"Wesley?"

Relieved, he twisted around to greet Anevai. Stephen ducked his head and edged away, setting that notebook on the floor beside him—the far side—making room for Anevai between them—

—and somehow Wesley felt no inclination to object.

Anevai set a tray of sandwiches and three mugs of—he took a sip of his and wrinkled his lip—*fruit juice* on the hearth, and following a whispered question to Stephen, laid a fire, showed Stephen how to use the start-cube and let him pull the key and toss it in. The resultant fire-flare turned Stephen's wide-eyed fascination to liquid gold and banished that strange mood at last.

"The admiral's gone," Anevai announced, handing Stephen a sandwich. "She said to tell you good luck."

Stephen thanked her politely, then picked at the bread, taking a single, nibbling bite, chewing slowly, apparently considering his stomach's quite audible complaints irrelevant. The juice roused substantially greater interest.

About the admiral's departure, he said nothing. He huddled down into the robe, sipping the juice and running an occasional listless hand through his hair, separating the strands, unconsciously taming the damp curls.

He didn't seem to notice when Anevai settled between them, or the tiny squeak that accompanied her. When she shifted, easing a squirming bit of blue from her shirtfront, he simply leaned aside to give her room.

"Hey, CodeHead," Anevai whispered, right into his ear, an insult not even he could ignore, particularly when combined with an elbow in the rib. "See what I found?"

Dark-rimmed, haunted eyes drifted from Anevai's face to the squirming bit of blue, and a slow smile broke through. Stephen set the mug down and wiped his hands on the robe before taking the pii'chum kit with exaggerated care.

"They brought them here from the barn. Mum says Cantrell's

people had all the animals moved out. Quarantined the area until they know..."

"They *know* all they need to know." Stephen pressed the squirming kit to his chest and rubbed his chin over the ungrateful furball. "I'm not pressing charges. They have no right to disrupt—"

"Stuff it, Ridenour." Anevai stopped him with a finger to his mouth. "Done is done, and if they hadn't, little junior wouldn't be here, now would he?"

Stephen buried his glower in fur, the kitten, if the audible purr was any indication, finding this arrangement thoroughly satisfactory.

Side by side, staring into the fire, equally VOSsed, one with a kitten under his chin, the other with a half-eaten sandwich lying forgotten in her lap: two truant kids whose escapades had kept him up all night and now they were going to just sit there?

"You two are about as exciting as a toothache." He pulled a leather backrest from the fireside stand, flipped it open facing them and settled; reached past Anevai for a sandwich—made it two for efficiency's sake and said, "Okay, children, out with it. What happened?"

Food, a bath, bed, in that order.

God, it had been a long day.

The Tyeewapis, Bennett, Liu: Cantrell gratefully relinquished the details to TJ and took the transport directly to her onWorld quarters—and found Paul's assigned guard waiting outside her suite.

She lifted an eyebrow toward the door. "He in there?"

Buck Buchanan nodded. "Said he wanted to talk to you soon as you got back."

"Wonderful."

"Had his supper delivered here."

Things were looking up. "Have they cleared the dishes yet?"

"Nossir."

Even better.

"You want me in there, sir?"

"I think I can handle it."

She knocked rather than letting herself in unannounced. The door opened on a rather distracted Paul Corlaney, who became a rather startled Paul Corlaney.

"Hello, Paul," she said. "Mind if I come in?" And to Buck: "I'll beep if I need help." She brushed past Paul to the table. He'd ordered enough for an army and barely touched it. Criminal, to her way of thinking. "I'm starved. This looks wonderful. Mind?"

He waved a helpless Go ahead.

"Thanks." She filled a plate, scrounged a breadstick and a handful of... "Where did you find sand—"

Bouquet of man-made glow, champagne on ice, wax-puddled candles, congealed sauces, limp salad, Albion sandberries (a favorite of hers since childhood)—and Paul slouched against the wall, sipping Scotch and glowering over the rim. "For me?"

He shrugged. "So much for surprises."

"I'm sorry, Paul."

"Not your fault."

"No, it's not. And you should have known better; but it's still sweet and I'm sorry I missed it."

He shrugged again and sauntered toward the table, the glower abating. "Not a total loss." Mouthing one of the sandberries, he slipped his arms around her and waited. She chuckled, dropped the breadstick and pulled him down to steal the berry, swallowed without losing contact, then kissed him for real, which tasted better than the berry. It had been a long time—a very long time.

But all good things...

"God, I'm tired." With a final squeeze, she broke away to seek out the sofa's soft cushions, taking the loaded plate with her. Paul popped the cork, brought the bottle and two glasses to settle beside her—close, but not crowding.

She took a sip, let the bubbles tour her tongue. "Very nice—local?"

He nodded.

"Hmm. Sandberries, Scotch-style whiskey, champagne—these Recons of yours do it all, don't they?"

He grinned. "Ian MacPhail would object to that. He's got a major paper ready for release—"

"When he's got backstock enough to export?"

The grin widened. "Impossible. Besides, makes no difference—he could name his price. That synthesized shit they pass off as drinkable Out There just doesn't make it, once you've had the real thing. Takes peat—or a RealWorld equivalent—to do it. The magic lies in the serendipity. —That's what Ian's paper's about."

"Serendipity."

He shrugged. "Speaking of—did you find the kid?"

She nodded. "Almost wish I hadn't."

"I won't even ask. —He's okay, though?"

"Better than he deserves."

"And Anevai?"

"Fine."

"Can I see her?"

She shrugged. "Why not?"

"Now?"

"Bit of a ride."

"She isn't here?"

"We left her in Acoma."

"*Acoma?* What is she—"

She held up a hand and, between bites and sips, told him the whole story: the kids' trek, meeting Bennett and Liu—even her suspicions regarding the researchers' condition—holding nothing back. No real reason to: he could find out easily enough, if he left this room a free man. And whether or not he left this room a free man depended on his responses to these very subjects.

"Is Sakiimagan at home? or did you arrest him?"

"At home—under surveillance. —Why?"

"I told you I'd talk to him—try to make him see sense—soon as you got back."

"It'll wait."

"But—"

"I don't think now would be a very good time. He and Cholena are—catching up on lost time."

"You mean they're actually speaking to one another?"

She grinned. "I imagine they'll get around to that, too—eventually."

He chuckled softly. "Good for them." And took another sip. "Got a problem, then, don't I?"

"Problem?"

His eyes dropped to her hand resting on a cushion between them.

"Free time. *Lots* of free time." He began tracing her hand with one, wine-damp fingertip. "Might get into trouble if I'm not kept busy."

She turned her hand, clasped his for an instant, then settled into the corner, tucking the cushion under her elbow, putting him at business-distance.

"All right, Paul, let's keep you busy. The Tyeewapis aren't the only people with things to settle."

He looked away. "I—don't know what you mean."

"You said last night you had something to tell me."

His lips tightened. He got up and moved to the glass door, using the rift-view to avoid her eyes.

"Time, Paul. No more lies, no more prevarications. In short—cut the bullshit."

He still refused to look at her, but his head dipped an acknowledgment.

"Hononomii Tyeewapi calls *Dena Cocheta* from the ship and gets 'Nayati' online. Anevai blames this Nayati for her brother's condition and vows not to let some *eons-dead lunatic* destroy her world. Wesley talks of *Cocheta libraries* hidden under the mountains. You still going to maintain we're talking teenage code words?"

"You really mean you haven't guessed?"

"I—avoid guessing, Paul."

A thought-filled moment later: "You asked me once why I chose HuteNamid rather than some other 'Tank. I—avoided answering. First of all, I was asked—politely. Second, it's out of the way—Council, the 'NetAT, SciCorps: as far as they're concerned, Paul Corlaney doesn't exist anymore, and that suits me just fine. Thirdly—" A shaky laugh. "We've found it, love."

"*It* covers a lot of territory, Corlaney."

"Dammit, Cantrell!" His voice crackled frustration, anger, maybe a little disappointment. "Give me a break here!"

"Hell if. I told you—I don't *guess*. Not anymore. Not where you're concerned."

He swung around, a dark bitter scowl marring his face. "Do the words sapient life form mean anything to you anymore?"

"Intelligent life?"

"About bloody time, Cantrell. Yes, intelligent life—of a sort."

"Do you mean nontechnological? That's all over the universe."

"Of course not. I mean, no live bodies. No cities. No artifactual continuum, at least that we've found so far. Only the Libraries."

"Libraries? As in books?"

"No books, Loro." The anger vanished in an enthusiastic researcher-esque glow. "Tapes. The machinery to operate them. We're—still working on reading them."

"Where are these Libraries, Paul?"

"I don't know. Only a few of the People do."

"Sakiimagan?"

"Among others. I'm not certain who all. The People found the Libraries, and it took me fifteen years to get them to trust me with what little I do know. I *want* to share it with you. I *think* I can get Sakiima's help, but that's why I couldn't let you take me up to that ship of yours. If you had, he'd never trust me again, and I can't show you a damn thing without him."

"If what you told me is the truth—"

"It *is*, dammit!"

"*If* it's the truth, the investigation can't be left up to amateurs. SciCorps Central—"

"Don't try to convince me Central is *better qualified* to orchestrate the probe. It's the first damned *time*, Cantrell. So don't give me SciCorps' patented *expert advisers* lecture."

"I wasn't about to. But you know there are people who've dedicated their lives to preparing for this eventuality. Isn't it possible those individuals deserve to participate? Don't you think their advice might just prove useful?"

"No."

"I've always known you were an arrogant bastard, Paul, but

this surpasses even my wildest expectations. You think the handful of rogue researchers and Recon colonials you've assembled here can guess their way through this better than experts in communications and ethnobiology?''

"Absolutely. Don't forget, I've met those experts—worked with no few of them—and *you've* yet to meet the *real* production crew here." He came back to the couch, knelt and clasped her hand. "Come with me tomorrow—"

"To these Libraries?"

He shook his head. "I told you. Not without Sakiima. —To the office. Let me introduce you—show you *why* this crew of rogue researchers can handle it."

She resisted the pull. "Not tomorrow, Paul. I'm returning to *Cetacean*. But I'll be back. I'll leave you here to convert Sakiimagan."

"Thanks." He groaned and buried his face in the cushions. "God, I'm too old for this."

She slid down beside him and patted his back. "You've got some time, old man. Cholena and McKenna have decided to consolidate. We're taking Bennett and Liu up to the *Cetacean*, Stephen and Smith will keep each other busy for days. But I want Nayati, hear? *And* I want *proof* of these Libraries." No answer, just a hunted look, and on a sudden impulse: "Come up with me tomorrow."

He twisted around and slumped to the floor. "Can't."

"Not much real chance you'll convert Sakiimagan, now you've made your stand with us. We'll find the Libraries without him."

"He'll listen—he must, after he's read Anevai's letter—she puts the blame for Hononomii's condition squarely on Nayati, and if it *is* like Barb and Will—you're convinced the similarity is real?"

"Much as I can be without direct corroboration." She shifted again, tucking her shoulder and arm in under him, smoothing her hand along his stomach. Unfair tactics, but the shifting tensions in his body were more honest than his face. The arm around her shoulders tightened convulsively, drawing her close. "I know Anevai blames Nayati—she also blames the Cocheta—and *she* doesn't consider the Libraries to be nearly as sacrosanct as you all seem to. She'd prefer to defer to her father's authority, but she's prepared to take me there if Sakiimagan refuses. And if they *are* the key—''

''Loren, I'm trying.''

''Are you? I'm beginning to wonder. Sakiimagan's a bit too canny for me to buy this altruistic coverup you suggest. Nonhuman intelligence, nonhuman technology. Potential gold mine, Paul.''

''Loren, that's not—''

''Isn't it? Is Smith's paper only the first of many? Is that why its precursors are so difficult to find? Is it because it *does* lie outside humanity's technological stream?''

No tension, just a shift away from her touch.

''I thought that's what your boy was here to find out.''

That sounded more like jealousy of Ridenour than guilt. She pulled him back into the curve of her arm.

''Just thought you might make things easier for us all.''

''Sorry, that's Wesley's business, and somehow I doubt he'll care to share it with a Del d'Bugger.''

''Oh, he will. One way or the other.''

''Hell will freeze first.''

She smiled. ''Somehow, I don't think so, Paul.''

''And th–then . . .'' Stephen's teeth chattered on the rim of his mug. He lowered the mug to his lap, practically on top of the sleeping kitten—''Then you . . .''—and yawned widely into a shaking hand. ''Scuze . . . sh–showed up with th' robe . . . and . . .''

His head nodded, he swayed; Anevai muttered a low curse and steadied him with an arm around his shoulders, took the mug away and set it on the stone hearth beside the hardly-touched sandwich.

Wesley noticed *she* showed no hesitation about—how had she put it?—putting *her* hands all over Stephen, but he curbed childish resentment and whispered hopefully, ''Need help?''

''Just rescue junior, will you? His mom's got a box in the kitchen.''

The kitten burrowed into the pile of his sibs, found a free spigot and mouthed it sleepily, ambition which faded rapidly.

Wesley ran a finger along the adult pii'chum's soft head, and whispered, "Take good care of him, mama."

Back fireside, other ambition was failing.

"I thought the sugar hit would be good for him," Anevai whispered, glancing down at Stephen's drooping head. "Looks like I was wrong."

"Not your fault, kid. He's been crashing planes and climbing mountains when he shouldn't even be on his feet. Let's get him to bed."

"Grandfather said to use Hononomii's room."

He nodded and touched Stephen's bowed shoulder. "C'mon, kid." Foggy confusion blinked up at him. "Bedtime."

But Stephen eluded his touch, twisting in Anevai's hold to grasp her arms and beg hoarsely, "Nayati?"

"Stephen, for crying out loud, don't start on that. I told you—"

"No time to nego—negotiate. Cantrell—gone. You, me, Wes—Nayati. *Please*, Anevai."

"Let *go*," Anevai protested. "That *hurts*!"

Stephen's hands snapped away, but his intensity didn't fade. "Please, Anevai?"

"All right! All right! But I'm tired, too. First thing tomorrow I'll—"

"What's this about Nayati?"

"Stephen insists he needs to talk with him," Anevai explained. "I thought he'd given it up—I *told* him Nayati's gone crazy, but—"

A pull at his arm demanded his attention. "Must talk with him, Wesley. Important!"

He patted Stephen's hand, but looked to Anevai. "He's not seri—"

She shook her head, flicked a glance at Stephen's increasingly obstinate expression, and said, "I can leave a message in our old tree. Chances are, he won't find it—will ignore it if he does—but it'll salve my conscience."

He looked down into those incredible eyes that were holding so desperately to awareness. "Okay, kid, whatever you want. But only if you shut up and go to your room quietly. Want me to carry you?"

"No!" Indignation incarnate.

He was very good—he didn't even laugh. "So, let's see you walk."

That indignation got Stephen to his feet—even held him there for a while—but for all the kid wasn't much bigger than Anevai, struggling to keep him upright soon had all three of them exhausted.

Going up the stairs, he let Anevai and the kid lead, staying deliberately at the rear—he even controlled the urge to help push—awaiting the inevitable.

A dizzy sway just short of the first landing, a perfectly timed tug, and the kid was draped over his shoulder. A whap on the rump shut him up, a threat to drop him on his head kept him that way till Wesley dumped him on the bed, where he bounced, rolled to the wall in a flash of bare legs, and up to his knees to face them, red-faced and gasping.

Unfair to carry a tired kid upside down with a shoulder pressed into his belly—probably seeing double or even triple.

"Stephen, I—"

"He'll live," Anevai interrupted, and to Stephen: "Stay!" and pulling Wesley back into the hallway: "Clothes in the dresser, blankets in the closet—whatever you need, help yourself—just get him warm—do whatever it takes to make him sleep. Promise him anything: we can renegotiate in the morning when he's ready to make sense."

Stephen, relaxed now he was alone, yawned and rubbed his eyes, caught him watching through the half-open door, and smiled. A shy, inviting smile that hovered around his mouth. Anevai's judgment call had been right on the mark—still, he couldn't help answering with a wink, and out of the corner of his mouth, "Warm and asleep, huh? My pleasure, darlin'."

"No it's not, Smith."

"Huh?"

A fist punched his ribs. "Dammit, Wesley Smith, don't you scare him."

He laughed and quit teasing. "Tell you what, love, I'll get him settled, then go crash in the den like I—"

"No!"

Stephen glanced up, a worried look; Wesley shushed her, reassured Stephen with another wink.

Anevai continued, tempering her voice: "Don't leave him alone. He has—nightmares. Sick as he is, waking up in a strange place, he could panic, maybe even hurt himself."

He glanced through the door again. Stephen had slipped off the bed to kneel on the floor beside the shelves containing the shell collection Hononomii had foisted off on his grandparents years ago, keeping his hands behind his back like a kid terrified of breaking something.

He sighed. "If you insist, kiddo." And when she still hesitated, jerked his head toward the stairs. "Go on, git. I'll behave myself."

ii

"What kind of shell is this, Wes?"

Wesley suspended rummaging through drawers to glance over his shoulder.

Stephen sat cross-legged on the bed, carefully turning a shell this way and that, his face a ludicrous blend of exhaustion and insatiable curiosity.

"Hell if I know, kid." He crossed the room to rescue the shell, registered the chill in Stephen's hands and said, "Ask Anevai tomorrow, if you must know. She knows all about that shit. Almost as bad as her brother."

"Hononomii?"

"Only one she's got. He collected all that garbage. This is his room—when he visits."

An uneasy glance around the room reminded Wesley of the horrific association Hononomii's name held for Stephen, and he said gently:

"Hey, kid, forget it. For now, give me the robe and hop into bed."

Tired eyes circled around to him, staring blankly.

"*Sleep*, kid. Ever hear of it? It's when your eyes close and refuse to open for hours. Healthy, so I've been told."

With a soundless chuckle, Stephen oozed off the bed and

shrugged the dirty robe into Wesley's hands. Nice shoulders. Very nice shoulders. Nicer even than the SportVids, now he had the leisure to examine them at close hand, even scratched and bruised.

A faint line of an old scar, the red of a healing one offered temptation to an exploring finger. A worried opal eye glimmered over one of those nice shoulders, and with an inarticulate murmur, the kid slipped back to the bed and into the corner, wrapping his arms against visible shivers.

Anevai's warning ringing in his ears, Wesley controlled his baser instincts, grinned reassuringly, and tossed the robe over a chair. (It slid off into a pile on the floor.)

The search for clean clothes—of which there were plenty—provided welcome distraction. Most looked to be castoffs of Anevai's and Hononomii's, a bounty which, from the range of sizes, had been accumulating for years.

A groan, quickly swallowed; a creak of bedsprings. He turned to a shapeless, sheet-draped lump in the middle of the king-size bed.

"Hey, kid, you want a blanket?"

Not that he needed an answer. The kid was frozen clear through. He rejected lightweight pajamas and tossed sweat pants (obviously from before Hononomii's current *au-then-ticity* phase) and a thick sweater onto the lump. "Here, sunshine, work your way into these."

The kid didn't even sit up, just—burrowed. Not quite the fit he was used to, considering the small fortune of painted-on pants and tailored jacket he'd worn to dinner, but Wesley heard no complaints, only soft, appreciative murmurs which faded into silence as the burrowing stopped.

Wesley shucked his own clothes into a pile on the floor and pulled on the rejected pajama pants. The shirt he tossed toward the dresser. (It slid off into a pile on the floor.) *He* wasn't cold, nor likely to become so any time soon.

Unlike the lump in the bed. Wesley found a comforter in the closet and settled it over the lump, folding the sheet down so he could see that face (sometimes neatness counted), mentally cataloging alternate ways of warming the lump up; methods

Anevai had vehemently nixed, then had the nerve to say *Stay with him. He has nightmares . . .*

Damned unfair to a frustrated old man, missy, he thought; and dropped into a chair, propping his feet on the edge of the bed and feeling a great deal older than his thirty-whatever years at the moment. Two days without sleep could do that to a man. Two days and a schitzy kid who insisted on taking his half of a very large bed out of the middle.

Frustrating, considering Ridenour's greeting in the bathhouse, his fireside come-ahead. But Anevai was probably right. In this environment, they could too easily lose their sense of perspective. *He* could recover it, of course; but he wasn't so sure about Ridenour.

He tipped his head, seeking a new perspective, and lost some of his regret in a repulsive surge of paternal instinct. Long dark lashes brushed wind-reddened cheeks. A hand, still lost in a knitted sleeve, tucked up against a sweetly curved, full-lipped mouth. Funny: awake, that face did a fair imitation of maturity.

Like the kitten burrowing into its mother's warmth, Stephen pressed his nose into the pillow until only dark curls remained visible. Not the kid's best feature, for his money; naturally it had been the first thing he'd noticed—but luckily, there was little else to remind him of Jean-Phillipe and that initial negative impression hadn't survived.

He frowned and slouched deeper into the chair, propping his elbows on the armrests, his feet on the edge of the bed, and found his head rather unwillingly replaying that first meeting with Stephen. He'd seemed just one more academy-clone pretty-boy out to play the game with whoever would net him the most political advantage. Circumstances had combined to dispel that image, but what if he'd acted solely on that first impression? Would the clone have remained?

Poor Stephen. It wasn't *his* fault. Not really. But somebody ought to tell him the charm he'd exposed here had infinitely more—influential-potential than the all-too-common Vandereaux Style. Of course, that intruding innocence could just be Ridenour's *own* Style—his own warped way of achieving the same ends.

Or maybe he was just chameleon enough to realize the Clone wasn't working here and was trying a new tactic.

Hands all over him, indeed, Annie-girl. Based on what? Sure, he'd mauled Stephen a bit at first, but that had been a— test. Had Stephen complained to her? If so, what about his actions downstairs—what about the bathhouse? If Cantrell's men hadn't been on the prowl . . . After all, Cantrell had said Stephen was headed to *his* room that night. . . .

He yawned and shook his head until his brain rattled, rubbed his face with both hands. If he'd had any sense at all, he'd have armed himself with the bawdiest book he could find in the Tyeewapi library.

Anevai was right about one thing. He did find the kid highly attractive. World-born children being forbidden SciCorps Researchers, relationships within the planetary ThinkTanks tended toward spontaneous and eventually grew distractingly incestuous. He'd partied with most of his fellow scientists and those he hadn't personally been to bed (or wherever) with, he might as well have been. He had hundreds of friends here—good friends— but Stephen was special.

The fact he was unattached, however casually, to anyone Wesley knew was part of it, but more importantly, Stephen *knew* the 'Net, the way he did. The way no one else ever had. . . . No one except Granny San, and she had long since left him alone.

Anevai had tried—God knew she had—and she'd provided invaluable insights to a revolutionary concept. But she hadn't the education to help him take it further. Stephen had. And someday. . .

A nodding near-fall from the chair later, he realized that he'd have to crowd Stephen a bit, or wake up on his head on the floor. Besides, he comforted his conscience, even old men needed their beauty sleep.

"Stephen," he said softly, easing onto the bed and working his elbow under Stephen's pillow for balance, "this is just me."

Dark curls gave way to a sunburned nose as Stephen rolled into the circle of his arm—

—and nearly pushed him off the bed. Wesley caught the headboard and maneuvered them both over far enough that he could release Stephen. If he cared to. Somehow, he didn't— care to, that was—and since Stephen only yawned widely and burrowed closer, tucking the sweater-enveloped hand between his cheek and Wesley's chest . . .

One temptation after another. He hugged Stephen's shoulders briefly. "That's the way, kiddo, make yourself at home."

Another ever-so-slight shiver.

"Still cold?"

"L'il . . . bit," a breathy whisper that brushed his chest with warm air answered, and: "Thanks." As Wesley tucked the quilt behind him and drew it around his head.

Stephen's breathing soon achieved hypnotic regularity. Wesley drifted with that rhythm, eyelids drooping, head nodding until his chin rested on silky curls. He moved his jaw lazily from side to side, savoring the sensation, desisting when Stephen stirred and murmured distressedly.

"Sorry, child," he murmured. "Go back to sleep."

Stirring stopped. Breathing steadied.

Child. He was, too, regardless of what the calendar said. How could anyone, even Mialla Shapoorian's devil's spawn, even think of hurting him? Bijan Shapoorian had been a too-rich, runny-nosed, mean-tempered, bit-brained punk when he'd known him at Vandereaux.

He doubted time had improved the model.

Poor kid. No one—no matter how frustratingly schitz—should have to put up with that shithead. On the other hand . . .

"What is it that makes *me* put up with *you*, Stevie-lad?" he whispered, brushing a stray curl back with one finger. "You know, I was ready to write you both off, you and Anevai?"

The question had been rhetorical. He'd thought the kid, whose head rested still as death against his chest, was asleep, but:

"You wouldn't. Couldn't." Surprisingly articulate for a corpse. "With us gone, who would worship at your oversized, but disgustingly brilliant feet?"

He chuckled. Answering laughter vibrated his side. He hugged the corpse and murmured into the curls, "Love you, Stevie-lad."

Silent laughter died in a caught breath. His stomach muscles twitched as a chill hand crept from the sleeve and snuck around to join its counterpart burrowing underneath him. Enough to make a man think Anevai Tyeewapi didn't know what she was talking about. Enough to dispel that childlike image from a man's mind once and for all in favor of more intriguing first impressions.

Anevai was, after all, only a kid from a delightfully guileless Recon world. Far cry from a lad who, though born Recon, had spent his *important* growing years in a far more sophisticated environment.

Could be, Ms. Tyeewapi had it all wrong.

Temptation gained a foothold. It had been a long time since he'd had new territory worth exploring. His hand drifted over Stephen's back, slowly, lazily, Stephen's arms tightened and thoughts of new territory or reasons vanished.

"My God, Stephen," he said, shifting onto his elbow, slipping his hands under the oversized sweater, "I *do* love you."

The kid froze. One slow breath. Another. A single violent shudder.

Then again, could be Anevai had it absolutely right.

Stephen's arms retreated, worked up between them, not protesting—not encouraging either.

"Stephen?" He carefully extricated himself, and Stephen turned to the wall, huddling around his pillow. "Stephen, what's wrong?"

"Why, Wesley?" Surprisingly steady answer, considering.

"Why, what, kid?"

"Why couldn't you just be my friend?"

"I—Good God, boy, I *am* your friend. I said I love you, I didn't mean—"

A chilling, over-the-shoulder stare. "Didn't you?" Bitterness. Profound disgust, though impossible to determine at what—or whom—it was directed. "You love me. Anevai loves me." The eye disappeared. "Everybody loves me. How nice."

"Stephen, I—"

With a heave that shook the bed, Stephen faced him, bracing on one sweater-draped arm.

"You love me, Wes? Well, I suppose I love you, too. —So—what?"

"So . . . What's your problem, boy?"

"I'm not a boy."

"Well, you're sure as hell not a girl."

Full lips tightened. Opal eyes glittered through dark, slitted lashes.

"Stephen, what's *wrong*?" He traced those hard lines with his finger. . . . "Too fast for you? You want me to—"

. . . and jerked his hand away as without warning those hard lines relaxed, and the tense body turned supple, slithering over him—around him.

"Wrong, Wes?" Warm breath brushed his ear. "What could possibly be wrong? To quote a very wise and clever fellow, 'You want me, you got me.' "

Not so long ago, he'd been absolutely certain he wanted Stephen Ridenour right where he was, doing precisely what he was doing; now he had him, those actions failed even momentary distraction. Those actions were too damned sophisticated for what the—*boy*—projected.

Warm breath against his neck, sophisticated motions growing harsh, fiercely intense—

—*Painful*, dammit!

An angry sweep of his arm flung Stephen thudding into the wall. He thrust himself off the bed, whirled to face harsh, rapid breathing: Ridenour, crouched in his corner among pillows and tangled covers.

Like some damned rabid animal.

"What's wrong, Wes?" The sarcastic whisper from that shadowed face grated on his adrenalined nerves. "Isn't that what you wanted? Don't you—love me?"

"You're mad! Stark, raving crazy!"

More gasping breaths, a sharp, bitter laugh. "Yeah? So what else is new?"

Frozen silence: an unbelieving moment in which revulsion overpowered thought. Another exhaled bark of laughter broke that silence, and Ridenour threw himself back down, face to the wall.

Wesley drew a few deep breaths of his own, unclenching his fists. He couldn't kill the bastard; he'd promised Anevai, after all. Besides, his promise to keep an eye on Ridenour had taken on a whole new importance: damned if he'd let this lunatic loose on the good people of Acoma.

"C'mon back, Wes." Nothing but a quiet, self-possessed suggestion... "You're safe from me. I won't touch you, so long as you do me the favor of keeping your hands to yourself." As though the whole thing was *his* fault.

"I'm fine right where I am."

The uncompromising back shrugged. "Whatever."

"What happened, Paul?" The last of the wine had gone flat. Cantrell stretched to set the glass on the out-of-reach side table. "Were you there?"

"After a fashion."

Hard to think straight, sitting on the floor next to Paul, her ears buzzing with fatigue and alcohol, harder still to keep one's mind off the hand tracing her shoulder and up her neck to her earlobe. But she had a report to give McKenna tomorrow. A report about two extremely out-of-touch-with-reality researchers.

"What fashion?"

"It was a party. A typical solve-the-burning-questions-of-the-Universe party. We'd all had enough even Wesley was beginning to make sense."

"Frightening."

"Exceedingly. Anyway, Wesley was planning his newest plan to disrupt the 'Net—"

"That's not funny, Paul."

"Sure it is. Wesley plans the destruction of the 'Net at least twice a week. It keeps him out of trouble."

"God."

"*He* thinks he is."

"Pan, maybe. Or Dionysus. —*Can* he?"

"How would I know? I doubt it. Even if he could, he wouldn't. Wesley talks about a lot of things. Carrying through is another matter. He's not malicious, Loro, just a bit crazed."

"God. God. And god."

He chuckled. "Anyway, Wesley was off on his tangent and Barb said something about the Libraries—I couldn't catch what—no one did except Nayati—"

"Hatawa was there?"

"Of course."

"There is no of course, Paul. No one's yet admitted the man exists."

"Hardly a man. Little more than a boy, really. Twenty-two—maybe three—'NetStan.'"

"At least two years older than Stephen, but you've all been fiercely protective of him and ready to condemn Stephen for a malicious spy. You do confuse a person, Corlaney."

His arm tightened around her shoulders. "I didn't know, Loren. None of us knew. Will you at least grant us that? With Ridenour's credentials, no one thought to check. Nayati is one of ours. His mother took ill when he was born—complications treated too late—his parents were among the true Reconstructionists."

"Those who've disappeared into the hills?"

"Literally. At least, his father did, after Nayati's mother died. Nayati was a child, five or six as I understand."

"His father left him here?"

He nodded. "With the boy's maternal grandparents. They died about ten years ago, but Nayati had attached himself pretty firmly to Hononomii by then and seems to have gotten on."

"And was Hononomii also at this party?"

"What par—oh, yes. The thing at the *Miakoda*. I don't know who all was there. Wes was carrying on. Barb made this comment, Nayati said something to her, she yelled no, and Will got into it, then she and Will were arguing, close to blows, Nayati was trying to calm them down, and before we realized anything serious was happening, Barb was down, Will had her by the throat and Nayati was trying to pull him off."

"And then?" she asked into an overlong pause.

"That's when they shut down."

"Shut down? Just like that?"

"Just like that."

"*Something* must have triggered it."

He raised a hand and from his concerned expression, she reckoned he honestly didn't know.

"And Nayati? What does *he* say?"

"He's as confused as the rest of us."

"You still think so? After Anevai's linked him with her brother's condition?"

"Yes, I do. If he *is* the cause, he doesn't realize it."

"Could be he's simply avoiding responsibility."

"Nayati isn't like that."

"You're certain?"

"Absolutely."

He looked exhausted. She let the matter drop and lay back against the pillows, urging him down where she could comfortably rub his head and temples with one wandering hand, absently pondering his strange ambivalence toward Stephen. At times, he seemed almost jealous, but jealousy wasn't like him. Why that crack about being *too old?* Could he truly feel threatened by Stephen's mere youth?

She ran her fingers through his silvery hair. There were those reports about dangerous side effects to the restoration virus. *She'd* never suffered any (felt better than she had at twenty), and he'd denied them, but could *that* be his real reason for never contacting her? Some chivalrous attempt to protect her from the truth? They'd been out of touch for years before his transfer here.

Paul stirred at her touch, kissed her wrist, then turned his attention to the parts of her body more nearly at hand. Or mouth, as the case might be.

"Why silver, Paul?"

"Hmmm?" he murmured against her neck.

She tipped her head back, encouraging exploration. "Why did your hair turn silver? Mine never did. In fact, the old color returned. Is there something you're not telling me?"

His mouth had worked its way to her chin, his fingers parted her robe, began some exploration of their own, and he was rapidly passing beyond coherent conversation. Moments ago, she'd been inclined much the same way. Now . . .

She worked a hand between them, pressed against his mouth, pushing him gently but insistently back. Opening her eyes and lowering her chin, she found him studying her with perplexed eyes.

"Paul, are you—all right? *Is* the virus all right?"

His mouth twisted behind her fingers. "Worried about your prescription, admiral?"

She moved her hand to stroke his cheek. "No, Doc. Yours."

A lopsided smile bent to kiss her palm.

"Thank you for that, my dear," he murmured and rolled away to reach for the glass on the sidetable. He took a sip, grimaced, and set it back down, scraping his tongue against his teeth. "God, that's awful."

"Well?"

He looked down at her, brows lifted. "Well, what?"

"Damn you, Paul Corlaney!"

She punched him hard in the ribs, and he grunted, then choked laughingly, "Okay, okay! I did it for you."

"The hell!"

"Monosyllabic, aren't we?" She glared at him; he grinned. "You always said the only problem with the Process was you'd never see how I looked with gray hair, so I—adjusted it."

"You mean chemically?"

The grin widened. "You might say that."

Suddenly she realized the implications of his answer. She looked at the flowers glowing softly on the dinner table among their naturally tinted wild-type relatives, then back to him.

"Good God, Paul, how many games have you been playing here?"

"Loro, I promise you, only the hair's changed. It was a totally harmless little experiment."

"With yourself as a damned guinea pig!"

"Hardly. I'm not stupid, my dear. I'd tried it on animals—remind me to show you Anevai's blue cat—and decided to give it a try, just in case you ever deigned to honor us with your presence."

He turned his head, affording her several different views, then grinned down at her again. "How do you like it?"

She stared at him in disbelief. "You—*idiot!*"

"But do you like it?"

Instead of answering immediately, she straddled him, propping her back against his raised knees. The last vestige of moonlight glinted on the hair in question. She ran her fingers through it, letting it fall where it chose. It had been a ridiculously frivolous chance to take, one out of character with *why mess with perfection* Paul Corlaney, but the effect was striking, and she found herself grinning like a fool.

"I *love* it."

He said softly, "Then do you think, my lovely lady admiral, we could possibly dispense with the chatter for . . . say . . . an hour?"

She let her hand drift down his cheek, followed the line of his jaw with her fingertips, up and around his ear and down his neck to his collar where she slipped a button.

"Make it—" She slipped a second. "—two."

The pillows responsible for the painful lump under Wesley's neck sailed across the room, bounced off the wall and sent Stephen's shell crashing to the floor.

A startled half-cry, quickly smothered, escaped the quilt.

God dammit, Wesley thought and swept a frustrated hand through his hair. "Stephen."

No answer, unless the quilt drawn higher over his head counted. Did the clone think him blind *and* deaf?

Clone. *What if he isn't, Smith?* he asked himself. What if Anevai was right? What if he was just a scared kid dealing with a Situation the only way he could figure? So what he had sheet-techniques out of hell? As Adm. Cantrell had so succinctly pointed out, Wesley Smith was the so-called adult here—

—and if Wesley Smith didn't want Adm. Cantrell on his neck, he'd better straighten things out.

He disentangled himself from the pile of blankets with some difficulty. Joints stiff, feet swollen—he wanted back down at his own altitude and in his own bed with someone uncomplicated.

"Stephen?"

The lump froze into unnatural stillness. He slumped down on the edge of the mattress and patted that lump. A solid pat: as impersonal as he knew how to make it.

Which was pretty damned impersonal the way he felt at the moment.

"C'mon, son. Talk to me. I'm sorry if I scared you. I'm *sorry* if I embarrassed you. I'm *sorry* if I hurt you. God knows, I never meant to do any of those things. Don't let it ruin what we've started."

A tremor under his hand.

"Please, son, *talk* to me."

An explosive, twisting lunge and suddenly Stephen was hugging him around the waist hard enough to surprise a grunt out of him.

"W—Wesley, *I'm* s—sorry. I—I didn't mean to say that. You want me to make love to you?" Stephen's head tipped back, revealing pale eyes that were only marginally sane. "I can, Wes. I *will*. Anything you want. Or, if—if you'd r—rather—I—If you I—like to—" His gaze shifted about the room as though searching the shadows for options. Blood wicked between teeth clenched on his lower lip. "A—anything, j—just please d—don't hate me." The curly head dropped against his chest. "Please, Wesley. Don't hate me."

He'd gotten himself a live one this time. Pretty. Definitely pretty, but melodramatic as hell. He patted the curls. "I don't hate you, kid. You're just not real clear in your signals, you know?"

"D—do you want me to . . . ?"

Liquid crystal eyes met his. Eyes that reflected the blue of the sweater, the reds and greens of the quilt puddled around them. Eyes that, according to Anevai, couldn't lie.

He touched Stephen's face, his tanned fingers warm and dark next to the boy's pallid skin. Skin that would be the envy of any Stationer, of any age, any gender: pearlescent and smooth, any hint of beard eradicated—if it had ever existed. He'd forgotten Stationer vanities. Perhaps he'd forgotten other things as well. Relationships in academies tended toward—unusual. He himself had done no few things once he'd find—distasteful—now.

But distaste melted as Stephen leaned into his touch, those telltale eyes closing with the desperate trust of a child.

Young—God, he was so young.

He ran his hand up into the dark waves, and Stephen relaxed against him, that smooth cheek brushing his collarbone, unsteady breaths warming his chest. He rubbed Stephen's back gently, losing all sense of time, concentrating on easing the residual tension. As those unsteady breaths grew regular, he settled them together into the pillows, Stephen shifting against him, easily, naturally, without a hint of that former desperation.

But:

Soft murmurs in some Recon language. Gentle hands floating across his chest. Ridenour was not asleep.

Young, yes, but not that young. And far from innocent.

"Stephen?"

"*Chto eta, otiets?*"

He grinned at no one and nothing in particular. Recon pillow-talk—he loved it—and a new flavor, at that.

Warm breath travelled up his neck, soft nuzzling that bore no resemblance to Ridenour's previous efforts.

"Stephen, are you awake?" he asked, suddenly suspicious.

"*Pochemu, otiets?*"

That difference and the strange, popping kiss in the vicinity of his chin should have warned him.

"Please don' hate me, *otiets*." Warm breath tickled his ear. "*Pozhalusta*, papa. Don' send me 'way..."

Papa?

"Shit!"

Stephen jerked awake, blinked cross-eyed at him, startlement and dismay chasing each other across his flushed face.

"Thanks, Ridenour. I'm a lot of things, but not..." The jest, too obviously lost on the horrified youngster, died in his throat. "Stephen, I'm sorry. I didn't mean..."

Ridenour pushed up on arms that shook, and pressed himself against the wall.

"Stephen, I—"

He stopped as Stephen's hand raised, the thick sleeve falling back to bare the thin, high-tendoned wrist. "No, Wes. It's me. *I* was wrong to—I can't—"

To what? Can't—

But before Wesley could ask, Stephen had escaped over the foot of the bed and slipped quietly out the door.

iii

The light winked off in Stephen's window and Anevai, with a sigh of relief, slumped down on the garden step, bracing her back against the rail, physically tired, but not yet sleepy, free (now) to enjoy this quiet reunion with her second favorite spot in the universe.

As her backbone settled, joint by aching joint, into a more natural curve, she realized just how worried she'd been about leaving those two together. While she had faith in Wesley's good intentions, she had none in his good sense. But Stephen *couldn't* be left alone—and there'd been no excuse for keeping them apart.

She tucked up a foot to rest her chin on her knee, straightened quickly at a sharp prick from her pocket and dug after the culprit.

A spark of moonlight in her hand: Stephen's button.

By now, this little chunk of crystal had more exchange value than ten shares of Albion Enterprises stock. Nayati had thrown it at her in contempt of her defense of Stephen, Cantrell's security had used it to link her to Stephen's disappearance, Cantrell herself had returned it to her—a pledge of good faith. Even Wesley had used it as the key to his file. She chuckled wryly. She could probably get those ten shares from Wesley—

She closed her fingers around the spark.

—if she were willing to part with her button.

He should have explained, but there was nothing to say. He should have known better... He'd done—something. Said—something. And now, he couldn't remember.

Wood cracked and settled; flames flared around his hand. Stephen jerked back, lost his balance and thumped to the stone hearth, bruising the last unbruised square centimeter on his body.

Can't do anything right, can you, Ridenour? he thought, cleaning singed fingers with a MediWipe from the pack.

MediWipes, concentrated food, self-warming blankets, even antibiotics and tablets to clarify water into good honest—tasteless—HOH. And pills. Lots of pills.

Hell, he could survive forever.

Survive, yes. Live? —He shuddered and settled his elbow on the pack, stared into the flames, while sections blackened and glowed, burst into flame or fell into the growing pile of coals. Strange use for so rare a substance . . . Anevai claimed this was windfall and useless for anything else, still it seemed—sacrilegious somehow. He concentrated on that morality, forced others from his mind.

Everything was as they'd left it. His almost-empty mug, the sandwich he hadn't dared risk . . . (though God knew he'd been hungry enough). Just not smart, trying something new right before, (he had to laugh) retiring. But the fruit juice had been safe—he'd recognized it from—before . . . Wesley's crumbs and mostly full mug.

He topped Wesley's mug off with the dregs from his and sipped. Warm, but still eminently palatable.

Working the pill pouch free of the pack's folds, he sorted out McKenna's prescriptions and took them in a single handful, choking them down with the fruit juice, wondering if Anevai would object to these as well. The girl had no concept of the chemical reactions his body had learned to handle over the years.

He dared not sleep—the nightmares were too surface-close tonight. If only he weren't so tired . . .

He tipped, caught his balance with a hand to the floor . . .

. . . not the floor. His copy of *Harmonies of the 'Net*, lying in the shadows. Careless of him to leave it there.

You left it open . . . Cantrell had tried to make such a big deal of that—security gaffe—as though it made a difference. So what if the janitor saw it? So what if anyone saw it. So what if *Smith* saw it? It wouldn't make any difference. Not now.

He tucked it into the pack, eased the diary free to make room. The poor thing's back, old and weak to begin with, was crushed from its recent harsh treatment. He offered a silent apology to young Zivon Ryevanishov and, opening it at random, found a drawing of a shell with an odd triple whorl and the accompanying passage written in that language he could no longer read, a picture which could have been a child's rendition of the shell lying in pieces beside Hononomii's bed, victim of Wesley's bank shot.

The book dropped to his lap, his hands gone numb.

It seemed everything tonight was designed to remind him of Smith . . . and his failed mission. He shuddered, drew his knees up and buried his head in his arms, not wanting to think about that, not wanting to think at all.

He knew one sure way to stop thinking. It had worked well enough, once upon a time, though he hadn't touched the stuff in years—

—until this morning, when he'd destroyed Anevai's budding friendship with the poison. She pretended otherwise, but she still mistrusted him, hated him for giving her the Eudoxin, however inadvertently. He couldn't say he blamed her, he hadn't exactly thanked those who'd introduced him to the stuff.

He'd never taken it alone—not for recreation—though he'd been told others did. He didn't really know why he'd brought it, unless his subconscious, more honest than his forebrain, had anticipated Wesley's true motivation all along.

Wesley had said he loved him—in the heat of close vicinity and frayed nerves. He'd known that sort of love and wanted none of it.

"Hypocrite," he berated himself. He could have—should have. Solve all his problems with Smith in fifteen minutes.

Except that it wouldn't. Wesley had a reputation—both here and at the academy—but it was one of open sexuality, his past partners universally endorsing his character and generosity. Wesley would never understand the Eudoxin, and the alternatives would disgust him.

As if he weren't already disgusted.

Thin, flexible vial. Red and blue pills. Large enough, he discovered, to snap into pieces. Cursing himself for a fool, he slipped one small bit under his tongue and leaned back, awaiting oblivion.

His tongue burned. He moved the drug around his mouth, spreading its bitterness. Stupid—doubly so, considering the threat of red-tinged bile earlier today. Should have eaten more. Should have . . . The last of the pill dissolved, and he gulped fruit juice, resisting the temptation to rinse it around his mouth and eliminate the pill's flavor altogether.

He'd forgotten how thoroughly he hated that taste.

His fingers found and caressed the diary. To take his mind off that repulsive flavor, he picked the diary up and began leafing through it, reading bits and pieces of his childhood; bits and pieces all too often obscured within that unknown language.

He turned to the picture of the shell, felt warmth spread through him: the fire, Eudoxin, or the memories that picture roused. He couldn't tell—

—and at the moment, didn't care.

His memory had betrayed him: this section wasn't written in that strange language at all. He could read it perfectly, could remember clearly the day he'd found that shell. . . .

Zivon cradled the shell against his chest, using both hands. Mama had said Never bring those dirty things in the house, but he didn't know what kind of shell it was, and Petros didn't know, and Granther didn't know, and Petros had said Papa was in the house, and if Papa didn't know, the only way they could figure it out was to look it up in the computer, and to do that, he had to have it to look at—didn't he?

He'd washed the shell in a bucket so it wasn't dirty anymore, but now it was dripping, and he was afraid Mama might be mad anyway, but Mama wasn't in the kitchen, so he couldn't ask her for permission and he had to find Papa so he tiptoed inside and down the hall to the den looking for Papa.

Papa was there, all right. So was Mama. Papa had his arms around Mama and was swinging her around in circles the way Zivon loved him to do, only Mama wasn't laughing. She scolded Papa—told him to put her down or he'd scare the baby right out of her.

Baby? What baby? Suddenly, Zivon wished he was Someplace Else.

Zivon knew about babies. Meesha had a baby when Milo was sent away 'cause he wasn't good enough to keep.

And Zivon had not been very good lately. Mama was mad all the time. He'd been very stupid and put on the funny hat— Granther had said so—and then he'd been very bad and followed Papa to the slaughterhouse, and he'd brought the shells into the house and made dirt all over, and he'd left the gate open . . . and now Nevya was dead—

And he wasn't Papa's.

Maybe he wasn't good enough to keep either. Maybe Mama

was going to get rid of him. Maybe Papa wanted him sent away, too. Papa was laughing as he set Mama down like a kitten, then knelt in front of her and pressed his face to her tummy.

Papa wanted the Replacement.

Papa wanted his own son—not Somebody Else's.

Zivon felt tears and rubbed them away with the back of his hand. The shell slipped, shattered as it hit the slate floor. Mama spun around, her skirts a red blur, Papa looked up.

They both looked mad. Mama looked at the shell·pieces and the wet puddle, and looked madder.

"I–I'm s–sorry, Mama. I'm s–s–s—"

"Zivon? What's the matter?" Papa didn't sound mad, but he turned and ran anyway. Ran down the hall and out the door. Ran to the barn and crawled up to the loft his secret way to burrow into the hay, holding his breath to stop snivelling. He heard Papa calling, but didn't answer.

Then he heard Mama say, "Let him sulk. He'll come out when he's ready. Don't let him spoil it, Stef."

And their voices trailed off in the direction of the fields.

They were mad and they were going to replace him, unless— unless he was very very good. Unless he could make them want not to send him away. There were all Papa's Round-tuits. The ones Papa laughed and said soon Zivon would be a man and able to do for her when Mama scolded Papa to do them.

If he was a man, the baby couldn't be a replacement.

He fixed the stall in the barn—no matter the boards were a little crooked and his thumb hurt where he'd hit it with the hammer. Three times. He stacked the equipment, sorted the box of leather bits, filled all the obatsi feed bins. He tried to clean the stalls, but the wheelbarrow refused to go through the mud. It fell over and he couldn't pull it back up so he kicked it and limped away, sure he'd broken a toe, and thinking Granthers' Bad Words.

At the house he weeded and weeded and weeded and hauled the weeds to the compost pile and put rocks around the edge of the garden like Mama wanted. The wheelbarrow was still stuck so he used the biggest grain bucket to haul fertilzer up from the barn. He tugged and hauled and pulled, inch by inch, until he was very tired and hurt all over, but he didn't care. Mama

*would be happy now and Papa would be happy and they'd stop
wanting to replace him . . . even if he wasn't Papa's.*

He was almost to the house when he saw Mama and Papa
coming up from the woods. They had their arms around each
other and stopped every few steps to kiss.

He pulled harder, heard Papa call his name and looked at
the house, at the not-quite-done-garden. He heard Papa's
running steps, pulled again. Hard. But his muddy fingers
slipped. He fell onto his backside, the bucket tipped and spread
muddy fertizler all over him.

"What have you done to my garden?"

She didn't like it.

Zivon bit his lip and looked down along the rather crooked
row of rocks, looked up at Mama and slowly stood up.

"Look at you! Get cleaned up, then go to your room.
—Don't you dare track that inside. —Down in the barn. —And
don't forget that bucket!"

Papa said, "Honey, he was only trying to—"

"I know what he was trying to do, but he pulled up every
vegetable in the garden! He's got to learn he doesn't know
everything and how to tell when he doesn't."

He limped down to the barn, the empty bucket banging
against his knee. He wanted to kick it down the hill. In the
barn, he rinsed the bucket and filled it again with clear water,
then sat beside it and scrubbed his hands, picking pieces of grit
out.

Back to the house, to the back door, hoping to sneak in. But
almost before the door was open, Mama's voice yelled Shoes!

He left his shoes to dry on the porch, climbed the stairs to
his room, pulled his nightshirt on, then sat on the edge of his
bed, picking more grit out of his palm and knee.

No supper; that was for sure.

He pulled out his diary and started to draw the shell from
memory.

It was the not-for-sures that mattered.

"Well, hello there."

Anevai jumped up from the step, crouched and ready to
defend herself against—

"—Nayati."

"In the flesh." He sauntered out of the moon-shadowed trees as she straightened. "Welcome home, love."

He reached for her; she stepped back.

He smiled disarmingly and held up his hands. "Truce, Annie-girl, truce. I'm sorry, I truly am. I've been a little—impulsive—of late."

"You do have a way of understating, cousin."

He held out a hand, ghostly glow in the moonlight, glint of silver at the wrist. "Friends?"

She grasped his wrist. "You were more right the first time. Call it a temporary truce."

His grip tightened. His shadowy head tipped to the side. "When did Cantrell let you go?"

Moonlight gave him the advantage: he could see her face—read her expressions.

She jerked free. "What makes you think she *let* me go?"

He laughed, loud and clear. "Long walk home, Annie-girl."

"Don't call me that. So happens we—" She bit her lip, trying to stop the anger that was making her stupid.

"We? *We* what?"

"Escaped."

"We? Who *we*?"

She raised her chin. "Me. And Stephen Ridenour."

Another laugh. "I *knew* it. So what's Cantrell's angle this time?"

She tightened her lips on another protest. She was too tired and too fuzzy-headed to argue sense into Nayati tonight.

"So, why are you out alone so late at night, little girl? Aren't you afraid the *tl'eehona'ai* will get you?"

"The 'one who rules the night?' High opinion you have of yourself these days, Hatawa. Besides, *Winema* rules the night here."

Nayati's teeth gleamed in the shadows. "So you claim. But something brought you out. What?"

"When did I need an excuse to enjoy the open air? I've been cooped with the canned stuff for too long, that's all." She glanced up at the dark window. Now was her chance to tell him. If Stephen really was that crazy . . . "Nayati, Stephen—" But of a sudden, she couldn't say it.

"What about little Stevie?"

Her hackles bristled. "*You* can damn well show a bit more respect, Hatawa. *Dr. Ridenour* is doing his damnedest to help us out of the mess *you* created."

"You're so pretty when you swear."

"Bastard."

"Speaking of bastards, how is Ridenour? Is he still around? Or did Cantrell cart him off?"

"How did you—" She bit her lip. He'd been using the 'Net without permission, been in files he wasn't supposed to be in, and might well know things about Stephen he shouldn't—but she wasn't about to give him the satisfaction of knowing that. "None of your business. —See you around."

He took the steps in a bound and planted himself between her and the door.

"And I'll see you to your room."

"Hell if."

"I'm wounded. I thought to say Hi to Ridenour. We are, after all, old friends."

"Funny notion of friendship you have."

"Oh, but we are, I assure you."

"You just stay away from him, Hatawa."

He grasped her arm. "You be careful what you tell that spacer, you hear me, girl?"

Black in this covered portico. Too black to see Nayati as more than a shadow, but the tone was serious. More the Nayati she'd grown up with than the tode who'd been in WetWare residence lately.

"What are you afraid of, Nayati?"

The shadowed stance shifted back to todish arrogance. "Afraid? I'm not afraid, girl, I just don't want to see our world turned into another Rostov."

"Rostov?" She searched her memory, found a connection. "Rostov was a shutdown: BiosSys crash with no funds for recovery. That *couldn't* happen—"

"Bullshit."

"What do you mean?"

A long pause, then the shadow shrugged. "Sure, why not? Rostov suffered a Bios crash all right, helped along by a few bombs from OuterSpace. But by that time, the 'Link was shut down, so nobody ever knew."

"But *you* do."

"Ask your father. *He's* the one who told me."

"I don't believe you."

"No? You're *negotiating* with people scared spitless of Recons and GravityWells—how do you think they'll react to the Cocheta who *are* the world?"

"So, the Cocheta are worlds, now? You're VOSsier than Ridenour."

"Think so? You let Cantrell in on the secrets of the Libraries and see how long it takes for xenophobia to set in. *I'm* ready. The Cocheta are. Are you?"

She edged toward the door. "Go back to your Caves and Cocheta gods. Do whatever you damnwell please, I don't care, but you keep away from me, and you keep away from Stephen."

She slammed the door shut behind her, for the first time regretting her people's rejection of outer locks. She scanned the dark kitchen for a weapon, but the door remained quiet, and when she snuck a look through the curtain, Nayati was gone.

She let the curtain fall and slumped against the doorframe. She'd tell Stephen she couldn't find him. Let Stephen and Wesley settle their business and get Stephen back to Cantrell before Nayati could get at him.

But maybe Nayati *should* get at him. If Nayati was right, if Rostov *had* been destroyed by phobic spacers, maybe she should listen less to Cantrell and more to Nayati. More worrisome was the possibility that her father *believed* . . .

She silenced the what ifs. She was tired, that was all. Her father would never knowingly set her up for arrest, not even to preserve his daughter from the annihilation of their world. Without her world, without her family, there'd be nothing to live *for?*

The stairs swam in and out of focus. Enough to make a person seriously consider closing her eyes. But then, the person might fall down the steps and have to start climbing all over again.

Fire crackled and snapped in the fireplace below. Strange. Should be out by now. She retraced a step and leaned over the rail.

Stephen. Sitting cross-legged, his diary in his lap, staring into the flames. The idiot was supposed to be in bed.

"Stephen?" she whispered.

He didn't even twitch. She sighed and went to him.

"Stephen?"

His lower lip trembled. One of the tears he denied crept down his cheek.

"Stephen?" She touched his arm.

He jumped.

"Stephen, what's wrong?"

"Anevai?" Spook-eyes sparkled through the tears. "I can read it."

"Huh?"

His notebook hit the floor. He grabbed her and hugged her breathless. "I can read it!" And he kissed her long and hard.

Bitter burning on her tongue sparked memory. No doubt this time what it was. She shoved him away and scrubbed her mouth with the back of her hand. "Ugh! You've been taking that—*stuff* again."

"But—you don't understand—"

"I understand plenty, Ridenour. You keep your hands off me until that junk is out of your system."

Radiance faded. His hands drifted down her arms and he withdrew to the far side of the fireplace, where he huddled, raking his fingers through his hair, rubbing his face hard. Then: "What are you doing here?" Cold. Abrupt.

"I like that. Not even *Hi-how-are-ya*."

"Hi-how-are-you. What are you doing here?"

"Sleepwalking, Grace-n-Charm." She crossed her fingers behind her back, asked to appease him: "What did you find in your book?"

He snatched the notebook up and cradled it in his arms, scowling at her over the top. "Nothing."

Appeasement turned to curiosity. "Not fair, Ridenour. —What did you mean you can read it now? Couldn't you before?"

"Never mind. You don't want to know."

"Do, too."

"Shit." He dropped his face into his hands.

At least he didn't immediately tell her to go to hell. She rose to her knees, edged over to his side. "Mind if I look?"

A shoulder hunched between them. She laid a hand on it. "Please, Stephen? Just to look at the pictures. Did you draw them?"

Another scowl faded to weary resignation. He opened the book, carefully angling it so she couldn't see the words. People, animals, rocks: a child's memories. She intercepted Stephen's anxious gaze.

"Diary, right?"

He nodded.

"Yours?"

Another nod.

She pointed to a picture of a woolly creature with a smaller one standing next to it. Made out a name, recalled it from one of his ramblings. "Meesha?"

A third nod.

His folks, poor, dead Nevyah, others he'd never mentioned. His mother's cats, and rocks, plants and wildlife. All done with careful attention to detail.

"Th–they're not very good, I'm afraid." Fear of derision— naked and unmistakable in those beautiful eyes.

"Better than I could do at that age," she reassured him.

He blushed. "Better than I could do *now*."

"I doubt that."

He traced the picture of a blond woman in a blue dress. "Mama was so much prettier. I never could get her right. . . ."

She lifted the following several pages and found a surprisingly familiar image.

"What's this?" she asked, flipping the page over.

"It's a shell I found. Papa couldn't find it registered anywhere."

"Interesting." She noticed writing on the side. In a language she couldn't read. "Is that what you can read now? What's it say?"

He shrugged.

"C'mon, Ridenour. Give."

"Don't know."

"So read it to me."

"Can't."

"You just said you could."

"Only with the help of the 'Doxin."

"Dox—? You mean that—"

His chin lifted imperceptibly. "That's right."

"Then it's not worth reading, Ridenour."

He scowled. "You don't know spit about it, Tyeewapi, so shut up."

"Stephen, how can you trust *anything* with that stuff running your neurons? Maybe you just *think* you understand. How can you . . ."

But he wasn't listening. He was staring at the book and off in VSpace again. VOSsed for sure.

Papa's head eclipsing the bar of light at the edge of the door.

"Zivon? Are you awake?"

He caught his breath in a sniff and rubbed the tears from his eyes as Papa set the candle down on the table by the bed. Papa was smiling, but Papa always smiled. That's why it hurt so much to disappoint him.

Papa sat down beside him, holding out his arms. He shook his head and wiggled away, too scared to let Papa touch him. He didn't know why—he'd never been scared of Papa.

"What's wrong, son? Won't you tell me?"

He shook his head so fast Papa's face blurred.

Papa was quiet a long time, but Zivon kept looking at his hands, trying not to waste tears.

Finally Papa said, "I saw what you did in the barn. Thank you very much. I don't know what I'd do without you, son."

He sucked his lips in between his teeth and bit down, sniffed and rubbed his nose, and eyes that kept leaking, wasting tears.

"You were trying to help Mama, too, weren't you?"

He nodded.

"You thought you were pulling the weeds?"

He nodded again.

"Zivon, —I need a hug real bad." Papa held out his hands and Zivon threw himself at Papa, hugging him as tight as he could.

"Please, don't send me away, Papa. Please, Papa?"

Papa squeezed him tight, then leaned away to look him in the eyes. "I'd never send you away. You're my son. I love you. What made you think otherwise?"

"Y–you're getting a new son. A Replacement for me. I heard Mama—"

Papa hugged him again. "My sweet, sweet Zivon, I couldn't bear to live without you. Yes, I'm happy Mama and I will have another baby, but it could never replace my Zivon, my bright, shining star. If you left me, who would watch the stars with me? —They're out tonight: sharp and clear. Shall we go see them?"

He nodded against Papa's neck, and Papa wrapped a blanket around him and carried him out to the telescope. They watched the stars until he fell asleep in Papa's lap. He woke to find himself still in Papa's lap, only they were inside now, by the fire. He snuggled closer, pressing his face against Papa's chest. Not caring when his tummy grumbled. Papa had forgotten he hadn't eaten. Papa always forgot things like that. But food didn't matter. Papa wanted him, not a dumb Replacement. He'd seen babies and they were no good. They couldn't even sit up. They cried and fell over. How could they watch the stars with their Papas?

Tears trickled down his face. So Mama had lied about that, too. But it didn't matter anymore. Mama was dead. Papa was dead.

No Papa to watch the stars with. No Papa to hold him. Never again . . .

("You like it, don't you, 'Buster-boy? I read about your daddy in that diary of yours. Started you early, didn't he?"

("No—no! Papa loved me—he did!"

("Sure he did, 'Buster-boy. Just—like—me. After all, you weren't really his. Just another pretty-boy for him to—")

iv

"No . . ." Stephen whispered. "Oh, God. Wesley. —Anevai, I—I've got to know . . ."

"For heaven's sake, Ridenour, just ask."

Swimming, wide-open spook-eyes swung around to her. "Was what P–Papa did bad?"

"Which—what, Stephen?" Anevai asked carefully, having learned caution regarding Stephen's rationality: he rarely made sense at first hearing.

"S–sometimes I—I wish I could remember everything. Other times, I—I don't want to know. But I remember the stars . . . the fire and P–Papa . . ."

Whatever words he needed weren't there. He waved a limp hand in surrender, stared into the fire, all dull-eyed exhaustion.

She said firmly, "You should be in bed."

A bleary-eyed glance at the stairs— "Not sleepy."

"Like hell."

—that shifted to her, dark and bitter. "Stay out of it, Tyeewapi."

Dammit, Smith, she thought, *what a sense of timing.*

"Okay, Ridenour, I can take a hint. None of my business." She hauled herself to sore feet. "I've got to go to bed. You want to come with me?" And at his look: "—To *sleep*, Ridenour. No strength for anything else. —And when you look like that, no inclination, either, so there."

The ugly scowl faded, and inclination underwent a momentary adjustment. He chuckled, a quiet, breathy release of tension. "Thanks anyway, Tyeewapi. I'm fine. Awake now. I'll read awhile—give Wes time to . . ."

Time to what, she wondered, but seeing no graceful way to ask; hesitant to leave him like this, but seeing no other options. She set a hand on his shoulder and murmured, "G'night, friend."

Deliberate echo of another time and place.

He smiled wanly up at her. "G'night, f—" He bit his lip and turned back to the fire.

She tightened her grip and he winced, for all it couldn't have hurt him. "What's this? Aren't we friends anymore?"

"Can't be, Tyeewapi. Not and do what we must. Please, go to bed. I'll see you in the morning . . . explain then." Muscle heaved beneath her hand. "Try to, anyway."

He opened his book, ignored her when she bent and hugged him, even when she whispered into his ear, "Friends, Stevie-lad. Until you give me a much better reason than that. G'night."

One hand on the stair railing, she glanced back at the fireplace. His knees were drawn up, the open book tucked in against his chest as he stared off into nowhere again.

Read? Like hell.

Retracing her steps, she pulled a backrest and a couple of pillows over to his side, sat down and tugged on his arm. A slow spook-eyed blink in her direction; a quiet collapse into her lap. . . .

He was asleep before his head hit the pillow.

"Paul, what *are* the Cocheta?"

At some point, they'd made it into the bedroom. Cantrell couldn't quite remember when or how, but somehow, she couldn't find the sleep her body so desperately sought.

"The Cocheta? I told you, the Library is all we've got. Tapes. Personalities."

"What do you mean: personalities?"

"That's the only way I—or anyone who's experienced the tapes—can put it."

"How old are they?"

"I don't know."

"How do you know the original owners aren't going to come home and reclaim their property?"

"I don't."

"Don't know much, do you, Paul?"

"Or too much."

She stopped stroking his hair. "What do you mean?"

"I've never hit anyone before, Loro. Not in anger."

She chuckled. "You mean Smith? Hell, Paul, he deserved it."

"Of course he did. But he has a dozen times before, too, from a dozen different victims. Why this time? Why me?"

"Always a first time, Paul."

"Maybe."

"You blaming it on those Cocheta tapes?"

He shuddered and shifted to burrow into the curve of her arm. "I wish I knew, Loro. I wish . . ."

Bare feet padded silently on carved-wood steps. Not that Anevai would notice, being far too preoccupied with the VOSsie curled in her lap.

Wesley leaned his elbows on the railing and chewed absently on one knuckle while trying to figure Anevai's unusual interest. It wasn't at all like her to tolerate crazies.

"What did you do to him, Wes?" Anevai's voice drifted up to him.

"My fault, is it?"

Her eyes opened to half-mast, she met his gaze in the mirror above the mantel.

"I'm not saying fault, Smith, only asking what caused this. He practically killed himself getting to you, now he won't even stay in the same room? *Something* happened, now what was it?"

"I didn't do a damn thing. He's the one started getting all snuggles."

Her eyes closed. Tears sparkled at the corners. "And you naturally took him up on it."

"Can you blame me?"

She shook her head. "No, Wes. No way you could have known. No way anyone could have known—"

Known what, he wondered. But she'd phased out again, staring into the fire as if Stephen's pet fascination had infected her. He worked his way slowly down the stairs, a deep, unfocussed pain in his gut. He knelt beside them, studying Stephen's sleeping face.

"What do I do, Anevai? What do I do to make him afraid of me?"

"I don't think it's you he's afraid of. I think he's afraid of what he feels for you."

And something in her face as she looked down at Stephen— "Anevai, did you and he . . ."

Her tender gaze turned to puzzlement. "Sort of."

"What the hell does that mean?"

"I can't explain. Not yet. —What happened? Why did he leave you?"

"*Nothing.* He fell asleep and when I got into bed—"

"Dammit, Wesley Smith, you promised—"

"I *told* you—" he objected, "—he'd fallen asleep." Even so, he couldn't quite meet her eyes. He'd never been less certain of his own motives. "Evidently, I woke him, and he—well, he seemed to think I was his papa." He propped his chin in his hand, felt like tearing his hair, but that would be—unrefined. And one wouldn't want to act unrefined in front of the kids. Depression lifted as Stephen murmured softly and shifted in Anevai's lap, snuggling deeper into the pillow. "I can think of worse things to be, if that's what the kid really wants. Hard to make the shift, though. He's a damned sexy little bastard."

"Not sexy, Wes."

"Not— Lord, girl, are you blind? *Look* at him."

"I am, Wesley. Have. Frequently. And I've made the same mistake—frequently."

"False signals. He's good at that, Anevai. Don't blame yourself."

"I suppose. But, I think I'm starting to figure him out. He wants—*needs*—to be touched, Wes. *Needs* to feel. I don't think he's allowed himself to feel much of anything for a terribly long time." She stroked Stephen's hair, down the side of his face. Even in sleep, he pressed his cheek into her touch, and Wesley's breath caught at the uncomfortably familiar, deceptively innocent gesture.

Anevai looked straight at him. "Sensual, Wesley. Not sexual. He's been hurt so often, everything frightens him now, though he tries to hide it. You know, I almost killed him on the way here because he wouldn't tell me."

"What are you talking about?"

"I forced emergency rations down him. He hadn't eaten, wouldn't tell me why, but he couldn't keep it down—practically turned himself inside out getting rid of it. You know he travels with a goddamn pharmacy? Because he *needs* it, Wesley. I can't imagine what it must be like. I mean, *look* at this." She held up his untouched sandwich. "He had to be starving this evening. He treats everything like it was poison. I thought at first it was some sort of Spacer insult to our cooking—but it's not."

"Sensible precaution with new food."

"But second nature—to the point of obsession—to a career *student*? Is the Vandereaux food really that bad?"

Wesley snorted. "Meals were the *only* educational part of the curriculum when I went there. I'd wager the head chef's salary at least doubled that of any prof, and I doubt that's changed; Vandereaux enjoys impressing visitors too much."

"So where'd Stephen get the reflex?"

"Who knows? Maybe the other students tried to poison him."

Anevai didn't smile. She gazed pensively down at Stephen and stroked his head. "Maybe they did."

Stephen curled halfway into her lap, his arms wrapping indiscriminately around the pillow and her leg.

"Go ahead."

He met Anevai's knowing gaze.

"Go ahead—try. He won't know the difference. Dead to the world, he is."

"Are you sure?"

She nodded.

He cupped that smooth cheek, and for a heartbeat it was the identical reaction. But suddenly:

"W–Wes?"

He jerked his hand away. Like hell the kid was asleep. That tiny catch of breath: the bastard ought to take out a patent.

Damned if he'd give a shit.

Ignoring Anevai's unspoken plea, he stood up and moved into the shadowy corner of the room to watch every elegant, beautiful movement—movements as sensual as those twists he once made in the gym. Someone should tell him he was overplaying his hand. People waking on the floor were awkward and uncontrolled, stiff, and ridiculous.

Eyes gleaming firelight gold flickered toward the stairs. A light whisper that nonetheless carried to his corner: "I could have sworn—"

"Stephen—" Anevai glanced toward Wesley's corner and shut up.

"I—I've got to go to him. See if I can—undo some of the damage." He gathered his pack up, stuffed some big notebook in, and disappeared up the staircase. A door latch clicked.

"Wesley?" A gentle, drifting whisper he refused to hear. Another click of the door latch.

Wesley stepped from the shadows. "Quite a performance."

"Wes, *don't*. For the love of human kindness, *go* to him. Give him a chance to explain. —Please."

He shook his head and passed her without slowing.

"Wes, where are you going?"

"Out."

V

"*Paul, —for the love of—Get up here!*"

He ignored her until Loren, laughing and gasping for breath, reached down for a handful of hair and pulled. Out of sheer self-preservation, he relented and stretched out beside her, laughing as hard as she. It had been a long time since morning had been this much fun.

Her arm wrapped around his neck to dangle fingers in front of his nose. He grabbed a fingertip with his teeth, held it captive long enough to lace his hand with hers, after which serious finger nibbling could get underway.

She chuckled and said into his hair, "Where did you—no, never mind, I don't want to know."

He finished with the fingers, and began on the wrist; shifted onto his elbow and started up the inside of her arm: "Liked it, did you?"

"M-m-mm, not in the least."

He chuckled and said against her throat. "Old man's turn now?"

An answering vibration against his mouth. "I think that could be a . . ."

When she didn't finish, didn't move, he transferred his attention to her ear, grabbed it between lip-padded teeth—

—and sensed an altogether different vibration. He leaned back, saw her distracted look, saw the finger tap behind the ear.

"Shit," he muttered, and rolled away, slamming his fist into a pillow as TJ walked into the room.

"He—he's in with Wesley now, admiral."

"*Is there a problem, Anevai?*"

"N—no. . . ."

"*You don't sound exactly convincing. I don't like this. I'll be honest with you: we tried to signal him on his beeper, and he didn't answer. I told him, either he uses that or he's coming back here. I'm sending a team to bring them both—*"

"No! Please, admiral, no. Everything's fine. They had a bit of a tiff last night—but that's only f—for the good, knowing them both. Clear the air and all. But that's probably why he didn't answer."

"*All right, Anevai, but since I'm to be out of pocket for a few days—*"

Taking Dr. Barb and Dr. Will up to *Cetacean*. Mom had told her this morning. Mom was going, too. Of her own accord.

So she said.

That's what *she'd* told her father a handful of days ago.

"*—if you need any help, contact Briggs. He's here. So's Sgt. Fonteccio. You got that? No heroics, no close judgment calls about what you can handle. There's too much at stake.*"

"I understand, admiral. I'll be careful."

"*And you tell Stephen Ridenour, TJ has standing orders to come and collect him if he doesn't answer that beeper. Last chance, Anevai. You copy that?*"

"I—copy, admiral. Believe me, I'll tell him."

"Dr. Smith?" Amazing how that light voice could cut through his most intense concentration. "Can we talk?"

Wesley let the novel fall to his lap, looked up through the V of his stockinged feet. The kid was standing in the doorway to the den, cool and composed as though nothing had happened.

He took a long swallow of gin and vermouth. "You ever hear of knocking?"

"Would you have answered this time?"

"Probably not." Ridenour's academy-clone mask didn't twitch. Wesley speared an olive with his toothpick, held it up. "Breakfast. Want one?" The clone shook his head. He shrugged and ate it himself, chewing and swallowing deliberately, waiting for Ridenour's calm to break, for any indication the young Recon really did exist within that cool exterior.

The clone still wore the oversized sweater, but the baggy sweatpants had been replaced with—

He raised an eyebrow and deliberately scanned the long clone-legs, encased now in soft—*tight*—leather and tall, fringed moccasins. "Nice pants, Ridenour. Where'd you get them?"

Apparent confusion played over the fine-boned features as Ridenour followed that look. Then his mouth twitched as if he were tempted to smile. Of course, being a clone, he couldn't: honest amusement wasn't a part of the Vandereaux curriculum. "Anevai gave them to me this morning, Said the sweats were an insult." His mouth twitched again. "I thought she meant they were too casual. Perhaps I was mistaken."

"Yeah. Right. *Mistaken*."

Ridenour took a step into the room—

"Hold it right there."

—and froze, one hand still on the door.

Wesley asked, "Ever consider *why* I didn't answer?"

"That's why I didn't knock. I must talk with you, sir."

"Not until you're ready to cut the crap, kid. No more games."

"I–I'm not p–playing any, s–sir."

He flicked the empty toothpick in the direction of the wastebasket. It missed. Joined several others on the floor.

"Sir? Dr. Smith? Give me a break, Ridenour. After where you had your hands last night? —Oh, a blush. Great touch, Ridenour. How *do* you manage it on cue?"

"I'm s–sorry for that, sir. As to my—form of address, I certainly meant no offense—"

"Well, it does offend." He dropped his feet from the desk, leaned forward waving his hand. "—What the hell. Sure. Come on in. Say your piece, do your thing, then get the fuck out. —What's your going rate?"

Ridenour, in the act of closing the door, stiffened. "R–rate?"

"Yeah. 50? 100? 1000? Hell, make it three. I can afford it. I might as well get *something* out of this forced vacation."

A puzzled, over-the-shoulder glance.

He plucked the book off his lap, snapped it shut one-handed and dropped it to the floor. It hit with a dull *thud*. Ridenour jumped.

Ruthlessly ignoring that leather-clad view, he said, "I've waited six months for time to read this thing and *it's* boring as hell. I trust *you* will do better."

Ridenour's knuckles grew white where he gripped the door, then his hand flattened and he pushed the door open again, said quietly, without turning, "I'm terribly sorry you've been—inconvenienced, sir. Please, enjoy your book."

Stephen leaned his back against the bed, elbows propped on his knees, his head in his hands. He'd grown soft; once upon a time, he'd have taken Smith's insinuations in stride, regardless of his physical condition. He would have this time if only—

His head fell back against the mattress.

—if only he hadn't been so certain Wesley would play by the rules, meet him halfway, given the parameters of professional courtesies.

He'd ruined everything. He'd gambled his career in coming down here, and now, due to his own stupidity, Wes would have nothing to do with him. He couldn't be angry, there was no one to be angry at except himself. He might as well call the admiral to come pick him up and take him back to the ship. *Let* them sift his brain dry, it was no use to him, anyway.

Just ask Bijan.

His gaze landed on his diary, resting on the bedside table.

(*"I think you ought to read it . . ."*)

Cantrell sitting at his bedside, his diary on her lap.

(*". . . You must understand, Stephen. Because Rostov is dead . . ."*)

His hands dropped and he straightened. Dammit, no! *Don't* ask Bijan!

Smith had not been his only purpose in coming down. Smith might be too insulted—or too stubborn—to deal with a 'NetTech Del d'Bugger, but the Rostov Recon had his own purposes.

Anevai wouldn't deal with him anymore. Wesley wouldn't. . . .

He reached for the diary—

—and the Eudoxin.

. . . Perhaps Zivon Ryevanishov would.

A kick at her instep: TJ's unsubtle reminder she wasn't alone in this airport-bound shuttle.

"Sorry, Teej," Cantrell apologized, and realizing his voice had been a background to her thoughts: "What was that?"

"I said, how far do you intend to play along with this Cocheta business?"

"Play along?"

Another kick to her instep. "You're not telling me you take this alien artifact bull seriously? What about Vandereaux's stone lattice? What about that Albion farmer with the rings in his wheatfield? *Every* planet's got their 'resident aliens.' Why do we believe these?"

"Other planets don't have Paul Corlaney—"

"Whom I trust about as much as I do Sakiimagan."

She scowled at him. "—endorsing the 'rings in the wheatfields.'"

"All right. Say Paul's telling the truth. So we've achieved 'First Contact.'" TJ's knuckles beat a frustrated rhythm against his thigh. "Just one more complication we don't know shit how to handle. We should get our collective ass back to Vandereaux and throw the whole mess into the Council's collective lap. Let *them* sort out which mess goes to SciCorps, what to the 'NetAT and what they want to keep for themselves!"

"I'm not saying one way or the other, TJ. If it were only Anevai's comments, I might be inclined to write it off to teenaged melodrama. But Paul? I can't believe anyone could hoax him, and he seemed quite positive. Either the Cocheta are legit, or—"

"Or?"

She thought of Survey scanning the planet nonstop since Corlaney dropped that little bombshell, and no longer felt inclined toward laughter. There wasn't a damned thing down there—up to and including the planet's core—they couldn't identify.

So far.

"—or Paul's become a far more accomplished liar than he used to be. I want you to keep a close eye on Ridenour. I don't count on him answering."

"He can't go far without our knowing. Can't open his mouth without our knowing."

That much was true. The Ears didn't catch all that went on in the house, but they'd heard enough to know Anevai Tyeewapi had been telling the truth. Smith and Ridenour had had an argument—a major argument.

"I still don't understand why you don't just haul them upstairs."

"Give them time. Stephen's safe enough for now. Maybe Smith can calm him down—get him back online."

"Why? What difference does it make?"

"The true origin of that paper of Smith's is no longer *just* 'NetAT business.'"

"You really think it might be Cocheta technology?"

She nodded. "If it is, and if it's just one totally new development of many . . ."

"Shit."

"Exactly. Determining that origin *is* Stephen's job, and he's far more likely to get the entire story out of Smith down here than aboard *Cetacean*."

"Take Smith up to *Cetacean*."

"And if he's . . . protected, the way Hononomii was?"

"Shit."

"Exactly."

An evil gleam touched TJ's eyes. "I could beat it out of him."

She bit her lip. "Tempting. Sincerely tempting."

"Zivon? Zivon! Wake up! Hurry now, or we'll be late!"
Zivon blinked the Sleep out of his eyes.
"Late? To where, Mama? Where are we going?"
"You must get up and get dressed, quickly. We're going to the spaceport. You get to take the shuttle up to the station. Won't that be fun?"
"Yes, Mama. Are you going too? Is Papa?"

"No, Zivon. Just you. You get to go to school in space. Aren't you lucky?"

He felt the Shivers start. *"Why, Mama? Why can't I go to school here?"*

"Because you're too smart, darling. The teachers don't know enough to teach you."

"H–how l–long will I be there?"

"I don't know. It's a wonderful opportunity. So get up and get dressed or you'll miss the shuttle."

He crawled out of bed and started putting on the clothes Mama was holding for him. *"D–does P–Papa know I'm g–going?"*

"Don't stutter, child. Of course Papa knows."

"C–can I see him before—"

"I doubt he'll be home in time, Zivon. Now hurry up. We've got to be on our way in ten minutes."

Mama left then, and the Shivers stopped. Someday had come. At least now he could stop wondering when.

He finished dressing and made his bed, smoothing the sheets with extra-special care. He looked around him at all the things that were his: the see-through rocks, the shells, the wooden puppets Papa had carved for him last winter. His bags were packed—he saw them by the door—so Mama probably meant he was to leave his Specials for his Replacement.

He thought of his Specials, of the new kittens and Meesha's new baby. They were all in his diary, anyway. He picked up the heavy notebook and went out to Mama, carefully closing his door behind him, taking the steps slowly and carefully so as not to make noise or fall.

Mama was seated at the desk, writing.

"Mama, c–can I take my d–diary with me?"

Mama looked up, frowning, and he hugged the diary to his chest. *"Please, Mama?"*

She said, still frowning, *"Of course, Zivon. Take anything you want. Are you ready to go?"*

He knew if Mama really meant him to take his Specials she would have packed them, so he squeezed the diary tighter and nodded.

A beeping in his head: insistent, hurtful, pulling his heartbeat to match the rhythm. He screamed and hit his head, trying to make it stop, trying to break the rhythm and get his own heart back.

The beep stopped.

Granther was waiting in the car. Mama put his suitcase into the back seat, told Zivon to get in the front, then squeezed in beside him, having to be very careful because of the Replacement. Granther smiled and hugged him.

They drove in silence for a long time.

"Mama?" he whispered.

"Yes, Zivon, what is it?" Her voice was sharp, and he shivered. "Speak up, child! Are you cold?"

"N–no, Mama." He tried to make his whisper be louder, but it just wouldn't. "Mama, c–can I h–have a p–picture of you and P–P–Papa? I don't have one, and I might not see you for a long time, and—" He broke off, catching his lip between his teeth.

"You mean you haven't told—" Granther started, and shut up as Mama looked a Mad at him.

"T–told me what?" His chattering teeth bit his tongue, making his eyes water. "Mama? What didn't you tell me?"

"Nothing, Zivon. You're going into space to study at one of the big schools. I want you to be very good and use the brains the good lord gave you and make us all proud of you. Do you hear me?"

"I h–hear you, Mama. I–I'll t–try."

"And stop stuttering! You'll be going to Vandereaux and your uncle Victor will be taking care of you. You remember me telling you about him?" He nodded. "Well, you be very good and do exactly as he tells you. You wouldn't want your Papa and me to be disappointed in you, now would you?"

"Ylaine, —stop it! You're terrifying the boy." Granther pulled the car over to the side of the road and set the parking brake, then took Zivon by the arms, brushing his hair back from his face. He hadn't had time to wash it and it was sticking out all over his head. He knew it was. He'd seen it in the rearview mirror. Now he knew why Mama hadn't scolded him about it. It didn't matter anymore. Not to Mama.

"Child, listen to me. This is an adventure. You get to go into

space. You get to do something Mama and Papa and Granther have never gotten to do. You get to go to the Capital of Alliance. Do you know where that is?''

He remembered that from the history lessons on the 'Net. *"V–Van–dro system."*

"That's right. And you get to go there. You get to go to Vandereaux Academy, out in space, and outside your bedroom window, the stars will be right there—you can reach out and grab a handful— Won't that be nice?''

So, Papa had changed his mind and decided the Replacement could watch the stars as well as Zivon could. He bit his lip and smiled at Granther. *"Yes, Granther, that will be very nice. M—maybe I can s–send Papa a s–star from V–V–V—"*

He couldn't get it out, but Granther hugged him and said softly, *"You do that, sweetheart."* And put him back on the seat, started the car again. Mama just stared out the window at the morning-pink clouds.

The pink was gone by the time they reached the spaceport. At the foot of the stairs leading into the big shuttle, Mama hugged him at last, and kissed him and called him sweetheart, which she almost never did. But she let him go too quick and somehow his fingers wouldn't let go. She pulled them loose, reminded him to behave, then gave him a card saying *Don't lose it. That it was his I-den-ti-fi-ca-tion and that it had his clearances to Van-dro on it.*

At the shuttle door, he turned and raised his hand to wave good-bye, but neither of them looked up. Mama was pressing a hand to her tummy; Granther was holding her up. The hand lost all feeling and dropped.

Inside, the man in the black uniform asked to see his Clearance. Confused, he whispered, *"I don't—"* Then he remembered the card Mama had given him. *"—is this—"*

The man grabbed it, shoved it into a slot on the wall, read a screen too high for him to see, then handed the card back and told him *Take any seat and stay out of the way.*

People were hurrying all around, inside and outside the shuttle. He pulled the sheet out of the pocket on the seat-back, read the instructions and carefully fastened his belt the way it showed. There was hardly anyone else on the shuttle, but they *were already starting the engines—he could feel it through the seat.*

Mama and Granther were walking back toward the terminal. Mama was crying, but that was because the Replacement was kicking her again. Zivon could tell by the way she pressed her hand to her round tummy.

Suddenly, Papa was there, running out of the terminal. He stopped at Mama, gesturing wildly.

"Papa?" Zivon whispered. Then, pressing his hand to the window: "Papa!"

The man who had checked his Clearance told him Be quiet—he was disturbing the other passengers.

"But—that's my papa." He pointed out the window. "He–he wants to see me. Please, sir, may I see my papa? See? He's right—"

But they were moving and the man said they couldn't stop, that they had a Schedule. So he shut up and just pressed his cheek to the window, pretending it was Papa. He couldn't see Mama anymore. Papa was running toward the shuttle waving his arms, but they didn't see him. Maybe only he could. Maybe Papa had gone away to become an invisible.

But Papa couldn't keep up and eventually Papa, too, disappeared from his window. Zivon felt the tears start, and he bit his lip to stop them—not to be stupid around these strangers— and whispered, "G'bye, Papa. I love you."

"Too late. Too late." Tears streamed down his face, but he didn't care, except to keep them from falling on the book. "No good. No **good**. Got to go back. Back to the hats."

Paper surrounded him. He was writing and writing and writing. A second notebook. Translations. Stephen stuff. What it *really* said. *Everything* that happened, not just the stupid Zivon stuff. But that memory was too recent.

Pounding. Banging. Voices.

Go'way! He screamed it, but the pounding didn't quit. It was in his head. He dropped his pen, gripped his head with both hands, willing the pounding to go away, willing the pain away, refusing to believe in it. The pounding stopped.

"Stephen?" A woman's voice. Soft. Sweet. From behind the

locked door. "Please, Stephen, won't you come out? I've got supper for you. I made it special."

A deep breath. Forced control. He edged to the door, and said past the dryness in his mouth: "Leave it there . . ." A name happened. A not-from-the-book name: "A–Anevai. I'm all r–right. N–need to be alone for a while."

A muttered *Shit*, then: "Okay, Stephen. Friends? You'll talk to me soon, right?"

Friends? He had no friends—it said in the book. And he couldn't talk to anyone. That's what Papa made him promise. That's why he had to know about the hats. So he wouldn't be sick anymore.

From outside the door: "Okay, Ridenour, you don't have to promise. Food's here when you want it."

The pounding started up again. He thrust it aside, yanked the door open. *"Anevai?"*

"Yeah?" Her head popped around the stairwell. "You want to—"

He shook his head, closed his eyes on the spinning corridor, the multiple Anevais. "Just, —thanks for the dinner."

He slid down the wall, pulled the tray into the room and closed the door.

"Sakiima, this is for you. I suggest you read it carefully. Your daughter makes a great deal of sense." Paul threw the envelope onto Sakiimagan's desk and himself into a chair.

"I sincerely doubt Anevai says anything I don't already know."

"Oh, I agree with you there."

Sakiimagan frowned. "I've told Nayati he must give himself up. What more can I do?".

"You can send the tribal police after him. And if he eludes them, you can tell Loren how to find him."

"Dammit, man, he's in the Caves."

"So?"

"So, she'd know everything."

It was the opening he'd been looking for, only somehow the words weren't there. He got up, paced Sakiimagan's office, really seeing it for the first time in twenty years. Sakiimagan had accumulated an outstanding collection of native plants, insects and fossils, their beauty forever preserved in crystalline spheres. The paintings on the walls, though stylistically similar to Sakiimagan's ancestors' sand paintings, were made of HuteNamid stone and shell and depicted not ancient legends, but real HuteNamid history.

Not a single visible reminder of the Spacer culture into which Sakiimagan had been born—even the computer display, superimposed on the woodgrain surface, was an integral part of the intricately carved desk.

"I wonder sometimes what would have happened even if you'd never found the Libraries," he said, out of that thought. "It's so simple to live here, day after day, and forget the Alliance even exists. The only time we willingly acknowledge its presence is when we want something from it: when a Nigan Wakiza wants to go work with Dr. Lanier's team on matter–energy interchange and can't because he hasn't the Academy credentials, or a Dolii Hata'li wants a chance to play professional Bracketball and she's refused a travel visa."

Paul leaned on the carved desk; thoughtful brown-black eyes met his.

"What if it were Honomomii who needed to go elsewhere to realize his potential? How happy would he have been weeding fields—or even hunting in the hills? I don't know about you, but I'm damned glad I came here. Sometimes that head of his is still so far out in Virtual Space I have to—"

"Paul, you confuse me. I thought you came here to get away from the Alliance and its politics. I thought you wanted to keep away from this Cantrell. And yet, the moment she shows up, you desert us and join her."

"I haven't deserted you, I'm trying to save you. You're right: the anonymity here suits me. But I've had my time, made my mark in history. What of the Nigans? the Honos? What of the Stephen Ridenours?"

"Ridenour's problems are not ours."

"Back to that, are we? What if he was your own son?"

"He's not."

"What if he were? What if Hononomii had had to experience the same horrors?"

"First of all, I would not leave him in such a situation. Secondly, *he* would not bend to their taunts. Hono is made of better material than that."

"Are you so sure of that? And what if you had no choice but to leave him?"

"There's always a choice."

"Is there? Are you so certain Stephen's parents would care so little?"

"Obviously, they did."

He'd anticipated difficult; impossible, he hadn't considered: Sakiimagan was determined to resist him. "Have you wondered yet where Stephen's from? Who his parents were?"

"I told you: Ridenour is irrelevant."

"What if I told you I knew them? Personally. Would that make his situation any more 'relevant'?"

"I doubt it."

He shook his head, too tired at the moment to care. "Read Anevai's letter, Sakiima. Perhaps it will change your mind."

"Paul?" Sakiimagan's voice caught him with his hand on the door. "Where *is* Ridenour from?"

He said without turning, "Rostov. He's Stefan Ryevanishov's boy, Sakiima. For me, at least, that makes him Family."

Were it not for the rise and fall of his chest, the blips and readouts from the monitors which indicated otherwise, the young man sitting statue-still in the middle of the hospital room might well have been a statue.

"How long has he been like this?" Cholena Tyeewapi showed considerable composure considering the handsome statue was her son.

"Like this?" McKenna answered. "A couple of days. Before that, in varying degrees since the interrogation."

"Eating? Sleeping?"

McKenna shook her head. "Not now. Definite downhill slide since his sister's visit. His file's in comp—I'll clear it for you."

"Were Bennett and Liu ever this bad?" Cantrell asked.

"Never," Cholena said. "But they weren't under Deprivil when they cracked either."

"Paul said they were at a party," she persisted. "Any drugs involved there?"

"Alcohol."

"I've been researching some of your ancestral customs, Dr. Tyeewapi," McKenna said. "Any chance some of the local hallucinogenic plants were floating around? What about those your people brought with them?"

"Those plants are cultivated for religious—and medical— purposes; and, yes, some native flora, too. But for casual use, never. It's not accepted, and not tolerated in those who lack the beliefs."

"You seem very certain of that."

"I am," Cholena said firmly. "You say my son came out of the catatonia once, admiral. Where? Under what conditions?"

"In this room. Watching the survey video taken of Hute-Namid."

"I assume you've tried that?"

"Of course. Those Bios just keep looping."

"Well, it at least gives us a place to start with Barb and Will. Keeping them in a calm, natural environment hasn't gotten us anywhere—"

"Perhaps because to spacer researchers, trees and flowers *aren't* natural, Dr. Tyeewapi."

A long, steady stare. Then: "I stand corrected, admiral."

vi

"Wesley, you've got to go talk with him. He's locked himself in there for three days. I've left food outside the door, but he's barely touched it."

"Maybe we'll get lucky. Maybe he'll have the decency to croak so we can all get back to work."

Not for the first time in the past three days, Anevai regretted her new resolution to control her fist. If ever anyone deserved to have his face used as a doorstop, Wesley Smith did. "Sorry to disappoint you, Smith. He's drinking fruit juice by the gallon. He could live forever."

Wesley glared at her.

She glared back. "You, Wesley Smith, are a self-centered, pompous ass."

The glare faded. His face took on a pensive air, then he nodded slowly. "That about covers it."

To hell with resolutions.

Papa took me to see the lights today. He said I'd done something new with the invisbibbles and he wanted to be sure was I all right....

"No, Papa! Please, no more..."

His own cry rang in his ears. His heart raced and he put the diary down carefully, afraid of inadvertently destroying irreplaceable memories.

He no longer trusted his reactions. Though the last of the Eudoxin was gone, he still felt the lingering effects, never knew when convulsions might start. There'd been none so far, but he'd pushed the limit—he'd had to: time was too precious. The voice beyond the door growing too insistent.

("Honey, I must. But you mustn't tell Mama. Mustn't tell anyone. If you try to tell it will make you very, very sick....")

His insides churned, remembering better than his mind the darkness, the lights, tingling through his body—

I think maybe Papa is trying to turn me into an invisbibble...

He stared out into the darkness. Were you, Papa? Am I an invisible? Is that why you didn't want me anymore?

Ridenour was sitting beside the open window staring vacuously into the darkness. Not that Wesley could *see* the vacuous expression, it was far too dim in the room, but he knew the body language, had seen it often enough in these Academy Pretty-boys. They had all the same moves—eachone a fuzzy RealSpace fax of the next.

And J. Wesley Smith could match Stephen NMI Ridenour for vacuous any day of this week or the next. He leaned against the doorframe and looked similarly Elsewhere.

"Anevai said you wanted to talk."

"She lied." Hoarse. Exhausted. Little wonder the lights were off in here. When looks were all you had going for you...

"Somehow I doubt it." Actually, she'd been so incoherent with relief at the clone's request, she'd simply demanded he make this useless gesture. On pain of death.

His.

"Never said *wanted*. I don't *want* things, Smith. *Needed*."

"Like hell."

Ridenour closed the notebook lying on his lap (*Reading?* In this light?) and carefully placed it on a neat stack of papers on the window seat, rose stiffly to his feet and limped toward the door, mumbling something about his foot falling asleep, making a sound he probably considered laughter as he stopped in front of him. "Dr. Smith, —look at me."

"I look where I want. I don't *want* to look at you."

"*Please*, look at me." The cultivated voice quivered around the edges.

Full of Good Touches, aren't you, Ridenour?

"Go to hell."

"D–dammit, Wesley." Hands gripped his sweater and shook at him. "You've got to tell me. C–can you see me? *Am* I an invisible?"

"Shit." He struck those grasping hands away, kicked the door shut and slammed the lights on. Ridenour cried out and cowered away, covering his face with shaking hands. "What the hell are you talking about? Of course you're not invisible."

Trembling hands fell, revealing a face haggard and hollow-eyed, and Wesley, painfully aware how that face could look, found his eyes slipping past it to the night-shadowed window.

"You see. You lied, too." Ridenour's whisper carried, light and hoarse though it was. "You *can't* see me. No one can." He slipped to the floor and buried his face in arms crossed on the bed's wrinkled surface. "Mama, why didn't you tell me? Was the truth so awful?"

"Stephen?" Knowing better—clones were into melodrama, this one more than most—he approached the bed, put a hand on the bowed shoulder. "C'mon, Ridenour. You've made your point. What do you *need* to talk about?"

Stephen twisted from under his hand, dropping to his butt, staring vacuously again. He buried a hand in a pillow and dragged it down to clutch against his chest. "I am, you know," he said tonelessly. "It's just that no one will ever tell me the truth."

"Stephen, you're *not* invisible. I can see you just fine, more's the pity. You're not exactly pretty right now."

A blind blink in his direction. No wonder he'd had the lights out. Those pale eyes were so dilated he probably didn't *need* light to read.

"Not *invisible*." The tone suggested a parent elucidating to an idiot child. "*An* invisible. I–I'm one of Th–Them."

God. The clone was flying in VirtualSpace and seeing ghosts. "Wake up, Ridenour. There's no such thing as—"

"Y–yes there is. —are. —a–am." Blind eyes squeezed shut, fists clenched on the pillow as he rocked back and forth. "Th–they g–get int–to your h–head and—a–and you f–feel them all through you when—" His eyes flew open. "*I'm not supposed to say that!*" A terrified crystalline glance toward the ceiling. "Please, God—I didn't mean—*No, Papa, no! Please, Pa*—" He screamed. Then coughed and heaved violently.

"Shit!" Wesley grabbed a towel draped neatly over a chair—whole damned room was meticulous—and when Ridenour had finished, hauled him out of the mess on the floor to sit on the bed. Holding him upright with a firm grip on his shoulders, he wiped the kid's face and tried to reason with him. "Stephen, why do you think you're one of these 'invisibles'?"

"D–don't th–think." The haggard face set with childish stubbornness. "Know."

"All right, how do you *know*? I see you just fine. Too well. You look like hell."

"That's because you're talking to me. Because you're mad at me. Even mama could see me when she was mad at me. You couldn't before. You only pretended."

"Now, Stephen, that's silly," he chided, certain, now, the kid was on something and hoping to cajole him out of the drug-induced VSpace. "Why would I do that?"

"Because I was talking. Sometimes people almost see me when I talk, but not usually. Usually only when I say something I shouldn't."

"That's—"

"Sometimes I thought I was, but I knew for sure on the way

to Vandereaux when *nobody* saw me, *nobody* talked to me except *Out of the way, Recon-brat*, when they ran into me and then they didn't look at me and at the station I sat and sat and sat for hours waiting and waiting and then everybody was gone." A haunted look searched every corner of the room. "The—the man at the desk was p–packing things away like he was leaving and I—I went to the d–desk and asked *Please, sir, c–can you help me f–find Uncle Victor?*" His trembling grew so violent, Wesley had to tighten his hold to keep him from sliding off the bed. Ridenour twisted like a snake and hugged him fiercely. "He never saw me, Wes. He heard me talk and yelled at me and I couldn't understand and I ran 'cause I was scared, but I had to go back and get my suitcase, but he couldn't see that either, Wes, and he didn't notice when it went away, and I followed the signs to the academy but they couldn't see me either."

"Who, Stephen? Who couldn't see you?" he asked, trying to deflect the runaway explanation that was rapidly gaining momentum in its own crazed course.

"Uncle Victor. At least he said he was but I wasn't to call him that and the teachers couldn't see me when I raised my hand to answer the questions and raised it and raised it but they only saw the Other and then they'd get mad and hit the Other and I never understood what we did, Wes, I never ever ever understood but they saw us in the dark, 'cause everyone saw us in the dark, just like the 'visibibbles,' an' now you can't see me, not 'nless I talk an' you won' talk to me, Wes, an' maybe if you never ever talk to me I won' be here a'tall."

Ridenour was cracking. He'd seen burnout—chemically aided and not—before; it was more common than graduation in upper-echelon academies—particularly Vandereaux. Ridenour's was more spectacular than most—less so than some.

He shook Stephen gently. "C'mon, kid, wakey, wakey. Time for RealSpace reEntry." But the monologue continued. "Shit." Holding Ridenour steady with one hand and he slapped him solidly with the other. "C'mon, doper, snap out of it."

Another slap and another, until his hand stung and its imprint shone white on Stephen's flushed face. The chattering faded to stony-eyed silence, but Ridenour gave no indication of recovered rationality. Whoever—or whatever—had been babbling had simply shut up to avoid being struck again. Rock-hard muscle beneath his grasp neither relaxed nor strove to escape.

Endurance. Survival. That was all the kid knew. Also common enough. Nonetheless, a wave of severe disappointment flooded through some starved, lonely part of him at this final, irrefutable evidence that Stephen Ridenour was just one more academy burnout trying to play the 'NetAT's game and come out alive. So what he was born Recon? That did nothing but add a new kink to an old equation: a constant, not a variable. He couldn't blame him, couldn't dislike him.

But damned if he could bring himself to like him either.

"What're you on?" Disappointment did nothing to lighten his tone. Not that it mattered: Ridenour's stony-eyed silence didn't flicker. "Shit."

He felt Ridenour's weird eyes following him as he searched the room. On the bedside table, three meticulous rows of vials and bottles, all carrying *Cetacean* Rx labels, all carefully marked and separated by daily dosages. He continued the search: drawers, closet, bookshelves—even pillowcases and ventilation ducts. The only other stash he found was the hip pouch containing Sudsies and five different digestive aids—three of them prescription-only.

"All right, Ridenour." He turned back to the bed. "Strip." Ridenour didn't move.

"Either hand it over or shuck 'em."

"N—not t–taking—"

"Like bloody hell." He grabbed at Ridenour's shoulder.

The kid dodged and scrambled across the bed to crouch in the corner. Wesley swore roundly and started after him, stopped when Ridenour held up a shaking hand.

"Wait." Those shaking hands pulled the sweater off over his head. The rest followed. Then he huddled in his corner like some feral creature, while Wesley inspected every pocket and seam.

Nothing.

He met that feral gaze steadily— "Get over here."

—and saw it crumble. Saw sanity reign at last as the mouth trembled and the huddle tightened, bare arms wrapping bare legs, ineffectually protecting what he realized now was a painfully thin, dehydrated body, the red and ragged edge of the still-healing legacy of his encounter with Nayati just visible in the skin below too-prominent ribs.

He'd nearly managed to steel himself against the responsive twist in his gut when that trembling mouth whispered, ''Please, Wesley...''

He swore and stood up. ''I see you, Ridenour. I don't much like what I see, but I see it.'' He swept the pharmacy into the hip pouch and headed for the door.

''*No!*'' A scream, more animal than human. A powerful blow to his back staggered him into the wall. Bony fingers clawed for the pouch. He jerked free of those talons, and used elbow and knee to fling Ridenour skidding across the floor, and up against the bed, where he collapsed, blood flowing freely from his lip, his breath coming in sobbing, panting gasps.

''I'm giving these to the Tyeewapis for analysis,'' Wesley said, coldly unimpressed. ''Meanwhile, we've got work to do. Tomorrow morning, in the den, 10:00. You're a Del d'Bugger, so come d'Bug. I've wasted too damn much time already.''

vii

''For God's sake, who wrote this garbage?'' Barbara Liu's voice, clear and precise, rang over the speaker. Her hand reached for the keyboard, stopped the slowly scrolling text—a sure, decisive keystroke.

Cantrell's heart jumped. In the Window, Will Bennett gasped, shook his head and slowly opened his eyes. For the first time since they'd been separated, his system was off instant replay.

Across the room, McKenna and Cholena Tyeewapi quickly scanned readings, compared notes. Cholena looked up, met her gaze, smiled grimly—

—and gave her an old-fashioned thumbs-up.

Ridenour was waiting: served the clone right. He should learn local—customs. Anyone could tell him Wesley Smith did *not* function prior to 11:00 CNS *or* Local.

Wesley kicked the door shut and dropped the heavy box of printout onto the desk. Ridenour rose from the couch and glided to his side.

He hurriedly stepped away and gestured toward the box. "There. Bathroom reading for the next fifty years, for all the good it'll do you. Go ahead—*find* your obscure references, find a deliberate attempt to avoid accreditation. Fat lot of good it'll do you. You'll never understand it anyway. Even if you do, it won't change a damn thing. I'll guarantee you're not going to make your rep here. Be lucky if the 'NetAT doesn't laugh you out of existence."

Ridenour wordlessly reached into the box and began sorting. Using what criterion, Wesley refrained from asking: he'd never been organized in his approach, and he'd been up at the unholy hour of 0700 making hardcopy of every possibly applicable file, backups and mems included, in deliberately randomized order. He'd even made printouts of his hand notes—damned if he'd waste comp time transcribing them: let the clone decipher the scrawl.

But the sorting continued, steadily and with apparent design. Ridenour flipped through each file, added some to a stack in their entirety, others he carefully pulled from their binding and split among several categories.

The piles grew.

And grew.

And Wesley grew—bored.

And Wesley headed for the door.

"Dr. Smith?"

"Shit." He turned, shoved his hands deep into his pockets. One more step and he'd have escaped. "What d'you want now?"

"Where are you going?"

"To take a leak."

"But you *will* be back?"

God. The clone took him seriously. *Remember, Smith, no sense of humor.*

"Look, Del d'Bugger, you don't need me. You've got everything in front of you. Find your connections, figure your angles, give me your report and I'll sign it so we can all get the hell out of here. Big fuckin' deal.''

"I do need you, sir. It's just—'' He lifted his hands helplessly toward the piles. "I'm not certain yet of the questions. If you would bear with me for just a few more minutes. I'm almost through here, and—''

"Through? What do you mean *through*? Five fucking years of my life and you toss it off in fifteen minutes? Pardon me if I don't buy it, clone.''

The next file shook slightly before it joined its ranks, but Ridenour's voice replied steadily, "I didn't mean through in that sense, of course. I only meant I've an idea now of what's here—'' Another graceful sweep of his hand above the desk. "What I need is what's—'' He tapped his temple. "—here.''

"Hah! Sorry, clone. Can't help you. I'm no shrink.''

Opal eyes widened and fell to the next file. "I meant in *your* head, sir, as we both know. I need to know how the operational aspects work. What assurances I can give the 'NetAT as to what's been done already, how long you think it would take to implement a new 'NetOS, what the mechanics of that switchover—''

"What the hell are you babbling about?''

"The new system. The one you wrote about in *Harmon*—''

"*Harmonies* is bullshit, boy, get that through your head first. And you're a damned idiot to imagine otherwise.''

The next file dropped to the table, unchecked. The hand that had held it shook visibly before it came to rest on a stack. "You know that's not true. *I* do. I *used* it!''

"Right. For my private use, boy. Means nothing if it's not free to be implemented.''

"Not—free?''

"That's right. Can't use the system unless I release the patent, and if anyone wants to argue the point, I'll keep it tied up in litigation for the next five hundred years.''

"Why?''

"Why not? Check into RealSpace, Ridenour. The 'NetAT's not about to change the existing 'NetOS—not until it collapses of its own chaotic weight, and by then it'll be too late.''

"Of course they will. They *must*.''

Desperation in that silky voice. A tone he'd heard all his life, from every scheming, coattail rider inside and outside the academies. "What did you think when you came here? Have dreams of a piece of the pie, did you?"

"Pie? What *pie*? I came here to—"

"Lord, spare me. The innocent's back. GrannySan made one of the biggest fortunes in human history with the patents on the NexusComNet system, and now I have my own pretty-boy showing up talking *new* operating systems—God! Those eyes of yours aren't opals, they're solid, Corelidon diamonds."

"My . . . eyes?" That desperation reached his face—made even its flawless lines ludicrous in his terror.

"Forget it. You won't get it, pretty-boy. Not a credit. Not even a byline."

"Forget what? *Why?*"

"It's mine, sonny-boy. —All—mine. That paper and its proper registration *makes* it mine—no matter the fake links you dream up—and *damned* if I'll turn it loose to that nest of self-aggrandizing hypocrites back at Vandereaux!"

Ridenour was quiet for a long, long time, his intense, narrow-eyed gaze focussed squarely on him. All hint of innocence or confusion vanished. "How could I have been so completely wrong?"

"Your first official question, Dr. Del d'Bug?"

"*Yes*, damn you!"

"Oh, good. Now we're getting somewhere." He tipped his head, getting a different perspective on the angry face. "Ooooo, you *are* pretty when you wake up."

"Answer the damned question."

He propped a leg on the desktop and leaned on the edge of the nearly empty box. "Which wrong? You're wrong about a lot of things."

"About you. —Your motives. —Your character."

He cupped his chin in his hand and smiled his best Cheshire-cat imitation. "What's that have to do with the price of—"

"*Damn you!*" Ridenour slammed his fist on one of his careful piles, swept it and several others off into confusion on the floor.

He craned his neck to see over the box. "You're going to sort them, Ridenour. Don't count on me to help."

"I don't." It was bitter disappointment marring the silk this time, and that tone hit him past all his defenses against Ridenour's kind, some seditious core insistently clinging to the mind he thought *Harmonies* had flushed. "I don't count on you for anything—not anymore. I've ruined myself, my career and my life trying to protect you from those 'self-aggrandizing fools,' and now I find you're no better than they are. Worse, if anything."

"Protect me? *You?* Shit. They won't touch me. They wouldn't dare. What the hell did you think *you* could do? You're nothing but a fucking Recon bastard who *happened* to get an education!" He jolted off the table and threw his hands in the air. "I don't believe this! My brain must be getting soft: I'm buying your whole fuckin' *line!*"

A viselike grip stopped him, spun him around to face an outraged, not at all innocent snarl. "I don't give a damn what you think of me, Smith. I'm not the one who wrote the most profound commentary about the state of the 'Net and the universe...you—you *fucking bastard*, —You made it sound like it came from some cloistered, misunderstood philosopher....*I* didn't write *Harmonies* and then *use* that publication to deny the universe the Harmony it strives for by the very nature that paper so eloquently describes!"

The clone ran out of breath at last. Wesley raised an eyebrow.

"Amazing sentence structure, clone. No wonder you liked *Harmonies*." He struck that vise-grip from his elbow. "Disabuse yourself of the notion you can shame me into changing my mind, *boy*. The only thing you'll get out of me is a promise to sue the pants off *anyone* who tries to use *Harmonies* for any purpose whatsoever."

Ridenour breathed deeply, regaining control. "I'm not *talking* economics. What about science? What about our understanding of the universe? About where ideas come from? Will you at least help me there?"

"Hell, no. Not *even* if I knew what you were talking about. And I've got news for you, boy, there is no difference. Science *is* economics."

"Then I'll ask Anevai."

Ridenour beat him to the door: fast, but not fast enough.

He slammed the door shut with the flat of his hand, buried a fist in that oversized sweater and backed Ridenour against the wall. "You stay away from her, Del d'Bugger. Nothing gives you the right to involve her. *Nothing*."

"She did. *You* did, when you sent that message and referenced her note."

"The hell! Nothing on record—*anywhere*."

"There damn well is. In my head. And a probe will get it."

"She doesn't *know* anything. Not of importance, anyway."

"What's the matter, Smith? Afraid I'll find the true mind behind *Harmonies*? Afraid I'll find out how it really works? Afraid—"

"*Shut—up!*" He rammed Ridenour against the wall—

—and pain exploded in his groin—his gut—his chin—simultaneously.

Or so it seemed. Perhaps it was relativistic comprehension. He was too busy collapsing to be altogether certain of his analytic capability . . .

The desktop jammed into Stephen's hip. He rolled across, into the chair and down to the floor, putting the desk between himself and Smith, then clawed at the chair back, pulling himself painfully to his knees, prepared for a counterattack that never came.

A low, cursing groan from the far side of the room. He peered over the desktop, across scattered papers to:

Smith, lying in a moaning ball on the floor.

He levered himself up, stifling a cry as his shoulder registered a protest, and worked his way cautiously around the desk.

"Here." He held out his right hand.

"Go away. Can't you see you've maimed me for life? God, you're a bastard."

"I've never claimed otherwise. But I assure you, you will survive—it's a long way from your heart. Give me your hand; I'll help you up."

"I said Go'way! Lemme die in peace."

He withdrew the offer, propped against the desk and rubbed his shoulder, hoping that slam into Smith's hard middle hadn't finished his ruination of Mo's work. "If I'd known you HuteNamids were this fragile, Nayati would never have—"

"F—*fragile?* Fuck you, Ridenour. How would you know?"

How would he know? Stephen felt a sudden, insane urge toward laughter and let it out. Anger and resentment glared at him from under shaggy, blond hair, and laughter ebbed to sour-edged bitterness. "Believe me, I know. That was a love tap. An hour or so, you'll have forgotten all about it."

Anger and resentment drifted to a puzzled frown. Then even the frown faded and with a muttered, *Shit.* Smith rolled—very carefully—upright, sighed and closed his eyes. He leaned his back against the door and drew his knees up for elbow rests, his hands hanging limp between them.

"I'm sorry, Wesley. I truly am. But, *dammit*, you had no right."

Smith's eyes opened to half-mast. One limp hand rose and combed the hair back from his sweating face. "Shit, kid, I probably deserved it. But—*look* at what happened to you in that hellhole. Do you really want to involve Anevai? Put her in the hands of the 'NetAT? Sakiimagan's kept her out of the infoflow for damned good reasons. For God's sake, —for Anevai's—keep her out of this."

"You still don't see, do you? All I want is to keep you *all* out of it." He extended his hand again. This time, Smith grasped his wrist and let himself be pulled to his feet where he transferred his hold to Stephen's elbow and steered him toward the desk.

"C'mon, kid. Let's get this over with."

"It's difficult to explain, admiral." Barbara Liu's voice was strained and hoarse, but at least she was verbal. Will Bennett's communications, while clear- (and single-) headed were thus far confined to computers. Not surprising: he was a mathematician before he—took up art. Nothing wrong physically, according to McKenna's experts, just 'missing a connection': *WetWare* problem, so Chet claimed.

But both researchers were doing their best to help. Had been since they caught a glimpse of Hononomii Tyeewapi. They'd been amazingly uncooperative prior to that revelation.

Cholena had taken them to the young man's room, but Cantrell had watched via remote...

My God. Was I really that far gone?

You want to watch the tapes? —See the medical reports?

Liu had glanced at her companion. He'd tried to speak— swept a frustrated hand toward Hononomii and reached for Liu's hand.

She'd avoided his touch like the proverbial plague.

And now:

"I remember we were at the party, talking about the Libraries—"

"Does everyone down there know about the Cocheta Libraries?"

Cover-up or hoax, the scope of the scam was increasingly difficult to comprehend. *How* had Sakiimagan's recruitment been so 100 percent infallible? Why, in twenty-five years, had no one ever slipped? Why had no one *ever* left?

"Everyone at the party. There are a few of the newer transfers who haven't been told yet, but most of us are here because of them."

"Why? Paul says most of the researchers have never even seen these Libraries—he himself went for the first time only three years ago."

"They're all waiting for their chance."

"Chance?"

"At finding a match."

"And did you get your—chance?"

A faraway look passed over Liu's doll-like features. "Oh, yes. Will and I—we've been working closely with our Cochetas."

"How?"

"Flying. Riding the winds of the planet with them."

Chilling echo of a young Recon's words—uttered moments before he VOSsed out completely.

"Who else was flying with you, Dr. Liu?"

"Nayati, of course." At least *she* didn't appear inclined to crash the way Hononomii had.

"Was he always there?"

"Usually. He was our guide."

"What do you mean 'guide'?"

"It's difficult to explain, admiral. But it's easier to come back to yourself if someone's there to guide you back."

"At the party—could you have gone flying without your guide? Is *that* what happened, Dr. Liu?"

She frowned. "What do you mean?"

"When Hononomii snapped, it was sudden and without conscious provocation. You said you took these trips under supervision. Could something have set you off? What are these *tapes* doing? Reprogramming minds? Giving them—I don't know—automatic sequencing?"

"That's what we're trying to find out, admiral. That's why we don't want too much done too fast. We *must* proceed cautiously." She glanced at a mirror, touched a hand to her cheek and looked away, shuddering.

"Dr. Liu? Are you all right?"

"I don't know, admiral. I honestly—don't know."

"Nothing I learned is true—none of it valid." Ridenour laid down his pen and sat back into the corner of the couch, staring blankly across the den. "What am I going to do? Everything I was taught is out of date."

"So learn," Wesley said, feeling less than sympathetic. Considering Ridenour's grasp of the concepts they'd been discussing for three days solid, his concerns now seemed ridiculous and self-indulgent. "Besides, I told you, the 'NetAT's not about to change a thing. Job security, Ridenour. Whatever you were going to do, do."

The bleak gaze swiveled toward him. "Knowing it's all wrong? Can *you* work with the old theories anymore? Could *you* teach concepts you *knew* were wrong?"

"Hell, yes, serve the bastards right. We're not talking courts here, Ridenour. You believe so much in *Harmonies*, —you want to play with ways to clean up the 'NetDB—*do* it. You can't publish it, or talk about it, or implement it, but—so what? Teach *their* system. Believe—*do* what you want."

Ridenour shook his head. "You don't understand. I can't. Once the logic goes, I can't see it—can't work with it. *Harmonies* is reality for me now. As long as some doubt remained, I could play Rasmussen's game by Rasmussen's rules. Now—I just *can't*, Wesley. I've tried, and it's gone. Even if you're wrong, even if the 'NetAT does decide to implement, they'll never let *me* take the time, never allow me to work with these ideas: too high profile, too potentially profitable."

"If you actually believe that, why'd you ever get involved? Why'd you agree to come? You already knew the theory was valid."

"But I *didn't* know. I *believed*, and the rest I hadn't considered. I—I know you don't believe me, but all I saw was a way to establish myself with the 'NetAT: right or wrong, so long as I did a good, thorough job. I never thought of *Harmonies* in those terms before—never thought of the attention it could bring—certainly not the wealth. Shapoorian and her crowd will never allow a Recon to—"

"Do it anyway."

A bleak laugh. "They'd love me to try."

"They can't stop you. Dammit, Ridenour, we're not *talking* money here. Not even notoriety. They won't stop you. There's no percentage in it for them. They can't use it!"

"And starve? I'm not rich, Smith. I've saved what I could out of the student stipend, but not enough for a lifetime. Not even enough to live on while I train for some other field: couldn't have if I'd wanted to. And the government isn't about to fund me for another ten years, or even two: they've been trying to run me through early as it is."

"That's ridiculous. You're the brightest thing they've conjured up in years; they won't drop you that easily. I've seen those scores of yours—hell, I've seen the test answers."

Yesterday, that admission would have raised startlement, a round of insightful questions; now Ridenour merely waved a dismissive hand, taking his knowledge for granted. "Even if you're right, it will work against me, if anything. Don't you see? They want me quiet—out of the public eye."

"So get an honest job."

A ghostly smile lightened the worried look.

"Meaning this isn't?"

"Hell no. ThinkTank researchers are the whores of science—" He laughed at Ridenour's shocked face. "What else would you call us? We think and create for the 'public good.' In return, our dear government sees we live happily ever after. —*Happily*. Hell, I pay more in taxes every year from the interest on my savings than I'll ever *make* at this job.''

''If you feel that way about it, why are you here? *You* certainly don't need to—prostitute yourself.''

He thought of the political and social games he'd left behind—games Ridenour even now reminded him of—and scowled. ''Some of us work for the freedom to work. That's not prostitution.''

Ridenour's fixed stare unnerved him. Spook-eyes, Anevai called the effect. If the chill he felt was any indication, she had it pegged.

''An honest job. —Like what? What do normal stationers do? And do you think any job would last once they discovered I was Recon? Because they would find out, Smith.''

''You're paranoid, kid. Stop worrying and start doing. You're fairly bright, relatively attractive: something will turn up. Hell, we're talking Vandereaux. They can stick you in one of their fancy new VRT's and have you trained as a plumber in no . . .''

Ridenour's intense stare went glassy. His hands started shaking, though he tried to hide the fact, burying them in his lap.

''Stephen? For God's sake, boy, it was a *joke*.''

He was shaking all over now, his legs drawn up, arms pressed tight to his stomach—an undeniable, gut-deep reaction that made Wesley forget all about the clone, made him want to take the child in his arms and hold him against that terror. But he resisted the urge—one's ego could stand only so many rebuffs, so many wrong calls. Instead, he said firmly, ''C'mon, kid, *talk* to me. What's wrong?''

''They—they put me in the VRT's.'' He had to strain to catch the words Stephen put together with such obvious effort. ''At first with Dep, but I'm allergic or something . . . made—made me s–sick—so they thought maybe time would do the trick. Lots of time.'' A quivering hand passed over the white face, pressed hard against his trembling mouth. ''S–sometimes I thought they'd never turn it off—that I'd go the rest of my life . . . They made me *live* in NSpace—S–sometimes, I think they forgot I was in there, and . . . and . . . and it felt so wrong—so very . . ."

"And they *were* wrong, weren't they?"

Opal eyes blinked at him. Focussed slowly. "Yes—they were."

"So much for their fancy new VRT's. Base the input on faulty equations and all you accomplish is a more effective way to create skewed thinkers. —I ought to know. I'd been beating my head against a conceptual wall for years, had *seen* things happen in the 'Net, seen the evidence for others—GrannySan had been collecting idiosyncratic data since the 'Net went up—and I was *still* hamstrung by Rasmussen's equations."

"*That's* what Anevai told you in the letter, isn't it?"

Wesley nodded.

"How'd she know, Wes? Please, you've got to tell me how she knew."

Hard to resist those eyes—but that was Anevai's to tell or no, and Cantrell had said *The more he knows. . . .*

"Sorry, kid."

Fists clenched. Stephen jerked to his feet, obviously intent on leaving. This time he didn't try to stop him. He'd warned Anevai. She'd said, Let him ask.

But Stephen paused for another unfocused instant, lost his momentum and slumped into a chair. "You're right: it's not fair to involve her directly. It's probably all a moot point, anyway. After what I've done here, it's most likely a total wipe and polishing the 'NetAT's floors for life."

"What are you trying to do, Ridenour?" *Hit me up for a handout?* he almost said, but something in the flickering spook-glance stopped him.

"Trying to do?" Quietly. Thoughtfully. "You know, it's strange. I'd almost forgotten . . . I came down here to convince you I could counter every move you made. To force you into staying off the 'Net."

That sudden, next best thing to sexual, thrill. "Can you?"

"Of course not!"

"Oh. —Damn." He fell back into the cushions, disappointed to his gut and striving, without much success, to hide the fact. "Struck out, Ridenour." He glanced upward, encountering a look which changed like quicksilver to the scared kid before he had time to read it.

You hypocritical bastard! he thought and crossed his arms. "So, what else do you *need* to know, clone?"

The scared kid stiffened and disappeared. Ridenour folded his hands on his lap, and said in a calm, steady voice, "I *need* you to quit fighting me, Dr. Smith. I *need* to know what to tell and what not. With what I know now, I can deal with the 'NetAT—explain enough to get their experts started. You've nothing to gain from getting directly involved; not until they ask you in—and you know they will. They'll find how little I really know and come begging. If you don't want them—if you don't want to go back—tell me how to do it. I can't protect you all—I haven't the power." Clone control slipped, taking the steady voice with it. Stephen leaned forward and slammed his fist on the desk. "Dammit, man, I risked my neck to get where you could advise me without the admiral's snoops, the least you can do is agree to keep the fuck off the 'Net and give me a chance to save your fucking hide!"

Suddenly, the kid was making sense. Suddenly, the whole situation seemed ludicrous. What difference did it make what motivated a Stephen Ridenour? What harm could it do to go along? He was fighting a system, making a statement no one was going to hear anyway. So he *gave* the clone his chance with the 'NetAT; at least he was a clever clone.

"Hell, kid, if *that's* all . . . All you had to do was ask."

viii

"Where is he, Wes?"

"Hell if I know, Paul." The stockinged feet propped on the Tyeewapi's kitchen table were at least the same basic color, even if only one had stripes.

Good thing they had Paul Corlaney along to handle Wesley Smith. If Smith had used that tone with her, Lexi might have felt compelled to teach him manners—an attitude they couldn't afford at the moment.

Cantrell had ordered TJ and her back up to the ship—wanted

Smith and Stephen as well. But while muscle might work with Smith, it never would with Stephen. She knew that, but it had taken her the entire trip here to convince the two men.

Dr. Corlaney said calmly: "This is no time to play hide-and-seek, Wesley. Ridenour's health is in danger. Dr. McKenna doesn't like the readings she got from Inyabi. She wants him back up there."

"Well, she can't have him. —Damn right, he's sick. Have you seen the pharmacy she was feeding him?" Wesley waved a hand toward the kitchen counter and at least a dozen pill bottles. "Inyabi's *still* checking out their interactions. Who knows what chemical cocktail is eating him from the inside out? He's operating on his own jets for the first time in years."

"You mean, he's not taking *anything?*" TJ demanded.

"Damn right. As of two days ago."

TJ went into listening mode: *Cetacean* had undoubtedly heard that.

"I'm not leaving, Corlaney." Ridenour, standing in the doorway. He looked terrible: tired, thin; but at the same time—energized. Maybe they *should* leave him here.

Smith's feet thumped to the floor and he went to stand protectively at Stephen's side. Stephen murmured something and Smith stepped past him into the hallway. But Smith didn't leave. She could see him clearly in the shadows, glowering at them as if daring them to make off with his—pet.

That intuitive perception disturbed her. Perhaps these two *should* be broken up before they had time to get any tighter than they already were.

TJ was still in communication mode. While he exchanged opinions with Cantrell, she edged over to Stephen. "You're sure you're all right?"

"I will be as soon as you let us get back to our work."

She drew back from that abrupt hostility, allowing him to see her disapproval.

He immediately reverted. "Lexi, I'm sorry. Really. It's just . . . things are going—"

TJ placed a hand on her arm. "Loren wants your opinion."

She looked from Stephen's tired, pleading face to the rack of pills on the counter. She was inclined to agree with Smith, better none than all those, but:

"You going to take McKenna's pills?"

"For God's sake—" Stephen's pale face flushed. "All right. All *right!* I'll take them! Just *leave us alone*." His voice broke and he rested his head wearily against the door frame. In a calmer voice: "Please, Lexi, a few more days, that's all I'm asking."

Lexi would bet her career that Stephen knew more than he was able—or willing—to say, and would extend that bet to 'willing.' He was onto something. Something important to him. He was a compulsive overachiever—and Anevai had said he wanted to do his 'NetAT report right, so she'd bet whatever he was onto was equally advantageous to Alliance.

She shrugged. "I'd say—leave him."

"Dr. Smith, could you—would you mind telling me something?" Stephen finished addendizing an addenda of a note in the chicken-scratched copy of *Harmonies* and closed it carefully.

"Only when you cut the *doctor* shit," he said, stretching a foot the length of the couch to nudge Stephen's knee. They'd been over every damned file in that box—twice. He'd been forced into far more intimate acquaintance with his thinking processes than he cared for and this one-jump-removed from a rug-rat Del d'Bugger had been doing the analysis. He was tired, and sick of the formalities.

The rug-rat-plus-one attempted a token smile. "W–Wesley. —Would you tell me why you hate me?"

"I don't hate you, kid. —Hell, I haven't beaten you for two whole days."

"Maybe not now, but you did, you know you did." His eyes dropped to the notebook, and he—caressed the cover. Kid had a fetish about *notebooks* and *organization*. Wasn't normal. *Couldn't* be healthy.

"News to me, kid. —What's this all about?"

"I—I thought once—that first afternoon—we might be friends, if I weren't—what I was. Foolish on my part, since *I* knew what I was—what I *am*. But even after you knew why I was here, you tried . . . for a while I thought . . . Why did you want me to come back? Revenge?'' His worried gaze lifted. "Please don't lie to me, Wes. It's okay if that was..."

Wesley shifted uneasily. Analysis of his neural pathways was one thing, personal motivation was something else, no matter the kid had proved at times quite charming—and always stimulating—company. "What difference does it make? We're fine now, aren't we?"

"I suppose.'' Stephen wandered over to the window, stood silhouetted against the afternoon sun. "What's that?''

"What's what?''

He pointed. "The sparkle—there—across the trees.''

"Must be the waterfall, kid. Big one. Good swimming hole—a lake, really. Get this nonsense over with and I'll take you.''

The silhouette shuddered. Or perhaps it was only light-ripple. "I—don't swim.''

"I'll teach you.''

Another ripple. "Thanks anyway. . . .''

"What's eating you, kid?''

"I *would* like to see the waterfall. . . .''

"Forget the damn waterfall!''

Most definitely a shudder this time. Shit. Probably shut him down for good. Damned sensitive . . . Anybody who couldn't take a good shout once in a while wasn't worth the—

—He softened his voice. "Stephen, what do you want me to say? You think people hate you for no reason?''

"N–no, I d–don't. It's just—I've never had anyone I could ask, and if there *is* something—something I can change . . .''

"Lord, we're talking in circles. Sure you've got some irritating quirks—who hasn't? But don't confuse those with what happened at Vandereaux. Or even what happened here. Danislav—the Shapoorian brat—they're certifiable asses. So is Nayati. So am I, for that matter—when I want to be. Just stand up to us; throw our asininity in our collective face.''

A slow turnabout. A concentrated stare that made his spine twitch. "You don't understand, Wes. It's not your fault—or Bijan's or even Victor Danislav's. Things happen when I want things—sometimes to me, sometimes—all too often—to others. There's an evil inside me that I can't control. So God does.''

Simply stated: as if he were commenting on the color of his hair or the size of his foot. For a moment, Wesley was speechless, then:

"That's—*stupid*."

"Is it?"

"I've been called a lot of things in my career, Ridenour, but *never* an instrument of God. The Other Guy, maybe, but—"

"Perhaps you're right—perhaps not God." Ridenour was drifting again. "Doesn't matter who or what—I'd just hoped there was a why . . ."

"Stephen, for God's sake—" He couldn't finish in the face of the boy's straight stare. "All right—*all right!* You say things happen. —Like what?"

Full lips clamped tight.

"C'mon," Wesley prodded. "Examples. Support your hypothesis, Dr. Ridenour."

With a low, reluctant chuckle, Stephen drifted back to the couch, where he pressed himself deep into the corner cushions. "I remember one Christmas eve . . ." His curly head cocked, perplexedly. "Do you know about Christmas, Wesley? I never know . . ."

"Yeah, kid. I've heard of it."

Stephen slipped his moccasins off and tucked his feet up on the couch, wrapping his arms around his legs and resting his chin on his knees: a childish position his supple body made— elegant. Wesley swallowed hard and concentrated on the wistful face.

"Christmas means—meant—a great deal to my parents. Had to do with their religion—I don't really remember. I never went to church—not since I got old enough to remember, anyway. I stayed home with Granther. He'd read the church lesson with me and then fall asleep. Usually I didn't mind. I—was fairly self-reliant—but this one time, he fell asleep and I remember running—it seemed like a thousand kilometers—in the dark, but I didn't need to see. I knew right where the church was . . ." Wistfulness grew dreamy. "In the spring, I used to go early every morning to watch the sun shine clear through and make colored patches on the ground outside."

"Why, Stephen?" he prompted, foolishly drawn to this melancholy sweetness. "Why did you want to go so badly?"

"To see the candles."

"To see *what?*"

"The candles. I'd heard mama talk about it—had seen pictures—but never the real thing. I snuck in the back and saw it all. The candles—everybody but me had one, and they were all along the aisles and on the altar—their light flickering off the statues and the colored glass—" His voice quivered, his hands clenched. "God, it was so beautiful. —Then someone saw me..."

Swimming eyes, shaky breath: damn, it was hard...

"What did you do?" He made his question matter-of-fact, reminding himself firmly: *a constant, Smith, —not a variable. He* was *a Recon. Find out what he is* now.

The eyes blinked, the breath steadied. Ridenour shrugged almost carelessly. "I ran. What else? I wasn't supposed to be there. On the way home, I heard sirens—saw a glow behind me. I found out later the back of the church had caught fire—on the spot where I'd been standing. And—and the stained-glass window I used to talk to had shattered. Papa said it was the heat, but I knew better—" He met Wesley's gaze calmly. "God would let me talk to the window from outside, but not from the inside, because I was an abomination: I wasn't Papa's and I did bad things all the time. I didn't mean to, but..."

"Stephen, you're not *evil*. That was just a coinci—"

A slow shake of his head. "Not coincidence, Wesley. A single example among a lifetime of examples." His eyes dropped. "Now I've let that evil touch you and Anevai. I didn't mean to, but it's happened, and I must take it away. *Must.*"

"There's nothing for you to take away," he maintained, surprising himself twice. Once for buying the boy's sincerity. Twice with his own stubborn denial of it.

"Yes, there *is*." Stephen fumbled for words, clenching and unclenching his hands, finally unfolding from the couch to pace the room, sleek and nervous as a caged feline. "How can I convince you?"

"Say I believe you. Who made you *my* keeper?"

"It's because you're a part of me—"

"What the hell—"

The pacing stopped and he swung around. "You are, Wes. The good part. *Please* don't let me destroy that."

He couldn't laugh at that earnest face. "What is it you're saying, kid? What do you want me to do?"

"I don't—"

"I know, I know. You don't want things."

"I can't, Wes. —But if I can help you be free to do the good things—"

"*What* good things, you idiot? What ever made you think I'm good for anything? I've very carefully made a career of not being—"

"You *are*." Stephen sat down again, leaning toward him, his hands clenched together. "People like you. They want you with them. You can make laughter. And—and love. But mostly, you can make the 'Net sing." Opal eyes glittered now with tears—and something so disastrously close to hero-worship it made his skin crawl. "I want to hear the 'Net sing, Wesley. I want the junk off it. The—'The discord eliminated, not overridden by louder cacophony.'"

He smiled reluctantly. His words. His allusions: from *Harmonies*. Such a wonderful piece of shit writing that was.

But it wasn't shit to Stephen. *He* could hear the 'Net the way it should be—

—or so he said.

"Want, Stephen?" He challenged. "Do you dare?"

Stephen bit his lip, nodded without losing eye contact. "You see? You've convinced me that's a silly superstition. *Chaff* to be eliminated from my thinking. If you can do that for me, just think what you can do for the 'Net."

He found himself drowning in those spook-eyes—unable to break contact. Unable—for all his better judgment—to completely ignore the invitation. "Child, you almost convince me. Maybe we'll install the SmitTee.Sys after all—whether the 'NetAT likes it or not."

A twitch. A downward glance that broke the spell. "Is that what you call it?"

"Yeah. Catchy, don't you think? I mean, I thought of SOS—" He paused, giving Ridenour time to get the pun, but he sat there like an academy-clone lump. He grumbled and explained: "Smith Operating System? SOS? Save our...oh, never mind. —But that would have left Anevai out, and I couldn't do that, could I?"

"I—suppose not." But the intensity, the animation had gone. He opened the notebook and picked up his pen. "Shall we get back to work?"

ix

"Did Dr. Hamilton get Stephen's report, admiral?"

"He certainly did, Anevai."

"Is it what you need?"

"Tell Stephen he's doing splendidly. He's made a believer out of Chet. The 'NetAT will be a breeze. —How is he doing, Anevai?"

"You've got his vitals from the grans."

"I mean, otherwise."

"Honestly, admiral, he seems happy. He's eating like a whole herd of ko'sii, and keeping it down, he's gaining strength—making Wesley work out with him—and he hasn't asked to see Nayati for two whole days."

Nayati? TJ stopped screen-flipping through Barbara Liu's file and exchanged a startled glance with Cantrell. She raised a hand and said:

"Good as that news is, Anevai, tell him to start packing. Time to come home."

Following a protracted silence:

I—suppose you're right. Goodbye, admiral.

"What the hell was she talking about?" she demanded, cutting the connection, "*When* did Ridenour ask to see Nayati?"

"First I've heard of it," Briggs said, his attention divided between her and the file on Barbara Liu. "Maybe I shouldn't have left him down there after all."

"Not your fault, Teej. Mine. I wanted you up here to discuss—" She nodded toward the monitor. "—that. Besides, he *swore* to me this escapade was about Smith, and he's *got* Smith. What would he need with Hatawa? Has he got a death wish?''

He glanced up from the screen. ''You don't want me to answer that.''

''I suppose not. But I still don't like *any* connection between him and Hatawa. Considering what Barbara Liu said, we've got to pull him up here fast.''

''Take it *too* fast and he'll bolt, Loren. Lex convinced me. Don't scare him into something stupid. Besides, you heard the girl: he's lost interest.''

''I suppose.''

''On the other hand—you could use him to *get* Hatawa.''

''Not on your life. I don't want *any* contact between them. If Stephen is somehow in league with Hatawa—hard as that is to believe—we'll discover it when he debriefs under Dep. If not, damned if I'll give Hatawa another chance at him after that report he just sent Chet.''

''So, you're going to put him under?''

''Damn right.''

''And if he reacts?''

She smiled, grim acknowledgment of his challenge. ''We'll just have to deal with it, won't we?''

''Good girl.'' She'd finally returned to her senses. ''He evidently thinks the Tyeewapi girl can contact him. We could pressure her...''

''Tomorrow's soon enough. I want you to talk with Liu.''

''Made a believer out of you, did she?''

She nodded once. Emphatically. ''Damn right. If we ain't got ET's, we got one damned interesting virtual substitute.''

Wesley lay down gingerly, tired muscles supporting exhausted ones, and hoped the sadist steaming in the bathroom down the hall would take his time.

Tomorrow, Ridenour worked-out alone.

On the sidetable, two notebooks stood propped between bookends, a third lay open: the Fetish in full flower. One was the kid's all-too-familiar copy of *Harmonies*. The other two—

He idly thumbed through the open one. A log; more properly, a diary, the chicken-scratch writing recognizable as the meticulous Stephen's only through the context. Half was positively illegible.

A memory of drug-hazed eyes, incoherent babbling about days past: maybe not log or diary. Maybe memoirs. Maybe what the kid was doing all that time alone.

A careful listen for the shower: it hadn't even started yet. Once it did, the kid would steam for an hour—easy. He propped the notebook on his lap and settled in for a little creative snoopery. . . .

Damn . . .

Pause for another listen: shower going strong.

. . . Damn . . .

No wonder the kid was messed up.

. . . Damn and—

"—Wesley, I've got it!" Stephen burst into the bedroom, steam-flushed and shower-damp. "I know how we could rig a high-bar. If we just—"

Bright, excited eyes flickered to the notebook in his lap, narrowed and returned to his face. The smile faded; a muscle in the jawline bulged.

Wesley closed the notebook, waffling between disgust with himself for getting caught and frustration with Stephen for barging in before he was finished. Torn between curiosity about what he hadn't read and wishing he'd never picked up the damned thing. "Stephen, I'm sorry. It was sitting open and—"

But Stephen, obviously not interested in reasons, justified or otherwise, held out his hands for the book, propped it carefully with the other two, then retreated to the window, his tense back to the room.

"Get out." Gone, the excitement. Even the cultured clone-tones. This was hissing, undeniable fury.

"Stephen, —"

"I said, *get out!*"

"Listen, son, I—"

"*I'm not your son!*" His hands shook with controlled rage, balled into fists, snapped open and balled again. "I'm not . . . any . . . body's . . . s–s . . ."

"Stefan Ryevanishov might—"

"Shut up, dammit!" The fists jammed deep into robe-pockets. "He's not—*wasn't* my father!"

"Good grief, Ridenour, you don't have to talk like he's dead."

A frozen silence. Then: "He is."

Well, Smith, he thought, *you've done it now, haven't you?*

"Yeah, well. Should learn to keep my mouth shut, shouldn't I?"

"Damn right." An angry mutter. An over-the-shoulder glare. "*And* your hands off other people's property."

"Yeah, I suppose." At least the kid wasn't trying to toss him out on his butt anymore. "But can you blame me for being curious?"

"Yes."

"Well—" he said, thoroughly helpless in the face of his first straight answer from the kid . . . "—Shit!"

The glare wavered.

"C'mon, kid," he pleaded, encouraging that chink, "give the old man a break, huh?"

With a rueful laugh and a rake of fingers through damp hair, Stephen dropped onto the foot of the bed.

"Damn you, Smith."

He grinned. "Too late, brat."

Stephen curled his bare feet up under the robe and leaned on the bedstead, his eyes focussed somewhere beyond the dark corners of the room. Something was eating at him. Something soul-deep.

"You still want me to leave?"

Slow shake of the dark head.

"You want to talk about it?"

Another slow negative that reversed polarity in midswing; Wesley didn't rush him.

"I—I t–told you things happen . . ." He drew a deep breath and started again, his voice stronger. "I never realized until Cantrell told me when I woke up aboard *Cetacean*—"

"That your father was dead?"

He nodded. "M–my mother as well. I'd been told they were relocated following the Bios crash. And–and it never even occurred to me—all these years—it *couldn't* have been the

268 • Jane S. Fancher

Bios: Rostov had been off them for years. I should have known—at least *suspected*..."

Ridenour paused, a determined search for control. The poor sod was dealing with the loss of his parents all over again.

"Mama...I always knew she hated me—at least resented me. I—she rarely took me anywhere. But I don't blame her, considering. I—I looked very different from papa even then."

Impassionate. Detached. As though it didn't matter...

"Pa—Stefan Ryevanishov told me he didn't care I wasn't his—that I would stay with him forever. I believed him. I figured once I was a man, the baby wouldn't be replacing me, so I'd be safe."

...Or had happened to someone else.

"Hell of a childhood, kid."

He shrugged. "Could have been worse."

How? he wondered, but knew better than to ask—now.

"One morning—Papa was gone hunting—Mama woke me up. I knew, Wes, somehow. Mama was due any day. She didn't want the hatred to touch the new baby, so I had to leave. It made sense, really...but..."

"But?"

"I wanted to yell No. Not till Papa's home. But it was too late. I was on the shuttle. The engines were started, and Mama and Grandfather were leaving."

Ridenour slid off the bed and over to the window, touched it with his fingertips, then pressed his palm hard against the glass.

"And then, Papa was there. I could see him through the window, yelling at Mama. I saw him run after the shuttle. I asked the man in the uniform—Please, sir, make it stop. That's my papa. He—he wants to see me. Please, sir, may I see my papa? He's right..." He leaned his forehead against the window. "But he didn't hear me, Wes: I was invisible, you see. I wanted to tell Papa I loved him and not to worry. That I didn't want my evil to hurt his new baby either. That I would grow up fast, get smart enough—good enough—so they would want me back. I wanted to hug him and say goodbye, but I should have known..." His slumped shoulders began to shake. "Maybe that's why he's dead now. Because what I want can't happen and as—as long as he was a–alive, there was a chance . . .''

That damned diary.

However, even as he damned his own vulgar curiosity, Wesley realized that much as he might choose to unknow what 'that damned diary' held, much as he'd prefer to reject the unwanted insight into that troubled psyche, he couldn't. Much as the obviously irrational, self-indulgent guilt might repulse him in an adult, he couldn't deny the pain of the child—the fearful strain the revelation of his parents' death must have put on an already overloaded karmic debt.

At least that damned diary could suggest a way to reach the child—the insight of a father who knew his shy son better than a spacer interloper ever could, who knew better than to offer comfort for the child's own sake. . . .

"Stephen . . . I need a hug. —Real bad.''

That slender hand, still pressed to the glass, clenched; the curly head lifted; and Wesley braced himself for another rejection as the boy registered that theft from his most private memories. But the fist relaxed, flattened again to the window before drifting free with the boy's slow turn into his waiting arms.

IV

i

Consciousness pulled at him. Eyelids no longer heavy, refused to stay closed. Muscles pain free for the first time in a week urged movement. But caution kept Stephen's eyes closed, his body quiet until his other senses assessed the situation.

"I told you—'' A whisper from the door: Wesley. ''—dead to the world. We won't see him for hours.''

"We *should* wait..." Anevai.

"Quit worrying. Give him a little breathing space." And lower still: "Give us a little."

He should let them know he was awake. It wasn't polite, listening in this way.

"I thought you liked him, Wes."

Silence—except for the delicate, laughter-edged breeze from the open window: children's laughter. He tried not to care when Wesley failed to answer immediately, told himself it didn't matter when the slow answer came:

"I do—sort of. I feel sorry for him. I'd like to help him. He's a nice kid." A pregnant pause. "He's also exhausting."
—C'mon, squirt, race you to the lake..."

The door closed.

A survey of the room through eyelash-disrupted slits confirmed he was alone.

Feel sorry for him... Well, Wesley could keep his pity. As for the other...

If Wesley was exhausted, it was his own fault. Last night Smith had encouraged him (at least the way he'd read it) to talk of things he wasn't supposed to talk about—had never *wanted* to talk about; but somehow, sitting on the fur rug, back to the bed, moonlight streaming through the window, and Wesley's friendly presence beside him, the words had come easily.

And somehow, only the good things had seemed important. Watching the stars with Papa, Mama's kittens and Meesha's baby walking for the first time. Wesley had asked about the fossil shells and he'd told him about exploring the edges of irrigated fields and sharp-edged ravines with his cousin Nevya for those evidences of onetime native life. Wesley's questions had even helped him remember good things about Vandereaux— his first ride in one of the interstation bubblecars, and that unforgettable first flight in the ZGym...

Somewhere, he must have fallen asleep, and this morning, he was alone because he was 'exhausting.' With a twinge he chose to take as relief, he showered and dressed and wandered downstairs.

The empty kitchen felt lonely, an impression he squelched

furiously. To tempt himself with unfounded what-ifs would only disrupt his concentration on the job at hand.

A job which neared completion. He had his notes, had all the necessary paperwork to prove *Harmonies'* lack of ComNet precedence except—

—except Anevai's letter to Wesley: the one he called the key to *Harmonies*.

A letter Wesley adamantly refused to give him.

He took his prescriptions in a gulp, washing them down with *memdi* juice, then belted the belt pouch securely as a reminder to take the next dose. He'd forgotten yesterday. Between Anevai's criticism and Wesley's insistent return of *all* the pills as a 'test,' he'd gotten careless. Carelessness he couldn't afford: if McKenna found out he'd been negligent with her handiwork, she'd kill him for sure.

And Wesley would kill him if *one* nonprescription pill was missing from the nightly count.

A wry chuckle escaped as he fixed a simple breakfast of toasted flatbread and fruit; maybe he should just slit his own throat and save everyone the hassle.

He settled into the window seat overlooking the wooded garden where Recon children tested their skills at self-destruction, feeling no concern when a flying dive from a tree-limb failed to flatten the unfeathered, would-be bird.

He needed that letter. Wesley had been so open about Anevai's input, had credited her so frankly in his files, he couldn't intend to deny her officially. So it had to be something in the note itself Wesley didn't want him to see.

"*Coffee . . .*" Leotii Wakiza, the clinic's night 'Tech staggered into the kitchen. "*Please*, tell me it's not my imagination— worse, an empty pot."

He waved a hand toward the freshly brewed. "Help yourself."

"Bless you, child." She filled a mug and slumped down at the table, grinning pleasantly and looking as if she expected him to make Conversation.

"You're here late today," he opened hesitantly.

"Ready to head home, assure you. Soon as I finish this." She raised the mug and took a long swallow. "Oh, my, that *is* wonderful. —One of the Etowa boys came in first thing this morning—tried to cut a couple of fingers off in the—'' She glanced at his plate. ''Sorry, —you're eating.''

He pushed the plate in her direction. ''Want some?''

''Thanks.'' Following careful deliberation, she nibbled a memdi slice, studying him over her fingers.

He shifted on the chair, the handful of words they'd exchanged over the past few days giving him no basis for their 'conversation.'

She said: ''I'd been hoping to get a chance to speak to you alone.''

He shifted again. ''Wh–why?''

''My brother asked me to give you a message.''

''Your—brother?''

''Sorry, thought you knew. —Nigan. He wants you to know he's very glad you're all right.''

He shrugged, confused and ill-at-ease. He should have recognized the name, he supposed, but Nigan had been just one more ephemeral element in his life. He hadn't thought about him since . . .

''He meant it, Stephen. —I know my brother. He's really sorry it happened.''

''Is that right?'' He swirled melted butter with a bit of toast. ''So why doesn't he tell me himself?''

''Are you kidding me?''

''No,'' he replied, wondering at her incredulity.

''Cantrell's got an APB out on all the Warriors—didn't you know that?''

No, he hadn't. ''Dammit, I *told* her—'' He broke off. Maybe Cantrell had her reasons—reasons he didn't know about. If Cantrell was after Nigan—if Nigan's sister knew where Nigan was—

''Told her what?''

But if Cantrell had Purposes, he thought, she should have told him, now shouldn't she?

''Not—not to prosecute—that I wouldn't be alive if it weren't for your brother's intervention with Nayati.''

Her head cocked. ''Truth?''

''Absolutely.''

Her smile was all the vindication he needed.

"Thanks, Stephen." She got up and headed for the door, leaving her cup beside the sink. "I—needed to hear that. I honestly didn't want to believe my brother was a willing participant in that—misunderstanding."

He felt the heat rise in his face. What had they done, reenacted the whole thing on the daily news? He wasn't exactly proud of his own role in those events.

"Will you tell Nigan something for me?" he asked.

She raised her chin, indicating agreement—at least it did coming from Anevai.

"Tell him . . . Just tell him thanks."

She nodded again, and left.

He finished the last of the toast, and straightened the kitchen, considering his options.

Time was running out. Cantrell was on a manhunt when she'd promised otherwise, and with that same disregard to promises, she could force him back to *Cetacean* at any moment. Wesley had kept information from him: key information the 'NetAT—if they took his report seriously at all—were going to demand to see. And if he couldn't produce it . . .

But he *could* get it. He knew now how to access the hidden HuteNamid files; better, perhaps, than Wesley realized. He could even infiltrate Wesley's personal files. Chances were, Anevai's letter was there.

A cup and a half of coffee later, he headed for the room he and Wesley had appropriated, and the 'Link it contained.

To use what Wesley had taught him in this way might very well ruin whatever chance at friendship they might have, but any friendship had been doomed from the start. He had the legal right—his mission granted that—and damned if he hadn't the moral right after last night's invasion of *his* private files.

But he had to get it before Anevai and Wesley returned, because neither morality nor legality would save him from Wesley's wrath if Smith caught him at it.

So he just wouldn't get caught.

The wild ko'sii drifted into range of the new bow. Nayati held his breath, waiting patiently for the right moment. He'd never killed a living creature before, though he sensed the ideal target for his arrow; and he demanded perfection of this first blood.

A shift of weight, a half-turn; Nayati drew a breath and held it, drew the feathered fletch to his ear and held it—

—A disturbance in his recondite reality. His bracing arm twitched and the shaft flew hopelessly wide. The ko'sii started and disappeared into the forest shadows.

Nayati cursed softly and stepped free of the undergrowth. Someone unwanted had infiltrated Cocheta files. That intrusion had ruined this perfect moment. That someone would pay.

Dearly.

Stephen threw himself back in the padded chair and scanned what appeared to be a completely useless file—a file he'd risked everything to see.

Anevai's letter said precisely what Wesley had told him: she'd had an insight after one of her late night head-thumping sessions with Wesley and she'd written the letter for fear the inspiration would escape by morning. Just basic 'seems to me's' and 'what if's,' all based on her one controversial insight of ignoring Rasmussen's equations and starting conceptually from scratch.

Exactly as Wesley had explained, except for one small reference . . .

>I think it works like the Cocheta links. . . .

>. . . I wish you could find a compatible, Wes. I wish mine hadn't made you throw up—I thought it would like you. . . .

>. . . It's not like the VSuits. You put on your helmet and start the tape and it's like two thoughts occupying the same synapse, one yours—one theirs—you get the feeling millions of minds could read the same synapse—but each would interpret it according to their unique Chaos Complex . . .

>. . . Do you think it's possible the compats occur only when there's enough overlap between your CC and the Cocheta's for you to—read its OS? . . .

Cocheta. The screen saver winked on, a soothing pattern of flowing water; and within those shifting fractal shadows, he saw shades of another kind:

(*Silver moonlight through leaves. Rough wooden siding against his shoulder, and Anevai's voice from the barn window overhead:* ("*I say again, we can work with Stephen—maybe even Cantrell—without endangering them . . .*)

And a moment later:

("*. . . Damn you, Hatawa, the Cocheta.*")

. . . without endangering them . . . So. These Cocheta were something both Nayati and Anevai wanted protected. So much so, Anevai had been reluctant to even say the word . . . *Damn you, Hatawa . . .*

Nayati had obviously been aware of his presence outside the barn by then; certainly Anevai had after she led him down there. He suspected that presence had been the source of her reluctance—and *Nayati's* insistence: justification—personal or to the gathered Recons—for his subsequent actions.

It was possible this 'Cocheta' was just some Recon project Wesley was respecting. It was also possible there was some more insidious reason for Wesley's withholding the letter—that the Cocheta held more significance for Wesley than for Anevai.

. . . you put on the helmet . . . two thoughts occupying the same synapse.

Other memories. Memories resurrected under Eudoxin influence. Confused and hazy, now he was sober, but written in the Book, along with the translations of the diary passages written in his childhood code . . .

I followed Papa and the others into the tunnels today. . . .

And his note:

Glowing walls. Tunnels. Dancing lights. Funny hats. Invisibles—in my head. No, Papa, no! Papa, it hurts. I won't tell, Papa. Won't!

Please, Papa . . .

His hand shook beneath his chin. He pushed himself upright never lifting his eyes from the scrawled pages, except to scan Anevai's displayed note.

Two minds . . . one synapse . . . Beyond Virtual Reality—even beyond Vandereaux's VRT's. A feeling—from Anevai's description—of *personality*.

...Invisibles in my head....

Is this it, Anevai? he thought. *Is this the elusive link between us?*

...Please, Papa, it hurts... and Anevai's Cocheta had made Wesley sick.

...I won't tell... Had Anevai likewise been constrained 'not to tell'? Had Nayati?

HuteNamid's Cocheta—Rostov's Invisibles. Technology imported from Rostov?

Cantrell had said civil war had killed everyone on Rostov. She'd once offered him the Rostov files; he wished now he'd taken her up on that offer. What she knew had become highly significant. If she knew of the Cocheta, if there were references to his glowing tunnels and funny hats in those records, *that* could be the basis for her fears that what happened on Rostov was happening here.

Or perhaps a more sinister note on tests gone awry? If the Recons *stole* that technology from the researchers... secret technology that Cantrell was here to prove they'd stolen and arrest them all... perhaps that theft was Wesley's real reason for hiding that letter. Perhaps *Harmonies* had its roots on Rostov as well.

Anevai said Nayati was going crazy. Certainly his own experience had left him less than sane over the years.

—Secret files.

—Rostov files.

—*Cetacean* Security files. He had the right to read them— Cantrell had given him that right. But she could as easily revoke it. She'd want to know Why now? and he couldn't tell her that—not yet. Not without knowing *what* she knew. Not without knowing if she had set him up—left him down here to expose Wesley and Anevai as frauds and felons without giving him the information he needed to do that job. Had left him floundering down here making a fool of himself—killing himself to remember what she damnwell could have told him.

If he contacted *Cetacean*, if he asked Chet Hamilton for

those files, he'd never get to see them. But there was another way. A way *he* knew that Wesley himself refused to see . . .

"*Stephen! Help!*"

Anevai avoided Wesley's grasp with a last-minute twist, and burst through the front door, laughing and clutching the jamb for balance as Wesley sprawled past her and thudded to the floor. Her laughter faded as she searched the entry and living room for sign of Stephen.

"Shit," Wesley said from the floor. "All that effort wasted."

"I was sure he'd be up by now." She gave him a hand up, then headed for Stephen's room.

"*Ste-ee-ee-ee-vie!*"

She missed a step. "*Wesley!* You trying to rouse the whole clinic?"

"Who's to wake? There's nobody there. —Never is. You people neglect the fine art of hypochondria."

"Check the house system, will you? See if he left us a note."

No Stephen; no note: not on the system, not even a paper one.

"His bed's made," Wesley commented when they congregated in the kitchen.

"He'd make his bed if he got up in the middle of the night to go to the bathroom," she responded absently. "He's had breakfast."

"How do you know?"

She nodded toward the counter. "Cleaner than I left it. Remind me to warn him: he'll blow my rep and the grans will expect it all the time. —Wes," she hesitated to tell him what else she'd discovered, knowing Wesley's feelings on the subject, "he's taken his notebooks."

"Shit." Wesley wandered to the window. "I'd hoped he'd gotten it out of his system last night. He spends too much time . . ." Sunlight glittered through the trees. "He's out there."

"I *bet* that was him I saw."

"Which time?"

"Ha. Ha. Ha. You'll get yours, Smith. What do you think?

You were with him last. Should we follow him or leave him alone awhile?''

He turned again toward the window. His eyes closed briefly and he looked tired. She followed him, touched his elbow.

"You okay, Wesser?"

His hand covered hers, and he grinned down at her. "Hey, kiddo, have I ever not been? —Hell, he'll be fine. Just wants some time alone. Gives *us* time to . . ." His eyes glittered. "—Classtime, brat."

"You've gotta be kidding!"

"Hell, no. The clone brought up some interesting questions." He plopped down on the window seat, pulled her down beside him. "—Now suppose you're wrong. Suppose the number of nests *is* infinite—"

"No way, Wes. —I tell you, you're crazy. A quantum universe dictates basic limitations on . . ."

"This is Leotii Wakiza's phone. If you really meant to call me—talk. I've pulled the vampire shift this month and I'm working very hard at being dead to the world right now, but if you really, really really have to talk to me, just punch twenty-three and this exceedingly nasty buzzer will wake me up. But I warn you, if it's not worth it, you'll be my next customer."

He waited anxiously for the beep, then hit twenty-three.

"Leotii? This is Stephen Ridenour." He bit his lip and strained to hear sounds from the kitchen, cupped the mouthpiece and murmured again, "Leotii, *please* wake up. I'm terribly sorry, but I *must* talk with you right away. *Please*, Leo—"

"Easy does it, Stephen." A yawn interrupted Leotii's live voice. *"I'm here. Where's the fire?"*

"I—" What was she talking about? "I don't know. *Is* there one?"

"What do you want?"

Angry. Not a promising beginning. Especially considering who was in the kitchen and the time he didn't have.

"I–I've got to talk to your brother right away. I tried his local BBoard listing, but it's offline. I thought you might know—"

"*And you think I'd tell Cantrell's man?*"

All her earlier friendliness was gone. He'd hoped...

"Please, Leotii. It's terribly important."

"*Sorry, Ridenour. I have no idea.*"

He bit his lip until he tasted blood; tried not to panic, not to think of what he'd found in those Rostov files. He *had* to contact Nayati. Nigan's sister had been his best hope.

"Could you—could you please just contact him? Ask *him* if he'll see me? M–maybe b–bring Nayati with him? I–I'll be—" He named the only place he knew. "—at the s–spring in t–ten minutes."

"*And have Cantrell's crew trace the call? Or maybe they'll just sit in the bushes and wait for Nigan to show up.*"

"I–I'm s–sorry. Never—never mind." He tried without much success to keep the desperation from his voice. "G–goodb–b—"

"*Stephen, I... If I see him, or—can think of a way to contact him, I'll tell him you want to see him, all right? Best I can do.*"

"Thanks, Leotii." This time, he didn't even try to hide his discouragement. "Sorry to wake you...."

"*Yeah, right. —See you tomorrow, Ridenour.*"

"Yeah, right."

The hand that hung up the phone was shaking. Stephen tucked it under his arm fighting for some sense of direction in a universe gone random vectoral, trying to rid himself of the pervading impression of impending doom.

Hard to believe any single individual could be quite so dim-witted... He knew better: persons of Cantrell's stature, even Wesley's, had far too much at stake to be honest to the likes of a Stephen Ridenour, but somehow Stephen Ridenour persisted in believing them.

Cantrell obviously had something to gain through his ignorance— had sought to confuse him once more. He didn't care about that. Not anymore.

Because while Cantrell might know about HuteNamid's Cocheta, she didn't know about Rostov's invisibles—at least, not from those files he'd pulled up. There'd been *nothing* about caves and hats. But there'd been much else—things she'd knowingly lied about.

Things like who really died and how. Things like why the commander of the Alliance Security investigating team had turned off Rostov's 'NetLink.

Things like who Stefan Ryevanishov really was...

Somehow, he doubted the files he'd found were the ones Cantrell had intended to show him.

Nayati was the key. Nayati and his Cocheta. Anevai had been unable—or unwilling—to contact him. Wesley wouldn't. Therefore...

He glanced at the phone and prayed the bait successfully cast.

...Stefan Ryevanishov's son would just have to let Nayati come to him.

ii

Getting out of the house proved easier than Stephen had feared. He'd been preparing to leave when Anevai and Wesley had returned—had taken his pack and notebook into the den closet with him, wanting the diary along in case Nayati required convincing. Wesley and Anevai were still deep in conversation when he slipped past the kitchen door—though he had to catch himself from correcting a statement Wesley claimed he'd made— and never even looked up.

Finding the spring was another matter. Too many well-worn and interconnecting paths headed in the general direction. However, eventually—rather more than his ten-minute estimate and totally due to luck—he sighted the sparkle of sun on water through the trees, heard energetic laughter on the breeze.

He hesitated at the forest's edge, but while some of those soaking in the steaming water saw him—even waved—no one seemed to object to his presence. He waved back, feeling more than a little foolish, since he didn't know any of them, but positioned himself on a rock on the far side of the irregular pool, in a little pocket protected from general view, knowing that otherwise Nayati would *never* show. Pulling his diary out, he settled in with all the appearance of studious occupation.

Seemingly respectful of his desire for solitude, the voices

faded away into the woods without a single person intruding on his haven.

Long after the last voice faded, Nayati still hadn't shown, and he began to despair of the plan. He'd feared it a long shot from the start, but he'd had to try. Still, he waited—who knew where Nayati was. It was too easy to think in terms of station complexes where one was never more than a few minutes' transit ride from . . .

"I hear you're looking for me, Spacer-man."

Stephen's heart jumped into his throat, his stomach flipped, but he kept either from showing as he searched the forest shadows for the source of the voice from his past.

"Who told you that, Nayati Hatawa?" Amazingly, his voice didn't shake.

"Perhaps it was a bird."

A Leotii-bird, he thought with an unconsciously triumphant smile.

"And did the bird tell you I'm not spacer?" he asked, not quite keeping that smile from his voice.

"I've heard you weren't born in space." The voice sounded closer. But that could be his imagination. "That doesn't make you one with your homeworld. And if you have no World, you're either of Space or nowhere. Take your pick."

Perhaps it should surprise him that Nayati had a better understanding of that subtlety than Cantrell, Anevai or Bijan Shapoorian, but it didn't. He was beginning to suspect that Nayati, in his odd way, could be his most unbiased critic. His most trustworthy mirror.

"I'm glad to hear you say that, Hatawa. I'd hate for any further lies to stand between us." He searched the nearest shadows again. "I don't suppose you'd care to come out and talk with me for a while. . . ."

"Make you nervous, do I, Spacer-man?"

He shrugged and sat back down, leaning his back against the rock, and opening his diary.

A snort of laughter, a rustle of leaves.

Close. Very close. His heart skipped another beat.

But that rustle had been a bit too deliberate: a warning, not carelessness. He heeded that warning and when the knife pricked his side, didn't twitch.

All else being equal, he'd match his school of survival against the Recon's any time, despite Nayati's greater weight and reach—but under the circumstances, if Hatawa chose to attack him, he'd lose. . . .

. . . if the engagement were physical. He didn't intend to let it get that far.

"Very good, Spacer-man." A familiar whisper; flashes of a barn and pain and incomprehensible questions. "Now, how 'bout you throw out all the fancy little bells and whistles the security boss gave you? *Then* maybe we can talk."

"Nothing but a pen, Hatawa." He set the notebook down carefully, ignoring Hatawa's pointed protest, then raised his hands above his shoulders. "Welcome to check, if you like."

The knife pressed a millimeter further. "Don't think I won't. You beeped?"

He nodded as a hand searched him thoroughly yet impersonally—a degree of polite conduct he hadn't expected. "Far as I know, simple signal sender. Far as I know, the real snoopers need special clearance. But I can't guarantee that."

Smug laughter in that same ear. "I can."

The point left him. Nayati circled to squat a good three meters away, his knife a flash of sunlight on his knee.

"I'm inclined to trust you, Spacer-man. I don't know why— I'm probably quite insane . . ."

"How do you know what style beeper I have in my head?"

"Why'd you want to see me?" Hatawa countered.

"The truth," Stephen answered quietly.

"Whose truth?"

"There *is* only one."

"That's where you're wrong, Spacer-man."

"Your truth, then."

"About what?"

"Why you're here right now."

"Truth for truth?"

"If I can."

"And if you can't?"

Following a rapid calculation of options: "You match me truth for truth. When I refuse, you can stop. Fair?"

"And if *I* decide you ask a truth I cannot share?"

"But you already have the advantage, Hatawa: this is your home territory; you have the knife."

Nayati smiled tightly. "All right, Ridenour. You're on. —Curiosity. Simple curiosity. I heard you wanted to see me, and I thought to find out why."

"Is that the truth *you* want?"

A nod. Sharp, direct.

"All right. Also simple. I've had a lifetime of lies. I want the truth about what's happening here. No one can give me that but Anevai, Wes, —or you. Anevai and Wes have been—reluctant."

"Good enough. Next question."

Somehow, he'd thought it would be simpler, that once he and Nayati were together, the questions—and the answers—would happen. Now, he knew the very questions he needed most to ask would drive Nayati away—

—or worse. He probed slowly:

"That night at the barn . . . Why did you want to kill me?"

"Because you were a spacer spy."

He shook his head. "That's an obvious truth, Hatawa. Doesn't count. Why me, personally?"

The knife flashed. His heart skipped a beat. He raised his chin a notch and dared Nayati. *Pushed* for that answer, knowing he might not survive to hear it:

"Was it to protect the Cocheta?"

A long pause. A delay he was frankly surprised brought no more than an abrupt thin-lipped nod, and: "Your turn, spacer. What *did* you hear?"

"I don't remember much . . ."

The knife threatened, blanking his mind.

"Ease off, Hatawa. I'm trying." He reBooted. "All I heard Anevai say was that you people could work with Cantrell and me without endangering the Cocheta." He took a deep breath, and taking a chance, asked the Real Question: "Nayati, what are the Cocheta? *Why* must you protect them?"

"You mean she's not told you?"

"Anevai? —No. Of course not. Nor Wesley, nor Cantrell— *no* one has."

A distant smile. "The gods of HuteNamid, spacer. And now they are ours. They speak to us—only to us. —My truth, now..."

They speak to us...

Two thoughts occupying the same synapse...

I think Papa is trying to turn me into an invisible....

No, Papa! They're in my head, Papa...

"No! No more games, Nayati."

"Are we playing one?"

"Dammit! There's no time—you must understand... Cantrell lied to me. She said they were dead and they aren't—but she said what happened on Rostov was going to happen here and..." Stephen fought to control his runaway mouth. He wasn't making sense, and he knew it.

"Rostov was a Bios crash. That can't happen here."

"It couldn't there, either. Don't you see? They'd been off Bios for *years*, that's what I never remembered—and I don't know *why* I never remembered, except Danislav told me to forget everything, but they were *proud* of the fact—I remember the celebration. That Bios crash—that's the cover story."

Nayati's cold smile cut his explanation in the middle. "I know it's a cover, Spacer-man. I *want* the *true* story."

There it was—in his lap. Just like that.

"Do you?" It was his turn to smile; to watch Nayati's satisfaction turn to something cold and blank but patently disturbed. "I can give it to you, Hatawa."

The question. The desire.

"How?"

The bait.

"The Rostov files. I can give them to you."

Eyes narrowed. "In return for what?"

"Truth for truth. The Cocheta. I want to—meet them."

"How will you give me the files?"

"Come back with me. Let me show you—"

"Walk into Cantrell's hands? What kind of idiot do you take me for?" He'd lost the fire of desire. "Forget it, Ridenour. Go home to Vandereaux. Stay out of our business."

"I *can't*." The advantage was lost, the desire now all his. "*Please*, Nayati, I've got to know—what are the Cocheta? *Where* are they? Can you take me there?"

Nayati grinned. A coldly satisfied grin. "If I tell you, I'll have to cut your tongue out so you can't téll. If I take you, I'll have to kill you."

"Do you have a 'Link there?"

The grin widened. "In a manner of speaking."

"So take me. If there's a 'Link, I can bring up the Rostov files there."

The grin faded slowly. "Forget it, Ridenour. Cantrell couldn't follow anyway."

"You mean the beeper." But he remembered Cantrell saying . . . "The signal. The first night—after the crash—it went crazy. Did *you* do that?"

Nayati's smirk returned . . .

"Then do it again so she *can't* follow."

. . . And again faltered. "Why?"

"This is for me. Not Cantrell. Not the 'NetAT. Will you take me?"

Nayati stared at him for a long time. Then he laughed and disappeared into the shadows.

"Stephen?" Wesley's voice echoed off the rocks on the far side of the lake, faded unanswered into the splash of water.

"Damn," Anevai muttered beside him, and swung the flashlight's wide beam across the lake's near shore. No Stephen. No one at all. "How could we have been so careless, Wesley? We should have come after him hours ago."

"He's a big boy. Besides, we were busy, kiddo. Sometimes— Wait!" He grabbed her arm and directed the light toward a stand of rocks. "Hold still." He ran along the beam and skidded to his knees at the pool's edge, fumbling in the shadows for the woven strap.

A sandwich. Two unopened cans of fruit juice, three empties— the kid loved the stuff—and his diary on top. No sign of what might have happened to him. Without a word, Anevai handed the pack to Wesley. He stuffed the spare jacket they'd brought into it and slung it over his shoulder.

Anevai sank onto a rock and cast the spot aimlessly around them. "This lake is so well used, it would be hard enough to track him in full daylight. If only he hadn't taken to wearing moccasins like the rest of us..."

"He might not be."

"What do you mean?"

"Stationer feet, remember? I found a pair of real boots for him—for when we went outside. They were a bit small, but he might be wearing those, if he used the sense God gave him."

"Always a first—" The spot caught a shadowed imprint between rocks. She jumped up and left him in the dark.

"Found him?" he asked, following her.

"One sharp-edged mark doesn't prove anything," she said. "Might not be a boot-heel at all. Besides, Stephen isn't the only person around who might be wearing boots."

She took a long stride, swept the spot across the ground. Another stride and repeated the motion. On the fourth such interval, she said, "Cross your fingers." And disappeared into the trees. He followed. There, the softer ground showed the marks clearly.

Anevai said positively: "It's Stephen."

"How can you tell?"

"Open your eyes, Smith. He's limping—those too-small boots..."

"I'll take your word for it. Let's go."

The trail led them steadily deeper into the woods. Anevai seemed uncommonly silent, and when new, painfully deliberate— even to Wesley's untrained eyes—tracks joined Stephen's, he touched her arm. She stopped and faced him, and though he couldn't read her expression in the dark, he knew:

"It's Nayati, isn't it?"

iii

(Glowing hands. Weird, purply-blue, rippling and flowing like rusalka hands. Shadows that weren't black, but a creepy-dark almost-purple.

(Papa and the others talking and laughing in the tunnel ahead.

(He wasn't supposed to be here: this was men stuff. But Mama had gone to town and his studies were dull stuff he already knew, and if only They would let him go back to school, he wouldn't be bored and lonely and wouldn't be being bad. But Papa said They said Not yet, so here he was being bad and Papa was going to yell if he caught him. . . .

(So he just wouldn't get caught.)

Another branching. Stone all around. Natural shapes, unnatural finish. A smooth finish he'd seen before, a million years ago: black with glowing lavender marbling across it, constantly shape-shifting with the heartbeat of the mountain above him.

Stephen staggered to a stop and sank to his knees, bracing a shoulder against the glow, shutting his eyes to that hypnotic pulse. Coach Devon's voice carped in his mind's ear. *Get it under control, Ridenour. Panic wastes energy, panting's inefficient.*

He slowed his breathing and relaxed, touch-searching the belt pouch for the sud'orsofan: a simple goal to force half-memories back into the recesses of his mind where they belonged—not in RAM messing up his LogicFlow. His fingers located the familiar vial, his thumb snapped the cap off. He shook out two of the tiny pills and recapped the vial without removing his hand from the pouch.

He'd fail Wesley's 'test' tonight for sure.

He'd followed Nayati to the brush-covered hole in the cliffside and once inside the tunnels, had discovered himself without options: the ambient light behind him faded making retreat insane, and at a given juncture, only one trail would light, eliminating any remaining doubt as to Nayati's intentions at leaving the clear trail through the woods.

He'd have been all right, if he'd kept his wits about him.

If . . . He swallowed the pills, and slumped to the floor, waiting for the synthetic boost to his flagging energy supply—hoping to keep terror at bay.

Terror these spirit tunnels had released: increasingly potent images which had overshadowed reality until now he was lost. Hopelessly, uselessly, lost. The automatic lights no longer guiding him. Chances were, he'd pulled stupider stunts, but he certainly couldn't think of any offhand.

Heart-rate rapid, but steady. He rubbed behind his left ear, feeling—for all he knew better—for the implant. He tapped the Spot.

Waited.

And tapped again.

Then he remembered Cantrell's explanation: . . . *no, you're left-dominant, aren't you? The right ear* . . .

Brilliant, Ridenour, he thought, and tried the right side, which generated an equally loud silence where Chet's answering signal should be. RealSpace ComTech: he should have known it would fail the one time it might prove useful. Maybe next time, Cantrell would mind her own business and not pollute someone's nervous system without asking.

"All right, Hatawa," he said, on a deep breath and clearly, scanning the surrounding stone. "Which way?"

Nayati had led him here for a reason—he had no illusions regarding his tracking talents—and if for a reason:

"C'mon, Hatawa, if you want me someplace: give me a lead. If not—if you lured me here for no better reason than to die in these tunnels, the least you can do is tell me. There's a lovely, very deep hole back there, I could save us all time and trouble . . ."

Sudden laughter surrounded him.

'All right, spacer. Come into my parlor.'

The glowing marbling disappeared down one branch.

"Oh, well, Spacer-man." Oddly disappointed, Nayati rose from the chair, aimless now Ridenour had ceased to be an issue. He'd lost the spacer for a time—had set him a winding trail, and himself, not requiring the light, come straightway to the control rooms. Somehow, in that short unmonitored interlude, the simpleton had gone off-track—had been lost to the Cocheta instruments until he spoke. Frustrating: the tunnels surely included movement sensors, but not that he'd found—

—yet.

He'd thought at first to let the fool wander forever—solve all their problems in one easy move: the spacer followed him, got lost ... but Ridenour's failure to crack when deserted in the maze, his crazed, matter-of-fact offer had resurrected the reluctant respect first kindled in the barn. Had Ridenour proved worthy—

"Dammit, Hatawa!"

Nayati swung back to face the monitor, leaned forward to rest his elbows on the control panel.

Ridenour stood, hands on hips, staring suspiciously around him.

"I've been jerked around by far more accomplished villains than you, Hatawa. I know it when I feel it. You want to be an ass: fine, be one. Just keep an eye to your rear, because I'm coming for you."

Laughter threatened and escaped as Ridenour whirled and marched back to the branch. Nayati straddled the chair, crossing his arms on the back as Ridenour entered the human-sense blackness of the other tunnel, warm glowing body drifting spiritlike against cooler, barely-there stone. Spirit strides attempted nonchalance at first, stumbled, and shifted to a more prudent path at the side of the tunnel, feeling for one careful step at a time, free-swinging hand seeking constant wall contact.

"Much wiser, Ridenour," he whispered, and sent the instruction to light the other tunnel.

Ridenour froze. His eyes closed for an instant, before he said, quite clearly, and with an ever-so-slight bow, *"Thank you, Hatawa."*

The spacer-spy was nearing the primary tunnels when an alert beeped: disturbance in the outer maze. Nayati opened a Door for Ridenour into the Primaries, and transferred his display to a small window on the main screen.

Cocheta sensors located the source for that disturbance. Cocheta core-memory identified the intruders: Anevai and Wesley Smith. Cocheta ears heard Anevai saying:

"... how Nayati got around so fast. I wonder how long he's known about those entrances."

"A long time, Annie-love," Nayati said to the surrounding air. "You just never listened to me."

The flashlight's glow entered visual range first, Anevai and

Wesley following close in its wake. The final players having arrived, he closed the Outer Door.

"Where the hell are we?"

"Wait a second." Anevai paused, leaned against the wall and closed her eyes.

"What are you—"

"Shush, Smith!" and a moment later: *"That way."*

"How do you know?"

"Trust me. I know where we are."

"You said you didn't know the entrance existed."

"I know where that entrance lies with respect to tunnels I do know. C'mon!"

Oh, my dear Annie, you hear, yet you persistently deny the Voice.

Suddenly, from Ridenour's Window:

"Oh, my, God."

(Colored lights through a round doorway. Wide, flat steps curving into a room of swirling colors he could almost see, sounds he could almost hear. Zivon watched, unable to move until the patterns began repeating and he grew bored.

(Shapes past the whirling colors. Beds. Row after row of narrow, lumpy beds. Papa and the other men were lying on those beds, wearing funny hats like it was a party. A very quiet party—not full of loud laughter and rough games like the one at school. But maybe adult parties were quiet. Certainly everyone was smiling. Someone even laughed aloud, somewhere on the far side of the big room. Maybe he hadn't had fun at the school party because he was becoming a man and maybe if he put on one of these hats—)

"—No!"

Ridenour twisted, tripped, fell and scrambled to his feet, tearing in mindless panic down the tunnel—

Away from the Library.

Nayati grunted. "Wasted my time after all, Ridenour."

The light above the door warned of Imminent Visitation.

"So long, Ridenour. You almost made it." He cut the monitor as Nigan Wakiza let himself in.

"Nayati, you got a minute?"

"What are you doing here? You're due home for dinner."

"Found something on the way. I've got to show you."

"I'm busy."

"Whatever you're up to, it'll have to wait. You've got to come with me, right now."

"I told you *no*!"

"You want the roof to fall in?"

"I'm not in the mood for jokes."

"I'm not joking. Get your butt out of that chair and come take a look."

"Shit." He flicked the sensors to auto-record and followed Nigan into the tunnel.

Wesley Smith was lost. Wesley Smith didn't *like* being lost. Especially with only Anevai's purported bump of direction to guide them, no matter she swore they were getting close to the main Library, and that she *knew* these specific tunnels.

Not that Wesley Smith had much choice in the matter now. He'd never find his way out on his own; how you told one Cocheta tunnel from another, only the Cocheta (and Sakiimagan's favorites—which Wesley Smith definitely was not) knew. Wesley had always come via the underground TransTube to—

"Papa, no! Please, Papa!"

The shrill echo chilled his blood. He knew the voice; he'd hoped never to hear the tone again. He darted around Anevai; her hand fastened on his jacket, jerking him to a halt.

"Dammit, it's *Stephen*! Let me—"

"Shut up and listen!" she hissed.

Running footsteps. A second cry cut off in midword.

"This way," Anevai said, and bolted in the opposite direction he'd headed. He followed her blindly.

A short sprint, a pause to listen, another short sprint, then she stopped and slapped a hand to the glowing wall. Dark spots appeared in the glow. Anevai tapped a pattern and part of the smooth surface slid aside, revealing another tunnel, this time of dead-black stone. She darted down the ragged path without switching on the spotlight she carried.

I sure hope you can see in the dark, kid, he thought, and

darted after her, praying the same gremlin that had opened the door wouldn't decide to close it again.

(The lights on the ceiling were making more pretty patterns— different ones, now he could see all the colors. He knew the names for some, but others were new; he couldn't even remember seeing them on Nevya's prism rainbow.

(His head itched. Fingers were running all over his head— then they were in his head. And they hurt.

(He screamed—and heard Nevya scream—but Nevya was dead—and heard Papa yelling to Get Granther—and he couldn't move. He was stuck in his hidey hole under the couch and couldn't move and Papa said Get Granther and he couldn't and Papa would be mad and—

(The fingers stopped, the hat was off and Papa was holding him and yelling What was he doing here? and How stupid could he be? and he was thinking Pretty damn stupid, like Granther would say, but Mama would wash his mouth out.

(But his head hurt and knives were cutting him into little pieces and all he could do was cry and say he thought it was a party—

(Which was even stupider, so he shut up and let Papa yell . . .)

Stone. Not the smooth violet shimmer-stone of—that—place, but wet, mineral-slick mounds beneath his palms, sharp-edged grit cutting into his knees. Stephen grasped at that sensory reality, shut out the memories threatening momentary lucidity.

He, Stephen NMI Ridenour, was on his knees in the blackness of the HuteNamid underground. He was not Zivon Stefanovich Ryevanishov, this was not Rostov-on-Don and his papa was not going to make him lie down and let the invisibles invade his mind and his body. Papa was dead. Rostov was dead. The admiral had told him so.

Except the admiral had lied.

Papa might not be dead. The Rostov files had said nobody but researchers. No Recons—dead, or alive. The admiral had lied—could, in fact, have brought him back to his old home. Nothing outside was the same. Only here in the caves. Could terraforming have wrought such changes in only ten years? Or perhaps *all* planets were like this—different above, underneath identical. Perhaps *that* was what spacers feared.

But those 'memories' could be lies as well. The VRTs created Reality—formed it according to the Coordinator's chosen parameters. Perhaps HuteNamid itself didn't exist. Perhaps Anevai didn't, and Wesley was nothing but the coordinator's creation to punish his persistent wrong thinking.

(*"Dammitall, Stef..."*) His father and mother in the far end of the house, believing—as parents throughout the ages have believed—that small, supposedly sleeping ears wouldn't hear:

(*"...we've lost too many like him already and I'm not willing to risk him if there's half a chance for him to realize his true potential—"*)

"Oh, God." He closed his eyes against the absolute dark, bit his lip on the sobs that threatened. He was losing Reality again.

(*"Potential? With Spacers?"*)

(*"Yes, Stef, if that's where his abilities lie, why not let him have his chance. His father—"*)

(*"I'm his father—the only one that counts—and I say he stays with us. He's bright. He'll adjust."*)

'He'll adjust.' —But he hadn't been given the chance to try. —Or had he, and was madness the result?

"There he is, Anevai. Down here!"

Voices. Voices which didn't fit the memories, but Voices which would take him back to that room of colored lights and invisible fingers nonetheless.

"God dammit, give me that light!"

Panic. Terror. Zivon leapt to his feet and ran, slipping and stumbling in the darkness.

(*Fingers weaving in and out: lightning between the squigglies of his brain cells.*

(*"Papa, stop! Please, Papa—"*)

Light flooded the tunnel. Blinding light, not rusalka glow.

(*"Is this what you call making him one of us, Stef?"*)

He tripped, caught himself against the craggy wall, sensed a dark side tunnel to his left and darted in, ignoring the imperative orders reverberating behind him.

(*Papa's laughter ringing through him. "One of us, Ylaine? Never. My Zivon's special."*)

"Stephen! Dammit—look out! There's a pit—"

("You've taken any choice out of it, Stef.")

The ground collapsed, stones rattling into nothingness. Instinct driven, midair twist; grasp the stony lip; let the momentum of that twist swing him back onto the stone path—

—and into his pursuer.

A dark shadow stumbling over him; a startled cry; a voice identified too late.

"Wesley!" he screamed, and threw out a hand, a blind scrabbling that hooked a strap. He closed his fist, and Wesley's momentum jerked them both to the edge and over.

A sharp pain stung his foot; his downward plunge ended, leaving him hanging head downward, the rocky lip pressing into his stomach, and Wesley swinging pendulumlike on the far end of that packstrap with a likewise one-handed hold, the blinding-bright flashlight in his other hand spotlighting a sickeningly endless wall below.

The strap slipped. He took a wrap with his other hand and relished the resulting pain: confirmation of Reality. An upward heave; the strap snapped free. He screamed again and felt an iron grip close on his wrist, let go the strap to clasp Wesley's arm as the flashlight tumbled a lightning-strobed course into the pit below, each spin catching the pack falling in its wake.

A sudden flash. An explosive pop and everything was still.

Balanced in uneasy equilibrium, Wesley's grasp numbing his hand, his foot, also rapidly losing feeling, wedged in some rocky outcrop standing between them and the flashlight's fate, Stephen no longer dared to doubt reality. Wesley began to struggle for a foothold, twisting in his grasp. Stephen felt their hands slip, and screamed at him to stop, his voice echoing endlessly in the darkness.

A hand grabbed his leg, another his belt: easement of the pressure on his foot. Anevai's voice told him *Don't panic.* And from another time and place: *Step at a time, Ridenour. Step at a time.*

A final tug and Wesley was out, the three of them tumbling back and away from the pit-edge, coming to rest in a confusion of arms and legs.

Stephen gasped beneath her. Anevai clutched him until her arms hurt. Wesley's arms squeezed her in similar desperation, his breath harsh in her ear. Suddenly realizing how close she'd come to losing them both, she buried her face in the back of Stephen's neck, rocking gently, startled how much that loss would have meant to her.

Wesley eased away, urging her to come with him. "He can't breathe, missy. Let him breathe."

Stephen, ghostly in the dim light from the Primary behind them, didn't move, aside from those heaving gasps. Finally, a hand crept out of the huddle, touched the ground where she'd been, only to disappear again into the shadows beneath him.

"Lies..." A breathy whisper of sound. "All lies...all ...'lone..."

Lies? All alone? She shook free of Wesley and reached under Stephen for that fugitive hand, and with Wesley's help pulled Stephen into her arms.

"Dead..." The word puffed against her arm. He was trembling, his body still fighting for oxygen. "All...dead. My...f–fault."

"Ridenour?" she said firmly, tightening her hold and rocking him gently. "C'mon, bit-brain. Snap out of it."

He slowly uncurled, his hand working tentatively up her arm until the featherlight touch reached her face. His head tipped back and spook-eyes, deprived of color to reflect, glistened like crystal in the light from the far tunnel.

"A–Anevai?"

"You're not alone, Ridenour, but next time you might be, so quit falling over cliffs, hear me?"

"I—I hear you, Tyeewapi." Still a whisper, but a stronger one. He rested his face against her. "I—I thought...'Tank..."

"RealTime, bit-head." Wesley eclipsed the light. "RealTime and almost Real Dead."

"Wes?" Stephen twisted and nearly fell, clutched at Wesley's steadying hands. "Oh, God, I thought—"

"Hey, kid, I'm fine." The sour note evaporated. "Everybody needs an adrenaline hit once in a while."

A confused attempt to read Wesley's shadowed face ended in

a gasping chuckle. "Th—thanks anyway, I think I've had—all I want."

"In that case," Anevai said, eyeing the black hole beside them, "d'you suppose we can move? I'd hate to sneeze and have to do it all over again."

They staggered and stumbled and held each other up like a trio of sots, but they made it to the lighted tunnel, where she got her first good look at Stephen.

"Gods, Ridenour. We no more get you patched together than you come in here and undo all our hard work. Whatever possessed you?"

"Nayati." He sank wearily onto a rock and braced his elbows on his knees, rubbing his shoulder. Probably got it good this time; Wesley was no lightweight. Served him right: if he'd keep his nose out of other people's business, he'd stay a whole lot healthier.

"He didn't force you here, Stephen."

"Did I say otherwise?" Shoulders heaved, a limp hand fanned the air. "Seemed like a good idea at the time. —Not so good, now."

Wesley said quietly, "Anevai, let's get him home."

"He'd never make it," she said, disgusted and letting it show.

"Don't I . . . havva say . . . in this?" Indignation, on several gasps.

"No!" she and Wesley unisoned.

"Sh—shit." His head fell back against the marbled stone, the rippling light casting strange patterns on his pale skin.

"Wait here," she ordered him, and grabbed Wesley's elbow, moving him down the tunnel for a conference. "If we could get him as far as—"

"Nayati? —Nayati Hatawa, where are you? I need a—"

"Dammit!" Wesley growled, and Stephen, already headed away from them, glanced back, then bolted. Wesley caught him easily enough and slammed him against the tunnel wall, pressing a hand against his mouth. "Shut up, you—"

Stephen struck out, a lightning move Wesley blocked and countered, then hauled Stephen back up against the wall.

Anevai, following at a far more leisurely pace, was still several strides away when Wesley snarled:

"You sonavabitch, you've been popping the bubbles, haven't you?"

Stephen took another swing, but this one was wild, far cry from his previous precision strike.

Wesley shook him again. *"Haven't* you?"

Stephen stopped struggling and stared off down the tunnel, ignoring them both, eerie desperation in the eyes shining above Wesley's hand.

She grabbed Wesley's arm. "Ease off, Smith. What do you mean, he's been popping bubbles?"

"Bubbles—sudsies—"

She shook her head, still confused.

He explained irritably, "Sud'orsofan. Speed demons. Finals fuel." And to Stephen: "You going to keep your trap shut, clone?"

Stephen's eyes flickered and dropped. His shoulders slumped, and Wesley took his hand away, leaving a bloodless imprint in its wake. Stephen licked his lips, worked his jaw back and forth as if that gagging hold had affected more than skin.

"Damned certifiable lunatic."

Stephen glanced up, shuddered, but otherwise ignored Wesley's growled assessment.

"Stephen," Anevai glared a threat at Wesley to keep *his* mouth shut, "you want to tell us what that was all about?"

A delayed shake of the head.

"Dammit, clone—"

She struck Wesley's arm; he turned on his heel, and retreated out of range. "Stephen, you obviously came here for a reason— but actively soliciting Nayati's attention—that's just plain stupid. Can't I help?"

Desperation wavered, but he shrugged, avoiding her eyes.

"C'mon, Stephen, *talk* to me."

"You don't want to hear what I have to say."

"For the gods' sake, Ridenour, we were *teasing*—"

He raised a dismissive hand. "Don't be ridiculous. Not talking about that. Not—" He had to pause for breath. "Not something you want me to know. Nayati . . ."

Fighting sudden, black suspicion, she asked, "What about Nayati? What did he tell you?"

"Nothing." His head tilted defiantly. "Figured it myself."

"Figured what?"

"The Cocheta. —Nayati was leading me to them."

"Bullshit, clone." Wesley stepped between them again, and she didn't stop him, too much happening too fast. "You're nothing but Cantrell's goon—*she* told you. Known all along, haven't you? Been nothing but—"

"Has *nothing* to do with Cantrell." The defiant spook-glare was more than half terror. "I got it out of *your* files, Smith."

"Like hell—"

"Got what, Ridenour?" she demanded, overriding Wesley's angry denial. And when he protested: "Shut *up*, Wes. Makes no difference where he got it. *No* difference."

"Please, Anevai," Stephen whispered. "I've got to know if it was real—see the hats—"

Never the best communicator, terror and desperation were overpowering this attempt. "What *hats*, Ridenour?"

But she didn't really need to ask. Somehow he knew, and that knowledge was driving him into that otherwhere state. "Must see the hats . . . the lights . . ."

iv

It *was* the same. Just like the fossil shell was the same.

Huge amphitheater: childhood memory given form and substance. Only the bodies on the couches and the lights on the high-domed ceiling were missing. Identical, he'd swear it, even to the exact number of softly padded couches with their attendant helmets held neatly in a cradle on the side.

Rusalka-lit, funnel-shaped tunnels: like elevator shafts from a hub. He knew—as surely as if he were standing in one—that the majority of these tunnels were lined with arch after arch of tiny alcoves stretching into infinity in every direction. He knew that architecture the same way he knew the eerily glowing dome overhead could come alive with images so dimensional the viewer's heart knew they were real, but so alien in design and concept, in colors the mind didn't know, shapes so distorted by energies the human eye couldn't see, the viewer's mind could be driven mad with the dichotomy of heart and brain.

If that mind were awake.

This time, Stephen was prepared. That dizzying jolt of *déjà vu* failed to send him bolting from the room, forced him only to tighten his hold on Wesley's arm.

Reality or VRT, this room *was* exactly like the invisible's cave, the way the shell was the same. Even if it was all some virtual reality imposed on him by the Vandereaux Coordinator, you still had to play the game by the rules of the Set. Any other choice courted madness.

"Stephen?"

But something inside him—something he trusted more than Papa, or Danislav or the VRTs—said it *was* Real. And of a sudden, he knew why God had brought him here. Of a sudden, he had Purpose.

"Stephen?"

Of a sudden that interview with Cantrell made sense. *Rostov is dead . . . the same thing could be happening here. . . . The answers may lie in that diary. . . .*

But it wasn't the diary. *He* was the link. *He* was God's way of preventing Rostov from repeating here. His purpose was not to . . . optimize the 'Net. He could only represent Wesley and Anevai in that now. The SmitTee.Sys was *their* purpose. But only he could draw the connection . . . give the warning.

"Stephen!"

"What is this place?" he asked.

"'Bout time you woke up." Strange: Anevai sounded annoyed. "We call it a Library. I don't know what the Cocheta called it."

Library. That was different—not a part of the previous program—but the Controller could add such whimsical details. . . . But that sureness inside chided his persistent skepticism.

"The Cocheta? Your people didn't build it, then?"

She shook her head.

And though the question was hardly necessary: "Are the Cocheta h–human?"

"Were, Stephen, —and, no. At least, not *human*-human."

"I should have known. I should..." The room started to fade, gravity to turn sideways. A hand grabbed his arm, sent a shock wave through him—

"Shit," —and Wesley's growl in his ear snapped him back to the 'Library.'

He moved away from that burning touch. Denied the proffered help with an accusation: "Why didn't you tell me?"

Wesley scowled and thrust his rejected hands in his pockets. "Tell you what, clone?"

"About the Cocheta's part in *Harmonies*?" he challenged, that deception hurting more than he was willing to admit.

"I don't know what you're talking about—"

"Dammit, Smith, I've seen the letter."

"How?" Wesley's hand gripped his arm—a painful grip he endured without objection. The question was rhetorical. Wesley knew the answer—felt righteous anger in that knowledge. "Damn you..."

"I had to know, Wesley. After all you told me... Is this where it really comes from? Is *Harmonies* nothing more than plagiarism of alien technology?"

"Is *that* what you think, Del d'Bugger?"

"What else can I—"

"You've got it wrong, Stephen," Anevai said, "*Harmonies* is just what you originally thought: Wesley's brainchild with useful input from a variety of sources."

Something in Wesley's face indicated disagreement with that statement, but it was no deliberate cover-up, of that, Stephen was sure. He dropped onto a step, the strength gone from his legs, and leaned his head against a stone banister. Anevai settled beside him, her hand on his shoulder.

Wesley scowled, rejecting them both.

"Is that why you left, Stephen?" Anevai asked. "Is that why you went into the woods alone? Why you followed Nayati?"

"Yes... sort of... No, not really..."

"That's what I love about you, clone," Wesley sneered, "your straight answers."

He pressed his lips together and stared at his feet. He was tired, he hurt and his head was whirling far too rapidly to organize the complicated chain of events and motivations she demanded. But he had to try.

"I came because of the Rostov files—to show Nayati—"

"Wait a minute," Wesley broke in. "*What* Rostov files?"

He pulled himself to his feet, tired of fighting Wesley, tired of explaining. "Anevai, is there a 'Link here?"

"Yes, but—"

"Where?"

She pointed with her chin toward the center of the room, a control panel and a desk he now recognized as an ordinary terminal desk. He brushed past Wesley, who stopped him with a harsh grip on his arm.

"What are you doing?"

"I'm going to show you."

"What?"

"The Rostov files. —I *tried*, Smith. I tried to keep you clear, but it's too late now. Someone else has to know, and you're elected."

"What files?"

"Rostov's P1's."

"Since when have you had Priority One clearance, clone?"

He knew what Wesley was asking—had led him to it.

"I don't."

And right on schedule, Wesley snarled: "Bullshit, Ridenour. I was on that system just before we came. If you'd infiltrated those files, the Tyeewapi link would have fried."

"Maybe." He smiled, feeling no humor. "And maybe not."

The suspicion on Wesley's face grew: "I thought we were on the same team, Ridenour."

"This is no game, Smith. There are no *teams*."

"For God's sake, clone, grow—"

"Shut up, both of you." Anevai stepped between them, and: "I said, shut up, Smith. —Stephen, what does Rostov have to do with anything?"

He slumped down into the chair. "I was *born* there, Anevai. I've been told a dozen different lies about what happened and they're all wrong because *none* of those lies included the Caves and the Hats, so I know I've either been lied to or They don't know—*none* of Them do, and if They don't know about that—''

"Stephen, you're babbling again. What 'caves'? What 'hats'?''

"Like these.'' He swung a hand wildly. "*They* are the link—they *must* be.''

"What link? Why?''

"Because there's nothing else!'' Stephen slammed his fist on the desk. "Rostov's dead, Tyeewapi. *D-E-A-D:* gone. Everybody wiped out. Researchers, stationers—everyone but the Recons.'' And in a rush of ruthless honesty: "And Cantrell said it was going to happen here.''

Her eyes widened. She backed a step—caught her balance. "I want to see those files, Ridenour. I want to see them *now*.''

He glared at Wesley. "I'll show you.''

Wesley held out a hand and said, "Truce, kid. I don't know how or why you're making these claims, but don't try—don't ruin yourself. You can't—''

"The hell I can't.''

"Then at least let me—''

"If I'm going to fry, I'd prefer to light my own pyre.''

Wesley stepped back, hands raised in mockery. "Far be it from me, clone.'' •

He scowled and turned to the keyboard, booted, then let his fingers rest on the keys for a moment, just letting the familiar vibration enter his system and calm his nerves.

"Well, what do you think?''

Nayati tempered his anger. The crack *did* look ominous, and no more than they understood about Cocheta engineering methods, it did bear checking. Nigan, damn him, had been right to pull him away from his monitors.

"Let's get back to the control room and I'll run some checks.''

"With *what*?''

"There's a file that might tell us. My Cocheta recognized it, anyway, which indicates it has to do with HuteNamid geology.''

Nigan took his eyes from the fracture in the corner of the Cocheta living suite and stared at him.

"How do you know that?''

Nayati shrugged. "I listened. Let's get back to the control room. I'll see what I can find out from there. Then you'd better go get Sakiimagan so he can have a look."

"Go get him? Why? Call him."

"With Cantrell's snoops around? *You* go and get him."

"Okay. Okay. We can go after dinner at my folks."

"You go. I'll stay here."

Nigan looked at him with that same odd stare. "Are you sure?"

"Of course I am. I want to continue to—monitor the system."

SECURITY ACCESS CLEAR

"There!" With something very close to a sob, Stephen lifted trembling hands from the keyboard and thrust himself away from the computer, shaking from the tension of ac cessing, unable to believe he'd gotten away with it twice, "Have fun!"

"Wes?"

The concerned note in Anevai's voice made him turn—to find Wesley staring at him with something akin to repugnance.

"You accessed *between* the security scans, didn't you?"

He shrugged, and Wesley bellowed, *"Didn't you?"*

Wesley had watched. He knew. He also knew that timing and ordering the accesses so they entered with that split-second precision required an act of faith greater than any sane 'NetTech ever operated on. "Sometimes, you just hold out your hands and trust the bar will be there."

"Except on the 'Net there are no spotters to catch you when you *miss*, you imbecile!"

"I've spent most of my life without spotters."

Wesley's gaze dropped pointedly to his shoulder. "And look what happened."

"Just read the damned files." He turned away, still shaking in reaction. Or perhaps it was the embarrassment of exposing this particular truth of his past that caused the sickness to rise in his throat.

"The *Aquila*. Whose ship is that?" Stephen heard Anevai's

whisper, chose to ignore it. He sank onto the steps, leaning his head against the rail, letting his eyes drift shut.

Sometime later: "No bodies." Anevai again. "What could have happened to them? *Could* there have been a Bios crash?"

"They'd been off Bios for years," he muttered. "Read the damned file, Tyeewapi. The Recons fried everybody. *My parents* did." Two pair of eyes turned to him reflecting the horror churning in his own stomach. "Check out the date." He knew the file they were reading. Transcript from a researcher's journal. A researcher who'd known his parents. "10.24.62. My parents—led the charge in honor of my birthday. Kind of them—"

His voice failed in the face of that continued horror. Two abortive attempts at speech later, he licked his lips, and swallowed hard. "So you see—looks like maybe you were wrong, Tyeewapi. I think, perhaps, I could be—quite dangerously mad. Sobering thought, really... Cantrell should never have brought me here... Perhaps you should have let Nayati..."

"Gods..." Her eyes widened. She fell back a step.

"Anevai, believe me, I don't think I'm homicidal yet! But then—" He felt panic rising. "—I suppose I *wouldn't* know—that's part of being crazy, isn't it?"

"Dammit, Ridenour, *give it a rest!*" Suddenly, Anevai's hands were on his shoulders and she was leaning over and saying right into his face: "Listen to me, Ridenour. You're *not* crazy! You're not even *going* crazy! I won't let you, hear me? Bringing up that file must have snapped your brain."

He was slipping. He knew it. Anevai did, and sought to stop his plunge over a different sort of cliff. "I—hear you, Tyeewapi."

"Good! Keep it up." She patted his face and straightened. "Because *whatever* happened on Rostov is damn well *not* going to happen here. I'm—*We're* not going to let it. Stephen, you said you know what goes on in the Libraries: How?"

He tried to answer. Couldn't get the words out. Felt the sickness rise—

(*"You must never tell, son. If you do it will make you very, very sick...."*)

"Ridenour? —Ridenour!"

(*"Won't tell, Papa. Won't! Won't!... Please, Papa..."*)

''—Damn.'' Hands seized his arms and shook him. One let go and slapped his face. Hard.

''Anevai!'' Wesley's voice, raised in protest.

Laughter bordering on hysteria usurped sickness. ''You're a . . . fine one . . . to obj–ject, Smith,'' Stephen gasped, raising his hand to a cheek still sore from Wesley's 'lovepats.' Swallowing sickness and hysteria, he said to Anevai: ''I *can't* answer. I want to, but I—''

''Never mind,'' she interrupted. ''Your people used the Libraries; *you* did, didn't you?''

He nodded, then closed his eyes against the room's disciplinary cant. *Mustn't tell . . . never tell . . .''*

Anevai's hold tightened, shook him to attention.

''Ridenour, listen to me. I don't think your people did the killing.''

''What do you mean?'' He gasped after breath. ''You *saw* the report! Of course it was—''

''Oh, I have little doubt the Recons were *physically* responsible.''

''Are you saying,'' Wesley said, ''that if they were using the Libraries, perhaps the Cocheta in some way—''

Her hands left him. ''It's what I've been trying to say all along, Wes, and nobody's listened! What *are* the Cocheta but personalities? You don the hat, put in the tape, and you're seeing things and feeling things in a whole new way. But not just *any* tape. You've got to find a compatible—right? Maybe it's a whole lot more dangerous than we thought. Maybe when you merge your senses with a tape, there's a lot more merging going on. *Something* changed Nayati . . .''

Stephen felt something inside him relax. She was onto it. He wasn't going to have to explain. Now, if something happened to him . . . He let his head fall back against the banister.

''. . . If Stephen's people changed the way Nayati has, and the Rostov researchers were as crazy-blind as the Vandereaux students—or even if they weren't that bad—only a . . . a . . .''

From somewhere he knew. From somewhere, insight supplied the term she sought: ''Threat,'' Stephen said quietly. ''I think that's what we are to Nayati. That's what we are to your father, your brother, to anyone who is—merging—with the Cocheta. Perhaps that's how the Cocheta perceive us—''

"Us, Stephen?" Wesley asked.

"Any—noncompatible. That's how they *must* perceive us. It's like the 'Net: you're a part of their—network, or you're an outsider, a threat."

"Why do you think *you're* 'noncompatible'?"

"Why?" He looked down at the console, touched the smooth, glowing surface with a fingertip. "I was sent away from Rostov-on-Don because I was . . . 'unfit for Recon life.' Meaning, I couldn't fit in with my people's increasing preoccupation with their—Cocheta. Maybe I couldn't handle the process—I just don't know. But Stefan Ryevanishov wasn't my *biological* father."

"Good, God!" Wesley threw his hands in the air. " 'Spacer' and 'Recon' mean nothing to the Cocheta. They're dead and gone."

"Are they?" He looked to Anevai, knowing she was tracking the tie-in to her own theory, even if Wesley wasn't, knowing that responsibility, too, was gone from his shoulders, knowing his survival was no longer necessary. . . . "How do we know?"

. . . Not knowing if that changed status was desirable or not.

"They aren't here, are they?" Wesley pushed again.

He shook his head, weary and out of answers.

Wesley scowled. "So what does any of this have to do with—"

"*I don't know!*" He slammed his hands on the console and swung away. "I don't know what the hell I'm talking about. I don't know enough—I *never* know enough." He pressed the heels of his hands to his eyes. "*God!* This is crazy!"

He headed for the exit endless stairs away, balancing against the bannister.

Wesley's voice followed him: "Where the hell do you think you're going?"

He didn't stop—didn't dare. "I must get back to Cantrell with this—"

"And just how do you plan to find your way out?" Anevai's faraway voice asked.

There was no breath to answer. And no plan, she knew that.

But he had to try. Another handful of steps managed, a pause, swaying despite a stranglehold on the rail.

"Optimist," Wesley said drily.

They weren't coming. He'd never make it back on his own.

"Anevai?" he whispered her name, trying to keep the desperation from his voice. Because someone had to get back. If not him—one of them. "Wesley?" The appeal stuck in his throat, but as the floor rose to meet him, two sets of hands cushioned his fall.

"Well, Nayati, I'm off for a decent meal—if Mom hasn't given up and tossed it out."

"Remember: get Sakiimagan and bring him here. And—" Nayati hid his amusement from Nigan, "—don't let Ridenour see you or follow you back. He's in Acoma, you know."

Nigan paused. "What would you do if he did?"

He couldn't resist. "I don't know, maybe give him precisely what he came looking for."

Nigan's laughter sounded hesitant. "You're kidding, right?"

"Sure, Nigan. —Enjoy your dinner." *Just go!* He thought.

"Nayati, are you all right?"

"Of course I am. Just not particularly in the mood for dinner parties tonight. Have an extra steak on me. And give Leotii a kiss for me."

Nigan frowned, then shrugged. "I'll do that. But I'm coming right back, Nayati. I'm worried about you."

Nayati snorted. "Don't waste your energy. Just remember that kiss—and, Nigan?"

"Yes?"

"—Use your tongue."

"On my *sister*? Gods, you're disgusting sometimes."

He laughed delightedly— "Just kidding, Nigan. Go on. Get out of here."

—and sobered the instant the door closed. Damned interfering PitA. How the same parents had produced two such different children . . .

He flipped the scanners on, searching for his players. Ah, they'd split up—

"Nayati—"

He blanked the screens with a sweep of his hand and swung around.

"*What now?*" he shouted; Nigan jerked to a startled halt just inside the door.

"Shit, man. Never mind. I'm outta here."

This time he flipped a switch and locked the door before he turned the screens on.

V

He supposed when it came to basic rest, 'comfort' attained a certain universality. A bed, a variety of cushions, blankets, a couple of contour chairs . . . what more could a man—or a Cocheta—want?

On the other hand, it could be the mortician's laying-out room.

Wesley sank into one of the contours with a groan of relief, plopping the notepad from the Library 'Link onto his lap.

Anevai was on her way back to Acoma, ostensibly to return with a posse; the kid was dead to the world on the cot along the wall; food from an emergencies-only storeroom, a sink in the corner, automatic air circulation, and since he couldn't find his way through the tunnels even if he *could* get out, the closed door made little difference. Far from an ideal situation, but they could last a fair while. Besides, if anything should godforbid happen to Anevai, they had a computer link that (in the *right* hands) could get a message to Cantrell's ship in seconds.

Of course, Cantrell would then have to secure Sakiimagan's aid to get here. He sighed again and opened a new file on the 'pad.

How he let himself get talked into these things . . .

"I don't recognize this room . . ." The hesitant whisper from the cot probably wasn't meant for him, but he answered anyway: "Any reason you should?"

"Everything else is the same—the Library, the tunnels, even the pit . . . There are other pits, aren't there, Wesley?"

"Hell if I know. They don't let me wander loose around here—wouldn't want to, thanks."

"Clever of you. Wish you'd used the same sense when you . . ."

He waited; then: "You ever finish a thought, kid?" when he didn't.

"Why did you follow me?" Short and to the point. For once.

Unfortunately, not a point worth investigating. "What makes you think we did? We were just out for a stroll—heard a banshee screech, and thought we'd check out the party."

A long silence. Then: "Wesley, I'm s–s—" The whisper stuttered into silence.

"Sorry?" He grinned generically. "For what? Standing up for yourself? For showing the old man up, and playing the 'Tap like a game of Galactic Gargoyles? Hell, kid, sure. Consider yourself forgiven."

"That's not—" The whisper died again. "Th–thanks, old man."

Not—? He dragged his chair over to the cot and leaned his elbow on the mattress, grateful at this point for any diversion. "Not what, Stevie-lad?"

"N–never m–mind."

He shrugged and leaned back, tapping the stylus on. He'd had more than his yearly quota of angst in the past week anyway.

The first sweep of the stylus across the 'pad was a joke: the simple egg-shape lopsided and pulling badly. Blocking in features only made it worse. His hands were shaking, he realized suddenly, now the excitement was over. He wiped the screen, hooked a blanket with his toe and pulled it into his lap. He hooked a second, and asked, "Cold, kid?"

No answer. No reaction at all. Maybe the thin-skinned spacer was hibernating . . .

Then out of the silent corner: "Don't start on me, Wes."

"Start? . . . You flatter yourself, clone. You're about as appealing as a sweaty fish right now."

A two-beat pause, then: "Why would a fish sweat?"

He laughed. "Humor. Give the clone a gold star. —Friends, Stevie-lad. Just a cold friend asking."

"Friends." Stephen's soft echo held a note of dawning

awareness. "That's why... I should have known better. Should never have wanted to keep you..." He propped himself up on an elbow, exposing a face pallid with pain, exhaustion—and fear.

"What are you scared of, son?" that look surprised him into asking. "Nayati can't get at you here."

"Not—" His eyes dropped. His fingers tightened on the pillow beneath his elbow. "Not for me. You. I'm sorry I got you into all this."

"Me?" He laughed— "Hell, kid, nothing's going to happen to me."

—Stephen didn't. "You. Anevai. The admiral. Everyone."

"You're creating spooks. Tired, that's all. Anevai's overreacting: Nayati may be crazy, but he's not stupid. 'Sides, what makes you think it's your doing?"

"I told you. Bad things—"

"—happen because of you. Yeah, brat, you told me. I don't recall agreeing with you."

"Doesn't matter what you believe. If I hadn't wanted Papa, Rostov wouldn't have died. If I hadn't wanted to keep you and Anevai safe..."

"We wouldn't be here now? Bullshit. I've got news for you, clone, the universe will go as *it* wants—whatever your desires or lack thereof—so you might as well start actively pursuing a few."

"I know now why mama sent me to Vandereaux."

"Because of this—curse?"

"If you want to call it that. Anevai was right, Wesley. I've *been* on those machines. I remember... Papa said I was—special. Mama said it was killing me. I—I think maybe mama didn't hate me. I think maybe mama sent me away to save me. Maybe to save her whole world. —Papa..."

"What about your father, Stephen?"

Stephen met his gaze squarely. "I think papa was trying to kill me. And I think—maybe—papa was right."

Anevai's feet beat a regular rhythm on the stone floor of the tunnel. The lights, responding to her recognized presence, barely got their glow started before she was past. Not smart to run in these outer ways, particularly when one's knees were beginning to bend backward. But she couldn't shake the sense of urgency—

"Shit!" —A body slammed into her from the side, throwing her to the tunnel floor.

"Better work on those reflexes, *olathe*." A hard-breathing whisper cut through the ringing in her ears, a heavy body pressed her into the ground.

"I'll *beautiful* you, you sonuva—!" She wrenched her knees up in a move which evoked a flash of morning sun on a mountain trail, a dozen other mornings, and practice games which made this weight a familiar one—a flash which undermined her concentration and made her blow lack conviction. . . .

Or maybe she found herself facedown in the grit, her cousin's knee grinding into the small of her back, her wrist imprisoned in one large fist and his other hand wound painfully in her hair, because Nayati was just that much faster than he'd been a week ago. . . .

Or maybe she was just that tired.

"Such language, m'love. One would think you were angry at me." The hand on her hair turned gentle, stroked it smooth, shifted to intercept the elbow she swung back at him.

"Dammit, Nayati, let me up!"

Nayati drew her to her knees, twisting one arm behind her: a deceptively gentle grip she was too smart to fight.

"What are you doing here, Nayati? Dad's expecting you in Tunica."

"As a sacrifice to the Alliance god of politics?"

"You know he doesn't mean—" She clenched her teeth as he twisted the arm.

"If he meant otherwise, he should have specified, now shouldn't he? And what, might I ask in return, are you doing here? Shouldn't you be in Acoma with your pretty Spacer-boy?"

She declined to answer. She knew that *he* knew that she knew that he damn good and well knew that she'd followed Stephen here. He probably even knew where Stephen and Wesley were stashed.

Nayati chuckled and stroked the back of her neck. She jerked away, stopped as her shoulder screamed objections. Nayati pulled his belt free, bound her hands efficiently behind her back, then turned her to face him, brushing the grit from her face and hair.

He touched her cheek, exclaimed at a cut over one eye. "Oh, my dear, don't you see how gravely you've been misled by these evil creatures from space?"

"Strange terminology you're using these days, Hatawa. They're not evil. Not even the enemy. If you'll only—"

"*No!* You're wrong, Sakiimagan's daughter. I'll show you!" Nayati grasped her elbow, pulling her to her feet.

"Wait, Nayati, please." She set her heels, resisting his pull. "I don't—I'm so tired. Can't you just tell me—so I can go home to bed?"

"Is *that* where you were headed?"

"I—" She was caught. She knew it. He knew it. And he knew she knew he knew it. Damn. More than enough to make a tired brain dizzy. More than enough to account for the upset in her stomach. "So what are you going to do now?" she asked.

"Convince you."

"Of what?"

"Your ignorance."

"*Dammit, Corlaney! Get your butt out of bed and open this door!*"

"Loren?" Paul groaned and rolled out of bed.

The banging stopped. The apartment door swung open before he'd found his robe. Loren. Alone—except for TJ listening through her head. "Dammit, yourself, woman," he muttered between yawns. "I finally get to bed at a decent hour and—"

"His signal's disappeared again."

"His . . . *Ridenour's*?"

"Of course, Ridenour's. One minute he was there, the next he was back to imitating a deepspace williwisp."

"Anevai. They're in the maze—"

"What maze?"

"The Libraries. They're a vast complex of caves and tunnels— some very dead ends."

"And the disrupted signal?"

"They have their own defenses."

"And have they also their own offenses?"

"Not that I know of."

"Truth, Paul?"

"Absolutely. We need Sakiimagan."

"He's gone."

"To Acoma?"

She nodded.

"He's after Ridenour."

"We expected as much. He's being held at his in-laws' clinic. TJ's people tracked Ridenour and those two cohorts of his into the mountainside."

"Still on their trail?"

"*Into*, Corlaney. Their trail disappeared into solid stone."

"Wes? Are you awake?"

Stephen's voice drifted from hidden speakers before his image solidified on a wall pulsating with a life all its own.

"Yeah, kid, what is it?" Wesley, somewhere off to the left, his crossed ankles just showing in the viewscreen frame.

Anevai started to speak, but Nayati's hand clamped over her mouth, and his voice whispered in her ear, "Wait."

Stephen rolled up on an elbow to face Wesley. Exhaustion and what Wesley called his 'sudsies' had left their mark: pale eyes glowed dully in shadowed pits, tightly stretched skin created hollows beneath high cheekbones.

"How—how long do you think Anevai will be? How long has it been?"

Anevai stirred, feeling the sting of that question. Nayati's hold tightened, reinforcing his whispered caution.

"I haven't the remotest, brat. Just go back to sleep so that you can state your case loud and clear to the admiral without collapsing at her feet. Poetic, but terribly gauche."

With a tired chuckle, Stephen settled back to stare vacantly up at the ceiling, slowly rubbing his arms. Then:

"Wes?"

"Yeah, kid?"

"I—I really am c–cold."

A low chuckle answered, and Wesley appeared to stand

beside the cot, blanket in hand. *"Figured. —Warm up faster if we share. Promise not to bite?"*

Stephen bit his lip, and nodded. Wesley motioned him off the couch so he could settle into the far corner, sitting up, his side of the blanket slung across his knees, the stylus and notepad he'd scrounged from the terminal desk propped on his lap.

"So—" He nodded toward the pillows and raised the blanket. *"Park it, brat."*

Stephen looked rather dubious, shivering as he stood hugging his arms to his chest. Wesley ignored him, holding the blanket, sketching with his unoccupied hand.

Stephen shrugged and slipped under, back to Wesley, burying himself in the pillows and pulling the blanket up around his ears. Wesley lent a hand, patted his shoulder, then returned to quietly scratching on the pad.

Scritch . . . Scritch . . . the occasional beep of erasure or saving.

Nayati's silencing hand eased, and Anevai felt compelled to object: "For the gods' sake, Hatawa, leave them—"

His raised eyebrow stopped her. His hand reaching for the control panel kept her silent.

"Wes?"

Stephen's nose appeared from under the blanket. Nayati's hand paused.

"MmmHmm?"

Scritch. Scritch.

"What are you writing?"

"Curiosity zapped the 'Tech, brat."

"Oh." The nose turned red and buried itself back into the pillow.

Wesley chuckled. *"Here."* A *beep* of closure, and Wesley lowered the pad in front of Stephen, who considered it in wide-eyed silence, before whispering:

"Is—is that r—really how you s—see me?"

"Yeah, brat. —At the moment." Wesley removed the pad and flipped it to the floor, screen side up. It was a sketch—what looked to be a child—a curly-headed, almost-child with long lashes and a bruised, sad look about the eyes. A caricature, as all Wesley's drawings were, but one of surprising sensitivity,

even to Anevai; and she could only guess the message he sent to Stephen through it.

"*So go to sleep.*" Wesley finished, holding out his arms. "*I'll wake you when Mama comes to take us home.*"

Whatever the message, Stephen moved willingly into Wesley's offered embrace and settled there with a little shiver as Wesley pulled the blanket up over his shoulders.

"Shit," Nayati said aloud. "Lousy show, 'NetHeads." He reached for the control panel, touched a sequence she didn't recognize.

"Nayati, what are you—"

"Wait and you'll see, my dear. Soon—very soon, now."

Within moments, Wesley's eyelids drooped, his head nodded, fell with a *thud* onto Stephen's.

"*Ow! Wesley, get—*" Stephen rubbed his head and Wesley's head slipped down to his shoulder with another thud. "*Dammit, Wes, wake . . . up. . . .*"

Stephen shook at Wesley's arms, but Wesley only draped like a corpse over Stephen's shoulder.

Anevai whispered, "What did you do to him?"

"Your friends will be fine. Amazing, really. Ridenour should have been long gone by now. . . ."

Stephen slipped off the edge of the couch, collapsed to his knees, face-to-face with Wesley. He fumbled at Wesley's awkwardly twisted limbs, trying to straighten the limp body, but couldn't seem to find the leverage. He slipped down, retching dryly, and Anevai, remembering his copious allergies to foods and drugs, felt sympathetic spasms twist her own gut and throat.

"Nayati, you've got to get him out of there. Can't you see? Whatever you put in there is making him—"

"Relax. He'll be all right."

But for all his seeming lack of concern, Nayati touched a button. A hiss of venting; the door slid open.

Nayati gestured toward the door. "After you, *olathe.*"

She stepped through the doorway.

Stephen's head came up. The look of betrayal in his spook-eyes prodded her to try something foolish—like throwing herself bodily at Nayati, for all the good it would do—but as he fought to his feet, white-faced and swaying, those spook-eyes focussed on her bound hands and that betrayed look vanished, leaving only the weary pride that kept him on his feet.

"I'm sorry, Spacer-man," she said ruefully. "I'm afraid I blew it."

She saw that ruefulness echo in his eyes as he lost the battle for balance and sat down hard on the couch, trying one last time to rouse Wesley.

Failing that, he said, "Never mind, Tyeewapi. I think—I think I actually expected it—"

vi

Taste of sickness in his mouth, pounding in his head...

Shit, Tyeewapi, if you want me to lie down and shut up... When you feel like this, Zivon...

Tranquillizer: a new brand, but he knew the symptoms. Any moment he'd be much too sick to be lying on his back, regardless the comfort of the bed. He would swear, if his mouth would cooperate.

"Damn you, Nayati."

Thank you, he thought.

And of a sudden, his head was surprisingly clear for the aftermath of tranq, the pain gone. He wondered vaguely if that secession was a side effect of the new drug. That would be a pleasant change.

But his eyes didn't want to get open yet, so he let them be closed.

Hands. Always hands. Hands on his arms, his legs, places he didn't want hands to be. And he couldn't move, though panic made the blood pound in his ears.

Cold steel against his skin, splitting him from throat to groin. But there was no pain, no hot flow of blood. His clothes fell away, exposing bare skin to chilling, drifting air currents.

And still, he couldn't move.

Fingers touched his side, probing recent injury, bringing pain and memory. . . .

(Dust motes in the dark. Coarse straw beneath his feet. Glint of curved steel in the moonlight . . .

("Ridenour, look out! . . .")

"Just as well this will heal scarless . . ."

A Voice, out of that memory, but not of it.

"I doubt he will care to account for it around a warrior's fire . . ."

The remains of clothing jerked from under him. A moment later, sharp snap of elastic against his waist.

"I trust your—sensibilities will not be offended."

And another voice:

"Surely you don't have to . . ."

"Oh, but I must. Nothing must come between the user and the suit."

"Whatever. —Nothing I haven't seen before, Hatawa." A laugh. *"I've done my time in the nurseries since I was ten. —You don't change much. Takes more than hormones to make a—"*

A sound—skin striking skin—a gasp of pain. And he was helpless to prevent it.

Again the touch of steel—this time at his hip.

(A cacophony of voices and laughter. A mouth closing on his: bitterness turning rapidly bittersweet.

(Hands. Hands holding him, hands traversing each muscle as it is exposed, leaving cold in their wake.)

Cognition returned as another touch swept from collarbone to crotch sealing him in warmth, and for a time he was too busy relishing that sensation to object when those hands pulled and pushed him.

"You're pretty handy at putting all this together, Nayati. Done it before, have you?"

"Once or twice."

"Like on my brother?"

Laughter. *"Feel free to move about. Ridenour's out for a good while yet."*

"Where are you going?"

"Guess."

The sound of the door closing.

"Anevai?" For a moment, he wasn't sure his mouth had cooperated, then:

"*Stephen? Can you hear me?*"

"Anevai? Where—"

"Gods. Nayati said you'd be out for hours. —Listen, Stephen, don't try to talk. Nayati's gone—for now. We're locked in here—"

"Wh–where?"

"I—I don't know what Nayati intends for you. This is a different room—a special machine . . ."

He tried to move; panicked when he couldn't.

Anevai's touch on his face steadied him. "Easy on, Stephen. He–he's got you strapped down . . ."

"F–feel s–strange . . ." He didn't know how else to put it. He couldn't feel restraints—only that inability to move.

"Stephen, I don't think we have much time. Nayati will be back any minute. You said you used Rostov's Libraries, but you didn't say how. The one in the main hall is like tuning in to somebody else's brain to watch a RecVid. This thing—Dad declared them off-limits years ago, so I don't think they can be real healthy. Gods, how much of this are you getting?"

Not much time. Nayati had to know . . .

"A–Anev . . . lis'n." He fought to explain. "M–must tell." And suddenly, he knew. "D–diary. Show N–N'ati . . ."

"Oh, gods . . ."

Sincerely upset. He hadn't meant for that.

"Stephen, I—Gods, I'm so sorry. The pack . . ."

The strap snapping. Wesley's grip closing on his wrist. Lightning strobed fall into blackness . . .

"G–gone?"

Another gentle touch on his cheek that was kind if unnecessary. If he could shrug, he would. Better the diary than Wesley. But that had been his only suggestion. He could no more bring up those Rostov files now than he could fly.

"Wh–what d–do?" he whispered.

"If you can just hold on—pretend you're still asleep, maybe I can delay him a bit. I left a note for the grans and—"

"Actually, Annie-love, I imagine your father will be heading in this general direction real soon now. Would you care to go meet him? Show him where to come?''

He'd know that voice on his deathbed.

A thud. Footsteps. A closing door. A rattle.

A hand gripped his chin and rocked his head left then right. It—hurt. Too much pain for the pressure. Despite Anevai's advice, he winced—at least his face muscles tried to contract, but unless his face was functioning more efficiently than the rest of him, Nayati wouldn't notice.

The hand left.

Before he could congratulate himself, the hand hit him. Quite hard. Quite painfully.

"Nayati!" Anevai protested vehemently.

Thank you, Anevai.

"Get 'em open, Spacer!" Nayati's voice ordered. "I know you're awake."

This time, his eyes opened willingly enough; possibly the added moisture helped. He blinked; the moisture dripped into his ear; his vision cleared—

—to Nayati's hand raised to strike again.

"Dammit, Nayati, *stop it*!"

"Thank you, Anevai," he said, his voice surprisingly cooperative. "I assure you, Hatawa, additional force is—quite unnecessary."

"I commend you, Ridenour." Nayati's face tilted above him, underexposed shadow against the ceiling's glow. "You had me fooled. You must have returned to us some time ago."

"Since I'm only recently cognizant, I can't very well accept the credit for prevarication, can I? —Strange. What was the gas? I'm familiar with the early symptoms, but I've never felt quite so clearheaded af—"

"Nor so damned chatty," Anevai muttered, and more loudly: "Don't you know when to shut up, Ridenour? —Shit. Researchers and questions."

He turned toward her voice, perplexed. His eyes were watering again, his face stinging quite amazingly. He said to her moisture-rippled image: "But I thought you said to delay—"

Her dismay was almost funny. "Ridenour, for the gods' sake!"

A bark of Nayati-laughter from the other side. "Not so sharp as you think, CodeHead."

"Oh, but I am, Hatawa." He swung his head back to that side, closing his eyes as the room spun sickeningly, swallowed hard and opened them again. "Quite thoroughly clearheaded. And since you obviously heard Anevai's advice, I thought I should at least make the attempt on some point of real interest. If we could isolate the exact combina—"

Nayati laughed outright this time. "I don't believe this! Annie-girl, I'm beginning to understand your affection for this lunatic!"

He asked, curious, in a rather detached way. "Does that mean you'd consider releasing me so that we can solve this dilemma in a civilized manner?"

"Sorry. I'm not *that* taken with you, Spacer-man," Nayati said, turning his back.

"Oh." He tried to keep the tremor from his voice.

Nayati laughed. "You said you wanted to meet the Cocheta— well, take a look around. Say hello."

Equipment surrounded him. Equipment he recognized, now he had the leisure. Looming overhead, not the hats of the outer hall, but a full-blown helmet, below, a contour couch and in between, a network of straps formed a harness holding him to that couch, and on his body—

Somehow, he was no longer quite so detached. A black second-skin covered him from the neck down. Across that skin-like surface, a complex design pulsed and rippled: the tunnel marbling in miniature, a single, iridescing thread wide, a spark of light at each branching.

Too short. It formed webs between his fingers, cut into his crotch and pressed his shoulders. But he welcomed those minor discomforts; they added a sense of reality to an otherwise unreal situation.

His heart rate picked up; he heard a beep match that pulse—like a medical monitor—and controlled it. Mostly.

"Nayati, don't you think . . ." Anevai's voice shook around the edges.

"No," Nayati said shortly. He was sorting something, a process Anevai watched with growing horror; a look which did nothing to help his blood pressure. But Nayati continued: "No—no . . . m-m-m–maybe . . . no! This one!" And pushed his selection into the control board.

"What do you mean, 'no, no, maybe and yes'?" Anevai cried, "You don't know whether the Cocheta on those tapes will agree with Stephen or not! You *can't*."

A hint of a smile. "Care to make a small wager on that?"

His heart skipped a beat, but he managed to ask quite steadily, "How, Nayati? How do you know?"

The ghost-smile turned to him and deepened. "What's knowledge but sensing what is and knowing it's right?" He held up one of the items he'd been sorting, and Stephen recognized it out of Zivon-memory. "My Cocheta knows who and what these symbols represent. I know what I want. When the two harmonize I—hear the music."

Anevai cried: "And you're willing to risk a man's sanity— possibly his *life* on your damn *taste in music*?"

Nayati's head tilted against the backdrop of lavender-glow ceiling, a positively warm smile appearing. "My taste in music. I *like* that. Thank you, sweetheart."

"I'm not your damn sweetheart! I'm not your damn sweet-anything!"

The position of Nayati's head did not alter . . . his expression did. "I'm sorry to hear that . . ."

"Nayati, if you don't mind—"

"Shut up, spy!"

Bound as he was, he couldn't even roll with Nayati's backhanded swipe. It snapped his head to one side, and he heard Anevai cry out. He opened watery eyes to find her watching him, and tried to mask his very real fear with a smile that shook and a half-wink that worked a little better.

She looked very worried—

A logic flow eminently reasonable to him.

vii

"Paul's here, governor." Leotii Wakiza's voice announced over the intercom.

"Tell him to come in, please."

Sakiimagan tapped the papers into order and closed the hardcopy file as the door opened on Paul, with Leotii on his arm.

"Here he is, sir," she said cheerfully, gripping his arm, apparently prepared to stay.

"Thank you, Leotii," he said firmly. "Leave us, please."

"Sorry, Doc." She tipped her head at Paul and shrugged. "On your own."

Sakiimagan followed her out, checked the waiting room, closed—and locked—the door.

Paul's eyebrow twitched. "To keep me from bolting?"

"No, Paul. Just to—slow up any unwanted interference."

Paul settled on the couch.

He retreated to the desk before asking, "Did you get Cantrell's people to stop the monitoring?"

"I didn't even ask. You should feel lucky you're not cooling your heels aboard *Cetacean* right now."

He drummed the desktop slowly with his fingertips. The one thing he'd asked... "Goodbye, Paul." He reopened the file and began scanning another of the letters it held.

But Paul didn't leave. "Not going to work, Sakiima. You know very well Loren would never consent to such an arrangement. Would you, considering what's at stake?"

"What's at stake?" He looked up, met Paul's challenging gaze. "I don't think you've any concept of what's at stake, Paul. You never have had."

"So enlighten me."

He didn't, waited instead for that condescension to break.

"Goddammit, what's the point?" Paul slammed his hands on the chair arms and jerked to his feet.

"Paul, wait."

Corlaney stopped just short of the door.

"The issue, my dear old friend, is Rostov."

"*Rostov!*" That brought him around. "Since when?"

"Since long before you came here, and I pray to all the gods that I'm right to trust you—and your Loren Cantrell—now. Sit down, Paul, please." And when he had: "Have you ever wondered how I developed my personal—network?"

"The recruitment program? I assumed it was all a part of IndiCorps admin—a part you simply utilized somewhat more creatively than other Recon governors."

Creative. If only that was all . . .

"Your admiral asked me once if I'd ever been offWorld." Sakiimagan breathed deeply and committed to Truth. "I sidestepped the issue then; I'm not now. Years ago, I was the People's senate observer. We were just starting the plans for the SciCorps buildings and determining our personal InterCorps charter."

Paul looked startled. "Senate observer? at Vandereaux? When?"

"I was thirty-six at the time. But I wasn't there long; I saw the anti-Recon bias already in ascendance, and soon realized how nonproductive my time would be. After speaking with other colonial representatives, I decided on a more fruitful use of that time and my observer credit allotment. I took a berth on a merchanter ship, went wherever they did and compared how various systems functioned. I met many people: merchanters, researchers, and colonials of all types. I *knew* Stefan Ryevanishov, Paul, long before you ever met him."

"You . . . knew him." Paul's face mirrored his inner struggle against anger. "All these years, and you never told me. *Why?* I thought we were friends."

"I've *told* no one. A few have guessed over the years, but I received no sanction from the Elders to leave Vandereaux; the opportunity presented itself and I took it. I stayed on Rostov longer than anywhere else. They had a good system—excellent interCorps relations at the time. Stef was quite young—eighteen or twenty—and more current on the Rostov SciCorps projects than most of the resident researchers."

"Well, it didn't last. When I was there, Stef was rarely around SciComp. I enjoyed his company, so I sought him out."

"Actually, Paul, he sought *you* out. He knew things were going sour—was trying to help salvage what he could of—"

"What did you *really* find at Rostov?"

"You don't at all realize—Stefan told you nothing?"

"Dammit, Tyeewapi, will you please stop talking in circles?"

"We didn't discover the Libraries by accident, Paul. I was looking for them—after I returned home."

He paused to let that sink in, relieved when Paul's antagonism faded to a much healthier curiosity.

"The Cocheta were on Rostov?" Paul asked.

"Does that surprise you? Personally, I'd expect to find evidence of their presence in each system of this cluster. We've no evidence they originated on HuteNamid—to the contrary—and they were obviously not star-tied."

"And Stefan knew of the Rostov Cocheta?"

He nodded. "They were a fairly new discovery at the time. There had been a few—disastrous mergers. Stef's people refused to allow researchers in."

"Why? If they were such a shining example of interCorps cooperation—"

"They refused to compromise their friends' honor. The option of the Recon patent umbrella did not then exist." He shifted in his seat, stretching tense muscle around a different cushion, used that movement as an excuse to avoid Paul's eyes. "Besides, the Cocheta do not encourage—notoriety. And there's the accountability."

"Accountability? As in explaining dead researchers?"

He nodded.

"Disastrous mergers," Paul repeated slowly. "Like Barb and Will?"

"I fear so, though I don't know the specifics of Rostov's problems."

"Did—did you ever hear from Stef—after I came? Anything to indicate any interCorps trouble brewing? Trouble such as would lead to civil war?"

"I heard from him, but nothing of that magnitude. I *did* hear about his son. And Zivon Ryevanishov is a primary concern right now."

"Why? I mean, it's nice Stef got his son, but—"

"Stef got more than a son." He leaned forward, pressing the HC-file flat with his elbows, wishing he could give them to Paul without that unseen listener's knowledge. "Paul, I'm worried. Ever since the admiral entered the system, the situation has deteriorated. Hononomii's arrest, the subsequent 'Net shutdown was only the beginning. And I couldn't put it together until you gave me the final clue."

"The boy's affiliation with Rostov."

He nodded. "Precisely. —If he *is* Stef's son. This *son* he speaks of and his 'special abilities'... somehow, I don't think Stef was referring to intelligence."

"You mean, you think Stephen's been in the Rostov Libraries?"

"I'm certain Stef's Zivon had been, for all Stef avoids saying outright."

"You keep saying 'Stef's Zivon,' as though Stephen is *not* Stef's boy."

"He might not be."

"You've never met Ylaine or you'd never say that."

"Physical alterations are simple, Paul."

"It's more than features."

"Careful training."

"I don't believe it."

"Stef would *never* have let that child out of his control."

"Perhaps he had no choice."

"Then if Ridenour *is* Zivon Ryevanishov, he is doubly dangerous to us. Who knows what Council has gotten out of his head—or put into it?"

("Please, Papa, no more. You promised...")

("One more time, son. Just one more time. So you'll be safe.")

("Safe from who, Papa? Bad men? Like the ones who hurt m--Mama?")

("I don't know if anything can make us safe from people like that, son. This is for the invisibles....")

The lights were making pretty patterns on the ceiling again, only there weren't so many colors as before and it wasn't the ceiling this time. This time his whole head was covered and the lights played inside this different hat and even inside his eyeballs.

("Remember, Zivon, you must never talk about your invisibles, or the caves or the hats. Not to me, not to anyone. Remember the way you feel right now. If anybody tries to make you tell, even if they hurt you, or give you medicines that make you feel the way you feel right now and try to make you talk,

you just go back to the time before you ever knew about the invisibles. . . ."

("Do you want me to lie, Papa? You said lying was bad. Please, Papa, I don't understand . . .")

His fingers hurt like his outgrown gloves and he hurt elsewhere—like his clothes were all too tight. A low buzz. Warm swept over his body and the Hurt went away and he was floating like the ZeroGym.

He loved ZeroG.

But ZeroG was Vandr'o. The lights were home and Papa.

("Papa, they're hurting me, the pills are making me sick. Papa, it's not about the invisibles, can I tell them? Even if it's lies? Please, Papa?")

"Ridenour, if you can hear me, say yes."

Ridenour? Who was that?

"I know you can hear me, Ridenour. Stop fighting, and let the spirit of the Cocheta enter your body—welcome him—he will take you to the height of sensory ecstasy. Go with him—ride the winds of freedom from your human limitations and remember it. Remember every moment to the depths of your heart and soul. . . ."

He felt his body begin to tingle—stimulation of nerve endings, one part of him (*That* was the Ridenour!) said. But Zivon believed the Voice. He believed the Voice because he could feel the fingers, the invisibles, crawling in his brain and up inside his fingers and his legs—and all over him.

"You must remember the ride clearly, Ridenour, because from now on, any time you are tempted to reveal the secrets of the Cocheta to the Enemy, your Cocheta will take you on that ride and you will stay there until I tell you to come down. Do you know who I am, Ridenour?"

Ridenour said, "Yes."

But I don't! What's a cheta? It's invisbibbles! They're running races in my tummy!

"Tell me who I am, Ridenour."

"N–Nayati. Nayati Hatawa."

Yeah. Well, Naughty Hatwa, you're dumb—real dumb. Can't tell a cheta from a 'visbibble. . . .

"That's right, Ridenour. So if you—"

"Dammit, Nayati, that's a death sentence! You won't be there—"

"Shut up, woman!"

Not nice, Naughty. Not nice to yell at ladies. Mama said never ever ever yell at ladies. You're not *a nice man, Naughty Hatawa.*

Naughty was still talking, but he kept saying the same things—besides, Papa had already told him the same stuff and he was talking about invisibles not chetas—so Zivon was bored so he quit listening. The invisibles walking inside him were making tickly patterns in his tummy and running down his legs and back up again. Zivon wanted to laugh but his mouth didn't work. Then the Ridenour began feeling awful things. Remembering worse things; things that made Zivon remember the researchers and Mama's crying. Made his body start to—

"No! Dammit, get out! Get out of my head! Leave me alone!"

Blackness.

Silence.

Sweat fled his pores, but his skin felt no dampness.

Air escaped his lungs and rushed back in, but he had no mouth and no nose.

Panic drove him, made muscles contract, but his feet felt no collision with the ground.

"Open your soul to your Cocheta. Be one with the World."

But he was not one with the World. Not any World. The Voice itself had reminded him, once.

Hands. *Pretty pretty 'buster-boy. We'll make you feel good.*

Hands in the dark. Not Papa's invisibles, not the researchers—Vandereaux's VRTs: *Pretty 'buster-boy. Tired? You want a break? A change of scenery?*

And more hands. *What's the matter, 'buster-boy? Homesick? We can make you feel better—help you forget all about home . . .*

"Ride with your Cocheta—feel the ecstasy . . ."

"No!" Running again in the sensory void.

"Become one with your World . . ."

Sensory image of a blue-green ball, of clouds and rain, of thunder and—Zivon shuddered—of lightning. But that was not his World. Neither was his world the golden-brown memory of Rostov.

His World—his Reality—was Space—total Space. *Not* Vandereaux's, not the VRT's. The older one. The Space that welcomed him, talked to him through tingling fingertips, that had no hands to rouse frightful sensations.

Running. But he could not outrun the Sense. Soon he would have no energy left to fight it and the blue-green ball would become Reality.

—Accept.

—Accept.

He stopped running and defied the Sense—repulsed the hands and the fear. But he was weakening. Sensation was too powerful, he'd given up to it too often in the past.

"Take him into your soul . . ."

"It's *not* my World!"

Beyond the Sense lay another. Aware now—of him and the battle he fought. The Other was Serenity. Safety. It told him so and reached for him. . . .

"What is it you want of me, Sakiima?" Paul's hoarse voice betrayed a sleepless night to match Sakiimagan's own. "I can't keep what you've told me from Loren—couldn't if I wanted to: she's already heard."

He took a deep breath. "I wanted you to read Stef's letters, Paul. I wanted to see you in private so you could—so I knew you had before *she* got them."

He held Paul's eyes, then dropped his own deliberately toward the desk. Trusting Paul would understand and respond accordingly. But when he raised his eyes again, Paul shook his head: there was no way. They had to depend on Cantrell's discretion, now.

He should never have delayed so long bringing Paul in. Now, it might be too late.

He sighed and asked, weary in every bone, "What do *you* want of *me*, Paul? My blessing? I can't give it to you. My permission? You don't need it. My understanding? You have it, for what it's worth. I'm too old, and the Cocheta have been my responsibility for too long, for me to truly trust anyone of your Loren Cantrell's position. Whatever you do, you must manage it on your own, but we have no army here to compete with her Alliance security troops—so do as you will."

"I want your help, Sakiima. Did you come here to kidnap Stephen? I can't believe you'd want him dead. —Not even if he were a spacer-spy."

"I just wanted to talk with him. Find out what he could—or has—revealed to Cantrell—determine for certain if he *is* Stef's Zivon. But he's not here."

"We know that. They're in the maze. We don't know why they've pulled this stunt. Stephen didn't signal *Cetacean*, so he's either deliberately disobeying Loren, or he had no choice. Either way, they're up to something and we don't have time to—"

"*I don't care who's with him! I've got to—*"

The sound of splintering wood. Nigan Wakiza burst through the office door, struggling in Leotii's grip.

"Dammit, boy!" she said, setting her feet and hauling him bodily back out the door. "You'll wait like a civilized Human Being! Now *sit!*"

A *thud* from the waiting room: the couch hitting the wall.

Leotii eased the door open on its ruined hinges and announced, somewhat breathlessly, "If you please, sirs, Nigan Wakiza is here with what he claims is an emergency. Will you see him?"

He shot a glance at Paul, soliciting opinion. "He's been in the caves with Nayati."

"Get him in here."

He nodded to Leotii, then added: "And Leotii? —Thanks. Above and beyond."

She grinned. "No problem, sir. I needed the practice—he needed a reminder." And from the outer room, "You may go in, Mr. Wakiza."

Nigan stalked through the door, rubbing his shoulder and glaring back at his sister, muttering: "Damn traitor. *Mr. Wakiza*, my . . ." Then meeting Sakiimagan's eyes, "Sir, you've got to go to the main Library. Nayati's finally gone round the bend and I'm afraid he's going to kill Ridenour if you don't hurry."

(*Fingers weaving in and out: lightning between the squigglies of his brain cells.*

(*He screamed and screamed and screamed for Papa to stop—to make them go away . . .*

(*His own bed, his own room and Mama holding him and telling him to wake up. The frantic beating of his own heart. His arms wrapped around Mama. His ear pressed to her soft breast. And Mama's heartbeat faint in his ear: the special rhythm that was and always would be Mama.*

(*"Is this what you call making him one of us, Stef?" Mama's voice, making her chest hum in his ear. Shivering through the air above his head. "What have you been doing to my son?"*

(*"He's mine, too, Ylaine." Warmth in his tummy at that, settling the invisibles, easing the pounding in his head. "Aren't you, Zivon?"*

(*He blinked stupid baby-tears from his eyes and smiled across at Papa, reaching for him. Mama's hold tightened. He protested, and she let him go. Papa tossed him in the air and caught him again, one hand slipping under his nightshirt to bare skin. He felt Papa's heart through that hand, the way he could now, strong and sure—like Papa; not fast and thumpy like his own.*

(*He wanted his to be like Papa's.*

(*He pulled at his nightshirt, heard buttons pop off as they caught in his hair, then he was pressed against Papa's bare chest, hugging as tight as he could, feeling Papa's heart, Papa's confidence. Feeling all the good feelings that happened in Papa's arms now. The feelings built and built until he exploded inside, the lights dancing in his head and only Papa's arms keeping him from falling into the black pit.*

(*Papa's laughter rang inside him. "One of us, Ylaine? Never. My Zivon is special. He's done something no one else can."*

(*"My God, Stef, what have you done to him?"*

(*Mama's hands on him again. A cocoon of blankets pushing*

*him back inside himself. He began to cry. Alone again, with the
pounding back in his head, worse than before.*

*("You've taken any choice out of it, Stef. I'm putting that
application through—calling in every bit of karma I can find.
I'm going to get him out of here before you destroy him.")*

"No, Mama, no . . . please, Papa, don't let her send me
away . . ."

"Stephen? Are you all right?"

Stephen? Did she mean Zivon?

"Mama?"

"Stephen!"

Nyet. Stephen. But—that *was* him. He was two people. He
was Papa's Zivon, but the Spacer-voice told him he was
Stephen Ridenour. For ever and ever and ever.

"Damn you, Anevai, shut up! Do you want to ruin everything?"

Nayati's hissed reprimand buzzed in his ears, driving the
Zivon memory elsewhere.

Stephen realized, in a vague and distant way, that he was
conscious. Sort of. It was all very strange. Strange, that the
sensations floating through him should conjure that particular
Zivon-memory. Strange, that the Ridenour wasn't more frightened. He remembered he had been. Once. Before the invisible
Other joined them and wrapped them in a safe Papa-esque
cocoon.

"Nayati, can't you see he's awake! You're going to—"

"He can't be—"

Remote awareness. Stephen registered that and ignored it as
superfluous. Zivon, the Ridenour, the Other: they were important.

Another flash of total Awareness—of total Dimensional Space.

The Other—invisible spirit, Cocheta machine, or its own
Self—probed delicately into the Body and Mind that had been
Stephen NMI Ridenour, hearing what the Ears heard, seeing
what the Eyes saw, feeling what the Body felt.

Zivon was frightened: he knew this machine, and associated
pain, accepted the machine and the pain, because the machine
meant Papa, and Papa had been gone for so long; but Zivon
knew the feeling, feared sickness that would follow, and that
after the sickness he'd be forgotten—a dim-string spinning
forever in space. The Other identified the association and

offered reassurance: no sickness this time. No mistakes. We know you. We won't corrupt the interface.

The Ridenour theorized the danger, knew what happened physiologically when the machine's intoxicating stimuli sensitized the Body. Could see and feel the blood coursing through veins, the electrical impulses firing between neurons, the clotting at a corpuscular hemorrhage. Recognized and could not prevent the Mind from extrapolating that Awareness to its Zivon-memory conclusion. And felt fear, knowing the force which had driven him close to the edge of sanity as a child—was back.

He should worry about these voices in his head, but he already knew he was crazy—had verification on the best authority: *Certifiable lunatic*, Wesley had called him. But it made sense—neural networking—interactive programming on the highest level. Just him, his other selves and the alien machine.

He'd never felt less alone.

The Other's cocoon enfolded them, holding him together like Mama's warm blanket, isolating him from too many others' input. Stephen welcomed its presence, reassuring Zivon and ordering the Ridenour to silent acceptance. And when the Awareness expanded to include colors human eyes should not register, sounds too low or high for human ears to distinguish, vibrations so fine human touch shouldn't feel them, that sound/touch/image gestalt made a beyond-analysis symphony.

Symphony. Harmony. Wesley had been more right than he could possibly imagine. This was the totality of Space—Reality as it was, not as others insisted.

And with the Other's help, his Awareness expanded—or contracted—to include the Sense, and the Sense's world became Real, gained substance as the mountain surrounding him as a living, breathing entity: an extension of his own body, and part of the Reality. But not all, the Other reassured him, guiding him into spacial organization—directories, the Ridenour called them, and the Other registered amusement. A careless hoof tracked the surface, sending a tiny cascade of stones down a slope, and the reverberations echoed through the mountain:

sounds which revealed shape and contour, density and composition. Grain of softness deep within stone. Identification. Zivon's elation at the diary's survival.

Someone tried to scan the mountain; the local Matrix expanded to include the energy source beyond the atmosphere: *Cetacean*, the Ridenour supplied. He felt the probing waves vibrating the stone—felt the mountain distort the return pattern, felt the Other's satisfaction at properly functioning safeguards.

"... *the enemies of the Cocheta must not learn of their existence. The safety and future of the Cocheta depend upon your ability to maintain their secret....*"

The Other's cocoon wavered. Panic. Anger. The Oneness at risk. The need to survive. Stephen struggled to maintain that sanctuary for Zivon and the Ridenour, but the Other's reactions were too powerful.

"... *When the Enemy seeks the Cocheta's secrets, you will join with your Cocheta and ride on the wings of ecstasy....*"

Probing, electrical fingers. Tingling threads of energy entering through his pores and hair follicles, coalescing in the centermost regions of his body. Zivon giggled at the invisibles, the Ridenour strove to Name the energy, the Other overpowered them both and responded as it deemed appropriate:

Survival. Reproduction.

(*Lightning-strobed blackness, hands and laughter in the dark ...*

("*Bijan says your kind like it rough. ... C'mon, 'buster-boy, let's see what you've got.*")

The Ridenour screamed.

(*The wonderful floating car whooshing over the pasture, obatsi scattering like wild birds. Laughter, his own and others. A hand touching his knee.*

(*A child's voice asking to go home. The hand moving higher, squeezing his leg.*

("*Not yet, pretty 'buster-boy.*")

Zivon screamed.

Terror. Pain. Betrayal.

("*Say Thank you to the nice men for bringing you home ...*")

("*The Board has determined the best interests of all parties ...*")

Anger overriding the Awareness. Anger at those responsible for the pain, anger at those who failed to protect the young.

The Voice no longer mattered. The Voice no longer controlled. The machines did not. The Other cut the Awareness, wrapped the Zivon/Ridenour in its cocoon of darkness, freed him of the terrifying sensations.

"Dammit!"

The Matrix localized. Remote awareness returned.

"Nayati, what is it? What's happening to him? —Stephen? Stephen!"

This time, the blow to the female-entity might have been to him. His Matrix stretched to include her pain, the sting in the male-entity's hand, the horror and frustration of the male-entity at his own lack of control. Knew when that same hand reached for the intensity dial, and shared the Other's frustrated impotence as increased sensory input overwrote the Universal Awareness and shattered its insulating cocoon.

But Stephen didn't need the Other now. He had fought this battle before.

Come to me, pretty 'Buster-boy, come to me when you want more . . .

Everybody uses everyone else, isn't that what you told me, Bijan? Consider yourself used.

Releasing the Self to the Eudoxin—letting the partner's feelings override fear—*using* those feelings to distract a too-aware mind: he *knew* this game. Knew the rules better, perhaps, than the Voice did.

The Voice began the litany of secrecy and enemies, of flying high and safety. He turned the feelings over to the Other; the Other understood them, would not panic. *He* controlled the association:

"The enemy. . ."

("Open it, Spacer-man." Moonlit pillbox. Nayati's face beyond. "One of us gets blown to hell, we both do . . .")

The Other objected: don't give the Voice power over you.

Stephen acknowledged the wisdom in that, and chose more carefully.

(A bare hip. The taste of blood.)

The Other again: grim satisfaction but caution against too shallow an image.

Stephen laughed and gave the Other the rest of the memory, felt the surge of anger and suppressed it. In this, he knew better than the Other: Bijan was a safe Enemy: understood—controllable.

". . . safety and future . . ."

("Stephen, I need a hug real bad . . .")

("One step at a time, Ridenour . . .")

("Remember what the admiral said about the 'NetAT's interest? Truth, kid. Absolutely.")

Odd, that his mind should conjure Chet's words along with Anevai's and Wesley's. Forlorn hope for the onetime dream? Or because truth, like safety, was relative? Cantrell had lied to him—more than once. But always for *someone's* benefit, if not his own. That did not make her the Enemy.

Just as Papa was not. He knew now what had driven Papa to program him against telling. It was not hatred for his non-son, as Zivon feared; nor was it heartless use of a valuable research tool, as the Ridenour suspected. It was the compulsion to protect the invisibles. Their own desire to be understood, to continue—to survive. And once touched, that compulsion overrode his affection for his non-son, as it would override his own sense of self.

Ultimate Security.

And with that realization came another. Nayati was no enemy. Nayati was acting out of fear, for preservation of the Cocheta Self and World. The Other surged at that, reinforcing Perception.

And in that instant, Stephen sensed the danger in that path: understanding Nayati, trusting the Voice. Not now. Not considering the next line of input:

". . . join with your Cocheta and ride on the wings of ecstasy . . ."

The Voice ended. The sensations rose to a new level, and Stephen's world narrowed to that Sensory Space. He strove to intellectualize, to anticipate and provide focus as before, but memory superimposed on reality at random.

(The drug entering his system, controlling his responses,

eliminating the fear and the cold—the absolute aloneness. All else, anger, pain, embarrassment, was irrelevant....

("Everybody uses everybody. Isn't that what you told me?")
("What would you choose, Ridenour? To go home?"
("I haven't a choice. Therefore, I don't choose.")

Fear and pain, synapse upon synapse overlaid with a homicidal rage—Stephen felt himself losing all control—felt the feedback loop taking sexual sensation into pain and terror into violent aggression, which found its outlet in sexual sensation into pain into terror into—

—and grasped at his last vestige of human awareness to disrupt the loop that was tearing him apart.

viii

Ridenour's scream reverberated through the room. His body convulsed and strained against the restraints. Nayati scanned the monitors, frantically seeking an explanation for this unprecedented reaction. The tape should bring pleasure, not fear. Cooperation, not combat.

"Turn the damn thing off! You're killing him!"

"Relax, Annie." He smothered his own panic, and prayed she was wrong. Ridenour's *death* had long since ceased to be his goal. "The tape's almost finished. You wouldn't want me to stop it before he—"

"Dammit, Hatawa! Turn it off!"

"Doesn't matter." The tape concluded, but Ridenour's reactions were *not* according to experience. The readouts made no sense. But the Inner Sense had seemed so positive. "Apparently even the Cocheta can't cure his brand of impotency."

"You don't have to be so crude." Anevai's expression as she tilted her head to search Ridenour's face roused a jealousy so blinding, Nayati had to turn away. He concentrated on Ridenour's vital signs, looking for evidence to explain that violent outburst.

But there was nothing. He was quiet—almost peaceful, though he'd be lucky to have any voice left after that single, spine-chilling scream. Fifteen seconds of fighting his restraints had bloodied his wrists and cut through the black suit, exposing skin where the binding straps crossed his chest, but he wasn't even breathing hard.

"He'll be a long time coming down out of this cloud." He rose and grasped her arm. "Come with me."

"No! I want to stay with him. He shouldn't be alone when he wakes up."

He felt a fear growing within him, a fear his Cocheta sense did nothing to purge. Ridenour should not have reacted as he did, yet his Cocheta gave him no solace, only a ghostly sense of—satisfaction.

He rejected the fear, replaced it with anger. Anger at Ridenour for his uniqueness, anger at Anevai for her concern. Anger—until he recognized and rejected it—at his Cocheta for betraying him at this critical moment.

"I said, he'll be fine! He won't even know what planet he's on for hours, maybe days, and I'll be damned if I'll sit here and wait. Now come with me."

Nayati and Anevai were leaving. Somewhere in his postbattle VSpace retreat, Stephen heard their voices, heard retreating footsteps and the whoosh of a closing door. His thought processes seemed quite rational—amazingly clear, considering the circumstances. It could be a side effect of the Cocheta gas, or (equally possible) he was not as lucid as he imagined. He'd heard Nayati speak, heard Anevai's answer, but failed utterly to understand them.

Sound was all he had; the rest of his universe was black: devoid of vision, devoid of touch. Or it could be that blackness was relative, a contrast to the scope of Before.

The Other was silent now, the Ridenour and Zivon settled into their own private niches. He was alone, limited to his own senses, and them on overload, exhausted from the battle.

Stephen counted to one hundred slowly, in time with the hiss of ventilation fans, allowing Nayati time to change his mind and return.

He counted a second hundred for good measure.

And a third because he didn't want to move. Didn't want to run the risk of Nayati returning and discovering him awake.

And because he was afraid. He was exhausted, in pain, and

deathly, paralyzingly terrified, the momentary high which had defied Nayati gone, the adrenaline spent.

And because he was a farce. He'd been proceeding as if he were the hero in some fantasy—glib, indestructible—and the fact was, his actions had not only endangered his own life, he'd put everyone else he cared about in jeopardy as well.

He was not doing very well since he'd decided to take control of his life.

About the only thing he *had* done right was uncover Wesley's System—and that, in view of what else they'd discovered here, would become relatively unimportant once the Rostov/Cocheta issue was resolved.

If the issue *could* be resolved, now he'd single-handedly managed to undermine negotiations between HuteNamid and the Council.

He should *never* have followed Nayati without informing Cantrell. If he and Wesley and Anevai all died before they could inform her of the truth behind his disappearance into the mountain and (more importantly) of his suspicions regarding Rostov, the Cocheta might wittingly or unwittingly destroy another planet.

Perhaps the wisest action was no action. Nayati claimed Sakiimagan would come. Cantrell's people would be investigating his failed signal—would have Tyeewapi under observation. She'd think of a way to find them—at least in time to save Anevai and Wesley. He sincerely doubted Nayati would harm either of them.

He had no illusions regarding Nayati's plans for himself.

There was undoubtedly some advantage in his being dead—or at least eliminated from the picture . . . any picture. So many people had, after all, wanted him eliminated from their pictures. And they couldn't all be schizophrenic megalomaniacs. If he weren't so used to the notion, it might have the power to depress him.

Since Nayati had already used Anevai's sympathy for him against her, perhaps they'd all be better off if he were dead. Perhaps when Nayati returned, he should provoke him to that end. Perhaps he could occupy Nayati long enough for Cantrell to arrive, and in that way atone for his error in bringing Anevai and Wesley here in the first place.

But if he died, he'd never *know* they were safe. If he were dead, he'd be no further use to Wesley and Anevai. Dying was the easy way out—crash and burn in a blaze of useless bravado.

This thing Nayati had just done was a death sentence to him—or so Anevai believed—but he knew what Nayati had tried and he could control it. Would not let it rule him.

So Anevai believed. God help him, he *couldn't* die. Not until he passed on what he'd learned from the Other to Anevai or Wesley.

Anevai and Wesley. Wesley and Anevai.

Even they had wanted him out of their picture once. But Wesley had wanted him to return, had *wanted* to work with him, had *wanted* to be his friend. And Wesley was trapped down here, in that madman's power—a madman who could well try to do the same thing to Wesley that he'd done to Stephen—and Wesley didn't have Stephen's built-in safeguards.

And Anevai was certainly in danger from Nayati: he'd seen how Nayati treated her in the barn—she was fighting him now more than ever...

...And for all he knew, Cantrell was never going to get here...

...and he was *damned* if he'd sit—or lie—here waiting!

"There, you see, Anevai? I told you he'd be all right, he's already wriggling around like a fish on a line. I must hand it to him: he's tougher than he appears."

She eyed Nayati in disgust. "Kind of you to notice something worthwhile about him. Why don't you just let him go?"

"Let him go? My dear girl, he's not been hurt. And I've noticed much that is worthwhile about him. This is an experiment—to see what he's made of. He can't possibly free himself—even if he did, he couldn't find his way out—but I'm curious to see how hard he tries."

Stephen's hand twitched, pulled against the restraints. His whisper drifted over the com: *"Naturally, Ridenour. The man nailed you down, don't you remember? Not so awake as you thought."*

Testing his other restraints, his legs slipped free with seeming ease. Mistake on Nayati's part? Nayati's smug expression indicated otherwise.

Beneath that form-fitting suit, Stephen's diaphragm labored. She thought of substance sensitivities and bruised ribs. If he threw up now, he'd choke for sure. "Nayati, you've got to—"

But Nayati leaned forward, elbows on his knees, the slightest of smiles on his face, and Anevai swung back to the screen. Suddenly, that panting ended, and with an effort which, if it didn't tear the hole in his side open again, he was luckier than he deserved, Stephen brought his legs up over his head, used his feet to work the helmet off, then kicked it aside, cursing under his breath and blinking as if the room lights hurt his eyes. The curse ended in a gasp and his legs dropped heavily back to the couch.

His face twisted in pain, he lay unmoving for several moments, his breathing slow and steady. Strangely, she could see his muscles relaxing one after another, from his face downward, until he lay limp as a sleeping pii'chum. His hands moved, leather rubbing bloodied wrists, and he lifted his head to investigate.

Another murmur: *"Glad I don't remember that one."*

The edge of white teeth appeared on his lower lip and he closed his eyes, pulling at the straps until his arms trembled from the strain. Then he relaxed, his hand collapsing to shapelessness as he worked, gently this time, within that leather restraint. Moments later, the process began again. Eventually, with the sacrifice of a bit more skin, his hands were free.

"Very good, Spacer." Nayati crooned. "What now?"

Nayati's patronizing tone made her want to break his face; Stephen had done very well for a comp-jock. But even though his legs and arms were free, his own narrow-waisted physique would never allow him to slip free of the harness that strapped him to the table.

"Well, I'll be damned," Nayati said. "Will you look at that?"

* * *

"Sorry, Dr. Mo," Stephen muttered.

Several good, deep breaths to oxygenate the blood, exhale, collapse the lungs and the rib cage, hands up over the head and collapse the torso, relax each joint and make a snake's undulating progress out of the webbing: Cogito Epiphenomenal Gymnastics 501.

At the last moment, the rebuilt left shoulder refused to fold the last, crucial centimeter. In desperation as his lungs began to fight and the room to spin, and trying not to think of what Dr. McKenna was going to do to him for ruining her handiwork, he gave one final pull, wrenching himself free and tumbling off the couch to the floor.

He rolled onto his right side, clutching the arm, waiting for the waves of pain to ebb. Not dislocated again—he knew what that would feel like—but ominously numb. McKenna would kill him for sure. However, his fingers still flexed—if inefficiently— and he could still move the arm—although he wouldn't trust it to support him.

And he was free.

With a silent thanks to weird Professor Luosan's Positive Self-actuation Therapy, Stephen levered himself up off the floor—

—and grabbed the couch to keep from collapsing again as pain ripped through his side. It shouldn't be that bad: the injury should be nearly healed by now.

A cold draft brushed his face and he turned slowly, seeking the source. The ventilation shaft. Closing his eyes, he allowed the chill air to wash over his face, driving the dizziness away.

As the pain in his side ebbed, he realized that his face was virtually his *only* body part experiencing that coolth. Only his head, neck, and the small strips of skin exposed by the tears in the suit detected that draft.

Neither could he *feel* the couch he leaned against—or the floor beneath his feet.

He'd had to remove that helmet to see how he was bound— touch had told him nothing—and he'd been unable to locate the helmet itself until he'd practically kicked his own head off.

He touched his arm gingerly, feeling that contact in neither fingertips nor arm. Somehow the suit he had on—which must have been the source of the machine's sensory stimulation—must be overriding his body's ability to feel beyond its surface.

And perhaps more than that. He thought of that strange extension of his senses; perhaps to amplify *internal* reactions. Perhaps that was why his side hurt so badly. Perhaps even, in some way, why his arm was going numb—like a feedback overload on the nerves.

It was a nice theory, anyhow. One he preferred over the alternatives.

He'd known isolation in many forms in his life, but nothing quite like this. He knew gravity pressed him down, that solid rock balanced that pressure, the joints within the suit attested to that fact, but nothing else confirmed it. His eyes confirmed his grip on the couch: the fingers, the palm, felt—nothing—not even their proximity to one another. Only the tension of the muscles.

For an irrational, terrified instant he wondered if perhaps it was not the suit at all, that his sense of touch had gone forever—burned out by the Cocheta machine.

Grasping the torn, bloodied edge at his wrist, he ripped his hand free and gingerly touched the couch once more.

Smooth, soft leather. Hint of imperfection. Bulge of a seam, soft fuzz of a thread's end. His fingers slipped over the supple surface. His breath caught. He freed the other hand, closed his eyes, and ran his hands over his face and back through his hair, profound relief flooding through him as touch corroborated touch, sweaty curls catching in ragged fingernails, rough callus scratching along a throbbing jugular.

A second chill as the stroke reached his collarbone and sensation vanished.

He fingered the strange suit, profoundly tempted to rip the rest off in the same manner, but his clothes were in shreds on the floor and freezing his ass off wouldn't help anyone. Searching for something else would waste time.

And he'd wasted far too much of that already.

ix

Funny how the information that the man you've been protecting all this time was responsible for frying your son's brain would shift a man's loyalties.

Thank God for Nigan Wakiza's corroboration of all they'd been suspecting.

Sakiimagan had stopped fighting. Consequently, Paul Corlaney found himself, along with several dozen others—mostly *Cetacean* security—three large transport bubblecars, and a handful of smaller express ones, at Transport Tube terminal MT402, somewhere deep under a very large mountain.

"... We've tested samples, and the rock seems ordinary enough, but the composition and configuration changes with each use of the gate. We've tried to track down the actual matter-energy transformer—the pad is only the signalling device— but have had no luck so far."

"Sure, Paul." Loren leaned back into the padded seat and waited. Five minutes later, Sakiimagan emerged from the shadows, the stone doorway unchanged. He came over to their bubblecar and leaned on the windshield.

"I don't know what's wrong, Paul. I've tried everything I know . . . Nigan has, too. We simply can't get it to respond. I don't know what to do now."

"Blast it," Loren said abruptly.

"But I tell you, that isn't necessary."

"We've wasted enough time, governor. If this is truly an entrance, either open it, or stand back while we do."

Sakiima's lips tightened, but he stood back and gestured toward the stone wall. "You're welcome to try."

"I doubt we have the firepower, admiral," TJ advised. "If that rock is more than a half-meter thick, we can't do it. Not with what we brought with us."

"What about the mining crews?" Paul asked Sakiimagan. "They have the disrupters. It'd take—what—forty minutes to get the equipment here?"

"We'd have to go outside to contact them. At least to the tunnel mouth. Within the mountain, the Cocheta blockade . . ."

"So—an hour?"

Sakiimagan nodded.

Loren broke in. "Let's do it—*now!*"

A lone figure running a weaving path down one dimly lit hallway after another: a logical path, a mark scratched at floor level at each turning. A path which might lead him out—in about ten years' time.

"This is wonderful!"

"Nayati, what are you doing? When will it be enough?"

"When the experiment is over."

"*Experiment?* Dammit, Nayati, this is no experiment. It's senseless cruelty. What's happened to you?"

"Cruelty? Is a mother protecting her children cruel?"

"But—"

"You told me he's not the Enemy, yet you heard him: he knows of the others. He's going to try to stop the Emergence. He *is* the Enemy."

"The . . . emergence? What 'emergence'? You *are* mad!"

"Am I? Perhaps. Then again, perhaps I'm more sane than you, my dear. It's all in your point of view, isn't it? But what of our test subject? Should I let him know we know? Oh, I think not: look where he's gotten to."

The lone figure had reached yet another hallway—one with doors lining both sides—and paused, leaning against the corner.

A soft exclamation escaped the speakers, and the figure began limping down the corridor. Limping walk accelerated to staggering run and ended in a skidding halt before one particular door.

Stephen searched the door's edge futilely: the spot where Anevai had accessed a panel of buttons was now only smooth, glowing wall. He backed away to reexamine the hallway—both ways. There—that was the Central Library—the 'Com—and the angle was the same—it *was*, dammit!

Pressing his ear against the door, he knocked lightly.

"Wesley?"

. . , and a second, sharper rap.

"*Wesley? Dammit, Smith, answer me!*"

An eye-level panel appeared as if by magic and slid back to reveal a small window.

It *was* the same room, and Wesley was still there, laid out in unnatural precision, but alive—if he believed the regular rise and fall of his chest.

If it wasn't some damned holo.

He had to get in there. For his sake as much as Wesley's. Together, perhaps they could find their way out of this maze.

Wondering what chance touch had opened the panel, he examined the door where his hand had been resting, but found nothing. Perhaps it wasn't *his* doing at all.

His 'being-watched' sense flared. He had to get out of here. Now.

Laying his hand flat against the window, he said softly, "Sorry, old man, but I've got to leave you for a while. Wait for me."

Halfway to the auditorium, the tunnel's ambient light faded and died.

"Nayati, *What have you done*?"

"What I had to."

While one part of her mind registered Nayati's strangely sober reply, Anevai couldn't tear her eyes from the figure cowering in the blackened corner beside Wesley's cell: ghostly image of a losing battle against terror. Horrified, she waited for him to break, waited for panic to send him tearing out into the maze.

"He'll die out there. . . ."

"Will he?"

Forcing herself to face her cousin, she was startled to discover her old friend and not the stranger. She appealed to the friend: "You *know* he will! He'll be completely lost once he hits the maze. Gods, man, think of the traps! He can't *see*, Nayati!"

"Are you certain?" He turned back to the screen. "I wonder— will he even try to escape? The experiment has reached its final stages, Anevai."

"What do you—"

"Wait," Nayati said, but it was the stranger who touched the button on the console; the stranger who said: "Very good, Ridenour. I didn't give your common sense enough credit. Stay there and Cantrell might even find you. Unless, of course, we tell her you've gone. Then perhaps your cowering skeleton will remain there to one day confound some alien archaeologist's theory."

Stephen's head came up, eyes wide and searching. Nayati's mockery continued, and he shrank farther into the corner he'd found, as though he could somehow hide from his invisible tormentor.

"I have no time for playing games. You see, there *is* a party on its way from Tunica. I fear they won't find the way in time to save your accomplices—these two who are traitors to their World, but you—*you* have earned the right to leave. Therefore I say: Join them if you can."

"*Wait . . .*" A thread of a whisper. Stephen scrambled to his feet, clutching at the wall to keep upright. "*Nayati Hatawa, wait! Dammit, man, talk to me!*"

"Have you something of interest to say?"

"*I'm . . . Anevai, are you there? Are you all right?*"

"Sorry, Spacer-man. That's not interesting. Good—"

"*Wait! I—Nayati, you don't really want to hurt Wesley and Anevai. It's me you want, isn't it? Let them go. Send them back to Adm. Cantrell—I'll stay here. Do what you want with me—but let them go, please, Nayati.*"

Anevai could stand Nayati's baiting no longer. "Stephen, dammit, shut—" Nayati struck her across the mouth. She spat blood from a split lip and glared at him.

"*Anevai? What's happening? Did he—*"

"She's fine, Spacer-man. Tell him, Anevai." With a warning glance.

She sighed and said, "It's true, Stephen. Just shut up, will you? No heroics. Just get your butt out of here. If Nayati gets his hands on you again, you're dead."

"*I—I know that, Anevai. Truthercon. The dice have been cast and I've only the cards I've been handed—if you will forgive the mixed metaphor.*"

"Dammit, Ridenour . . ." Her voice gave out on her this time, and Stephen, casting a despairing look around him, rubbed a hand across his face and up through his hair, scrubbing hard. A gesture she knew well now, as she understood the desperation it disguised.

"Please, Nayati. Let her go. Wake Wesley up and let him go, too. Let me use the terminal. I'll send a message to the admiral—you can vet it first—I can explain I'm staying of my own free will. I have that right. My transfer is on file regardless of what they intended. And I'm legally IndiCorp: HuteNamid wouldn't have to explain my death—simply record it."

"You have a high opinion of yourself, don't you, Spacer? Think you're worth Anevai and Wesley in fair trade?"

Stephen's head dropped. *"Nowhere but in this market, Hatawa. I only hoped—"* His head came back up, but proudly this time, without the fruitless searching. *"You have all the Aces, Hatawa. I only hoped you would prefer to have a direct hand in my death—a small enough thing, but then, letting two innocent people go isn't very much to ask, either."*

A flicker of a smile crossed Nayati's face. "Well, you're wrong, Spacer. Your *life*, at this moment, is of far more interest to me. So live, Spacer. Live so that your—friends—can live as well. For *their* sakes, since your own life means so little to you, find your way out—warn the admiral to stay away—to leave us in peace. For if she makes it here, they will surely die—I promise you that. And, Ridenour—"

"Yes?"

"Do us both a favor. Stay off the 'Links. —Goodbye, Spacer."

"Nayati? Nayati Hatawa!"

Nayati cut the transmission.

"What do you mean he's worth more to you alive than dead?"

Nayati slid down into the chair next to her, rested his elbow on the counter, and said, with convincing sincerity, "It's true, Anevai. I meant it when I said he interests me. He's got guts—in his own weird way. And he has the power, if only he'll listen."

"And will you really kill Wesley and me if the admiral makes it through?"

He reached out, stroked her cheek gently with the back of

one finger. She didn't flinch from that touch: pride, and because something in his expression held her steady. "I don't know, love. I honestly don't know. I think I might have to. You both know so much, in your own ways. I'll be honest with you—it depends very much on what your Spacer-boy does."

"You're asking too much of him, Nayati."

He looked at her enigmatically, then toward the ball of humanity cowering in its dark corner.

"And you, sweet Annie, don't expect nearly enough."

Stephen felt his *out there* state of mind threaten and fought against that retreat. He curled against the wall—thankful now for the alien suit which confined the chill air to his hands and face—and tried to resurrect the way out. Taking advantage of the surrounding darkness, the freedom from input the suit provided, he let his mind drift, regressing step by step to build a picture in his mind of the seemingly endless journey which had brought him here.

But the memories were too hazy—too overlaid with periods of partial consciousness. Much clearer were the older images— images of another underground maze and wrong turns which hid deep holes, dead ends and worse. He thought of Wesley's near-death and the idea of braving these tunnels in the dark set the hand on the wall to trembling. That trembling increased as he drifted further and further from the reality of darkness and stone, and deeper into that memory, a *thrumming* echo vibrating through him, drawing him into—

He jolted awake—the echo of that strange heartbeat still with him—shuddered and pressed closer to the wall, wishing he could feel its solidity against his shoulder. To validate its existence, he moved his hand along that strange surface. Or thought he did. Suddenly, he was unsure *where* his hand was or what it was doing, where it ended and the wall began.

He jerked the hand away. That . . . *that* was the source of the heartbeat. No, not heartbeat. It was more, and less, than that.

The Other's sense: sounds, vibrations in the rock, so much else unnameable that had made him a part of the mountain and its world, had made him aware of the shapes and contours as he was aware of his own body. More so—he didn't know the currents and courses of his own blood as well as the currents of air and water through this mountain. But that had been *recorded* sensory input—controlled, as the VRTs were controlled—hadn't it?

If it wasn't—if it *was* RealTime . . . If he could—somehow— return to that state—*let* the Other feel . . . He swallowed hard, trying not to count on that ability. But he *was* still wearing the suit. And if there was a chance—

"Nayati?"

Silence.

"Nayati Hatawa, I know you're listening!"

Another silence. Then, Nayati's deep voice from the velvet blackness:

"What do you want, Spacer?"

"Dammit, stop calling me that!"

"Goodb—"

"Wait! —What if she won't?"

"What if who won't what?"

"What if Cantrell won't go back? Or Anevai's father brought her—"

"He would never *betray the Cocheta!"*

Betrayal. Survival. *Protection.* Keys, if he could only find the right doors . . .

He asked carefully: "What if she already knows about the Cocheta, Nayati? What if it's not me she's come after? If I find her and she insists on coming to the Library anyway? They have instruments that could follow my trail back . . ."

"Not if I don't let them."

"But—Wouldn't it be best for the Cocheta if you could show her *why* you protect them? Solicit—solicit her protection as well. *Show* her what they can do, get her to help—"

"We don't need her help. Besides, the Cocheta won't talk to such as she."

"They spoke to me."

Silence. Hard to argue with that.

"If—if I find her, bring her back here, will you talk with her? Just Cantrell, you, and me. Please, Nayati, it's important."

He held his breath, waiting. If there was a chance, any

chance at all to get Cantrell and Nayati together, especially here, where the machinery would back his memories . . .

"Nayati, do you *want* Rostov to happen here?"

But to voluntarily cede his very self to some other awareness . . . What if he could never come back? Was any of it even possible without the machine itself?

'All right, Spacer. You get back here with Cantrell, we'll talk. Just you, me and the admiral. Either of you alone won't do.'

"Thank you, Hatawa." And he meant it—

—until Nayati's laughter rang in the darkness. *"Not much of a gamble for me, Ridenour. It was a brave wager—a good try—but you'll never make it back. —Goodbye, Stephen Ridenour."*

Stephen set his jaw, controlled anger and the twitch of terror those words invoked. Nayati was counting on that terror. Trying to inject doubt of self.

Well, he'd put up with that all his life. Damned if he'd let it win now.

Pressing both palms against the stone, he systematically shut down other sensory input, as he had before. As before, the vibrations and echoes within the stone resonated in his flesh and bone. He tried to remember his RS-physics—the relationship between frequencies and densities, the equations which could tell him what the signals all meant—but those equations grew into chants which blended with the thrumming and he felt himself once again drifting out of associations with his body and into the mountain.

His fist slammed into the wall, breaking the thread, and he collapsed once more, his heart reverting to its own terrified rhythm. Drive him insane: undoubtedly. Get him out: never.

But he couldn't simply sit here and let Nayati win. Keeping one hand on the wall, he staggered to his feet. He at least knew how to get out of the Cocheta tunnels and into the rock maze—unless that rock door had disappeared. All he had to do was get back to the main amphitheater . . . and it was that—no, *that* way.

X

"Where is he, Nayati?"

He hated to admit: "I don't know."

Ridenour had somehow managed to move beyond the range of the Cocheta sensors. He should never have shut down the MT402 section. But it had been the easiest way to slow Cantrell. He'd never considered the possibility that Ridenour would get that close.

He'd underestimated the Spacer again.

Vaguely uneasy at the knowledge his Awareness had failed on this crucial instance, he checked the monitors again for Smith's room. But Smith was sleeping quietly; Ridenour long since beyond that sector.

"So what do we do now?" Anevai, admirably steady, asked.

"We wait."

The stone throbbed beneath his hands in time to his sobbing breaths, pulling his heart into irregular syncopation. He hugged the stony outcrop, resting his cheek against it, closing his eyes to the blackness surrounding him.

What difference do you think it makes, Nayati Hatawa? he thought, closing his teeth on borderline hysteria. *Light or no light, I'm hopelessly lost anyway.* Light had merely created an illusion of Place. This way, he could easily convince himself it was all a dream—forget Anevai, forget Wesley. Here, only the throb of the mountain existed, echoing tons of stone above and . . . below and . . .

And nothing holding it up! Any moment now it was going to crash in around him—tons and tons of rock and earth leaving nothing but blood and calcium oozing between minute fragments of alien soil. . . .

Running. Blackness surrounding him. Jarring halt against stone—rebounding stumble over irregularities, feet skidding on crumbling gravel, falling . . . falling endlessly. Falling into the black pit he sought against all parental threats of reprisal . . . a pit in which a falling stone never reached bottom. A pit which had swallowed his diary and now wanted him.

Consciousness returned: momentary relief preceding a fervent wish to return to that place of nonfeeling, nonthinking peace, free of pain, free of this inability to save himself or his friends, and to pass quietly out of existence. He was so tired of fighting what he could not understand—had no power to change—and here, where no one would ever find him, he could die and they'd never know how thoroughly he'd failed.

"I'm sorry, Papa." His whisper echoed loudly in the darkness. He pressed his hands over his ears, ashamed of that whisper, ashamed of the frightened child who'd uttered it. But the child was not ashamed. The child refused responsibility for saying it. Somewhere, long ago, a fierce will to survive had been kindled in Zivon Stefanovich Ryevanishov. Zivon remembered that challenge *So deserve to live, Spacer-man,* and whispered it in his ear, over and over and over again.

There *was* another choice. He'd felt the Other fighting for predominance once before: it was not about to let this body die senselessly. The Other *was* inside him and it had the ability to interpret those signals the mountain radiated where all his science failed him.

But only if he could listen—only if . . .

Stephen rolled to his knees, pulled himself to his feet and leaned against the stone, palms flat, cheek pressed against rocky chill, willing the rhythm into his body—but it was not enough—he needed more. Through the holes in the suit, he felt the rhythm seeking entrance and he carefully began increasing that exposure a centimeter at a time, pressing against the stone after each new tear.

It was a gamble—he was as certain as he could be of any of this that the resonance within the alien suit was part of the experience; that to eliminate the suit altogether was not the answer. And the instant the insulating fabric no longer stood between his heart and the stone, he knew he was right. For an instant, he could sense the shape of the mountain. For an instant he knew the way out—

How? . . . he thought, and abruptly the awareness collapsed.

Momentary panic before he realized his own thinking had inhibited the Cocheta awareness. He must cease being a free agent. He had to sense the presence of the invaders—Cantrell, Paul Corlaney, and whoever else was with them, and go to them like—like a white corpuscle to a sight of infection. Or, more appropriately (he chuckled, more than a little light-headed), sperm to an egg.

But he knew now the ability to sense the mountain lay within him. The answer was really quite simple: Fourth Echelon Stephen Ridenour simply had to release his hold on the science he'd fought to understand all his life, to curb the human wonder which had collapsed the matrix.

Simple, except that Science had been the one stable force in his life, the one trustworthy absolute—

—Until Wesley and *Harmonies*. That stability had faltered months ago, if he were honest with himself.

Closing his eyes, he willed himself into that region of otherwhere, opening himself, in the only way he knew how, to that Other's control—focusing his mind on Loren Cantrell and freedom from the tunnels, felt Sense waver and revised *from* to *within*: he was not a prisoner within the Cocheta's protective maze, he was a part of it.

The flatbed spilled Recon miners before it stopped moving. Even Loren, observing this operation from the corner of the landing, nodded approval as the crew adjusted face masks with one hand and received disrupters from those still aboard with the other. One man in *Cetacean* teal climbed out of the second miner flatbed and joined Loren and TJ on the narrow ledge.

Paul stayed in the transport.

The ledge filled rapidly, and Loren ordered everyone not actively involved in cutting through the stone barrier back into the growing row of vehicles. After a brief conference with Sakiimagan and the team foreman, she left TJ and newly arrived crewmen adjusting masks of their own and dropped into the seat next to Paul.

He felt a twinge of uneasiness, seeing those masks, and helping Loren pull the bubblecar cover down and latch the air-seals. Disrupters and explosives made him nervous anyway; in this closed tunnel, considering the turbulent emotions running rampant . . . "Are you sure this is the only way?"

Loren threw him a wry look. "Fine time to ask, Corlaney. Don't worry. These men know what they're doing. TJ's no novice, and Melrose—" She nodded toward the crewman. "—is our AlphaGeoTech. They'll be— Scuze me." She tapped behind her ear. "They're ready."

She handed him a pair of dark goggles, adjusting a similar pair over her own eyes. He settled them on his nose, pulled the strap tight—too tight. He muttered a low curse and pulled them off again as Loren signalled the go-ahead.

"Sorry." He rubbed an itch on his nose, shrugged an apology at TJ waiting patiently on the far side of the bubblecar's clear top, and beyond TJ . . .

He rubbed his eyes and looked again. The stone wall continued to shimmer and undulate.

"Loro!" He grabbed her arm. "Loro, look. *Look at the wall!*"

By the time she had the bubblecar open, the stone barrier had disappeared altogether. Even expecting it, the sight was un-nerving. Stranger still was the almost familiar figure which slowly gained substance in the darkness beyond.

This time, Paul joined Loren, the miners piling back into their car to free space on the landing. That problem, at least, appeared solved.

"Stephen?" Loren called to that strangely quiet entity. "Stephen, is that you?"

"TJ—"

It was difficult to connect the ghostly figure with the young graduate. More difficult still when their spots hit full on his face and he didn't even blink, just stared at them with unwavering tranquility. That serene face, his hands, a bloodied stretch of skin across his chest, seemed to float in the dark, only an occasional spark of silver corroborating the rest of his body's existence. Even as he approached, the blackness covering him seemingly absorbed the light, making him one with the shadows behind him.

His voice was as colorless as his face. "Adm. Cantrell. Please hurry. Anevai and Wesley need your help."

Without another word, he turned full about, began striding down the tunnel. Loren, looking decidedly puzzled, called, "Stephen? Wouldn't you like a light?" And to a crewman carrying one of the big spots: "Crank that up—get it on him."

The light threw Ridenour into high relief against his own shadow. Slow, deliberate turn, blinking, a hand raised to shade his eyes from the glare. Dark brows knit. He took a half-step toward them, staggered badly and grabbed the rock at his side.

Paul brushed past Loren, who seemed frozen, and ran to the boy's side. His eyes were closed, his body swaying, not as though he were about to fall, but rather as if in time to some unheard melody.

He had to be pried away from the outcrop; but the instant his death-grip on the wall broke, Ridenour collapsed. Paul controlled his slip to the floor, balancing him against his chest. Loren came up behind him and took the hand still reaching for the wall in her own.

"Stephen? Come on, boy, wake up."

"Loro . . . ?" That one word, on a hard-won breath, and then a sigh. "Thank God . . . I found . . ." His eyes drifted shut. Loren gestured to the *Cetacean* medic, who hurried up to them, a mobile analysis unit out and ready.

A part of the unit buzzed and whirred on a blood sample, leads touched here and there sent arcane readings to the MAU. While they waited on the results, Loren said, "Come on, boy. Stay with us. Don't fall asleep on me again."

The slack mouth twitched and tightened, hazed eyes blinked. "Is that . . . propo . . . sition, admiral?"

She grinned. "You better believe it, handsome." And to the medic: "Well?"

"Some unusual trace elements in his blood, but nothing the Unit's worried about. Mostly your basic exhaustion." He gave the boy a mild stimulant. "But take it easy."

"Understood."

As the drug took effect, Ridenour tried to sit up, murmuring an apology when he fell back.

"Don't be silly, boy," Paul reassured him, and wrapped an arm around his shoulders, holding him steady. "Delighted to find you in one piece. You said something about Wesley and Anevai. Where are they? Safe?"

"I—as far as I know, they're all right." A dazed brush of his hand across his face. "Nayati has them. Demands that you go away or he'll kill them."

"He does, does he?" Sakiimagan emerged from the spotlights.

Ridenour straightened his shoulders, brushed his hair back with a shaking hand in a pathetically futile attempt to assume his Academy manners. "Sir, I had no idea you were here."

"Good, perhaps my undisciplined nephew will prove equally surprised. —Admiral, I'm going on. I'll not be intimidated by such threats, but should you choose to return, now that Dr. Ridenour has been restored to you, I promise to deliver Nayati to you."

"I have no intention of returning without your daughter and Dr. Smith, governor. Nor, for that matter, without Nayati Hatawa." She gestured to Lexi. "Take Stephen back—"

"No!"

"Not a debate, Ridenour."

"No, admiral, it's not."

But Ridenour's admirably steady voice failed to shake her resolve. "Lexi, take him back to the complex. Sit on him if you have to."

The boy's shoulders dropped in weary resignation. "Admiral, listen to me. How will you find them? I can show you..."

"So can I, Ridenour," Nigan said, stepping into the spots, chin high, tone and stance radiating skepticism.

Stephen struggled to his feet, and Paul rose with him, keeping a steadying hand under the boy's elbow. "Admiral, what's *he* doing here? He's Nayati's right-hand man!"

"Was, Ridenour. Now I wonder who Nayati's new man is. Who's your new tailor?"

"Ease off, Nigan," Paul said sharply, catching Stephen as the boy's knees gave. But Loren's warning pressure on his arm silenced him, and Nigan, encouraged, continued:

"How did you get free? Nayati's in no mood to release *you* for good behavior. How did you find your way through the maze? This sector was shut down: the gate was off, the lights—how did you get here? How did you open the gateway?"

"I—" Stephen broke off, eyes locked on Loren's cold face, then turned that beseeching look on him. "Dr. Corlaney, *please*, I must go along. Nayati might—might *kill* them if I don't." He brushed the back of his hand across his sweating brow. "He said something...I can't remember exactly what . . . I—I don't know how to explain how I found my way here. It was the Other who . . ." His voice faded, and he shivered violently against Paul's arm.

"The 'Other,' " Nigan repeated scornfully. "Admiral, you can't trust him. That's a Cocheta suit. Sure as hell, Nayati's had him on the machine. He might believe everything he's saying, but it's Nayati's plan, not his."

Loren rose to her feet, looked from one young man to the other, then grasped Stephen's arm, pulling him gently away from Paul. He went without resistance, the fight driven out of him at last.

"Take him back, Lexi." And to Stephen: "Boy, you're out on your feet. With the best of intentions, you'd be nothing but a liability. Go with her. Wait for us. Trust us to bring your friends back safely."

He moved a quiet step or two, then said to her, "If you'd just have the medic give me another shot . . ." But she shook her head; his lowered in defeat, and he walked slowly through the miners and security officers to Lexi's side.

"Let's go," Loren said, and the small group moved past Paul, with Nigan and Sakiimagan in the lead and Loren's crew falling in behind them, the miners staying behind as insurance, ready to blast through the gate should it close behind them.

"Paul?" That was Loren calling for him.

"Yeah, I'm coming." And with a final backward glance, "Hang tough, kid. We'll be back soon."

It was wrong. He knew it was wrong, and all he could do was stand there as the last light disappeared down the tunnel.

"Come, Stephen." A gentle tug at his arm. Let's get you home."

Home? People said such strange things. Pat phrases. Meaningless words. But nothing Nayati had said was meaningless. Somehow, it was important for him to return with Cantrell. Somehow, there was some test he had passed in getting here, and if Cantrell's group showed up with Nigan and Sakiimagan as guides and no Stephen, Cantrell would lose.

He couldn't stay here—certainly couldn't go back with Lexi. But lacking immediate options, he moved quietly to the hindmost bubblecar, the Recon miners gathering in quiet groups in the cars, ignoring them after the first curious glances.

He caught his balance against the windshield, and closed his eyes against the resultant bobbing. "Lexi, would—would you go in first, please? I'm feeling a bit—dizzy—could use a steady hand in there."

Lexi studied him a long moment. He did his best to sway uncertainly (not a particularly difficult act), and she shrugged and stepped in, her back to him. A teal-blue back with a rifle slung over the right shoulder.

Almost without conscious thought, he grabbed the rifle strap and jerked back, pulling the gun away. She spun off balance; he hit the emergency return switch and threw himself backward, slamming the top down as he fell.

Brakes screamed. He scrambled to his feet and stumbled toward the Cocheta tunnel, the rifle banging against his side. He heard shouts, heard the bubbletop hydraulics whine as his shoulder struck the edge of the doorway and he recoiled into the tunnel.

"I'm sorry, Lexi!" he yelled, loudly as he could, and punched the code which re-formed the stone in the doorway. He didn't stop to think why it worked or how he knew the code. He just did it and ran down the blackened tunnel, lights flickering alive at his approach, dying rapidly behind.

"Dad's with them."

"I have eyes, woman." Nayati growled, a muscle clenching spasmodically in his jaw as he watched the parade enter the Library. "Ridenour's not."

"He was behind them—we saw him pass that monitor—"

"He's not now." He glared at her. "He's double-crossed you, Annie-girl. Could have saved you and chickened out. You still care what happens to him?"

She jerked her head toward the screen. "I'd say you'd better consider what you're going to do with them before you worry about Stephen."

"I don't know!" She was mocking him and he hated her for it. Hated her for the threat which had forced him to tie her to the chair as the others' arrival had grown imminent. Hated all of them for forcing his hand. Hated Ridenour for failing him. Hated Sakiimagan for betraying him. And setting all that hate aside for later, he said mildly, "I don't know. Nothing much—put them under, perhaps, plant a few suggestions, then turn them loose to take those back to the Alliance."

"Do you plan to—operate on them all? Won't that take a while? And do you intend to take them by yourself?"

He shrugged. "I can flood the Library itself and they can simply stay that way until I get to them."

"Flood the Library? Manufacture that shit out of thin air, do you?"

He just looked at her, knowing truths she did not.

"My father as well?"

"Sakiimagan as well."

"What about me, Nayati?"

"What do you suggest?"

"What if I offer to join you?"

Tempting, but: "N-n-no, I don't think so."

Voices whispered over the speakers. He swung to the panel and struck the volume control.

Voices flooded the room.

"Nayati!"

That imperative could only have come from Sakiimagan.

He grinned tightly at Anevai and whispered, "It's showtime!" And to the microphone: "I see you, Sakiimagan Tyeewapi."

"I'm ordering you to surrender yourself at once."

"Forget it, Tyeewapi. I'm through playing by your rules. Your rules have put the Alliance watchdogs in the middle of our most precious treasure."

"Why speak through walls? Come out—or are you too much the coward to face those you accuse?"

"You'll not get me that way, Tyeewapi."

"On my word, you'll be safe, nephew."

"Safe? To do what? Bow again to the will of petty Spacers? That's not safety, uncle, that's slavery. The Cocheta are *our* legacy, the Spacers aren't fit to share them. We have seen that time and again: not even those superior examples you hand-picked can successfully interface. Barb and Will were their best, and they have broken."

"Broken? Or did you booby-trap them as you did Hononomii?"

"Booby-trap? Oh, that's rich, Sakiima. I didn't booby-trap Hono—any more than you booby-trapped Corlaney and all the others."

"What are you talking about?" Dr. Corlaney's voice, from out of the shadows.

Nayati laughed. "You mean you haven't told him? Tell him, Sakiima. Tell him where I learned my methods—and on what guinea pigs."

"Nayati, what are you talking about?" Anevai hissed, and he pressed her shoulder, tacit warning against further reaction. This was between Sakiimagan and himself. He was tired of the hypocrisy.

"Ask him to tell you why you've never wanted to leave here," Nayati said into the darkness that housed Paul Corlaney. "Ask him to tell you about your *first* visit to this Library, then ask him *why* you don't remember it."

Corlaney exited the shadows, his face dark with anger. *"Sakiima, what's he talking about?"*

And Sakiimagan, satisfactorily broken: *"I'm sorry, Paul. It was the only way I knew to protect—"*

"Adm. Cantrell!" Nayati interrupted. Doubt had been planted. For the present, that was sufficient. "Where's Ridenour?"

Cantrell answered: *"Safe, Mr. Hatawa."*

"Don't try to fool me, admiral. He was behind you in the tunnels. Now where is he?"

Startlement. They hadn't known. He'd swear to that. But why—

"I'm right behind you, 'Buster."

Two pairs of eyes turned simultaneously toward him: black, golden, widening in welcome, narrowing in fury. On the monitor behind them: Cantrell and the others in the main Library.

Nayati turned from the console. "Well, Ridenour. Again, it seems I underestimated you."

"I hope you continue to do so, Nayati. That oversight could get us all out of this." He leaned against the door frame, the stolen weapon balanced in what he hoped was proper heroic style. He thought he'd even figured out how to fire it.

Aiming it was something else.

But Nayati didn't know that. And with luck, he wouldn't have a chance to find out. He gestured with the rifle. "Over there, Hatawa, and behave yourself." Amazingly, Nayati did as directed and Stephen dropped to his knees beside Anevai, working her wrist restraints one-handed, keeping the heavy weapon levelled with his right.

The third time the strap slipped from his numb fingers, he muttered a curse and shifted the rifle to that marginal grasp, praying he could hold it there long enough to free her. But:

"Stephen, don't—"

Peripheral vision caught the movement: he twisted and rolled with Nayati's attack. The rifle barrel struck the floor; he pulled it with him, their combined weight whipping the rifle stock into Nayati's face. The knife clattered to the floor. Nayati collapsed onto him, his elbow absorbed the shock, numb fingers dropped the gun.

Unable to free himself of Nayati's weight, unable to reach the rifle, he kicked as hard as he could, heard the weapon skid toward the door as Nayati pushed himself up, shaking his head dazedly.

Stephen rolled from under him, flattened again as a moccasined foot flew over his head, catching Hatawa full on the chin. Nayati's head snapped back, his body following in an awkward slow-motion tumble to the floor.

"Got him! —Damned careless, cousin, forgetting me like that."

Stephen rolled up onto his elbow, panting for breath, blinking the sweat from his eyes. Nayati lay unmoving on the floor.

"Heads up, Stevie-lad, my hands're going to sleep and Nayati won't be out for long."

Fumbling fingers located Nayati's knife without much help from his brain, but his head cleared as he cut her free, saying breathlessly, "Thanks, Tyeewapi."

"Hey, man, don't mention it. Just remind me to give you some lessons in basic self-preservation before we head out on another adventure? Like once you've got 'em, disarm your captives?''

"An excellent suggestion, Ms. Tyeewapi." A quiet voice drifted in from the darkened corridor. A hand reached down and swept up the rifle, and Lexi stepped through the open door. Lexi, complete with a miner's disrupter slung over her shoulder.

She settled the rifle on her hip, swung around to—

—Nayati: crouched, ready to attack—

—and flipped the safety. "I wouldn't, Mr. Hatawa."

Stephen said, "Sgt. Fonteccio, I'm—"

"Dr. Ridenour," she interrupted, "it appears you were correct. You were needed here. —You did quite well, you know."

"Did?..."

She grinned at him. "You were quicker than I gave you credit for—almost got away from me."

And suddenly he realized: "You *let* me escape."

Her grin widened.

"Why?"

"Seemed like a good idea at the time—but don't you think we'd best advise the admiral on the state of affairs here?"

He handed Anevai the knife. "You take care of him?"

"With pleasure," she said grimly. She tucked the knife into her belt at the back and looked positively disappointed when Lexi handed her a pair of restraints, muttering, "I was looking forward to using the rope."

Following a quick study of the control panel, Stephen flipped a switch.

"Admiral?"

Cantrell's image spun about, searching the shadows.

"Stephen? Good God, boy, what are you doing here?"

"I told you, I had to come. Everything is under control up here. Sgt. Fonteccio is with me." No need to fill them in on *all* the details at once. "Nayati is under restraint, Anevai is safe. We'll meet you down there."

It was an oddly civilized gathering, considering—

—considering who would like to do what and to whom.

Stephen sat on one of the Library couches propping up an

exhausted Anevai (Or maybe it was Anevai doing the propping; he was too tired to know the difference.), his crossed ankles resting on the neighboring couch beside a soundly sleeping Wesley.

The poor sod had been inhaling the Cocheta gas all this time and kept nodding off despite the EMT's stimulant. He murmured and started to wiggle. Stephen shifted his foot, sticking a toe in Wesley's side to prevent him from rolling off. Wesley swore, blinked sleepily at him and smiled, then wrapped an arm around his ankle and rubbed it with his cheek, drifting off again in that awkward position.

It would be—nice—if he could feel as well as see that silly gesture.

They awaited—among other, security-related procedures—the construction of three litters. If it weren't that Anevai and Wesley had both demanded a lift back, he'd have protested. Vehemently. Every moment they delayed here was another moment for *something* to go wrong.

And something *was* going to happen—as surely as Anevai was seated next to him, for all he couldn't feel her.

His hand sought hers, as if on its own. Her fingers wrapped and squeezed, reassuringly Real, and he relaxed a degree. The suit had him on edge, that was all. He couldn't feel things properly, so his imagination was making things up.

Nayati had worked himself into a passionate frenzy. Seemingly oblivious to his manacled hands, he strode back and forth, raving: "... perfectly well survive on our own, we and the Cocheta. We don't need or want Spacers who cannot hear the universal heartbeat. They offer nothing we don't already have."

"Listen to me, Nayati." Governor Tyeewapi reached to stop him. "It's not like that. Adm. Cantrell has offered to carry our case personally to the Council. She has sworn to keep all Cocheta references Secured to the highest level. That only a few handpicked experts—"

"*No!* They want to steal the Cocheta from us. But the Cocheta have *chosen* us. They speak to *us*. Only to us! Are we to allow these intruders to interpret what we know in our hearts? Our souls?"

Nayati jerked free and continued pacing.

Last he'd heard, Sakiimagan Tyeewapi had been pushing for very similar conditions. That, like so many things, seemed to have changed in the past few days. If he hadn't been so lost in his own strange universe, perhaps he'd have known. . . .

Stephen gathered his breath and said, with what authority he could muster, "Only to you, Nayati? Are you sure they've chosen no others?"

Nayati paused, turned slowly to face him. "We are not afraid to *admit* that we hear."

Stephen had no response for that. Nayati knew he could only have found the admiral by listening to the Other—that was the test Nayati had given him and challenged him now to acknowledge. But he couldn't. Not until he understood himself what had gone on in his head and body for those lost minutes.

Nayati laughed derisively and lost interest in him, turned instead to Sakiimagan, his chin high, his tone challenging:

"You ask me to reveal all I know to *these*? In return for what? Theft of my Cocheta? More of their kind invading our sacred places? I will *never* agree to such a treaty."

"Sacred places? Speak for yourself, boy," Sakiimagan objected. "Not all the People would agree with that assessment. Nor is yours the only agreement to be considered. Many of our people *do* want what the Alliance has to offer, not the least of whom are Barb and Will—"

"They are researchers. They are not the People. Otherwise, they would not be as they are."

"And Hononomii? Is he not *of the People*, as you, in your great wisdom, define them?"

"Cantrell is to blame for Hononomii."

"Is she? Not according to Hono. Not according to Nigan."

"Nigan." Nayati's voice held more loathing than Stephen had ever heard, and over beside the first litter, Nigan ducked his head.

"From what I heard," Paul Corlaney said, a bitter edge to his voice, "Nayati's not the only one to blame. —I want to know, Tyeewapi: am I going to end up like Will?"

The governor, looking profoundly disturbed, said, "It was only a mild suggestion, Paul."

"To accomplish *what*? Why'd you have to fuck with my head?"

Nayati laughed, a loud, triumphant shout.

Cantrell grabbed Corlaney's arm and hissed, "Cool off, Paul. Nayati's trying to create factions. Don't pander to him."

"I don't *create* factions," Nayati said smoothly, "I point them out."

Paul shook Cantrell off, and confronted Tyeewapi. "Anevai said Nayati's changed. Have I? What about the violent outbursts? Is your tampering responsible for those as well?"

"I simply don't know, Paul," Sakiimagan answered calmly.

"Dammit, man, after twenty goddamn years—couldn't you have trusted me?"

"No," Sakiimagan said. . . .

Another friendship destroyed because of him. Cantrell and Corlaney. Nayati and Nigan. Tyeewapi and Corlaney.

Perhaps if he'd known, none of this would have happened.

". . . Not with something this important."

But if he'd never followed Nayati, never gone on the Cocheta machine, he'd never have realized:

"It's not his fault, Dr. Corlaney," Stephen interjected quietly, rather disconcerted when all attention centered on him.

"Mind your own damn business, 'NetHead," Corlaney snapped.

Sakiimagan just stared at him, and he addressed that canny, narrow-eyed face rather than Corlaney's anger.

"You did it to protect the Cocheta, didn't you, sir?" he asked. "Because you *had* to."

"Had to?" Sakiimagan echoed. Then nodded. "And do you understand that compulsion, Dr. Ridenour?"

"I—" He couldn't explain all Nayati's machine had done—at least, not yet—but: "That's what happens, isn't it? The Cocheta want to be safe, protected. Once you've experienced that machine—the personality of a Cocheta—can you feel any differently? How can you *not* do everything in your power to keep them safe from perceived threat?"

"You're very perceptive, for someone who has only experienced the Cocheta a single time."

Sakiimagan's tone was encouraging, not accusatory. Perhaps

it was paranoia, perhaps exhaustion, but something told him this was not the time to prevaricate.

"It—" He swallowed the sickness. "It wasn't the f–first t–t—"

Sakiimagan smiled, set a hand on his shoulder. "I thought not. Did your father also perceive a threat?"

He nodded, grateful to release that burden to someone else. And to Corlaney:

"Don't you see, sir? All Nayati did—all Gov. Tyeewapi did—was try to keep them safe. The Cocheta—reinforced those efforts until they *had* to. Anevai says Nayati's acting out of character. Well, my father did, too. He did what he had to do once Mama had put in my application to Vandereaux. He wouldn't have threatened my sanity, even my life, if something beyond his control hadn't—"

Of a sudden, hands gripped his shoulder, thrust him about to face Nayati's dark suspicion. "Who the hell are you?"

The following instant, Lexi was on them, pulling Nayati away, but Stephen stopped her. "It's all right, Lexi." And to Nayati: "I'm Stephen Ridenour. And I'm a Vandereaux graduate. That's who I am. I was born Zivon Ryevanishov, to Recon parents on a world called Rostov. That's what I am."

"That Recon shit's a cover-story, spy. Rostov was burned off—"

"What are you talking about?" Cantrell broke in. "Civil war—"

"Bullshit. —Tell them, Sakiima. Tell them the truth."

"I don't know what that truth is. I *speculated*, Nayati. I *feared*. I never *knew*."

"Bullshit."

"Dammit, Ridenour," Anevai whispered in his ear, "straighten them out!"

He sighed wearily. "You're all wrong."

Cantrell scowled at him. "Stay out of this, Ridenour."

"It's *my* homeworld you're talking about. My family. *They* destroyed it, Nayati. Not the researchers, not the Security Team sent to investigate. No civil war. That's what I wanted to show you. No dead Recons. Only dead researchers. Massacred. No reason. No fight." He slid off the couch, rousing a muffled

Wesley-curse he silenced with a touch. "Even the stations were shut down—remotely and with all personnel aboard—and no one knew it was happening until too late." He faced Nayati squarely. "You tell me what happened, Hatawa. You tell me who started the war—and why. Tell me where the Recons got the power to shut a station down remotely."

"Why should I answer to you?"

"Because we both know. . ." He hesitated, still unwilling to admit what he'd experienced. But that obsession with survival, the implied threat to oneness with the universe that had made the Other lose control, was a force too powerful to be ignored. "There were Cocheta at Rostov. *I* know the Recons were experimenting with their Cocheta machines in ways you haven't yet imagined. If those experiments ran amok—if they. . . It wasn't a war, Nayati. The Recons went crazy—killed everyone—researchers, support teams—even the stationers. And if Cantrell is right—if it's happening here— Don't you see the danger?"

"You're lying."

"No, he isn't, Nayati," Sakiimagan said, taking a step toward his nephew. "He *is* from Rostov. He's Stef's boy. Stef got him away—before the shutdown. Don't you see? He could be the one—"

Stef's boy? What 'one'? What did Sakiimagan Tyeewapi know of Stefan Ryevanishov's son?

Wild laughter; a quick avoidance of Sakiimagan's hand that brought Nayati up abruptly against the Cocheta console. He clung there with his manacled hands, and sneered, "So *that's* why you're so solicitous of the spy, now. Hononomii failed you, now you can replace Hononomii with Stefan Ryevanishov's mystery-child. Well, I wish you joy with him." His head dropped, a mass of black hair obscuring his face for a long-drawn breath. When he looked up again, his face was calm. "Gods of earth and sky, you're a fool, Sakiimagan. You've overlooked a real son for years just to mold a fool into your own foolish image. I could understand had you overlooked me for Anevai, but for *Hononomii*?"

Anevai jumped down, fire in her dark eyes. Stephen grabbed her, held her even against her protests.

"Why do you talk like this about your brother?" Sakiimagan asked Nayati.

"My *brother*? Hononomii isn't my brother, he's my cousin."

"He certainly thought of you as—"

"If he was my brother, *you* were my father. But you were no more a father to me than my own ever-absent gene-provider."

"Cholena and I opened our house to you—what more did you want?"

"I never wanted your house—never wanted your son." Nayati's voice took on a pleading tone. "All I wanted— all I *ever* wanted—was for you to see *me*. *Me*. I did everything you wanted in a son and still you denied me."

"You were my son's friend and brother. Wasn't that enough?"

"No! My father deserted me—where were you? Where were the other men of the tribe? The *Dineh* took care of my mother—who took care of *me*?"

"You were the leader. The self-sufficient Nayati to whom—"

"Well, it wasn't enough. It was never enough."

Stephen shuddered, feeling an unwanted empathy, felt Anevai's resistance turn solicitous, and shook his head, stopping her query as Sakiimagan said sadly:

"I'm sorry, Nayati. I can't be other than I am."

"You could have tried."

"Could I? Could you?"

"No!" Nayati exploded. Two jumps had him around the Cocheta control panel. He struck down sharply with his manacled hands, smashing several levers, pushing one to a full-down position. The lever broke off, fell clattering to the floor, and energy arced down and around them: man-made lightning for an endless moment. Then everything went black. A siren blared and a strange, musical voice called out meaningless sounds.

And above that voice, Nayati's: "Goodbye, Sakiimagan. Your mind has grown too Alliance. You do not deserve the Cocheta."

Violet light surrounded them, the radiation alarms on the Security personnel beeped warnings of their own into the general cacophony. An instant of minor chaos, before Cantrell's voice directed a civilized retreat to the tunnel. Spots flared, hands grabbed Stephen, dragging him into the flow of bodies. Ahead of him, Wesley's head bobbed bonelessly over someone's shoulder.

"Nayati! *Where's Nayati?*" Sakiimagan's voice, louder than the alarms.

"We can't worry about him now, governor," the admiral's voice answered.

"Dammit, *what about my son?*"

"Sakiima," someone else roared, *"not now."*

Darkness.

A flare of Cocheta light that dimmed.

Honest, shadow-casting human spotlights.

Everything was bouncing. His stomach felt decidedly unhappy. Wesley raised his head—difficult against the jolting—and saw Stephen staggering head-down between two teal-uniformed individuals. Terrible thing to do to a man: fall asleep with a pleasant armful of Stephen Ridenour, wake up to a madhouse.

Damned fools couldn't stay out of trouble for . . .

"H-h-h-h—" He tried to check in. Stephen looked up and he quit trying to talk—settled on a grin, and a raised hand that flopped a greeting in time with his trusty steed's stride.

Solid fellow—he was no lightweight. No reason the man getting a hernia, however, he was perfectly capable of walking. "L-l-l—" He inhaled deeply. "L-me down!"

The shoulder beneath his belly heaved. Jolted him. "In a—"

"Wait!"

Stephen's voice. Startled. Demanding.

And Nigan: "He's right. There's a structural flaw—"

Stephen again: "It's ready to go!"

And the human tide changed its course as the tunnel ahead collapsed. Wesley no longer worried about getting down—just held as still as he could, interfering as little as possible.

"This way!" Anevai in the madness, this time. And: *"Turn off the damn lights!"*

Blackness again. Cocheta glow, flaring as Anevai created a Door into another, older tunnel. The Door closed behind them. Blackness again. Disturbed murmuring when the lights refused to work. Silence. Gentle vibration through the stone. But for that, the turmoil a step away might have passed unnoticed. It was—spooky.

"It's all right . . ." He recognized Stephen's voice even in its hoarse whisper. "We can rest now."

Tacit agreement from the others. A low murmur as they all caught their breath.

"Stephen?" His head surprisingly clear now, Wesley worked his way down the human mountain he was riding, thanked the mountain, and reached in the general direction of Stephen's last position. A chill hand met his and clenched, and he found himself pulled into a powerful embrace.

Damn, the brat was a strong one. He closed his arms around the slender body, and almost let go the next instant. Felt like the kid hadn't a stitch on—except he didn't feel like skin, and his fingers tingled where they touched him—as if his hands had fallen asleep. . . .

"I—I c–can't f–feel . . ." Stephen's breath caught, his weight shifted, and his hands moved along Wesley's arms to his face. Not exactly ready to give this crowd a floor show once the lights came back on—if they did—he covered those hands with his own, then pulled them away, squeezing them, advising caution.

"Case you hadn't noticed, brat, it's dark in here, but—" Down the darkness, the self-generating spots began to glow. "—that might change."

A throaty chuckle. "I'll try to control myself. —Are you all right?"

"Why wouldn't I be? My belly's been bounced to mush, I can't see a damn thing, the lights won't work and we're trapped under a gazillion tons of rock. Hell, I'm wonderful."

The word came down the line that the foremost light was working and they began a slow exodus. He put his arm around Stephen's shoulders, but the boy slid out from under it—took his hand instead with a cryptic "Want to feel you."

Couldn't say he objected—the kid's hand, at least, didn't tingle.

"Hope this isn't a dead end," he said conversationally.

"It's not."

"Ho—ho. And how would we know?"

"I feel it."

He laughed outright. "Like you felt the 'Net, right?"

"I—no. The Other is . . . Y—yes. Like the 'Net."

He laughed again. "That's my Stevie. Not a straight answer in you. —Just say you feel it in your bones, laddy-buck."

"I feel it in my bones, laddy-buck."

This time, the rest of the vulgarly eavesdropping group laughed with him—laughter which became a full-out cheer as the big spots flared.

V

i

Nayati was gone. Not dead, just gone. Word had come down from the hills he'd been sighted, but if anyone knew where he was, they weren't telling.

The full extent of the Library cave-in was still being determined, but the miners had made it out safely.

Hononomii was improving. They were using a voice sim to speak for Nayati, trying to undo Nayati's handiwork.

Thanks to Stephen, her father and Paul were reconciled—at least enough for their working relationship. Deciding what to do about her father's manipulation of the researchers would take a while longer, but she knew the researchers better than her father. Like Paul, they'd understand.

Wesley had recovered with nothing more than a hangover.

Everyone was alive and relatively well, except—

"Anevai? Are you here?"

She ignored the soft query from the barn entrance. Maybe Stephen wouldn't notice her and go away. But straw rustled and a shadow appeared at her side, leaning elbows likewise on the railing and gazing into the empty stall.

A handful of days and a lifetime ago, they'd stood in these same spots looking into this same stall. Only then, it hadn't been empty. Then, a baby ko'sii, Dr. Paul's attempt to re-create the ancestors' horse out of HuteNamid fauna, had staggered on unsteady legs and nibbled Stephen's hair.

"He's dead, Stephen." Surprisingly, her voice didn't break. So small a loss in the midst of such gain, but sometimes economics didn't make much sense.

"I'm terribly sorry, Anevai."

Tears threatened in earnest. It was the first anyone had deigned to recognize her loss. She'd had to discover what had happened from the livestock records. "They moved him out of the stall—took him down into the valley with the herd. We had a special set-up for him—Dr. Paul and I—we knew from the first-trimester tests that the first few months would be touch and go. If we could have gotten him through that, his own immune system might have handled it. But Dr. Paul forgot. They moved them so the Security team could get in here and work. Bego contracted something from the other animals and he died overnight—everyone was too busy to notice. —Even me. When I saw the kittens, I should have known. I should have . . ."

Out of the corner of her eyes, she saw Stephen's head drop before he turned to face her, one elbow draped on the fence. "Can't the female have another?"

"Not like Bego. He was an experiment. Dr. Paul was trying a combination which, after the first-trimester tests, he revised. There's no reason to make another: Bego was only marginally viable. Oh, we have sample cells in the 'Bank so his Code isn't lost, but there's no sane reason to make another like him. Another who would run the same risks."

She propped her chin on the rail, remembering hours of struggle just to keep breathing. "And Bego was a fighter; who really knows what made him that way? Another might not live even as long as he did."

Stephen turned back to the rail, leaning his forehead against his crossed arms, his hair almost Amerind-black in contrast to the white bandages on his wrists. "If only I'd had sense enough to stay away that night, he might still be alive."

If he'd stayed away that night, a whole lot might be different. But that was her loss thinking, not her heart. She shrugged and turned away from the stall. Leaning her shoulders against the rail, she shoved her clenched hands deep into her pockets.

"Doesn't make any difference, really. Some experiments just fail, that's all. We all did what we had to—when we had to. Even Nayati. He experimented hoping to build safeguards, and because of his paranoia, my brother is up there—" She glanced up in the general direction of *Cetacean*. "—trying to find his way back to RealSpace and Nayati it floating somewhere out there—" A second glance, this time toward the mountains. "—in his homemade VirtualSpace."

Long after Anevai assumed the subject closed, Stephen murmured, "How fortunate Bego was. He knew, from the moment he was born until he died, that he was understood for what he was and for what he might become. That's very important for an experiment, Anevai: to know that what it's experiencing has a purpose."

She knew that comment was meant to comfort her, however: "Bego isn't the only experiment you're speaking of."

It was his turn to shrug.

"What about love, Stephen? Doesn't the experiment need that as well?"

"I suppose." He frowned: concentration on a puzzle: something else she knew about Stephen Ridenour. Now. "But loving is so basically simple a thing. My parents loved me, I suppose. But I was too different and they didn't love me enough to discover in what way I was different, or to understand and love those differences."

She headed him toward the doorway—to the morning sunlight and life outside this dark, increasingly morbid cavern. "Do you really believe that, Stephen? What about all the stuff you told my dad and Paul?"

"I think the Cocheta drove Papa to protect them. I think, maybe, they also drove him to investigate—in any way possible. I think *they* want to be understood. I don't think Papa had any real option, just as Mama had none when she sent me away. Humanity's sense of protection is pretty well developed, too. She didn't know she was sending me into—hell. She did know she was saving my life."

They settled side by side on a bench outside the door, and she said, "There must have been another way."

"Another way wouldn't have brought me here." He reached for and squeezed her hand. "It's funny how rapidly priorities change. A few days ago, I made a very eloquent, philosophical speech to Adm. Cantrell all about purpose and the 'NetAT—somehow, when I was on that table, and later, in the tunnels, *Harmonies* and the 'NetAT never entered my mind."

"Survival is real nice, Stevie-lad."

He chuckled. "Beats most alternatives, doesn't it? —But not my survival, Anevai. I've been living on borrowed time for too many years for my life to be worth much on the exchange. Yours and Wesley's, on the other hand, are well worth any price. And Nayati didn't ask so very much, after all."

She didn't know what to say to that. Nothing she could say, no matter how profound, would change that opinion of his overnight, and today, she was anything but profound. She turned his hand over and played with his long fingers, watching them curl, seemingly of their own volition, around hers, then rolled back beside him, pulling his arm over her shoulder and leaned her head against him. "I wish you'd known Nayati the way I did. He didn't always have that—problem. I think the Cocheta had some *real* head problems—ones that don't inter- face with humans real well."

He chuckled softly. "I'll second that."

A dark curl floated into his eyes. She reached a hand to brush it back; he looked away and muttered something about a haircut.

"You do, Ridenour, and I'll chop your barber's hands off at the elbows."

He laughed reluctantly and held out his bandaged wrists. "Better chop away, now, Tyeewapi. Save yourself some time."

"Cut it yourself, do you?" Somehow, that didn't surprise her. The surprise was that he didn't seem to mind her playing with the curl now. But he didn't seem to enjoy it much either. She let go his hair in favor of his hands and wrapped them around her neck. "Then I'll just have to keep your hands busy, won't I? The Wesser wouldn't approve of you typing with your toes." She hugged him and whispered in his ear, "Please don't, Stevie-lad. It's such pretty hair. It deserves a chance to live, too."

He laughed shakily and pulled away. "All right, Tyeewapi, all right. Give me a break. I promise not to touch it until I'm headed home."

"Dammit, Ridenour." She punched him in the ribs. Hard. He protested and grabbed her wrists. "This *is* your home. We want you here! Wesley wants you. I want you. Even Nayati did. He said—"

He shook his head and leaned back. "Sometimes, we can't have what we want, Tyeewapi." But his fingers winding into hers tempered the sting in his words.

"Stephen, how *did* you find your way back to the admiral? Nayati said you had the power—if you would only listen."

"I—" He squeezed her hand, and rose stiffly to his feet. "Luck, Tyeewapi. Sheer, unadulterated, for-once-in-my-life luck. C'mon. Let's go find breakfast."

She let him pull her to her feet. He relaxed his grip, but she laced her fingers through his as they started up the path to the Researcher Condos.

A spark in the bushes caught her eye. "Wait a second, Ridenour."

ZRS winked up from her dirty palm. She caught Stephen watching, a melancholy expression on his face. It *had* been a lovely outfit, but for all his predilection for fancy clothes, she somehow suspected the ruined coat wasn't the source of that sadness.

She walked slowly over to him, picking the dirt from the grooves, gently rubbing them clean. "Wonder how the admiral's security team missed this?" she said, and held them out to him.

Stephen shook his head, closed her hand over them. "Some things are gone and best forgotten. You keep it. Make something new."

"I'll do that, Ridenour." She wrapped the button into a bit of only slightly used tissue from her back pocket and tucked it safely away, before linking arms with Stephen and starting up the path again. "And every time I wear it, I'll think of someone who's *not* gone forever, and best *remembered*."

He stopped, struggling to say something, then gave up and pulled her to him. She hugged back, and his arms tightened. And tightened. Of a sudden, her back popped. Audibly.

He released her abruptly. "Are you okay?"

She twisted to the right, and the left, then grinned at him. "Thanks Ridenour. That stupid vertebra's been driving me crazy for weeks. C'mon. The food'll be gone before we get there!"

For the third time they started up the pathway, edging closer together with each stride, linking hands then elbows. Finally, she slipped her arm around his waist, his hand on her shoulder drew her closer. She sighed contentedly, let herself sway to the motion of their stride. "You *will* come back to us, Ridenour, won't you?"

Before he could answer, Wesley appeared in a second-story balcony, waving at them frantically.

"C'mon, you two. We're *dying*!"

A hand-in-hand walk broke into a trot and finally into a laughing head-to-head sprint.

Wesley Smith grinned and said without looking back, "So, admiral, you going to leave the brat down here while Hononomii recoups?"

Ignoring TJ's for-her-ear-only grunt of disapproval, she asked, "You really think it would be beneficial?"

Smith jerked his head toward the couple who'd gotten distracted and were playing touch-tag around a tree. "Answer's obvious." He turned full about. "The boy's got a confidence problem, Cantrell, we both know that. Let Anevai and me finish what we've started. He'll do a better job for the 'NetAT— and for you—I promise."

"And that access of the Rostov files?"

"Scared him spitless, Cantrell. He won't do it again."

"*I've heard that before*," TJ growled in her ear.

"How'd he do it the first time?"

Smith smiled and shook his head. "Luck, admiral. Luck and good instincts for the internal functioning of the 'Net. Theoretically, anyone could do it. *I* could, if I started at the absolute right instant.''

''He did. Twice. How?''

''He claims he felt it—it's an old 'Tech's tale, admiral. He thought he could feel some vibration in the 'Net through the keys. Thought all 'Techs could. He operated on that assumption.''

''Blind faith.''

And in her ear: *''The mind boggles.''*

Smith nodded. ''Coupled with desperation. Now he's discovered no one else *really* feels it, he's begun to doubt himself. He won't try it again. So whadaya say, mama, can he stay?''

''Can't stay. He's got some explaining to do to McKenna, but once he clears with her—well—we'll see. He might not want to come back. If he does, Smith, and he comes anywhere *near* a terminal, your ass is—''

''—still gorgeous,'' he finished with a grin and vaulted the railing. *''Steeevie.''*

TJ joined her at the open door.

''So. You going to tell her about her brother?''

''And spoil her party? —Look at them.'' She gestured toward the exuberant reunion taking place below. ''You'd think they haven't seen each other for years.''

TJ said nothing until Wesley had insinuated himself between the two and hauled them into the building. ''Simulates sanity pretty well, doesn't he?''

''Which one?'' she asked.

A deep chuckle. ''Ridenour. Smith's a shit, but he's sane.''

''You think Stephen isn't?''

''Not a bit. He wasn't before all this started. You've seen Hononomii. Nayati had a go at Stephen. What happens if *he* blows...'' He glanced toward the sky. ''...out there?''

She leaned on the railing. ''Those reports he gave Chet are all we need. If he blows...he blows.''

''You don't really mean that.''

''Did it to himself, Teej. Played a fool—reaped the consequences.'' She turned to face him. ''Of course I'm concerned, but what can I do?''

''Waste him.''

She burst out laughing, took his arm and led him into breakfast.

Winema rose, ethereal in her naked beauty as the stars set about reweaving her silver robe. Another pattern repeating.

The World had changed in this cycle—but it was only a convolution within the broader pattern, repetition of a far more ancient cycle.

Nayati smiled into the cosmos and pressed the pouch containing the precious Cocheta tapes to his chest. Most were gone, buried within the heart of the mountain. But these key entities survived.

And for those who Sensed the Matrix, there were always other Libraries.